THE TWO-HEADED
EAGLE

The Two-Headed Eagle

A novel by

JOHN BIGGINS

ST. MARTIN'S PRESS ❧ NEW YORK

THE TWO-HEADED EAGLE. Copyright © 1993
by John Biggins. All rights reserved. Printed in the United
States of America. No part of this book may be used or
reproduced in any manner whatsoever without written
permission except in the case of brief quotations embodied
in critical articles or reviews. For information, address St.
Martin's Press, 175 Fifth Avenue, New York, N.Y. 10010.

Library of Congress Cataloging-in-Publication Data

Biggins, John.
    The two-headed eagle / by John Biggins.
        p.   cm.
    ISBN 0-312-14751-1
    1. World War, 1914–1918 — Aerial operations,
Austrian—Fiction.   2. World War, 1914–1918 —
Campaigns—Italy—Fiction.   I. Title.
    PR6052.I34T96   1996
    823'.914 —dc20   96-8482
                                                       CIP

First published in Great Britain by Secker & Warburg

First U.S. Edition: October 1996

10   9   8   7   6   5   4   3   2   1

ABBREVIATIONS

The Austro-Hungarian Empire set up by the Compromise of 1867 was a union of two near-independent states in the person of their monarch, Emperor of Austria and King of Hungary. Thus, for the fifty-one years of its existence, almost every institution and many of the personnel of this composite state had their titles prefixed with initials indicating their status. Shared Austro-Hungarian institutions were Imperial and Royal: 'kaiserlich und königlich' or 'k.u.k.' for short. Those belonging to the Austrian part of the Monarchy (that is to say, everything that was not the Kingdom of Hungary) were designated Imperial-Royal – 'kaiserlich-königlich' or simply 'k.k.' – in respect of the monarch's status as Emperor of Austria and King of Bohemia; while purely Hungarian institutions were Royal Hungarian: 'königlich ungarisch' ('k.u.') or 'kiraly magyar' ('k.m.').

PLACE NAMES

Since border changes resulting from the two world wars have altered beyond recognition many of the place names used in this story, a glossary is attached giving those most commonly used in 1916 and their modern equivalents.

The names given here attempt to follow Austrian official usage of the period. However, most of the story takes place in the regions where the old Danubian Monarchy bordered Italy, and in no other part of the Austro-Hungarian Empire – except perhaps for Transylvania – was there such complete anarchy as regards local place names. Virtually every settlement above the size of a hamlet had three names – Italian, German and Slovene – and there seem to have been no hard-and-fast rules, even in official documents, about which one would be used; except that in 1916 German or Italian would still normally be preferred to Slovene when the speaker was an educated person. Thus the small town which is nowadays called Bovec was quite likely to have been referred to as Plezzo by an Italian- or as Flitsch by a German-speaker.

The use of place names in this story should therefore not be taken as implying endorsement of any territorial claims, past, present or future.

Adelsberg	Postojna, Slo.
Arbe I.	Rab I., Cro.
Asinello I.	Ilovik I., Cro.
Bozen	Bolzano, It.
Brixen	Bressanone, It.
Bruneck	Brunico, It.
Caporetto	Kobarid/Karfreit, Slo.
Castagnevizza	Kostanjevica, Slo.
Cherso I.	Kres I., Cro.
Dornberg	Dornberk/Montespino, Slo.
Eger	Cheb, Cz.
R. Eisack	R. Isarco, It.
Flitsch	Bovec/Plezzo, Slo.
Feistritz	Bistrica, Slo.

Görz	Gorizia/Gorica, It.
Klausenburg	Cluj/Koloszvár, Ro.
Laibach	Ljubljana, Slo.
Leitmeritz	Litoměřice, Cz.
Lundenberg	Břeclav, Cz.
Lussin Grande	Veli Lošinj, Cro.
Lussin Piccolo	Mali Lošinj, Cro.
Lunga I.	Dugi Otok, Cro.
Marburg	Maribor, Slo.
Monte Vecchio	Sveta Gora, Slo.
Monte Santo	Skalnica, Slo.
Monte Nero	Krn, Slo.
Meleda I.	Molat I., Cro.
Neumarkt	Egna, It.
Oppachiasella	Opatje Selo, Slo.
Prerau	Přerov, Cz.
Pago I.	Pag I., Cro.
Ranziano	Renče, Slo.
Selva di Ternova	Trnovski Gozd/Ternauerwald, Slo.
Santa Croce	Sveti Križ/Heiligenkreuz, Slo.
Selbe I.	Silba I., Cro.
Sansego I.	Susak I., Cro.
Tolmein	Tolmin/Tolmino, Slo.
Trautenau	Trutnov, Cz.
Trient	Trento, It.
Toblach	Dobbiaco, It.
Ulbo I.	Olib I., Cro.
Wippach	Vipava/Vippaco, Slo.
Wocheinersee	Bohinjsko Jezero, Slo.
Veldes	Bled, Slo.
Zara	Zadar, Cro.

HANSA-BRANDENBURG CI

LLOYD CII

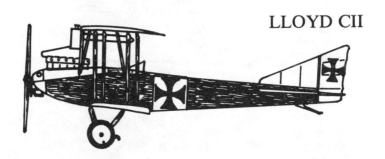

LOHNER TYPE "L"

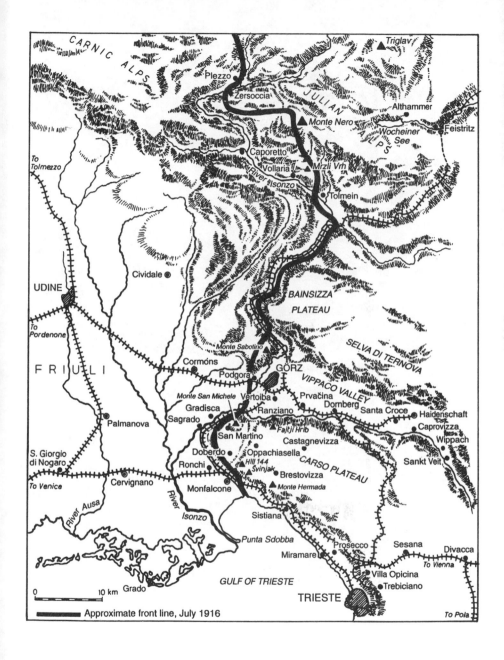

CARNIC ALPS

Triglav

Plezzo

Zersoccia

JULIAN ALPS

Althammer

Monte Nero

Wocheiner See

Feistritz

Caporetto

Vollaria

Mrzli Vrh

To Tolmezzo

River Isonzo

Tolmein

Cividale

UDINE

To Pordenone

BAINSIZZA PLATEAU

SELVA DI TERNOVA

Monte Sabotino

FRIULI

Cormóns

Podgora

GÖRZ

VIPPACO VALLEY

Monte San Michele

Vertoiba

Prvačina

Gradisca

Ranziano

Dornberg

Santa Croce

Haidenschaft

Sagrado

Fajtji Hrib

Caprovizza

Palmanova

San Martino

Castagnevizza

Wippach

S. Giorgio di Nogaro

Doberdo

Oppachiasella

CARSO PLATEAU

Sankt Veit

Ronchi

Hill 144

Svinjak

Brestovizza

To Venice

Cervignano

Monfalcone

Monte Hermada

River Ausa

Isonzo

Sistiana

Punta Sdobba

Prosecco

Sesana

Divacca

Miramare

To Vienna

River Isonzo

GULF OF TRIESTE

Villa Opicina

Trebiciano

0   10 km   Grado

TRIESTE

To Pola

Approximate front line, July 1916

THE TWO-HEADED
EAGLE

1

TAKE-OFF

Recorded at
SS of the Perpetual Veneration Old People's Home
Plas Gaerllwydd
Llangwynydd
West Glamorgan

Undated – probably autumn 1986

Strange, I always think, how the pettiest and least significant things – some banal tune playing on the wireless, the smell of the floor polish they once used at your old school – can set off a train of recollections; even when one has not thought about the matters in question for decades past, and even in someone like myself, who has never been one of nature's chroniclers or – at least until lately – much addicted to reverie, never even kept a diary except when required to do so by service regulations.

It was the television that set it off, yesterday evening in the residents' lounge: that draughty, high-ceilinged hall converted (I would imagine) from the one-time drawing-room of this dilapidated Victorian mansion, built out here on the tip of peninsula so as to be as far as possible upwind of the Swansea copper-smelting works which provided the money for its construction. I was sitting near the back of the room, in the armchair where Sister Elzbieta parks me each afternoon and which I occupy by virtue of my position as the Home's eldest resident: a hundred and one next April if I last that long. I was sitting there with a blanket over my knees, trying to read a little, in so far as cataract allows me, and to absorb some of the feeble warmth radiated by the Plas

Gaerllwydd's monstrously inefficient central-heating system. My young friend Kevin the caretaker fired up the boilers the day before yesterday to counter the autumnal chill cast by the Bristol Channel fogs, but one would be hard put to it to notice any difference.

It was only just after supper but the television was already jabbering away at the front of the room, surrounded by its circle of devotees intent on their evening act of worship. Normally it disturbs me little. My English is quite creditable – as well it might be, considering that I began to study it about 1896 and that I have spent the best part of half a century in exile in this country. But I find that programmes in what is still (for me) a foreign language are something that I can easily shut my ears against. In fact, since the Sisters moved me down here from Ealing in the summer the position has been doubly satisfactory in this respect, since a good half of the programmes each day are in Welsh, of which I think that I may be forgiven for not understanding a single word.

It never ceased to amaze me even back at the Home in Iddesleigh Road how the residents there (I try hard not to call them inmates) would cheerfully spend sixteen hours a day, seven days a week, watching programmes in a language which many of them still barely understand. So what shall I say of them down here in south Wales? No, I sat undisturbed and thought, and read a little, then thought again: all the long-forgotten events which have been coming to the surface these past few months, like oil and wreckage from a sunken ship, since the photograph album turned up and they brought me to this place and I began telling these improbable yarns of mine to young Kevin. I could have continued like that until they came to put me to bed. But then the insufferable Major Koziołkiewicz strode in on his bandy cavalry-man's legs and, without asking anyone, walked over to the television set and turned up the volume (he is deaf in one ear and half deaf in the other, but the vanity of old age prevents him from wearing a hearing aid). Bored with my book, and wishing anyway for some respite from memories which were not always entirely welcome, I sighed and turned resignedly to watch the programme.

2

It was a poorly made pulp-thriller film of early-1970s vintage: the usual turgid, best-seller-made-into-film stuff of which the chief characteristic is that, after the first two minutes or so, no one could care a button what happens to any of the characters. This particular offering was worthy of note only in that it contained in the very first five minutes an example of one of the most verdigris-encrusted of cinematographic clichés: the one where the air hostess emerges from the door of the flight deck with an anxious look on her pretty face and asks whether any of the passengers is either a doctor – preferably a consultant toxicologist – or a qualified pilot. At this point, as Charlton Heston (who, naturally, just happened to be both) rose from his seat, I gave up and returned to my book, knowing only too well what rolling vistas of tedium would now unfold themselves before me.

But still this episode, ludicrous in itself, had set my mind working. For the truth is, I think, that more often than we care to admit life impersonates art and real events take on the character of a B-feature film. I imagine – admittedly on the basis of no evidence whatever – that there must be occasional Tarts with Hearts of Gold who address their clients as 'dearie'. And years ago there were unquestionably Scottish ship's engineers (I once met one) who wiped their hands on cotton waste while informing the bridge that their engines wud nae make it thru this storm. And believe it or not, something very similar to the situation that I have just described did once happen to me; though in the event it was not to turn out quite as the film version would have it.

It was in the summer of 1959, I remember, when my English second wife Edith and I were living in Chiswick. The telephone had rung in the small hours of the morning. It was Edith's younger sister calling from the island of Jersey. Their mother, then aged ninety-six or so, had moved from Suffolk to live with her a few years before and had been in poor health for some months past, bedridden and half paralysed by a stroke. Her condition had suddenly worsened during the night and the doctor's opinion was that she was unlikely to last much longer. She was asking for her children to be at her bedside, so in the end there could be no argument about it: we would have to get there as quickly as possible even though it meant the expense of an air flight. I say 'we' because Edith, even though she had been a VAD with the Serbian Army during its terrible winter retreat through the Balkans in 1915 and might therefore be reckoned to have been immunised for life against fear, was still extremely nervous about flying and would certainly not board an aeroplane without me to accompany her. So a taxi was summoned, overnight bags were hurriedly packed and at first light that Saturday morning we set off for Waterloo Station, driving across a city still barely stirring from its sleep.

The trains were still steam-drawn in those days: glossy dark-green carriages with varnished panelling inside and nets over-head for luggage, pulled by curious boxed-in locomotives like enormous baking-tins. We arrived at Eastleigh Aerodrome (as it was still called) about breakfast time, and just managed a ham sandwich and a cup of tea in the wartime hangar that served as a passenger terminal while my travel documents were examined by the airport officials. Jersey was British territory, but this was only fourteen years after the end of the war and the Home Office still demanded that I should show my identity papers before embark-ing upon air flights: 'Ottokar Prochazka (formerly Prohaska) – British-Protected Person Resident in UK – Born Austrian Subject 1886; subsequently Czechoslovak and Polish Nationality – State-less Person since 1948'. They scratched their heads politely over this for a couple of minutes, then stamped it and allowed us out on to the airfield. Our tickets had been waiting for us at Eastleigh, booked in advance by Edith's sister, so there were no further formalities to be gone through as we hurried out across the brown-scorched grass of that blazing summer, one of the hottest that I can remember during all my long years in this country.

The aeroplane standing before us, completing its fuelling, was a delightfully graceful little twin-engined De Havilland: twelve passengers plus pilot and cabin stewardess. And as we walked out across the field, bags in hand, I knew that despite my wife's misgivings I was going to enjoy this trip. People flew but rarely in those days, even the moderately well-off like ourselves, and my last flight had been sixteen years before: at night, over the darkened countryside of Bohemia, in the belly of an RAF Whitley bomber with a parachute strapped to my back. As we neared the aeroplane steps and the smiling hostess bade us good-morning and asked for our boarding passes, dim half-forgotten memories were stirring of such summer mornings many years before, and walks out across the grass of distant meadows to climb aboard other flying machines, far more primitive than this one and bound on much less innocent errands.

We were shown to our seats, one row back from the flight-deck bulkhead athwart the propellers, and sat down one on each side of the gangway. Poor Edith was already pale and tense as I reached across the aisle and squeezed her hand to reassure her. For myself though, I settled back into my seat – so much more comfortable than the creaking wicker cat-baskets which had cradled my backside when I first started to fly – and looked out of the porthole at the sunlit field and the cloudless blue sky. A curious feeling of contentment spread over me. Despite the distressing circumstances of our journey I knew that, for me at least, this part of the outing would be a wonderful lark and a most welcome diversion from the rather monotonous daily round of old age. I could only hope that some of my eager anticipation would communicate itself through our clasped hands to Edith, for whom flight was anything but a happy adventure.

The remaining passengers took their seats, the pilot appeared at the front of the cabin to wish us a pleasant journey – about forty-five minutes he said – then disappeared like a magician behind the dark-green curtain that masked the flight-deck door. The hostess showed us how to put on our life jackets (Edith winced at this and shut her eyes tight), then we fastened our seat belts as she took her place at the rear of the cabin and the pilot started the engines. I heard vague quackings from the wireless up forward, and after some minutes a light winked from the control tower to signal us out on to the concrete runway: 'Ausgerollt – beim Start,' as we used to say in the k.u.k. Fliegertruppe.

5

I have lived over a century now, and experienced many wonderful and terrible things. But for me there are still few moments as exhilarating as that of leaving the ground; as exciting even now as it was for me that first time I took to the air, in a wire-and-bamboo Etrich Taube some months after the *Titanic* went down. I cannot be far away now from my own long-postponed death; but if the sensation of passing from this world into the next is at all like that of take-off in an aeroplane – as I suspect it may well be – then I shall not mind it one bit: the gathering speed, that sudden rush as the air starts to bite, the shudder as the wings begin to lift, the feeling of being pressed back in one's seat even in a slow piston-engined aeroplane, that invariable missing of a heartbeat or two as the wheels leave the ground – and the equally invariable worry (no idle anxiety in my younger days I can assure you) that the pilot will exhaust his supply of runway before we are properly airborne. I was so engrossed in all this that I almost forgot my wife, white-faced and trembling across the gangway.

We were soon clear of Eastleigh Aerodrome and climbing steadily into the summer sky, the pilot giving rather more throttle than usual (I thought) on account of the thinness of the already warmed-up atmosphere, but otherwise as smoothly and as pleasantly airborne as one could possible have wished. I settled down to admire the view: the chimneys and cranes of Southampton Water below us; with two transatlantic liners in the ocean terminal and a lavender-grey Union Castle ship manoeuvring to dock; and away to port the fretted coastline of Portsmouth Harbour, its gleaming silver expanse dotted with warships – for whatever the sad realities might have been back in 1959, Britain in those days still looked almost as great a naval power as when I had first visited the place over half a century before. We passed over Calshot Spit, with its flying-boat hangars and its endless rows of laid-up minesweepers, and were soon climbing gently to pass over the Needles and head out across the English Channel. Within a couple of minutes the western tip of the Isle of Wight had slid away below us and we were out over open water, heading for St Helier, about half an hour's flying time

6

away. Edith seemed to have calmed down for the moment, so I sank into a pleasurable state of reverie, lulled by the steady hum of the engines and the gentle rush of wind along the aeroplane's fuselage. Pity that it had to be so short a flight, I thought.

This blissful, almost infantile state of contentment continued for another ten minutes or so; until I began to notice, while looking at an oil tanker far away on the shining sea, that the aeroplane was beginning to yaw gently from side to side, then to pitch up and down in a long, soft undulation like that of a large ship riding the swell from a far-off storm. I looked out of the cabin window again. Air turbulence? Surely not: the weather had been very hot lately but we were far from land and there had been little wind that morning when we took off. After a couple more minutes of this meandering progress – so gentle as yet that none of the other passengers appeared to have noticed it – the air hostess put down her magazine and bustled forward to disappear behind the flight-deck curtain. And when she emerged once more, a minute or so later, I saw to my alarm that she was wearing that bright games-mistress smile which among the English is supposed to convey reassurance, but which I must say has on my morale rather the effect of smoke oozing from under a door, or water starting to drip from a bulge in the ceiling. Prochazka's First Law, based upon more than half a century's observation of the English, states that when a nurse sits down by the head of the examination couch and starts making light conversation with you, it usually means that you are about to be given a spinal tap without benefit of anaesthetic.

'Well,' she enquired brightly, 'everyone enjoying their flight I hope?' She spoke – as did all air hostesses in those days – in the carefully cultivated tones of the J. Arthur Rank Charm School: the sort of well-groomed débutante-cum-Esher diction which was so perfected by the late Jessie Matthews and which seems almost to have died out now, along with elocution classes and the Court Turn. We all agreed that we were enjoying the flight. I sensed that the man in front of me already seemed a trifle uneasy; but the other passengers appeared not to have noticed anything amiss so I nodded with the rest.

7

'Splendid, super.' Then there was an ominous pause, although the smile remained as fixed as ever. 'I say, I wonder whether anyone has ever flown before?' By the murmur of assent I judged that about half the passengers had in fact flane befaw. A faint, barely discernible shadow stole across the radiance of the smile. 'No, no. I meant, has anyone actually flown an aeroplane before. You know: *flown* an aeroplane, not flown *in* an aeroplane.' The significance of this question appeared not to have sunk in, so she persisted. 'I mean, is any of you actually – er – a qualified pilot?' This question produced a sudden chill in the cabin – accompanied as it was by a distinct and ominous lurch to starboard. I looked across at Edith, who was staring in a sort of trance with tiny drops of sweat already breaking through the face powder on her forehead. Quite clearly, something was badly amiss. I raised my hand – and saw the young woman's smile freeze as she glanced at me.

'Excuse me young lady, but I am a qualified pilot.'

She looked at me, struggling valiantly to conceal her dismay. I was a well cared-for old gentleman I suppose, in my early seventies and still (I imagine) with some vestiges of the stiff-backed bearing of a one-time career naval officer of the House of Habsburg, without a walking-stick or even spectacles. No, I suppose that it must have been other factors that did it: the Central European accent and the bristly white moustache and the rather squarish, high-cheekboned Slavic cast of countenance. One of the least endearing traits of the English, I have often had cause to observe – now quite as much as in those early post-imperial days – is their total inability to take any nationality but themselves seriously; as if Englishness were some God-ordained ideal state of humanity of which all the other peoples of the earth fall short to a greater or lesser degree. And in my case of course, being an Austro-Czech by birth placed me immediately in a sort of third-class compartment of risibility some way below Belgians and only just above the Portuguese and the Greeks: remote, quaint and absurd, probably untrustworthy but basically harmless; bracketed for ever in the realms of operetta along with Rupert of Hentzau and the late Richard Tauber, complete with monocle and silly accent.

The hostess's response to my intervention was at any rate the normal reaction of the English Lady when confronted with anything alarming or unwelcome: that is to say, she simply ignored it and went on as before, raising her voice this time and craning to look over our heads as though she suspected that Captain Lindbergh in full flying kit might be aboard, concealing himself behind the seats for a joke.

'I said, is anyone here a qualified pilot?'

Well, I can be stubborn too, and matters were clearly getting serious: the aircraft's pitching was now so pronounced that she was having to hold on to a seat-top to steady herself.

'Excuse me, young lady, but I said that I am a qualified pilot.' She looked at me as if I had just made an indecent suggestion, but still with that glassy smile. Feeling that my credentials were being called into question I decided to elaborate. 'In fact I have held a pilot's licence since the year 1912, though it has not been renewed since before the last war . . .'

'Oh really? How very interesting. I said, is there anyone here who . . .'

'. . . I was one of the first pilots of the Austro-Hungarian Naval Flying Corps, and I flew as an officer-observer with the Imperial and Royal Flying Service for five months on the Italian Front in 1916. It is true, I have not piloted an aeroplane since that year, and I think that twin-engined aircraft might give me some problems at first. But I am quite confident that I could still handle a small piston-engined aircraft like this with no difficulty whatever . . .'

If, until now, the full gravity of our plight had not fully dawned upon my fellow-passengers, it certainly did at that moment: the sudden, awful realisation that they were several thousand metres above the middle of the English Channel in a small aeroplane with no co-pilot and with some unspecified but dreadful emergency taking place on the flight deck. And as if that were not bad enough, that their only hope of survival should now rest in the hands of a decrepit old Mitteleuropean zany who claimed to have

9

last flown with Prince Eugen of Savoy during the War of the Spanish Succession. As if to underline the point, the aeroplane suddenly leant over on to one wingtip for a second or two, causing the hostess to lose her balance and land in my lap with a squeal of alarm.

'I said, I am a qualified pilot . . .'

'Shut UP, you horrible old man!' she hissed as the aeroplane came level again and she got up, smoothing her uniform and trying to reassume her smile as near-hysteria broke out among the passengers (Edith, mercifully, had just fainted). In the end my qualifications were rejected and she scrambled through the curtain dragging after her the passenger who had been sitting in front of me: a large, mild-mannered commercial traveller in carborundum wheels who (it transpired) had been a flight engineer in a Halifax bomber during the war.

We heard later that while the aeroplane had been standing on the field at Eastleigh a large bumble bee had flown in through the cockpit window to escape the heat and had remained dozing behind the instrument panel until we had passed the Isle of Wight, whereupon it had flown out in alarm – perhaps realising belatedly that it was bound for a new life in the Channel Islands – and stung the pilot on the bridge of his nose. He was one of those people who have an allergy to bee stings, and within a few minutes the poor man had become woozy while his face had swollen up to a degree where he could barely see out of his eyes. In the end though, assisted by our flying carborundum-wheel man, he recovered sufficiently for us to make a safe if bumpy landing at St Helier, where fire engines and ambulances were standing by to receive us. As we descended the steps – myself following Edith, who was being carried out unconscious on a stretcher – the air hostess stood at the foot of the steps, a model of well-groomed composure once more. As the passengers filed past she bade them a smiling farewell, making the expected apology for 'the unfortunate incident' and hoping that they had otherwise had a pleasant flight. And the passengers for their part – who not twenty minutes before had expected to be entering the Eternal Kingdom – assured her as the English will that yes, it had been a pleasant flight and that it was no bother to them at all to have narrowly missed nose-diving into the sea. My turn came, last in the queue. But for me there were no comforting words: only a suddenly frozen smile and the reproachful stare reserved for someone who cannot really be expected to behave well, but who has still contrived to act in a base and cowardly manner – letting the side down even though he could never have aspired to belong to the side.

'I'm afraid,' she said, 'that your behaviour back there was simply disgraceful – there are no other words for it – and you must never, never, do you hear me?, *never* do that sort of thing again. If you can't restrain yourself from upsetting the other passengers with your silly jakes then you really shouldn't fly at all. I'm afraid that in this country we just don't behave like that.'

I have often had cause to wonder, both then and since, at that effortless tone of authority which seems to come so naturally to the English upper-middle-class female, whether the genuine article or (as I suspect in this case) one promoted from the ranks. I spent over half my life as a career officer at sea, on land and in the air; leading men under fire aboard ships, in the control rooms of submarines and on a dozen battlefields from the hills of north China to the Paraguayan chaco. Yet I could never hope to equal the faultless self-confidence of that young woman's voice: as if only a moral degenerate or a person utterly devoid of decency could possibly fail to do as they were told. I suppose it was the result of three centuries of being able to lay down the law to the natives wherever the guns of the Royal Navy could reach. What a pity, I think now, that she should have been born into an age when the natives were fast acquiring bigger and better guns of their own.

When we arrived at my sister-in-law's house we discovered that Edith's mother had already been dead several hours, so we might just as well not have bothered. Not surprisingly, Edith insisted on returning by sea, saying that she would far rather remain on Jersey for the rest of her life, sleeping under hedges if necessary, than ever fly again.

A silly incident really, and I must apologise for having rambled on so and bored you with it. But I was reminded of it by that silly film on television. And it made me cast my mind back even further to events forty years earlier still: to my brief but hectic career in the summer and autumn of 1916 as a flier for thc Noble House of Austria: not quite four months with the Austro-Hungarian Army Flying Service, followed by a period of nine weeks with the Imperial and Royal Navy's air arm. After Sister Assumpta had helped me up to my room that evening (I can still manage the stairs on my own but they prefer someone to be with me), I took out my old photograph album and began leafing through the pages.

The Sisters brought me down here in May, after I had suffered so badly from bronchial asthma in Ealing the previous summer. It was to have been only a short seaside holiday, but they have shown no disposition to move me back and anyway, a lengthy military career has taught me that nothing lasts quite so long as a temporary posting. No, I suppose that I might as well die here as there, almost on the shore of the great ocean which is now the only fatherland to which I feel any attachment whatever. And anyway, we have to be practical about these things. I understand that the Sisters have a cheaper-by-the-dozen concession with the Swansea and West Glamorgan Co-op and receive no less than ten books of stamps for each funeral, which makes no small contribution to the Order of the Perpetual Veneration's finances over the course of a year. They are not allowed to do it back in Ealing because the Order's chaplain, a ferocious old bigot called Father Czogala, holds the Co-operative retail movement to be a part of the worldwide Jewish-Bolshevik-Masonic conspiracy. But down here they are far enough away from his rantings to have some discretion about their trading arrangements. I have enquired of Mother Superior whether she could get the Co-op to bury me at sea – no nonsense about a coffin; just a seaman-like shroud of canvas and a couple of bricks tied to my feet – but she is dead set against the notion, I fear. Being a land-locked people the Poles like to have a grave to mourn beside (though no one at all is left to mourn beside mine), and anyway, she tells me that the local Co-op are reluctant to do sea burials after a distressing incident a few months ago, when hake fishermen trawled up a coffin off Tenby. So I suppose that I shall just have to be content with being devoured by worms like the rest.

But there, I am wandering again. Yes, what about the photograph album? Well, the photograph album covers the years 1915 to 1918, kept with the Imperial and Royal War Ministry's permission as the basis for a post-war book about the career of an Austro-Hungarian submarine. It was restored to me back in May by a quite extraordinary stroke of luck after it had turned up among the possessions of a dead Ukrainian émigré in a west London bed-sitter. Most of the surviving photographs detail my career as a k.u.k. U-Boat captain: Linienschiffsleutnant Ottokar, Ritter von Prohaska, submarine ace of the Mediterranean theatre and holder of Old Austria's highest military honour the Knight's Cross of the Order of Maria Theresa. It was these faded pictures that provided the background for my reminiscences when Kevin and Sister Elżbieta prevailed upon me to tape-record them some weeks ago. But one photograph – and one only – remains from those months in late 1916 when I was taking an enforced break from submarining and instead doing my best to get myself killed in the air. I gazed at it that evening by the light of the bedside lamp.

Faded and sepia-grey with the passage of seventy years, it shows a group of men standing in front of an aeroplane on a sunlit, stone-littered field fringed by a few wooden huts and canvas hangars. By the foliage on the trees in the background, it looks like early September or thereabouts, and in the distance one can see a low range of eroded, bare mountains. The two men are wearing leather flying overalls with helmets and goggles, and are accompanied by four mechanics in the baggy grey uniforms and high-fronted peaked caps of Austrian soldiers. The taller of the two airmen is clearly me as I was then: erect, confident, with binoculars slung around my neck and a map case under my arm, every centimetre the Habsburg career officer. The creature standing beside me however is barely recognisable as a human being at all: at least a head and a half shorter, hunch-shouldered, bandy-legged, with a prognathous beetle-browed face scowling out from under the brim of his flying helmet like something from a zoo cage or a fairground side-show. This is – or was – my personal chauffeur, Feldpilot-Zugsführer Zoltan Toth – or Toth Zoltan as he would have styled himself back in his native Hungary.

As for the aeroplane behind us, even if it were not for the black Maltese crosses on the tail and beneath the lower wings, one would scarcely need to be an expert on aviation history to identify it as one of that numerous family of German-designed two-seater reconnaissance biplanes of the First World War: a large, squared-off, uncompromising machine without much pretension to grace or refinement, only the sturdy utilitarian good looks of a well-bred carthorse. It stands there behind us on that field, rearing up in indignation on its large-wheeled undercarriage as if to say 'What the devil do you mean?', its short nose occupied by a six-cylinder inline engine, and with the space between that and the upper wing's leading edge occupied by the clumsy box-radiator which gives it away to the expert as an Austrian machine: to be precise, a Hansa-Brandenburg CI.

In fact, if the expert really knew his stuff he might be able to date the photograph to 1916 or thereabouts by the fact that the aeroplane is still not in camouflage paint but left in its natural colours: gleaming varnished plywood for the fuselage and clear-doped linen for the wings, the latter so translucent (I now notice) that if I look carefully I can just make out the black crosses on the upper wings showing through on the underside. One can also just see the number on the fuselage side, 26.74, and the name, 'Zośka', bequeathed to us by some earlier Polish crew. Curious now to think that this was probably the only aeroplane in the entire history of aviation ever to have been flown in Latin.

Strange also how merely touching the grainy surface of that faded photograph evokes all the smells of those months so many years ago, rather like one of those children's ornamental stickers

14

(Mr Dąbrowski's great-granddaughter showed me one last summer), where scratching it with a fingernail liberates a pungent odour of peppermint or cinnamon. I have only to touch it and back come all the various scents of seventy years ago, flying over the now forgotten battlefields of the Austro-Italian Front: the smell of early-morning dew on the tyre-crushed grass of the airfields; the smell of petrol and cellulose dope and lubricating oil on hot engines; the warm sweet-sour perfume of mahogany plywood; the reek of cordite and fresh blood; and the nauseating rotten-egg stench of anti-aircraft shellbursts. And the smell of burning wood and linen left hanging in the thin, cold air, flavoured sometimes with a sinister taint like that of fat burning in a frying-pan.

I never spoke or even thought much about it in the years that followed: we had lost the war, while I had lost my country and my career and had a new life to build for myself. Many of the memories were distressing – in fact are painful to me even now, a lifetime after the events. And to tell you the truth, I very much doubted whether anyone would be at all interested. But young Kevin and Sister Elżbieta tell me that I am now one of the very few left who remember it all. So perhaps now that I have at last committed my U-Boat reminiscences to posterity I might as well tell you about my flying career as well. It may perhaps interest you; and if nothing else it will help me to pass the time before the undertakers come to screw down the lid on me. You will probably think some of the tales a little improbable, but there you are, I am afraid that I can do nothing about that: Austria-Hungary was a rather improbable sort of country, and in the year 1916 flying was still a decidedly eccentric sort of thing to be doing, so much so that the psychiatric tests which became de rigueur for aspirant fliers in the Second World War were held to be completely unnecessary in the First since, by definition, anyone who volunteered to fly must be not quite right in the head – or if he was not already, very soon would be. I hope that these yarns of mine may at least entertain you, and perhaps give you some idea as well of what it was like to go up in an aeroplane in those few brief years when men took to the air wearing the two-headed-eagle emblem of the Holy Roman Empire.

15

2

KNIGHT ON A BICYCLE

I first began to notice it that morning about an hour after dawn, as the train stopped to take on water at the station in that wide, high, wind-swept defile known to us in those days as the Adelsberg Pass, where the railway line from Vienna crosses the last range of mountains before Trieste. It seemed to bounce to and fro between the scrubby, eroded slopes of limestone and come at us from all directions at once: not a distinct rumbling or booming as I had expected but a faint, sinister, barely audible shuddering of the air, irregular but incessant, as if some vast sheet of tin were being shaken somewhere away over the mountains. It told me – as if there should have been any doubt on the matter – that we were getting near to the war zone. For this was the last week of July 1916, and only a few score kilometres away, along the valley of the River Isonzo, the Italian armies were preparing for their next assault on the lines guarding the south-western frontier of our great multi-national empire. I was now approaching the zone of the armies, which began just beyond Adelsberg. Soon I too, like perhaps thirty million others, would become a subject of that new state which had been carved out of the body of Europe over the past eighteen months: the Front, that strange linear kingdom hundreds of kilometres long, but sometimes only metres wide, which now snaked across northern France and through the marshes of Volhynia and along the crest of the Alps – a curious country, where the inhabitants were exclusively male and, although mostly under twenty-five, suffered a mortality rate so high that the population could be kept up only by constant immigration; a strange topsy-turvy land where men lived under-

16

ground, worked by night and slept by day, and courted instant death if they appeared in the open for a couple of seconds. It was a hungry land as well, one that produced nothing whatever but which consumed so prodigally that the entire economic life of the world was now devoted to feeding it. Soon I too would cross its borders and become one of its subjects. For how long exactly remained to be seen.

The train moved out of the station once more in a haze of lignite smoke, and was soon clanking through the five successive tunnels beyond Adelsberg, where the line burrows through a series of mountain spurs. Before long we were squealing to a halt alongside the low platform of the station at Divacca. I had changed trains here many times during the previous sixteen years, for Divacca was the junction for the line down the Istrian Peninsula to Austria's principal naval base at Pola. But this morning it was to be different: my rail warrant extended only as far as Divacca, where I was to get off the train and carry on to an obscure little town called Haidenschaft some twenty-five kilometres away, thence to a doubtless even more God-forsaken place called Caprovizza, so out-of-the-way that I had been unable to find it even on quite large-scale maps of the Kustenland region.

The other difference that marked off my arrival that morning at Divacca from all the previous ones was that I was now stepping down from the train as someone else. On all previous occasions I had been travelling as a plain, ordinary naval lieutenant called Ottokar Prohaska, the son of a Czech postal official from a small town in northern Moravia. Now though, even if I was still only a Linienschiffsleutnant as regards service rank, I was altogether something far more exalted in social standing: Ottokar Prohaska, Ritter von Strachnitz, the most recent recipient of the very rarest and most prized of all the Old Monarchy's honours for bravery in action, the Knight's Cross of the Military Order of Maria Theresa, awarded to me a few days previously at Schönbrunn by the Emperor himself, in recognition of my feat one night a few weeks previously, when I had shot down an Italian airship off Venice and then, for good measure, torpedoed one of their submarines as

17

well. And to be honest I was finding it more than a little hard to get used to my sudden fame and elevation to noble rank. I had tried to leave Vienna quietly the previous evening – not least because I had got married only two days before. But quiet farewells to my wife had not been possible, not with the crowds which had somehow gathered ahead of me at the Südbahnhof, and the autograph hunters, and the popping magnesium flashes and the children being held up on their fathers' shoulders to get a look at me. In the end, unused to such celebrity, I was heartily glad when the train steamed out of the station.

But even as we clanked southwards through Graz and Marburg I was not to be left in peace. As I made my way along the corridor to the meagre wartime buffet car, brother-officers had jostled to shake my hand and slap me on the back and wish me well in my new career now that (according to the Vienna newspapers) command of a U-Boat had become too humdrum for me and I had volunteered for flying duties, '. . . as the only field left in which he may provide fresh evidences of his matchless valour in the service of Emperor and Fatherland'. When I was at last able to find some peace back in my compartment I looked down once more at the decoration pinned to the left breast of my jacket. It seemed a small enough thing to be making such a fuss about, I thought as I gazed at it lying in the palm of my hand: a small white-enamelled gold cross with a little red-white-red medallion in the middle, encircled by the word FORTITUDINI. Such a small thing, yet within a few hours it had turned my life upside-down to a degree where I was already beginning to suspect that malignant fairies had substituted someone else for me while I slept.

Nor was there to be any respite at Divacca, that bleak little township up on the arid limestone plateau above Trieste. Word of my arrival had somehow travelled ahead of me during the night and the townspeople – mostly Slovenes in these parts – had arranged a reception for me. As I appeared at the door of the carriage to descend to the platform I saw a crowd waiting. Before I realised what was happening the town band had struck up the 'Radetzky March' and I was being hoisted on to their shoulders to

18

be carried through the station vestibule into the square in front of the building. A crowd cheered and the Bürgermeister stood holding a large bouquet of flowers as the band played the 'Gott Erhalte' and the local gendarmery and fire brigade presented arms. The houses were bedecked with black-and-yellow and red-white-red bunting, while on the opposite side of the square a banner proclaimed:

VIVAT ÖSTERREICH – NIEDER MIT DEN ITALIENERN!
ŽIVELA AVSTRIJA – DOL S ITALIJANI!
VIVA AUSTRIA – A BASSO GLI ITALIANI!

With that little ceremony over, I am afraid that the whole thing rather ran out of steam. If you are carrying someone on your shoulders you have to be carrying them somewhere, and the welcoming committee clearly had no idea of what to do with me next. So after the Bürgermeister had made a short patriotic speech and the crowd had applauded I was unceremoniously put down on the cobbles of the station forecourt while everyone dispersed to go about their daily business, leaving me holding the bouquet and a scroll of paper giving me the freedom of the commune of Divacca – surely, now as then, one of the least desirable privileges on the whole of God's earth.

I went back into the station, which had resumed its normal wartime bustle of men proceeding on leave and men returning from leave. I took out my movement order and looked at it: 'Report at 1200 hours 24/VII/16 to HQ Fliegerkompanie 19F, flying field Haidenschaft-Caprovizza.' Well, it was now just past 8.00 a.m., so I had four hours in hand. But how to get there? The order took me only as far as Divacca by train, so how was I to get myself and my belongings to Haidenschaft and then to Caprovizza, wherever that might be? Clearly, expert advice was called for. I entered the station offices and eventually found a door marked PERSONNEL MOVEMENTS – K.U.K. ARMEE (COMMISSIONED AND WARRANT OFFICER RANKS). They would surely know in here. I opened the door and entered to find an unkempt and rather shabby-looking Stabsfeldwebel dozing with his boots resting on a paper-littered desk. A copy of the dubious Viennese magazine *Paprika* lay open beside him, while the walls of the office were decorated with numerous bathing beauties, evidently cut out from this same magazine, whose sumptuous padding had not yet been reduced to any noticeable degree by the privations of wartime. I coughed. He stirred, looked at me with one eye, then got up and made a perfunctory salute while fastening the topmost buttons of his tunic.

'Obediently report, Herr, er – ' (he gazed at my three cuff-rings for some moments in puzzlement) – 'Leutnant, that you've got the wrong office: naval personnel movements is upstairs.'

'I'm not concerned with that. I have been seconded to the k.u.k. Fliegertruppe, Flik 19F, at a place called Caprovizza near Haidenschaft. I've no idea where it is or how to get there, so I would be grateful if you could help me. Do you deal with movements of flying personnel or only with ground troops?'

'Obediently report that both, Herr Leutnant.'

'Excellent. So how do I get from here to Caprovizza?'

He rubbed his chin – he had not yet shaved that morning – and rummaged beneath some papers. It was quite plain that he felt it to be really no part of his duties to assist anything that wore blue instead of field grey, even if it did have the Maria Theresa pinned to it. At length he answered.

'I'm afraid that's not going to be so easy, Herr Leutnant. Normally there's a lorry comes up here mornings and evenings to collect people for the Vippaco valley airfields. But the rear axle broke yesterday evening so there won't be any transport now before about nineteen-hundred.' He paused for a while. 'Tell you what though, Herr Leutnant, I could help you perhaps. Strictly outside regulations of course, but . . .'

So in the end, once I had reluctantly parted with a precious tin of cigarettes, a way was found of getting me to Haidenschaft by midday. It appeared that a despatch rider's motor cycle had to be returned to my new posting's parent unit, Flik 19 at Haidenschaft. The reason for this, I learnt, was that the previous day, on the station platform, a Hungarian soldier proceeding home on leave had sought to demonstrate to his comrades the utter unreliability of Italian hand-grenades, using a captured example which he was taking home as a souvenir. The result had been three onlookers dead and seven more or less seriously injured, among them Flik 19's despatch rider, who had been standing nearby waiting to collect a packet of documents from the Vienna express. The motor cycle had to be returned to its unit, but since it had been moved to a shed on the other side of the town I would have to wait while an orderly was sent to fetch it. There was time for refreshments.

As I made my way to the station buffet I began to grasp for the first time exactly how strange a territory it was that I was entering, this Zone of the Armies which I had heard and read so much about while stationed down at Cattaro, but which I had never visited. The station was thronged with soldiery from every nationality of the polyglot Army of the Emperor of Austria and Apostolic King of Hungary: Magyars and Slovaks and Bosnians and Tyroleans and Ruthenes and Croats, all reduced now to a weary sameness, not only by their shabby grey uniforms, and the rust-red mud of the Isonzo trenches which still caked the boots and puttees of most of them, but also by that glazed, apathetic look which I was soon to learn was the inevitable consequence of a prolonged spell at the Front. It was a look which I was to see again a quarter-century later in the Nazi death camps. The men going home on leave jostled wearily on the platforms as the provost NCOs bellowed at them, loading them into the trains that would take them back for a few brief days with their wives and children in their mud hovels in the Hungarian puszta or their cottages in the Carpathian valleys. For many of these gaunt-faced peasant soldiers with their drooping black moustaches it would no doubt be their last leave. After the failure of our offensive on the Asiago Plateau in May, the Italians were preparing a counter-blow of their own on the Isonzo. The men now clambering down from the returning leave trains at Divacca would be in the front line to face it.

When I had at last fought my way into the crowded station buffet – reserved for officers but still packed to standing – and purchased the glass of tea (in fact dried raspberry leaves) and slice of kriegsbrot that would be my breakfast, I had leisure to look around me. It was only then that I realised quite how much the Imperial and Royal Army had changed in two years: how the great battles against the Russians in Poland in the autumn of 1914 had torn the heart out of the old k.u.k. officer corps, and how the numerous gaps in the ranks had been filled with hurriedly commissioned pre-war Einjährigers or youths straight from secondary school. I noticed that one chair was free at a side table, and moved over to ask the other customer, a young Leutnant, whether I might sit down. He could only have been twenty or so but he looked much older, tunic dusty and torn by barbed wire. He did not answer; in fact seemed not to notice me as he stared into nowhere with sunken, dark-ringed eyes. I saw that his lips were moving slightly as he talked to himself, and that his hand shook as he continuously stirred his tea, mechanically, like a toy in a fairground, as if he would go on doing it for ever unless someone pressed the stop-button.

I finished my breakfast just as the orderly returned with the motor cycle. I signed the appropriate receipts, then fastened my luggage to the carrier and set off, glad that in this dusty summer weather I had brought my pre-war pair of flying goggles with me from Vienna. It was a Laurin und Klement machine I remember, with no kick-starter so that I had to run alongside it down Divacca's main street and leap into the saddle as the engine began firing. I was soon glad though that I had chosen to make my own way to my new posting instead of waiting for transport. It was a beautiful morning, too early yet for the July heat to be shimmering among the limestone boulders and myrtle thickets of this bleak plateau. I puttered along the smooth metalled road at a leisurely speed as I enjoyed the view, leaving a cloud of white dust behind me as I droned through Senosetsch and then down from the Birnbaumerwald into the Vippaco valley, a sudden ribbon of greenness among the bare, grey mountains of the Carso.

*

Curious, I thought, that there should be so little traffic on this road. Here we were, only kilometres behind one of the major battlefronts of the greatest war in history, yet there seemed to be little more movement than in peacetime, when the only vehicles would be those long, narrow-bodied farm carts, with the horse harnessed to one side of the single shaft, which characterise the Slav world from Slovenia to Vladivostok. Most of the supplies for the Isonzo Front came either down from Laibach or up from Trieste along the branch railway line to Dornberg; so apart from the airfields at St Veit and Wippach this winding valley road was not much used by the military. I passed a few motor lorries throwing up choking clouds of dust, and one or two columns of marching men, but otherwise saw little sign of the war except when I had to stop for a gang of Russian PoWs engaged in road-mending. They seemed a cheerful enough lot and waved in farewell as I went on my way, having dispensed my remaining tin of cigarettes among them as largesse. They were supervised only by an elderly, bearded Landsturm reservist who (I observed) left his rifle in the care of one of his charges as he went into the bushes on a certain errand. Otherwise the scene in the Vippaco valley was one of immemorial peace, the summer-shallow river winding half-heartedly among banks of pale grey limestone pebbles and the twittering of the birds in the willow thickets quite undisturbed by that constant ill-tempered rumbling in the distance.

I have always found journeys to be conducive to thought; and that morning I was particularly grateful for solitude and the opportunity to think things over, after the dizzying succession of events over the previous week. Last Wednesday morning I had been a national hero. The hurrah-patriotic press had worked itself up into a frenzy of adulation over me – 'one of the greatest feats of arms of the entire war' the *Reichspost* had called it – not least because the performance of Austro-Hungarian arms elsewhere that summer had been so uniformly dismal. But being created a Maria-Theresien Ritter had not been my only engagement that week, for on the Saturday I was to have been married in the Votivekirche to a beautiful Hungarian noblewoman, the Countess

Elisabeth de Bratianu, to whom I had been engaged since the previous autumn and who was working as a nurse in a Vienna military hospital. But Fortune's wheel was to turn with bewildering speed. By three o'clock that same afternoon I had found myself standing in the War Ministry before an unofficial court martial, accused of having sunk a German minelayer submarine off Venice in mistake for an Italian boat – and of having killed my own future brother-in-law, who had been among the German vessel's crew. Elisabeth's relatives had immediately forbidden the wedding on pain of disinheritance. But it had gone ahead just the same – not least because (as I now learnt for the first time) she was two months pregnant with my child – and we had got married the next day in a registry office while she was duly disinherited by her family.

As for myself, the War Ministry was in a quandary. Though unconvinced that I had sunk the German minelayer, they were in no position to resist Berlin's demands for my immediate court martial. The best that they could do in the end, short of having me shoot myself or pushing me under a tram, was to get me out of the way by posting me to the k.u.k. Fliegertruppe on the Italian Front. This (officialdom felt) would put me beyond the German Admiralty's reach at least for the time being and quite probably for good, soon reposting me either into the next world or into an Italian prison camp for the rest of the war or – most probably – to join my elder brother Anton in that indeterminate category 'missing in action'. One way or another, I had been placed in Austrian bureaucracy's favourite desk-tray: the one marked ASSERVIERT, or 'pending'.

It was only after asking for directions from townspeople and from soldiers on the streets that I was able to find my way to the headquarters of my parent unit Fliegerkompagnie 19, based on a rough meadow some way to the west of the little town of Haidenschaft (or Ajdovščina or Aidussina as its largely Slovene and Italian inhabitants called it). It was near midday now and already very hot in this trough in the karst mountains. But my reception in the orderly room at k.u.k. Fliegerfeld Haidenschaft

24

brought an immediate chill into the air. I had expected a certain reserve on my first arrival here. The Austro-Hungarian military and naval air services were largely self-contained forces under their own commands and did not generally have much to do with one another. The Navy's aircraft, it is true, did give a great deal of support to the Army on its southernmost flank during the later Isonzo battles, bombing Italian batteries and shooting up the enemy in the trenches. But since the Navy's aeroplanes were exclusively flying-boats, for obvious reasons their pilots were reluctant to take them very far inland. So for most of the time the two air arms kept themselves to themselves. A few army pilots had flown with the Naval Flying Service, but so far as I knew I was the first naval officer to serve with the k.u.k. Fliegertruppe.

Even so, I felt that my reception at Haidenschaft flying field broke all bounds of civilised courtesy. As I arrived at the gate, stiff and caked in dust, I noticed that the sentries did not salute me. I was just about to demand the meaning of this when the Adjutant appeared from the guardroom. I saluted, introduced myself and presented my compliments – prior to giving him a piece of my mind on the standard of his sentries, who appeared not to recognise a naval officer when they saw one. But before I could gather breath he merely grunted:

'Hmnph! That's our motor bike isn't it? What d'you think you're doing with it?'

'I was asked to return it from the station at Divacca.'

'About time too and all.' He seized the handlebars from me and began to wheel the machine away as I tried to unstrap my valise.

'Wait a moment,' I said. 'My orders are to report here to the Kommandant of Fliegerkompagnie 19 and then proceed to your sub-unit 19F at Caprovizza.'

He paused and turned round. 'We don't have much to do with that lot here, and as for Hauptmann Heyrowsky I doubt whether he'll be very pleased to see you. If I were you I'd just push off and not bother him.'

'Very well then,' I said, trying to sound as dignified as I could while removing my luggage from the carrier. 'Since you clearly can't spare the courtesy to receive me as befits a brother-officer I shall consider that I have reported here as ordered and make my way now to Fliegerfeld Caprovizza. Might you be so kind as to give me directions?'

Without turning round the Adjutant pointed over his shoulder with his thumb in a vague southerly direction.

'Other side of the road, over the level crossing and past the cemetery . . .' He paused as if a thought had just struck him. 'Feldwebel!' he shouted into the guard hut, 'bring out that bicycle would you? We've got someone here who's going to join those bastards over at Caprovizza.' The bicycle was wheeled out from behind the hut and thrust at me. 'Be a good fellow and take this with you, will you? Hauptmann Heyrowsky saw it in town and thought that it might be a nice present for your Herr Kommandant. He said to tell Hauptmann Kraliczek that if he's feeling in a particularly daring mood one day he can come over here and we'll teach him to ride it.'

'Might I request that comment in writing, if you wish me to convey it to my commanding officer?' I said, as stiffly as I could. 'You understand I'm sure: duels and courts of honour and all that sort of thing.'

The Adjutant smiled. 'Certainly. There's a note under the saddle springs already. As for duels between our CO and yours, I doubt very much whether it'd ever come to that. But if it did I certainly know where I'd place my bet.'

I felt after this last insult that there was little point in prolonging this sour and uncomradely exchange. So I swung myself on to the bicycle – which mercifully still had rubber tyres instead of the hemp-filled canvas tubes which were now being supplied as substitutes – and pedalled away down the side road and across the railway line as instructed. Soon I was skimming along a level, poplar-fringed road among the flat maize fields of the valley bottom: one of the very few bits of the Vippaco valley (I soon discovered) level enough for airfields. A couple of kilometres outside the town I stopped and shaded my eyes against the sun to watch the approach of an aeroplane, coming in low to land at

Flik 19's flying field. It was a Lloyd two-seater by the looks of it. As it roared overhead I saw that a good half of one of its lower wings had been reduced to a chaos of splintered ribs and tatters of trailing fabric. Dark drops plopped into the dust of the road as the aeroplane passed overhead, and one of them splashed warmly on to my forehead. Damn it! Engine oil, I thought, hoping that none had got on my clothes. I wiped it off with my handkerchief – and saw that it was not oil but blood.

I arrived at k.u.k. Fliegerfeld Caprovizza at sixteen minutes past twelve, according to my wristwatch. Not that anybody seemed to mind very much. I made my report to the duty warrant officer and was led to my quarters – a distinctly threadbare tent – by a private soldier. The base of Flik 19F was not at all an imposing sight: a stony stretch of more-or-less level field on the edge of the River Vippaco with four or five canvas hangars and two wooden ones under construction, a Stationskanzlei hut, a small marquee which I took to be the officer's mess and a few rows of tents for accommodation. At the edge of the field stood a row of log-and-earth shelters whose purpose entirely escaped me. A motor lorry and one or two horse-drawn wagons stood near by; likewise a field kitchen and a couple of barrows with petrol drums for fuelling aircraft (standing dangerously near the field kitchen, I considered). The only aeroplane that I could see was a Hansa-Brandenburg two-seater being rolled out of one of the canvas hangars. Otherwise the place seemed deserted in the midday heat that wobbled above the field, stilling even the cicadas in the riverside thickets and making the barren karst hills to southward appear to dance and undulate like the waves of the sea.

I put down my bags on one of the two camp-beds – the soldier obediently reported that I would be sharing the tent with a certain Oberleutnant Schraffl – then washed and brushed the dust off my clothes as best I could, combed my hair and straightened my bow-tie before making for the mess tent. I found it to be deserted except for one officer in flying kit smoking a pipe with his back turned to me. The mess cook reported that dinner had finished half an hour past and that the Herren Offiziere had all gone to rest in the shade of the cypress trees on the other side of the field. As for food, there was only some tinned meat with cold potatoes and some warmed-over mehlspeis. I took this as courteously as I could and sat down at one of the trestle tables.

The officer in flying kit turned round – and we both recognised one another. It was Karl Rieger, late captain in the 26th Jäger Regiment and a close friend of my elder brother Anton. We shook hands and embraced, not having met since 1912 or thereabouts. My first enquiry was after my brother, who had been missing in Serbia since August 1914, when the 26th Jägers had been wiped out in the fighting around Loznica. Since then I had questioned every survivor I could find in the faint hope that my brother might have been taken prisoner. But Rieger could offer no help: he had gone down with dysentery just after Potiorek's army had crossed into Serbia and had been lying in a hospital bed back in Sarajevo when the regiment had gone to their doom. Having no unit left to rejoin when he came out of hospital, he had volunteered for the Fliegertruppe and had served as an officer-observer on the Russian Front before training as a pilot. He was now the recently formed Flik 19F's 'Chefpilot': in theory the only officer in the unit apart from the Kommandant who could fly an aeroplane, since all the rest of the pilots on the strength were NCOs.

'I haven't been here that long myself,' he said. 'Only arrived last month when they split us off from Heyrowsky's lot over at Haidenschaft. As you can see, we're still using canvas hangars and the pens are only half finished.'

'The what?'

'The pens: those log-and-sandbag things over on the other side.'

'Please tell me – what on earth are they for? Surely you don't expect the Italians to start shelling the place: we must be a good twenty kilometres behind the lines here.'

'If it was only shelling we had to worry about! They're against the bora. It's not too bad now in summer, but believe me, come the autumn the wind'll be howling along this valley like anything. Flik 4 had their entire aircraft strength written off in five minutes last winter because they left them outside with nothing but tentpegs and a few sandbags to hold them down. One of them blew so far away they still haven't found it. I can tell you, Mother Nature's not going to catch us like that: we've taken enough losses from the Italians lately without having to worry about storm damage as well.'

'How are things on this sector then – in the air I mean?'

He drew reflectively on his pipe before answering.

'Not too bad until the past few weeks. In fact for the first twelve months of this war we had it pretty well our own way over the Isonzo: hardly saw the Italians at all, which is scarcely surprising, since I believe they came in with only about fifty serviceable planes in the whole country. But since about Easter things haven't been so bright. They've been setting up aircraft factories over there like nobody's business and buying up everything they can lay their hands on abroad, so now we're pretty well equal as regards numbers. But I'm giving away no secrets if I say that the quality's got much better on their side these past few months. I reckon our fellows have still just about got the edge, man for man. But the Italians have been getting Nieuport single-seaters from the French lately and, believe me, they're a handful if you meet one when you're flying one of our old furniture vans: nimble as a bluebottle and climb so fast you wouldn't believe it. We've had a hot summer of it so far in Flik 19F: forty-one aircrew joined the unit so far, of which twenty-three killed, wounded or missing and ten aircraft written off, five in crashes and five from enemy action. But that's enough of me rambling on, Prohaska. Tell me, what's our newest Maria-Theresien Ritter doing honouring our humble unit with his presence?'

'Sent here at short notice I'm afraid.'

'Extremely short: I was over in Kanzlei before dinner and we still haven't got your posting papers, only a telephone call from the War Ministry. What have you been up to, old man? Caught in bed with the Heir-Apparent's wife or what?'

I smiled. 'No such luck I'm afraid: just a minor disagreement with the Marine Sektion. It looks as if I shall be off U-Boating for a while. I'm here as an officer-observer I believe, though I can fly if needed: I've had a licence since 1912.'

'Splendid – you'll certainly find that useful. All the pilots except for me are rankers.'

'What about the Kommandant?'

Rieger smiled wryly. 'Herr Kommandant? Oh, not him I'm afraid: he says that flying would get in the way of his duties as commanding officer.'

'What duties? Surely in an air unit the commanding officer's main duty is in the air?'

'Perhaps so in most units. But not in ours. I suspect that our man would get dizzy standing on the edge of the kerb. Anyway, you'll see what I mean when you meet him, so don't let me prejudice you. But going back to what I said before, I certainly advise you to get some flying time in on your own as soon as ever you can, even if you only intend flying as a passenger. Life's getting pretty hectic now and more than once we've had officer-observers landing their own plane when their pilot's been knocked out. Oh yes, my dear Prohaska, I assure you that flying over the South-West Front is no easy number these days: we live fast here in the k.u.k. Fliegertruppe.' He rose and picked up his leather flying helmet. 'Anyway, can't sit here all day. I hope that you'll excuse me but we'll talk further this evening. The Kommandant presents his compliments and says that he'll see you at fourteen-fifteen hours when he gets back from Haidenschaft. He's been at the printers it seems, looking at the proofs of a new form for us to fill in. As for me, I've got to go and look at a machine with the Technical Officer. It came back from the repair shops only this morning and I want to see that everything's as it should be before I sign for it. Auf wiederschauen.'

Rieger went out, and I was left on my own. The mess orderly brought me a cup of that black, bitter infusion of roasted acorns described as 'kaffeesurrogat' and I picked up a day-old copy of the *Weiner Tagblatt*. I felt a good deal happier now than I had done after my oafish reception at Flik 19 a couple of hours before. I had just walked into a tent and had immediately run into someone I already knew, so perhaps this would be a congenial posting – at least for as long as I survived to enjoy it. I glanced at my watch: five-past two. I would go back to my tent and change out of my travel-grimed uniform into field dress for my interview with the commanding officer.

I emerged from the stuffy mess tent into the glaring sunlight to be greeted by the drone of an aero engine. An aeroplane was coming in to land on the field: a Hansa-Brandenburg CI to judge by the characteristic inward-sloping wing struts. It lined up to land, about fifteen metres up and as steady as could be. But as I watched, something went terribly wrong: the aeroplane suddenly lurched over on to one wingtip, which struck the ground with a splintering crash, kicking up a cloud of dust. I thought that the pilot had managed to right the aeroplane, but the thing simply cartwheeled into the ground before my horrified gaze, nosed over and then skidded crazily across the field to end up in the bushes on the bank of the river. I ran towards the wreck, joined on the way by a number of ground crewmen. But as we neared it, whumpf!, the whole thing went up in a bright orange puffball of flame. We ducked and stooped about the bonfire, eyebrows singeing from the heat, coming in as close as we dared to peer into the blaze and see whether the pilot might still be dragged clear. In the end we were driven back by the crackle of ammunition going off in the inferno.

By the time a hand-pumped fire engine had been brought up and a thin spray of water was playing on the wreck there was hardly anything left to burn, just a smoking tangle of bracing-wire and steel tubing jumbled up with glowing embers, a blackened engine and the upturned, tyreless bicycle wheels of the under-carriage. Gingerly we approached it, fearful of finding what we knew we must find. In the end I almost tripped over the ghastly thing before I recognised it for what it was. It lay twisted and grinning horribly, smoking gently as its charred fingers gripped the smouldering remains of the steering wheel. Fighting back a desperate urge to be sick, I knelt down, trying not to smell the stench of burning bacon. Only the boots and the steel goggle-frames remained intact; that and the metal identity tag hanging on a chain around the shrivelled throat. Without thinking I bent to pick it up – and yelped with pain. In the end I had to lever a stick under it and twist. The chain snapped and it went flying, to land hissing in the damp grass by the edge of a streamlet. I walked over and picked it up. It was the usual Austrian identity tag: a small metal case like a girl's locket, embossed with the two-headed eagle and containing a little booklet giving the wearer's personal details. I prised open the case, and found the paper toasted brown by the flames but still legible. It read, *Rieger. Karl Ferdinand. Oblt Geb. 1885 Leitmeritz. Rm Ktlsch*. Not fifteen minutes before, I had been chatting in the mess with this fire-blackened obscenity smouldering among the embers. As he had so recently observed, in those days we lived fast in the k.u.k. Fliegertruppe.

I left the scene of the crash feeling very weak at the knees. The birds had now resumed their interrupted chirping in the undergrowth by the riverbank, and two ground crewmen – both Poles I could hear – were heading towards the wreck with the tarpaulin-shrouded handbarrow reserved for such errands. They did not seem unduly awed by the solemnity of their gruesome task, which I learnt later they were often called upon to perform. As they neared the site of the crash they met a fellow-countryman coming the other way.

'Carbonised this time, Wojtek?'

'Completely. But never mind – it was only an officer.'

Hauptmann Rudolf Kraliczek, commanding officer of Flieger-kompagnie 19F, was not at all pleased that I had arrived three minutes and twenty-seven seconds late for my interview with him. Still shaky from the terrible sight I had seen only a few minutes before, I blurted out my apologies and reported that I had just witnessed a crash on the other side of the flying field. He waved my excuses aside irascibly.

'Herr Linienschiffsleutnant, please refrain from bothering me with such trifles.'

'But Herr Kommandant, your Chief Pilot Oberleutnant Rieger has just been killed . . .' He rolled up his eyes in despair behind his pince-nez. 'Oh no, not another one. Rieger, did you say?'

'By your leave, Herr Kommandant, Oberleutnant Rieger.'

'Are you sure?'

'Perfectly certain, Herr Kommandant: burnt beyond recognition. I saw his remains with my own eyes and removed his identity tag myself.'

He got up from his desk and selected a crayon.

'Which aeroplane was it?'

'A Hansa-Brandenburg just back from repairs. It seemed to go out of control just as he was coming in to land. From what I could see of it . . .'

'Be quiet,' he snapped peevishly, turning to face a board which covered the entire back wall of his office and which was itself covered by twenty or so sheets of squared paper with jagged rising and falling lines of various colours and with a rainbow-hued array of bars. He had a red crayon in his hand and seemed to be talking to himself.

'One more officer-pilot down and one aeroplane less. Oh gottverdammt, it's really too bad: how can they expect to keep orderly returns if they behave like this? Let me see: Effective Against Nominal Establishment for July should have been here . . .' he traced a line on the graph, '. . . and now it'll have to go here. Why couldn't the idiot have crashed next month?'

While Hauptmann Kraliczek was thus engaged, rubbing out and correcting lines on his beautifully drawn charts, I was able to get an uninterrupted look at the man. And really, even if I have never been much addicted to what might be called the 'male-model' view of military leadership – that an effective fighting man should necessarily look like a Viking chieftain or a Greek god – I have to say that he did seem a remarkably odd specimen to be running a front-line flying unit in the middle of a world war: a most unsoldierly-looking soldier. Not that he was deficient in military smartness: rather that there was too much of it. Although he was kitted out in the standard field-grey service tunic I noticed that this

33

was immaculately brushed, and entirely free of the patches and darns that were increasingly widespread among front-officers now that we were approaching the third year of the war. I also observed that instead of the breeches and puttees which were de rigueur nowadays, he wore pre-war salonhosen of the General Staff pattern, dark grey with a double red stripe, impeccably pressed, and leather shoes rather than field-boots like the rest of us. As for the man inside this get-up, he had more the air of a rising deputy bank manager than of a military officer: pale, sleek and be-spectacled, with neatly manicured little hands which looked far more accustomed to wielding a pen than a stick-grenade or a pair of wire cutters. I saw also, as he turned to face me, that although he wore the balloon-badge of the Fliegertruppe on his collar patches behind the captain's three stars, he had neither the wings of a pilot nor those of an officer-observer. He brushed the eraser-crumbs carefully off his tunic before speaking.

'Well Prohaska, I have to welcome you to Fliegerkompagnie 19F. I think that you will find it, though but recently established, to be one of the more efficient air units of the Imperial and Royal Army. And I can assure you that it is my intention to make it the most efficient. Tell me, Prohaska, at what time did you arrive at Fliegerfeld Caprovizza?'

'Fifteen minutes past twelve or thereabouts, Herr Kommandant. My movement order said twelve a.m., but there was no lorry from Divacca so I had to borrow a motor cycle, and my orders instructed me to report first to Flik 19 at Haidenschaft . . .'

He pursed his lips in a curiously spinsterish expression of disapproval.

'Herr Linienschiffsleutnant,' he said quietly, as if I had just committed some unspeakable solecism, 'I believe that I just heard you refer on two occasions to hours of the military day as "fifteen minutes past twelve" and "twelve a.m.". Such a slipshod method of denoting time may be acceptable in the k.u.k. Kriegsmarine, I cannot say; but I must ask you never to use it here. You must accustom yourself without delay to the clockwork precision with which the k.u.k. Armee conducts its affairs. The correct military formulations are "twelve hours fifteen" and "twelve hours" respectively and will be used *at all times* while you remain with this unit. Is that clear?' I replied that this was clear. 'Very good: until further notice, and pending the arrival of your posting papers from Vienna, your duties with this unit will be those of an officer-observer.'

'Herr Kommandant, by your leave . . .'

'Yes, what is it?'

'Herr Kommandant, I obediently report that I am a qualified pilot and have been for nearly four years past. Given a little training in flying modern land-based aeroplanes I am quite capable of fulfilling the duties of an officer-pilot, and before he died Oberleutnant Rieger said that I ought to get some flying hours in on my own . . .'

He had turned even paler than usual as I said this. 'Herr Linienschiffsleutnant, pray contain yourself and reserve your helpful suggestions for when I ask you for them. Your substantive post here, I understand, is to be that of an observer-officer; so as far as I am concerned, until I receive further orders that is what you will do even though you should be the last qualified pilot left alive in the entire Dual Monarchy. Quite apart from anything else, to permit otherwise would be to make absolute nonsense of the manning establishments laid down for this calendar quarter by the Imperial and Royal War Ministry. Anyway, that is all that I have to say to you.' He sat down at his desk and took out a folder of foolscap sheets densely covered in figures, along with a pencil and ruler and pocket reckoner – a thing rather like a pepperpot where one twiddled knobs in the top and read off the figures in a little window at the side. He looked up. 'Yes, have you anything more to say?'

I rummaged in the breast pocket of my jacket.

'I obediently report that before I departed from Flieger-kompagnie 19 this morning the Adjutant there gave me a present for you from Hauptmann Heyrowsky: a bicycle, to be precise. You will find it leaning against the back wall of this hut. He also gave me this message for you.' I handed him the envelope which had been tucked under the bicycle saddle, then saluted with as much irony as I could risk without ending up on a charge of insubordination. He took the envelope. I saw that his hands were trembling slightly.

'Er, was there any verbal message accompanying it, by any chance?'

'I have the honour to report, Herr Kommandant, that there was; the gist of it as conveyed to me by the Adjutant was that Hauptmann Heyrowsky is prepared to teach you to ride the bicycle if you so desire.'

He smiled nervously and slit open the envelope, then pulled out the sheet of paper inside. He swallowed hard as he read it, then looked at me with a sickly grin.

'Yes, yes, Prohaska, Hauptmann Heyrowsky and I are old comrades – always pulling one another's legs; you mustn't take what he says too seriously. He is a fairly capable officer even if he is lamentably lacking in military precision. We have a great deal of respect for one another, I can assure you. Anyway. . .' (he tore the letter up into minute scraps and dropped them into the waste-paper basket), 'if you will excuse me I must get on with my returns. We are already into the last week of the month.' I saluted once more and turned to leave. 'Oh, by the way, Prohaska.'

'Herr Kommandant?'

'I am assigning you to fly with Feldpilot-Zugsführer Toth for the time being. I shall expect you to manage the man with a firm hand. He is totally lacking in discipline and respect for military order: to a degree in fact where I am considering whether a posting to the trenches or even a court martial may not soon be necessary. Aerial discipline is already lamentably lax in the k.u.k. Fliegertruppe and I shall make it my principal concern while I am in command of this unit to tighten it up. As far as I am concerned the fewer unruly degenerates like that we have in the Flying Service the better it will be for Austria.' With that he adjusted his spectacles and set to work on his papers, apparently blind to my departure.

I learnt over the next few weeks that, before the war,

Hauptmann Kraliczek had once been one of the brightest rising stars of the Imperial and Royal General Staff. His tour of duty as an infantry Fähnrich had been lacklustre to say the least of it, marked only by a regrettable incident during the 1906 summer manoeuvres in Dalmatia, when he had fallen off his horse in front of the Archduke Franz Ferdinand and several thousand onlookers – then remounted with the wrong foot in the stirrup so that he ended up astride the beast facing its tail. But his career as a military administrator had been far more promising. After obtaining the highest marks ever recorded in the 1910 Staff College examinations at Wiener Neustadt he had been posted straight into the Military Rail Movements Directorate, the department of the War Ministry responsible for the Austro-Hungarian version of those vast, minutely detailed mobilisation plans by which the gigantic conscript armies of the European Powers would be moved to their appointed places in time of war. This was extremely exacting work in those days before the computer. In fact it used to be said, not entirely without truth, that the best brains from the Staff College went into the Eisenbahn-truppe and ended up in padded cells before they were forty.

Kraliczek had shone at this arduous work. But when the fateful day finally came, at the end of July 1914, these elaborate plans were found wanting. The Monarchy had two microscopically detailed mobilisation timetables, worked out to the last second and the last soldier's bootlace: one for a war against Russia with a holding force to take care of the Serbs; the other for a war against Serbia with only a holding force against the Russians. What the plans had failed to take account of however was the possibility of a war on two fronts. The result was a month or more of indescribable chaos as the two plans ran foul of one another: of trains of cattle trucks rattling past empty while exhausted soldiers trudged along beside the railway tracks laden down with their entire kit and supplies; of gunners being sent to Serbia while their guns went to Poland and their ammunition to the Tyrol; of troop-trains clanking day after day across the sweltering Hungarian plain at eight kilometres per hour – then burning out their axle boxes as they tried to storm the Carpathian passes at express-train speeds. A cousin in Cracow – where enthusiasm for a war against the hated Muscovites bordered on the hysterical – told me years later of the scene as a flower-bedecked trainload of Polish reservists had left the Hauptbahnhof for the front one morning early that August: how the soldiers had climbed into the bunting-draped carriages laden down with presents of tobacco and chocolate, then steamed out of the station before a wildly cheering crowd as the band played the 'Gott Erhalte' and the Polish national anthem. The Cardinal Archbishop was there in full canonicals to sprinkle them with holy water from an enamel bucket and to assure them that they were off to take part in a God-sanctioned crusade against Tsarist tyranny and Orthodox heresy. The train disappeared around the bend, he said – then promptly reappeared, steaming backwards into the station, where the whole patriotic effect was somewhat undermined, to say the least, as the entire complement disembarked on to the crowded platforms.

The outcome of all this had been a series of notable thrashings for the k.u.k. Armee at the hands of the Russians and the Serbs – followed by a discreet purge among the staff officers who were held to have been responsible for this appalling mess. Heads had to roll if the prestige of the Dynasty was not to suffer, and poor Kraliczek – whether justly or not, I cannot say – was among those upon whose necks the axe fell. In fact it was only by expressing a sudden interest in flying that he had been able to escape immediate posting to an infantry-reinforcement battalion on its way to the Carpathians, where the Russians looked about to batter their way through the passes into Hungary.

Thus the immediate danger of bayonet fighting with wild Siberians had been averted. But in the end poor Kraliczek had found himself faced with the prospect – perhaps even more frightful to someone with his retiring nature – of being required to soar thousands of metres above the earth in a fragile, unreliable contraption of wood and linen driven by some reckless castaway suffering quite probably from the long-term effects of serious head injuries. Urgent requests to transfer out of the Fliegertruppe had been turned down, so in the end the only way out for him was to seek command of an air unit and use his seniority to make sure that his immaculate footwear stayed firmly planted on terra firma. His method for accomplishing this would become clear to me over the next few weeks.

In brief, it consisted of avoiding flying duties – so far as I know he never once took to the air – by filling his entire waking life with administration. God alone knows there was enough paperwork in the old k.u.k. Armee: endless forms to be filled in, returns to be made, authorisations to be sought, derogations to be obtained in regard to an intricate mesh of often contradictory regulations that governed every aspect of service life, down to the precise daily ration scales for the cats employed to catch mice in military supply depots. Yet Kraliczek had somehow contrived to add to even this mountain of paper, inventing reports and statistical compilations of his own, even going so far as to design and print at his own expense official forms as yet undreamt of by the War Ministry. Thus ensconced, spider-like, at the centre of a dense administrative web which only he fully understood, he clearly hoped to be able to sit out the entire war in his office, sixteen hours a day, seven days a week, eating at his desk and taking his few hours' nightly rest on a camp-bed in the orderly room, retiring long after the nightingales had gone to roost in the willow thickets by the river. How could he do otherwise, he would argue, when the Fliegertruppe could not even supply an adjutant to help him? What he failed to mention here was that each of the three adjutants who had arrived at Caprovizza since May had left after a week or so with nervous prostration. Questions would be asked one day. But the Imperial and Royal military bureaucracy moved slowly even in wartime, and with any luck it would all be over before he was smoked out of his burrow. Then he would be able to return to what he called 'proper soldiering'; that is to say, sitting once more behind a desk in Vienna compiling mobilisation timetables and calculating his pension entitlement.

My first official engagement as a member of Fliegerkompagnie 19F took place the next morning in the cemetery at Haidenschaft.

It was a ceremony that I was to attend on many occasions over the next few months – though somehow I always managed to avoid appearing in the leading role. Rieger's coffin was lowered into the grave while we stood by with bared heads. The priest finished his prayers, the guard of honour fired off its three salvoes into the summer sky, and we then filed past to toss our handful of earth on to the lid of the coffin, the smell of incense still not quite managing to mask the faint odour of roasted meat. The k.u.k. Fliegertruppe had been here not quite three months, yet already a row of twenty or so wooden crosses stood beneath the black cypress trees against the cemetery wall: crucifixes in which the cross-beam was made from a cut-down aeroplane propeller painted white and inscribed with the name and rank of the deceased. The non-German names looked faintly odd in black Gothic lettering: Strastil and Fontanelli and Kövess and Jasiński. We used to call it the 'Fliegerkreuz', I remember. It was a frequently awarded decoration, and one which – unusually for the Imperial and Royal armed forces – was distributed to officers and other ranks without distinction.

3

FLYING COMPANY

For me, as someone whose mother tongue was not German, one of the most curious things about the old Austrian variant of that language was the way in which its extraordinary regard for titles, and its endless inventiveness in creating jaw-breaking composite nouns – monstrosities like 'Herr Obersektionsführerstellvertreter' or 'Frau Dampfkesselreinigungunternehmersgattin' – was balanced by an equal facility for cutting down these same sonorous titles to hideous little truncated stumps like 'Krip' and 'Grob' and 'Frop': names which to my ear always sounded like someone being seasick. It was as if a man should wear himself out and spend his entire substance equipping an ordinary house with marble staircases and balustrades worthy of a palace, then spend his time entering and leaving the house and getting from floor to floor within it by a system of makeshift scaffolding and rope ladders hanging from the windows.

The Imperial and Royal Austro-Hungarian Flying Service in the year 1916 was particularly rich in these uncouth acronyms. The basic unit, the Fliegerkompagnie, was cut down in common parlance to 'Flik'; while the workshop that undertook care and maintenance for each group of Fliks, the Fliegerettapenpark, was reduced to 'Flep'; and the units which supplied men to the squadrons, the Fliegerersatzkompagnien, were 'Fleks'. The rear-area supply unit, the Fliegermaterialdepot, was the 'Flemp'; while the flying-schools for officers and for other ranks came out as 'Flosch' and 'Feflisch' respectively. There were also entities called the 'Febsch' and the 'Flobsch' – though God help me now three-quarters of a century later if I can remember what on earth they signified.

In the summer of 1916 each of the thirty or so Fliks of His Imperial, Royal and Apostolic Majesty's Flying Service consisted (on paper at least) of eight aircraft – six operational and two in reserve – and a total of about 180 men: a commanding officer, a Chefpilot, a technical officer, an adjutant, eight or nine pilots and a similar number of officer-observers and, beyond them, about 150 ground crew. The trouble here though was that since in the years before 1914 the k.u.k. Armee had always been too strapped for cash to call up more than about half of its annual contingent of recruits, and since the losses in the early battles of the war had been appalling, these manning levels were never anything like met in practice.

Nor were we any better off as regards aircraft that summer on the Isonzo Front. Always conservative in outlook as well as financially hard-up, the Imperial and Royal Army had paid very little attention to aeroplanes in the years before the war. Indeed, that the Dual Monarchy had an air force at all worthy of the name was almost entirely the work of one tireless officer, a Croat major-general of Sappers by the name of Emil Uzelac – 'Unser Uz', as we used to call him. Uzelac – whom I met on several occasions – looked the very archetype of all the numerous gallant Croatian dimwits who had formed such a high proportion of the Habsburg corps of regimental officers over the previous three centuries: a square-skulled, wooden-countenanced man in his early fifties with a sweeping moustache and an air of permanent indigestion. But in reality old Uzelac had a remarkably lively and flexible mind. In the mid-1900s he had taken up sailing – and then taught himself marine navigation to be able to take a merchant master's ticket, which he did at the first attempt. The flying bug had bitten him about 1910, and although he was already well into his forties he set about learning to fly; then, once he had obtained his pilot's licence, got to work remorselessly hounding the sceptical War Ministry to allocate money for building up a military air service. In this though he was only partially successful, for whenever he did manage to wring a few miserable kronen out of the Ärar for the purchase of an aeroplane he almost always had to go to France or Germany to buy it.

It was not that the Dual Monarchy lacked good aircraft designers; it was rather that it seemed incapable of using them to any purpose. Igo Etrich, Kurt Sablatnig, the immortal Dr Ferdinand Porsche – all very soon grew tired of trying to squeeze money out of the Austrian bureaucracy, whose attitude to aviation was probably that if God had meant Austrians to get both feet off the ground at once he would not have created the Habsburgs to rule over them. One by one they had left to work in Germany, where the official attitude to these things was much less blinkered. An Austro-Hungarian aircraft industry of sorts had begun to put out shoots by 1914, but it was always a feeble and sickly plant. Industrialisation had anyway come late to our venerable Empire, and when the war arrived it was far too late to make up the arrears. By the end of it, Austro-Hungarian aircraft designs were by no means bad: I understand that the Phönix two-seaters of 1918 could give even the much-feared Sopwith Camel a run for its money, and Austro-Daimler aero engines were outstandingly good. But the numbers of aircraft built were always miserably small, and production of engines was anyway very fitful as the wartime shortages spread and the electricity supply was cut off for much of each day. When the Armistice Commissioners arrived in 1919 I believe that they found entire hangars full of finished airframes waiting for engines that never arrived.

A good deal of the trouble, I think, was that the enormous Imperial and Royal bureaucracy, though undeniably conscientious and hard-working enough in its way, was simply unable to adjust mentally to the twentieth century: in fact seemed never to have been entirely comfortable with the nineteenth. Even as I arrived there at Haidenschaft in July 1916, almost two years into the most desperate, bloody war in the Monarchy's long history, the official doctrine was still that it would all be over before long, and that there was thus no call to crank up war production unduly for a conflict that would soon have ended. No cutting of corners, no reduction of paperwork, no lowering of pre-war standards was still Vienna's motto. Not the least of Uzelac's difficulties in getting half-way decent aircraft in sufficient quantity was that right up until the end of the war the government department responsible for aircraft procurement was not the military itself but a civilian organisation called the k.u.k. Fliegerarsenal, at Fischamend just outside Vienna. Nobody and nothing in the world seemed capable of moving this body to speed up its majestic pre-war pace and authorise construction of modern aircraft – not even collective threats from bodies of front-fliers in 1917 to come along with bags of stick-grenades and conduct a general massacre of the officials. Long, long after all the other warring nations had realised that aircraft would be built in production runs of thousands at a time – and would often be obsolete almost as soon as they rolled out of the factory – Fischamend still clung obstinately to its pre-1914 belief that aeroplanes would be ordered individually like ships and that, like ships, they would last for a quarter-century. Even in 1915 Austrian aircraft were still being given individual names.

The Fliegerarsenal also hung on far longer than most to the idea – already fast waning in 1916 – that an aeroplane was an aeroplane was an aeroplane, capable of being used equally well for any purpose that required a flying machine, whether reconnaissance, photography, artillery-spotting, bombing, shooting up ground troops or bring down enemy aircraft. It was a belief that had already been comprehensively shot out of the skies over France, where in late 1915 it had only been their limited numbers that had prevented the notorious Fokker Eindeckers – the world's first effective fighter aircraft – from wiping out the entire British and French air forces with their forward-firing machine guns. Aeroplanes were already beginning to split up into specialised types, and even here on the Austro-Hungarian South-West Front the first moves were beginning to be made towards setting up air units with special tasks.

This was why I had joined not Flik 19 but Flik 19F: the 'F' stood for 'Fernaufklärung', or 'long-range reconnaissance'. Previously all front-line Fliegerkompagnien had been attached to an infantry division, for which they provided artillery-spotting and air photography and a little (usually not very effective) bombing and close support for the troops. But in February a daring experiment had been tried. Early one morning a flight of three Lloyd two-seaters had lumbered into the air from Gardolo flying field, in the Alps north of Lake Garda, and had flown a four-hour round trip to bomb the city of Milan. The results had been so gratifyingly out of proportion to the meagre investment – mass panic in a city that until now had thought itself far away from the war – that the Austrian High Command had decided to make further experiments in this direction. After all, the war had never been very popular in Italy – their parliament had been manoeuvred into it in May 1915 by something little short of trickery – and it was quite possible that a few more daylight raids on Italian cities might shake public morale to breaking-point.

The only problem here was our Emperor. The Old Gentleman was by no means the kindly grandfather of popular legend: he was as hard-boiled as most monarchs of the old school and was said to have been quite unmoved by the carnage at Solferino, whilst his adversary Napoleon III was violently sick when he saw and smelt that ghastly field the following day. But though seriously under-stocked in the imagination department, Franz Joseph was unquestionably a man of principle, and by his limited lights dropping bombs – even accidentally – on to unarmed civilians was something that he would never countenance, least of all in a city like Milan, which had been an Austrian provincial capital within living memory and where (it was rumoured) he still had an account at a military outfitters. In fact the very word 'bomb' was said to produce a noticeable agitation in this otherwise phlegmatic and rather dull old man: perhaps because he had spent so much of his long life having them tossed at him by would-be assassins. Arguments that bombing-raids would be directed solely at military targets – barracks, arms factories, railway yards and the like – had completely failed to budge him; maybe because, although not especially intelligent, he possessed a good deal more common sense than most of his advisers and knew instinctively what we airmen had yet to find out: that dropping bombs from two thousand metres under fire with primitive bombsights is one of the most inexact sciences of which it is possible to conceive.

Unimaginative though he was, the old boy perhaps knew in his aged bones what we young men did not: that when we staggered into the air in those feeble wood-and-linen biplanes of ours with their ludicrous bombloads we were in fact taking off on a flight which would lead via Rotterdam and Dresden to end amid the vitrifed rubble of Hiroshima.

Anyway, the outcome was that when a specialist long-range bombing squadron was created – after long delays for the appropriate paperwork to be completed, naturally – it was split off from an existing unit, Flik 19, and disguised as a long-range reconnaissance unit. It was a rather neat piece of duplicity. But in the end it created as many problems as it solved, both administrative and personal. The parent unit, Flik 19, formed in the spring of 1916, had already built up a reputation as one of the best and most enterprising Austro-Hungarian flying units; largely because of its remarkable commanding officer Hauptmann Adolf Heyrowsky, the man who had not been able to meet me when I arrived at Haidenschaft and who it seemed was conducting a running campaign of insults against my own commanding officer Hauptmann Kraliczek.

Heyrowsky was the very model of the Old Austrian career officer, one of the few survivors of a species which had been largely destroyed in the autumn of 1914 at Limanowa and Kraśnik. A superb fencer, skier and marksman, Heyrowsky – though not especially bright – was a man of exemplary courage, unshakeable loyalty to the House of Habsburg and spotless personal integrity. Although completely without experience in the air, he had insisted on flying as an observer from his first day with Flik 19, and within a month had bagged two Italian aircraft with a Mannlicher hunting rifle. And as if this were not enough, during the Fifth Isonzo battle in May, when the weather had been too bad for flying, he had volunteered to fight evenings and weekends (so to speak) as an infantry officer in the trenches.

Such a man as this was no more likely than his imperial master to take kindly to the idea of running an air unit designed to drop bombs on cities far behind the lines. Quite apart from the risks to civilians, he held it to be the duty of fighting airmen to fight in the closest possible support of the men in the trenches. But there was also the administrative insult offered to him by the existence of Flik 19F. Flik 19, you see, remained under the command of its nearest corps headquarters – the Archduke Joseph's 7th Corps at Oppacchiasella if I remember rightly – while we, being a strategic flying unit, came directly under 5th Army Headquarters far away in Marburg. Now, there is nothing that a professional officer loathes more than to have responsibility for a unit but no operational control over it – rather like being responsible for one's wife's debts when she has been living with another man for years past. So quite apart from the personalities involved, Hauptmann Heyrowsky could scarcely have been expected to look with any favour on this bastard offspring of his.

But the fact is that quite apart from his professional dislike of Flik 19F, Heyrowsky nursed an almost homicidal enmity towards the wretched Kraliczek, whom he despised as a desk-soldier of the most abject kind. It was not poor Kraliczek's fault, I suppose, that his name was a Germanised version of the Czech word for 'little rabbit' (a fact of which Heyrowsky was well aware, since he spoke that language fluently along with six or seven others). But it was a pity that the man's timid, grey, burrowing, nocturnal nature should have corresponded so exactly with his name. The very sight of such a creature might well be expected to arouse in a warrior like Heyrowsky feelings – well, feelings like those of a weasel confronted with a rabbit. I was told in fact (confidentially, since it had had to be kept quiet at the time for fear of a court martial) that, a few weeks before, there had been a disgraceful scene when Kraliczek had arrived at Fliegerfeld Haidenschaft to visit Heyrowsky on some business or other and had emerged from the Kanzlei hut after a few minutes pursued by Heyrowsky, with his sporting rifle, firing shots around Kraliczek's boots as the latter scurried towards his staff car and shouting, 'Run for your life, bunny rabbit!' Since then scarcely a day had gone by without some elaborate insult – like the offer of bicycle-riding lessons – being conveyed from Haidenschaft to Caprovizza: all with perfect impunity, since Heyrowsky knew that any complaint by Kraliczek would involve the latter in a court of honour and the choice either of fighting a duel or of being cashiered in disgrace.

Quite apart from its shortcomings as regards supply of aircraft and organisation, the k.u.k. Fliegertruppe when I was seconded to it in July 1916 still suffered from yet another crippling disadvantage imposed on it by the intense conservatism of its superiors. This was the doctrine, still held to by the War Ministry even if it was beginning to break down in the field, that it was the job of an officer to command an aeroplane and the job of an enlisted man – a sergeant at best – to fly the thing. The trouble was, I think, that even if k.u.k. military officialdom had by now grudgingly accepted that it needed an air force of some sort, it was damned if it was going to let the exigencies of flying get in the way of the famous Old Austrian discipline which, over the previous two centuries, had caused the Habsburg Army to be kicked about the deck by a succession of enemies ranging in size from France to Montenegro. In particular it would countenance no dilution whatever of that sacred entity the Habsburg officer corps, twin pillar of the Dynasty along with the Catholic Church.

By 1916 this was frankly a crazy notion: ever since the 1870s the old Imperial aristocracy had been withdrawing from military life and its place had been taken by ordinary people like myself, grandson of a Bohemian peasant. Even before 1914 the k.u.k. officer corps had been a thoroughly bourgeois body, and the terrible losses of that year had made it even more so by bringing in huge numbers of hastily commissioned cadets and one-year volunteers: youths who would have been pharmacists and school-teachers but for the war, and who would certainly go back to dispensing pills and teaching French grammar once it was over. Yet still the War Ministry behaved as if we were all Schwarzenbergs and Khevenhullers, and as if tying on the sacred black-and-yellow silk sword-belt (which large numbers of newly commissioned officers were now not even bothering to buy) was the next best thing to being anointed with consecrated oil by the Pope. Meanwhile men from the ranks – without the all-important

Matura certificate which allowed them to apply for a commission – were debarred absolutely from becoming officers, no matter how able and energetic they might be. So far as I know, no ranker-pilot in the k.u.k. Fliegertruppe was ever made an officer, though I believe that as a special mark of esteem the Hungarian ace Josef Kiss was promoted to officer-aspirant in 1918, once he was dead and safely out of the way.

The results of this imbecility were plain enough to see as the war went on. Our fliers invariably fought bravely, but the level of initiative and enterprise, it has to be said, was generally not high: not when compared with the German Flying Corps – which had once been as caste-conscious as our own but had changed its ideas under the pressure of events – and certainly not with the British on the Piave Front in 1918, when our Air Force had rings run around it by a handful of RFC squadrons whose pilots were almost all second lieutenants and whose daring was quite legendary. Certainly the mind-numbing routine of the old pre-war k.u.k. Armee – lots of drill and parades, because they cost less to put on than proper exercises, impressed the populace and required very little mental effort – was no very good preparation for a type of fighting that required the utmost qualities of self-reliance and initiative.

So it was that in the afternoon of my second day with Flik 19F, after returning from Oberleutnant Rieger's funeral, I made the acquaintance of the man who was to be my own personal coachman in whatever desperate adventures lay ahead. The Operations Warrant Officer had informed me that I was to make my first operational flight the next morning, to photograph ammunition dumps near the town of Palmanova at the urgent behest of 5th Army Headquarters. So I naturally felt it to be important to prepare for this quite lengthy flight over enemy territory by at least being introduced to the man who was to fly me there and (all being well) back again.

I came upon Feldpilot-Zugsführer Zoltan Toth engaged in

playing cards in the shade of a hangar with the ground crew of our machine, a Hansa-Brandenburg two-seater like the one that had incinerated poor Rieger the previous day. It was just after dinner and the men were enjoying their regulation hour's rest. They got up reluctantly and saluted as I approached. I had already met Feldwebel Prokesch, the craftsman sergeant in charge of the aeroplanes' six-man ground crew – but this creature . . . there must be some mistake. The man who stepped forward scowling to salute me and shake my extended hand . . . no, surely not. Few people, I think, would feel completely easy at first about entrusting their life, four thousand metres above the enemy lines and without a parachute, to the care of a complete stranger. But to a complete stranger who looked like an artist's reconstruction based on a jawbone and cranial fragments recovered from a Danubian gravel-bed? Prognathous, bow-legged and barrel-chested, this frightful apparition – altogether one of the ugliest, most ungainly-looking men I have ever seen—glowered at me from beneath his beetling brows: or to be more precise, a single protruding brow like the eaves of a cottage. Offhand, I was not quite able to remember the minimum height requirement for the Imperial and Royal Army, but I was still pretty sure that even in wartime this man fell short of it by a good head; that even if he had stood up straight, so that his trailing knuckles had not come quite so close to the ground, his head would barely have reached my shoulder. To describe his appearance as 'simian' would be grossly defamatory to the monkey tribe. I half expected him to swing himself up into the rafters of the open hangar and start jabbering and pelting us with nutshells. This was bad enough, to be sure; but Zugsführer Toth had not yet opened his mouth to make his report. When he did the effect almost managed to make me forget his appearance.

What on earth could these frightful sounds mean? Was it German or Magyar, or some other quite unknown tongue? Was it human speech at all? No, I decided at last: the words were approximations to German; it was just that they seemed to have been chosen at random by sticking a pin into the pages of a dictionary.

50

In theory, the language of command throughout the old Imperial and Royal Army was German. Even if less than a fifth of its men in fact spoke German as their native language, and even if most regiments conducted their internal business in the language of the majority of their men, every soldier of the Austro-Hungarian Army, no matter how illiterate or plain stupid, was supposed to learn at least a basic German military vocabulary: the famous Eighty Commands of the Habsburg Army. But in the purely Hungarian part of the Army – the Honvéd regiments from which Toth had transferred to the k.u.k. Fliegertruppe – the merest lip service was paid to German, and sometimes not that much. Even in the last years of the war there were cases of Hungarian full colonels who could barely understand German, let alone speak it. The Flying Service had been hurriedly put together from volunteers gathered from all nationalities of the Empire, so it was only to be expected that the standard of written and spoken German should often be very shaky. But even so, Toth's German there that morning was in a class of its own for sheer incomprehensibility. In the end we had to exchange our formal courtesies through a young mechanic who came from the Burgenland, east of Vienna, and knew both German and Magyar. It was also plain at this very first meeting that Feldpilot-Zugsführer Toth did not greatly care for officers as a class, whatever their nationality.

That evening in the mess I had my first real opportunity to talk with my brother-officers in Flik 19F; all, that is, except for Hauptmann Kraliczek, who had not been present at supper since he had to work (he said) on his statistical abstracts. I learnt that he usually took his meals alone in his office, so now that Rieger was dead the mess presidency devolved by right of age upon the Technical Officer – the TO – Oberleutnant Meyerhofer. Franz Meyerhofer was a good deal older than the rest – a year older even than myself in fact – and was a pre-war reserve officer who had been called to the colours only in 1915. A Jew from the Sudetenland, his normal job was as manager of a machine-tool company in the town of Eger. He had volunteered for the Fliegertruppe out of a wish to fly, but had been securely grounded ever since for the simple reason that, in the k.u.k. Armee, officers with such a thorough knowledge of engineering were extremely scarce; far too rare at any rate to be risked in flying operations. A solid, calm, reassuring sort of man, I took an immediate liking to him for reasons that I cannot quite define.

The other old greybeard in the mess was Oberleutnant Schraffl, my tent-mate. He had been a professional officer before the war, in one of the crack Kaiserjäger regiments, and his route into the Fliegertruppe had been that followed by a great many other flying officers in those years: that is to say, he had been too severely wounded to be able to serve any longer in the infantry, but was still able to hobble out to an aeroplane and climb into it. In his case he had been shot through the knee at Przemyśl in 1914, and then bayoneted for good measure by a passing Russian as he lay in a shell hole. An aluminium kneecap allowed his leg to bend (more or less), but he had to walk everywhere with a stick and needed a mechanic to help him into his seat. I must say that I got to know him very little. He was a rather reserved man; and in any case, there would not be the time.

The other three officers – Leutnants Barinkai and Szuborits and Fähnrich Teltzel – were extremely young: none of them more than twenty and straight out of gymnasium into the Army. I must say that I found them rather tiresome; not least because only Barinkai (who was a Hungarian) knew any language other than German. Relations were cordial enough I suppose, but these young men lacked tact, I felt, and had a disturbing tendency to admire everything German while disdaining the empire whose badge they wore. I had been a Habsburg career officer for sixteen years, but never in all that time until now had I ever heard it suggested in any gathering of officers at which I had been present that a Czech or a Pole or an Italian was any less loyal a soldier of the House of Austria than an ethnic German or a Magyar. Now I heard it all the time: allusions to the Czech regiments which had gone over to the Russians on the Eastern Front and the stories that the Heir-Apparent's Italian wife Zita was in secret contact with the Allies. On occasions I even suspected that these young sprigs were mimicking my Czech accent. But I supposed that perhaps I was growing sensitive on the point.

I made all my preparations that afternoon for the next morning's photographic mission to Palmanova: checked my maps, compass, pistol and so forth and drew my suit of leather flying overalls from stores – noting with some dismay as I did so that the breast of the jacket bore three none too discreetly patched bullet holes and that the lining was still stained profusely with blood. Then I had set off for a conference with my pilot, to discuss the route and our plans for tomorrow, even though I might have to use the young ground crewman as an interpreter. I was met on the way by Hauptmann Kraliczek.

'Ah, Prohaska, where are you going if I might enquire?'

I was tempted to tell him to mind his own business – he and I were after all equivalent in rank, while I had several years' seniority. But he was the commanding officer, so I remained courteous.

'To speak with Feldpilot Toth, Herr Kommandant.'

'With Toth? About what, might I ask?'

I was becoming rather irritated by this obtuseness, but I managed to contain myself. 'About the flight tomorrow, Herr Kommandant.'

'The flight, Herr Leutnant?' He looked puzzled. Was the man deliberately trying to annoy me, I wondered, or was he really as out of touch with events as he seemed?

'The flight, Herr Kommandant: the flight over Palmanova tomorrow morning to take photographs for Army HQ. Surely you remember.'

'Oh yes, of course, that flight. But why should you wish to discuss it with Toth, for goodness' sake?'

'I obediently report, Herr Kommandant, that Zugsführer Toth is to fly me there and back tomorrow. I wished to outline to him the purpose of the mission, to show him the route we might take and to ask for his views on it.'

He paused for some time and looked at me in bewilderment. 'Herr Leutnant,' he said at last, 'Herr Leutnant, do my ears deceive me or are you seriously suggesting that you, an Austrian officer, should *discuss* your plans with a ranker?'

'Why of course, Herr Kommandant: it seemed to me the merest common sense to tell the man what we are setting out to do and work out with him the best way of doing it. After all, I am not just a newcomer to the Fliegertruppe but to the South-West Front as well. Toth has been here several months I believe and has crossed the Italian lines on numerous occasions, so he should know better than most people what the hazards are and the best way around them.'

'Herr Linienschiffsleutnant' (he always used the cumbersome full form of my rank when he wished to annoy me), 'Herr Linienschiffsleutnant, while I cannot say what the custom is in these matters in the Imperial and Royal U-Boat Service – for all I know you may take it in turns with the cook to command your ship – in the k.u.k. Fliegertruppe the regulations are quite specific: the officer-observer is there to give the orders and the ranker-pilot is there to carry them out, even if he is ordered to dive at full speed into the ground. Toth has neither the right to his own opinion in the matter, nor any need to have one. He does not need to know where to go because you will direct him. And you will direct him because you are an officer and that is what officers are for, is that clear?'

I discussed this conversation with Meyerhofer after supper.

'Yes I know,' he said, 'stupid way to run an air force if you ask me. But I warn you, watch out for Toth: that man's got a mind of his own and he's done for one officer-observer already.'

'Who was that then?'

'A fellow called Rosenbaum, at the end of May, over Görz. Seems that Toth was manoeuvring the Brandenburger – your *Zośka* – a bit abruptly to dodge a Nieuport and Rosenbaum just fell out. He dropped through the conservatory roof of a convent you know – just missed a nun who was watering her begonias. Funny thing, but you'd have expected him to have splattered like a Roman candle, what with just having fallen from two thousand metres, but when they picked him up there was scarcely a mark on him. Anyway, there was no end of a row about that: seems that Toth had just done a bunt-turn and flicked him out of the cockpit.'

I should point out here that a bunt-turn is rather like performing a loop, except down rather than up, so that the pilot is on the outside of the loop, not the inside. It is still a court-martial offence I believe in all the world's air forces because of the brutal strains that it places upon an airframe.

'How did Toth get off?' I enquired.

'Luck. On the way home he met an SP2 artillery spotter. They're an Italian-built Farman pusher: you'll see a lot of them before you've been here long. I pity the poor buggers who have to go up in them because they're quite helpless when attacked: more blind spots than you'd think possible. Anyway, Toth decided not to shoot this one down, just got under its tail and kept tormenting it: nudging the tail down when the pilot tried to dive and bumping it underneath when he tried to climb and generally chivvying the poor sod around, further and further from home, until he ran out of petrol and had to land at Sesana. I gather that the observer was really cut up about it – the Principe Umberto di Cariagnano della Novera or something: really posh cavalry-regiment type. Said that he'd been forced down by unfair means – presumably it would have been all right if Toth had just shot him – and demanded immediate repatriation under a flag of truce. Then he got a look at Toth, who'd just landed alongside, and that really did it: carried on like a lunatic about him, a nobleman, being forced down by a "trained orang-utang", as he put it.'

'What happened then?'

'Oh, Toth just lost his temper and walked over and caught him a beauty under the chin – knocked him clean out. Of course, there was no end of a row about that: a ranker punching an officer and a nobleman into the bargain, especially after he'd just lost an officer of his own. They disallowed him the victory, then Kraliczek stepped in threatening court martials. In the end, rather than lose a pilot for a month in the cells, they gave him eight hours tied to the stake. We said that Kraliczek couldn't, but Kraliczek knows his regulations and pointed out that Toth's only a titular sergeant and therefore he's as liable to corporal punishments as a junior NCO when on active service. I tell you, though, it went down very badly here, to see a fine pilot like that standing for eight hours in the sun with his wrists tied above his head like a Ruthenian ploughboy who hadn't bothered to clean his rifle.'

This left me very sad and (I confess) not a little apprehensive. The k.u.k. Armee was not alone in 1916 in having a range of humiliating field punishments. I understand that the British Army of the day made a habit of leaving defaulters lashed to wagon wheels for hours on end. But to apply them to a sergeant-pilot in a front-line unit seemed to be going too far. Toth had tipped out one officer already by accident. Might the next one perhaps not fall to his death by design?

Later in the evening, before I turned in for the night, I spoke with the young Hungarian lieutenant Barinkai.

'Oh yes,' he said in his lisping Magyar-German, 'Toth, yes. I haven't spoken much with the man but I believe he transferred from a Honvéd sapper unit. From what I can gather it seems that he was once a monk, believe it or not; or rather a seminarist, in the abbey at Esztergom. I believe they threw him out after they caught him on top of a nun in the abbot's marrowbed. Luckily for him it was the week of Sarajevo, so he just came into the Army and no questions asked. Funny really how the war worked out like that for some people. I'd just ploughed my Matura second time around, and I'd borrowed a lot of money for cards and there was a housemaid being troublesome about a kid she said was mine. Then suddenly hey presto!, war declared, into uniform and goodbye exams, goodbye debts, goodbye housemaids for the duration. The papers say that this war's a disaster for the human race. All I can say is, blow the human race: for Feri Barinkai it couldn't have come at a better time.'

4

LITTLE SOPHIE

Oberleutnant Schraffl and I were up and dressed at eight bells –
sorry, 0400 hours – next morning, wakened by our shared
soldier-servant Petrescu. Petrescu was an illiterate Romanian
peasant from near Klausenberg in Transylvania – my wife's
birthplace – and we had been introduced only the day before. His
eyes had widened with wonder when he saw me standing with
Schraffl. I had been wearing my blue naval jacket with field-grey
breeches and puttees, and I later discovered that within a couple
of hours he had broadcast it about the entire district that I was a
British officer – the son of the English King no less – whom 'der
Herr Lejtnant Schraffl' had just shot down and was holding
prisoner until a ransom could be paid: a harmless enough yarn I
suppose, except that the following week, while I was out for an
evening stroll, a posse of rustics armed with pitchforks surrounded me and sent for the village gendarme in the belief that I
was trying to escape.

   We ate a hurried breakfast of coffee and bread, then walked out
across the flying field to where our two aeroplanes, their pilots
(Toth and a Czech corporal called Jahudka) and their respective
ground crews were waiting in the pale, faint-shadowed light of an
early summer's morning, long before the sun's rays had begun to
stream over the mountain pinnacles that loomed above Haidenschaft to the north and east. In the distance the rumbling of
artillery was growing louder by the minute as the daily round
began in the Isonzo trench lines. It had been decided the previous
evening, following intelligence reports of a new Italian single-
seater squadron near Udine, that instead of proceding alone

on our mission we would fly with Schraffl's aeroplane about five hundred metres above us as an escort.

Our own aeroplane, number 26.74, named *Zośka* – 'Little Sophie' in Polish – was a Hansa-Brandenburg CI built under licence by the Phönix company at Stadtlau. This was a matter of some comfort to me on my maiden combat-flight, since the 'Gross Brandenburger' was generally reckoned to be the best of the Austro-Hungarian two-seaters. Able to perform most front-flying tasks at least competently, it was easy to fly, immensely strong, stable enough to make a good reconnaissance aircraft yet sufficiently fast and manoeuvrable to give it at least some chance of survival if attacked by a single-seat fighter. One of the better products of that brilliant if patchy designer Ernst Heinkel, we owed the Brandenburger – like so much else in the Imperial and Royal armed forces – to a succession of administrative accidents and half-decisions; but also to the foresight and imagination of the Trieste-Jewish financier and aviation enthusiast Camille Castiglione who, when war broke out in 1914, had solved the Dual Monarchy's aircraft industry problem – that is to say, the almost total lack of one – at a stroke by simply buying up a complete factory in Germany along with its chief designer. The Hansa-Brandenburg plant near Berlin produced the designs and the prototypes, and these were then licensed out to be built by Austro-Hungarian factories. It was far from being an ideal system: the k.u.k. Fliegertruppe tended to get only those designs that Herr Heinkel had been unable to sell to the German Air Force. But it was better than nothing, and in the Hansa-Brandenburg CI it gave us a reconnaissance two-seater which served us faithfully right up to the end of the war, fitted with ever more powerful engines. In fact I recall that the Czechoslovak Air Force was still flying a few of them in the early 1930s.

The machine that stood before us in the half-light that morning at Caprovizza was a sturdy-looking, squarish, rather uncompromising biplane with curious inward-sloping struts between the wings. Its 160hp Austro-Daimler engine and attendant radiator completely blocked the pilot's view forward, so that Toth had to crane his neck out and look along one side of the nose like an engine driver peering out of his cab. The two of us were to sit in a long, shared cockpit. For defence to rearward I had a stripped-down Schwarzlose machine gun mounted to slide on rails around the cockpit edge, while for attack – that is to say, something getting in front of us for long enough to be worth a shot – Toth had a second Schwarzlose, complete with water-jacket this time, mounted on a pylon above the top wing so that it could fire ahead over the radiator and propeller. Looking at it that morning I was not at all sure that this second machine gun was worth the trouble of lugging it along with us. Thanks to the lack of forward view for the pilot, the sights consisted merely of a brass eyelet and a pin fixed into the interplane struts while the firing mechanism – since the weapon was way above the pilot's reach – was a lavatory chain and handle.

As for the photography which was our business that morning, I foresaw little problem. The previous afternoon I had received such instruction as was considered necessary for an officer-observer to be able to work an aerial-reconnaissance camera, and really there was nothing to it. A warrant officer from the army photographic laboratory at Haidenschaft had bicycled over to Caprovizza to tutor me in the principles of air photography and, when he learnt that I had been a keen amateur photographer from about the age of ten, had kindly agreed to omit the introductory parts of his lecture (properties of light rays, refraction through lenses, chemistry of the photographic plate, etc.) and just show me how to work the thing: so simple, he assured me, that even cavalry officers had been known to master it. The camera was about a metre high and was fixed to look downwards through a little sliding trapdoor in the belly of the aeroplane just behind the observer's position. It had a magazine of thirty photographic plates, and all that I had to do was to wait until we were flying level over the target, at the prescribed height and a steady speed, then keep pulling a lever until all the plates were used up. The lever would operate the shutter and then, on the return stroke, allow the exposed plate to drop into a collecting-box while loading a fresh one.

It looked like being a simple enough operation. Our orders were to be over Palmanova at 0630 precisely and then to fly northwards along the Udine railway line at exactly three thousand metres and a hundred kilometres per hour, taking photographs at precise five-second intervals. The reason for all this precision (I learnt) was that the Italians were stacking artillery shells alongside the railway line in preparation for the great Isonzo offensive that was expected any day now. The intelligence officers at 5th Army Headquarters were keen to know exactly how much ammunition the Italians were accumulating, which might give them some indication as to which side of Görz the blow would fall. We were to photograph the ammunition dumps at a precise time and height so that, by taking the altitude of the sun at that moment and measuring the length of the shadows cast, it would be possible to work out exactly how high the stacks were. To my mind this seemed a rather futile exercise: if you have ever been on the receiving end of an artillery bombardment (as I have several times and devoutly hope that you may never be) then it is largely of academic interest whether the enemy has a thousand shells to lob at you or only 973. But there we are: Old Austria was much addicted to such meaningless precision; and anyway, orders are there to be obeyed no matter how inane they may appear.

Hauptmann Kraliczek's remarks notwithstanding, I used the services of our young Burgenlander mechanic to hold a brief conference with Toth, pointing out the proposed route on the map and signalling by dumb-show what we were to do. He grunted and nodded his head and appeared to signal his agreement, so we clambered aboard and made our pre-flight checks: guns, camera, compass, altimeter and the rest of the rudimentary equipment considered necessary for fliers in those days. As we finished the first rays of the sun were reaching over the bare limestone peaks of the Selva di Ternova. Up there the shepherds would soon be piping to gather their flocks as they had done every summer's morning for the past four millennia, still living a life that would be entirely familiar to their counterparts in Ancient Greece. Yet here we were, only a few kilometres away in the valley, about to take

60

off on an adventure at the very forefront of the twentieth century, doing something which even in my not so distant youth had been completely unthinkable: the very crime for which the gods had punished Icarus. It was all extremely dangerous; but I have to say that at the same time it was marvellously exciting.

The checks completed, I turned to wave to Schraffl in the other Brandenburger. He waved back, and I slapped Toth on the shoulder to signal him to get ready. Given our problems with language, it was at least some comfort that speech would soon be entirely redundant; since, once we were up in the air, we would be able to communicate only by hand signals or at best by notes scrawled on signal pads. Toth nodded, and I leant out of the cockpit to call to Feldwebel Prokesch and the two mechanics waiting by the aeroplane's nose.

'Ready to start?'

'Ready to start, Herr Leutnant. Electrical contacts closed?'

I glanced at the switch panel. 'Electrical contacts closed: suck in.'

Prokesch turned the propeller to suck air-and-petrol mixture into the cylinders.

'Sucked in, Herr Leutnant. Open contacts now if you please.' I indicated the ignition switch to Toth, who flicked it down.

'Electrical contacts open. Start the engine.' With that, Toth began cranking the little starter magneto – 'the coffee grinder' – on the cockpit bulkhead while Prokesch took a swing at the propeller. It fired first time, the engine roaring into life as gouts of smoke and blue-green flame rippled from the six stub-exhausts. I let it warm up for a minute or so, looked to make sure that Schraffl's engine was also running, then waved to the ground crew. The mechanics pulled the chocks from in front of the wheels, threw them aside, then ducked underneath the aeroplane to sprawl themselves forward over the lower wings, one man lying on each side just inboard of the struts. The reason for this was that, with the engine and radiator completely blocking the pilot's view forward, Brandenburgers were notoriously tricky to taxi on the ground and were always piling up against posts or running into other aircraft.

The mechanics were there to give directions to Toth as he opened the throttle and the aeroplane started to lurch across the stony grass field.

We turned into the wind – a faint westerly breeze this early in the morning – and Toth gave full throttle as the two mechanics waved to signal 'All clear ahead' and slid back off the wings. The air began to sing past us as the Brandenburger gathered speed, wheels bouncing on the bumpy field. Take-off runs were minimal in those days when aeroplanes started to lift off at near-bicycle speeds: 150 metres or less if the aeroplane was lightly laden. Soon a faint lurch and sudden smoothing of the motion signalled that we had left the ground behind. Toth lugged back the control column – not a modern joystick but a backward-and-forward post with a small wooden motor-car steering wheel on top – and soon we were climbing away from Fliegerfeld Caprovizza, banking to port to make the regulation two circuits of the airfield: a precaution against engine failure, since the probability was that if a piston was going to seize, it would do so now rather than later on. Meanwhile Schraffl and Jahudka had climbed into the air astern of us. Once I saw that they had made their circuits too I fired a green flare to signal that all was well, and we set off down the Vippaco valley, heading for the town of Görz and the enemy lines in the hills to west of it. We were on our way. Whether we would make the same journey in the opposite direction would become clear during the next ninety minutes or so.

We climbed gently as we flew down the broad, uneven valley of the Vippaco, heading for the point where that river joins the Isonzo just south of Görz. Our aim was to cross the lines at about three thousand metres, then head north-east towards Udine for a while to confuse the Italian observers on the ground, who would telephone our height and direction as soon as they saw us pass overhead. We would then turn south-westwards and circle round to approach Palmanova from the direction of Venice, hoping in this way that we would be taken for Italian aircraft and left alone by any anti-aircraft batteries around our target. I checked my map and ticked off the towns and villages of the Vippaco valley as we flew over them: Santa Croce and Dornberg and Prvačina and Ranziano; not so much for navigational purposes – we were following the railway line and river anyway – as to memorise their appearance for future flights when visibility might be poor and there might be no time to consult the map. How considerate it had been of previous generations (I thought) to have built so many hill-top monasteries around Görz – Monte Vecchio and San Gabriele and Monte Santo. As a sceptic I doubted their religious efficacy; but there was no denying that as air-navigation beacons they took some beating, stuck up there on their mountain-peaks and painted white and yellow to stand out against the dark green pine forests. Meanwhile, away to westward, the guns flashed from time to time among the wooded hills across the Isonzo.

The sun was well up as we passed over the town of Görz: still largely undamaged despite the closeness of the lines. The castle and the twin-domed cathedral were clearly visible in the early-morning light, and the silvery ribbon of the Isonzo branching and rejoining among the summer-dry banks of pebbles as it made its way towards the sea. Then we crossed the trench lines, which here climbed up from the valley floor to wind among the devastated forests of Podgora and Monte Sabotino on the west bank of the Isonzo. It was around here if anywhere that we would meet flak artillery fire. I peered ahead apprehensively – then saw three quick red flashes and puffs of dirty black smoke in the sky far ahead of us. A feeling of intense relief surged through me. Utterly feeble: so typical of the Italians and their charming incompetence. If that was the best they could do then – It was like a sudden, heavy kick in the backside: three or four shells bursting below us with a concussion that knocked the air out of my lungs and tossed the aeroplane around much as a number of badminton players will bat a shuttlecock from one to the other. I clutched the cockpit edge in alarm as Toth looked down, snorted in disgust and began to weave the aeroplane from side to side to put the gunners off their aim. I looked up and saw that Schraffl – now well above us – was doing the same. Other shells followed, but none came as close as that early group, and within a minute or two we were well beyond the lines and out of reach. A few puffs of smoke hung in the sky astern as if to say 'You are lucky this time, porci Austriaci, but there's always another day . . .' Twenty minutes later we were approaching Palmanova from the west.

Because everything happens so much faster, and in three dimensions instead of two, air navigation has always been a rather hit-or-miss business compared with position-finding at sea. I imagine that this is still largely true even now; and in those far-off times seventy years ago it was true – how do you say? – with brass knobs on it. Even so, it would have required a complete imbecile not to have recognised the town of Palmanova, because I think that in the whole of Europe there can scarcely be another settlement so instantly recognisable from the air. I whistled in admiration as we flew over it, so lost in wonder that I almost forgot to check the time and line us up for our photographic run along the railway line. I suppose that in the years since, the growth of suburbs and factory estates must have blurred its outlines; but as I saw it that July morning it still possessed that pristine purity of form in which its builders had left it: a perfect Renaissance fortress-town laid out like a star of David with successive rings of earthworks – lunettes and ravelins and bastions – surrounding it in what could well have been an engraving from a Leonardo da Vinci treatise on the art of fortification. It was so perfect that I half expected to see a scrolled cartouche in the fields near by with a pair of dividers, a scale of yards and a copperplate legend: 'Senatus Serenissimae Republicae Venetii castrum et oppidum Palmae Novae aedificavit anno domini 1580', or something similar. It suddenly occurred to me that Toth and I were among the very few people who had ever had the privilege to see the place from above, exactly as its architects had designed it.

But we had more important things to do that morning than study sixteenth-century military engineering. More technologically advanced and far less aesthetically pleasing ways of killing people were our immediate concern as we lined up to run along the railway track leading towards Udine. Toth brought us down

64

until the altimeter read exactly the three thousand metres prescribed by our orders. I pulled back the cuff of my flying overall and glanced at my wristwatch. Even in July over Italy the air was near-freezing this high up, and I felt the cold suddenly bite at my exposed skin. Right on time: the seconds hand was just sweeping up towards 0630. Really this was too easy. I glanced down and saw the dark oblong stacks of shells piled up neatly alongside the railway track for a good two or three kilometres. Then I bent down to slide open the hatch in the cockpit floor. As the hands of the watch touched 0630 I pulled the lever for the first exposure.

My attention was not entirely devoted to working the camera lever every five seconds: in fact ever since we had left Caprovizza I had been ceaselessly scanning the sky above and astern of us for the first sight of anything suspicious. I must say that I was somewhat apprehensive about this. Being a naval officer my eyesight was excellent; but I suspected that the skills of a good U-Boat look-out – like the trick of never looking directly at the horizon but always slightly above it – might not be entirely applicable in the air. I had also, I must admit, something well short of total confidence in the means by which I was to defend us if we were attacked from behind.

The 8mm Schwarzlose had been the Austro-Hungarian Army's standard machine gun since 1906 or thereabouts, selected after an exhaustive series of competitive trials in which it alone had been able to meet the War Ministry's stringent specification as regards price. I suppose that the thing might have been just about adequate for a peacetime army, but for fighting a world war it was a very dubious contraption indeed. Whereas most other machine guns in service around the world were operated by muzzle-gas, Herr Schwarzlose had chosen to make his design work by recoil – and had then (for some quite unaccountable reason) decided to dispense with the locking system generally considered necessary to hold a machine- gun breech shut while each round is fired. These twin eccentricities meant that the Schwarzlose had to have a very short barrel – and thus mediocre range and accuracy, not to mention a picturesque gout of flame as each round left the muzzle.

It also necessitated a massive breech block, like a miniature blacksmith's anvil, so that its inertia would prevent it from being blown back into the gunner's face. This in its turn meant a further loss of range, because so much of the energy from each shot was absorbed in kicking the breech open. As a result its rate of fire was poor: about four hundred shots per minute on paper but barely three-quarters of that in practice.

And that was just the army version: the air Schwarzlose, which now rested behind me on its rails ready for action, was a still further declension of mediocrity. Unlike the excellent Parabellum – standard observer's gun in the German two-seaters – it had no shoulder-stock to allow the gunner to keep his aim however violently the pilot was throwing the aeroplane about the sky. Instead it had a pair of handles like those of a child's toy scooter. The water-jacket had been removed to save weight; but this had only made the aim even more uncertain since it abolished the foresight, and also meant that we could fire bursts of only twelve or so shots at a time, for fear of burning the barrel. As for the ammunition feed, it consisted of a canvas belt of five hundred rounds coiled in a metal drum on the side of the thing. This belt would always absorb some damp in the early mornings, waiting out on the airfields, and even in summer this would often freeze in the upper air, causing the gun to jam. This was bad enough, but our gun that morning was an early model – pensioned off no doubt from the Army – in which each cartridge had to be lubricated by a little oil-pump as it went into the breech so that the empty case would extract afterwards. This oil would become sticky in the cold, so that even if the gun would still fire it would slow down to two hundred rounds or so per minute, making it sound like an exhausted woodpecker on a hot summer's afternoon. All things considered, I think that a Singer sewing machine would have been about as much use for defending ourselves – as well as being a good deal lighter.

In the event though it looked as if the wretched Schwarzlose might not be needed that morning, there in the summer sky above the Friulian Plain. I pulled the lever to expose plate number thirty, heard it clack into the box and then turned thankfully to Toth to tap him on the shoulder and signal 'Finished – head for home'. I was glad of this, because cloud was coming in fast from the west: white cauliflowers of cumulus which were for the moment above us, but which seemed to be coming down to our altitude. I looked up, and saw Schraffl's aeroplane disappear into the cloud above us, reappear for a moment and then vanish again as we turned for home. He had seen us I was sure, but to make certain that he knew we were finished I fired a white flare just before we lost sight of one another.

When I next caught sight of an aeroplane, about three kilometres astern and slightly above us, it took me some moments to realise that I was not looking at Schraffl and Jahudka's machine. I could not see exactly what it was, but head-on it was most certainly not a Brandenburger, whose inward-sloping struts gave it an unmistakable appearance when viewed from the front. It was a biplane, but of what kind I could not say except that it appeared to be somewhat smaller than ours – though still too large for a Nieuport – and that it was most certainly closing with us at speed. Then I saw another one, at the same altitude but about two kilometres astern of the first. Whoever they were, they had seen us and were gaining on us fast. Heart pounding, I turned around and seized Toth by the shoulder. He looked around to where I was pointing, and nodded casually. I signalled for 'Full throttle' by thrusting my fist forward. He nodded, and eased the throttle lever forward a little. Meanwhile I had turned to fumble desperately with the machine gun, releasing the clamp which held it still on its mounting-rails and jerking back the cocking lever. Damn them, where were Schraffl and Jahudka? They were supposed to be escorting us and ought to be manoeuvring now to drop down on the Italians as they came in astern of us. And why were we moving so slowly? Surely a Brandenburger could travel faster than this at full throttle.

The leading aeroplane was close enough behind us now for me to get a good look at it. It was most definitely an Italian two-seater. Of what make though I have no idea at all, except that it had a rotary engine and a gun mounted on the top wing to fire over the propeller. They were still out of range, but weaving about slightly in our wake in an effort (I suppose) to confuse us before they moved in for the kill. The Italian was smaller and evidently rather more manoeuvrable than our *Zośka*, and also looked as if it might be slightly faster. Although I had no way of knowing it at the time, he was about to use what would become the standard technique for shooting down a reconnaissance two-seater. He would make a series of feints like a boxer to put me off my aim, then drop down into the blind spot under our tail until Toth had banked away – say to starboard – to let me take aim. Then he would dodge away to port before I could fire, and use his higher speed and tighter turning circle to come up on the other side as I was desperately trying to lug the gun around on its rails. There would then follow a short burst fired at perhaps twenty metres' range into the belly of our aeroplane; a burst which, even if it were not to kill the pair of us, would certainly knock out the engine, or hack out a wingroot, or rip open the fuel tank to send petrol pouring over hot engine and sparking magneto and send us spinning down in flames to our deaths.

In the event though, both the Italian pilot and I had reckoned without Zugsführer Toth. He banked us a little to starboard as expected. I caught a glimpse of the Italian machine – a mottled greenish-buff colour I remember – under our tail and was just about to loose off a few shots at him when he disappeared back under it. In panic I turned to Toth – and felt my stomach and liver hit the top of my skull as Toth suddenly gave full throttle and dropped into a power dive. Then I was squeezed to the floor as the whole airframe squealed in protest about me: Toth had wrenched the control column back to take us up in a tight loop! I was not strapped in of course: the observer's folding seat had shoulder-belts, but to fire the machine gun I had to stand up with nothing but gravity to hold me into the aeroplane. I still shudder to remember the sudden, stark terror of finding myself upside-down, three thousand metres above the meadows and woodlands of Friuli, clutching convulsively at the cockpit coaming as the engine coughed and faltered at the top of the loop. Then, just as I felt sure that I must let go and fall to my death – I was already hanging in mid-air like a gymnast performing a somersault between parallel bars – the nose dipped down as we dived out of the loop. As we did so I saw ahead of us the Italian, taken by surprise, trying to execute the same manoeuvre.

I see it now as vividly as in that split second one summer morning seventy years ago: the perfect plan view fifty metres ahead; the black V-marking on the centre section of the upper wing; the red-white-green Italian colours on the wingtips and tailplane; the observer swinging his machine gun up in a desperate attempt to get a burst at us as we passed. In the event though it was Toth who fired first. Given the extreme crudeness of our gunsights and the primitive firing system I think that it must still be one of the finest pieces of aerial marksmanship on record. Our forward-firing Schwarzlose clattered, and the hot cartridge cases showered back over us. The burst of ten or so shots hit the Italian just as he was into the tightest part of his loop, and therefore when the airframe was under maximum stress. I think that our bullets must have smashed the main wingspar, but I cannot say for sure: all I know is that as we hurtled past, swerving to avoid him, the Italian aeroplane seemed to pause in its abrupt climb and hang motion-less for a moment as though undecided whether or not to go any further. Then it began to fall backwards as its wings crumpled like those of a shot partridge, dropped back out of its loop, then nosed over and began to spiral down, transformed in a couple of seconds from a neat, fast, fighting biplane into a confused jumble of fabric and snapping wood. As we lost sight of him plunging down into a cloud he was already breaking up, leaving sections of wing and strut drifting behind him.

That left us to face the other Italian aeroplane, which was now upon us, apparently undeterred by the fate of its companion. Toth had put us into a shallow, banking dive and I was just swinging the gun around to port to bear on the Italian – who was some way above us still and about seventy metres astern – when I suddenly realised that things were dreadfully amiss. It was a curiously unpleasant sensation; the queasy realisation that something had gone terribly, unaccountably wrong: the way in which all the normal noises of flight except for the engine – the hum of the wind in the wires, the rushing slipsteam – suddenly ceased as we began to fall out of the sky. The patchwork fields and woods below started to whirl crazily before my eyes as the ghastly truth dawned upon me. We had gone into a spin.

I suppose that in those early days of flying there was no condition, except death by burning, that was quite so dreaded as a spin. But even a petrol fire was susceptible to rational explanation: the peculiar horror of the spin was that it happened for no apparent reason. One moment the aeroplane would be flying along without a care in the world, the next it would be spiralling down to destruction, falling like a cardboard box and suddenly, bafflingly immune to whatever desperate measures the pilot might be taking to try and get it flying once more. Left aileron; right aileron; elevators up; elevators down; full throttle until the engine screamed itself to pieces – none of them were the slightest use. The only thing to do was to watch in horror as the ground came rushing up. Very few people had ever survived a spin, and those who had emerged from the wreckage alive usually found that their nerve had gone and never flew again. It was as if the gods of the upper air had condemned all of us fliers to death for our impudence in defying gravity, but were graciously pleased to keep to themselves the precise moment when they would execute sentence. All that I could do was to cling desperately to the cockpit edge as we fell and shut my eyes tight, waiting for the final smash.

I think that we must have fallen a good thousand metres. Then, as suddenly as it had stopped flying, the Brandenburger groaned and creaked a little then began to fly once more, straight and even in a shallow dive below the clouds. As for our Italian attacker, there was no sign of him. Toth scanned the sky above us as I picked myself up, white-faced and trembling, from the floor of the cockpit. He seemed not to be unduly bothered by our terrifying experience, and certainly showed no particular gratitude for an escape so miraculous that even I was tempted to think – for a while at least – that there might be a god after all.

As for the two men in the Italian aeroplane we shot down that morning, I can hardly think that they could have survived such a fall. I was sad afterwards for them and their families, once I had leisure to think about the morning's events. But there: what would you? It was kill or be killed in those days before parachutes, and I suppose that the Fliegertod was at least preferable to choking with gas in some stinking dug-out or being casually blown to bits by a chance artillery shell. It is a noble and glorious thing, the Latin poet observes, to die for one's country. But given the choice I think that I would still prefer to make the other fellow die for his.

We landed safely at Caprovizza about 0800; much to my relief, since our poor *Zośka*'s racked frame was creaking and sagging in a most alarming fashion as a result of the brutal strains imposed upon it by Toth's aerobatics. From the observer's seat alone I could count a good half-dozen snapped bracing-wires. We had come out of it alive — even contrived somehow to escape from a spin. But having had a taste of Toth's flying I could now quite understand how Leutnant Rosenbaum had met his end over Görz. If I had been a fraction slower about letting go of the gun and seizing the cockpit coaming when we reached the top of the loop I would now be embedded half a metre deep in some Friulian cow pasture.

I saw as we came in to land that a motor-cyclist was standing by, waiting for the camera to be unloaded so that he could collect the box of photographs for the dark-room in Haidenschaft. We taxied to a halt and Toth switched off the engine as the ground crew came running across the field towards us. The sudden silence was stunning after nearly two hours of engine drone and roaring wind. As Toth lifted up his goggles I saw that his eyes too were bloodshot from the strain placed on our circulations by our violent manoeuvres over Palmanova. We were both pale and tired from a combination of excitement, altitude, exertion and inhaling petrol fumes in the freezing cold. As I climbed down to the field I noticed that my knees were unsteady and my heart still fluttering from the after-effects of the brief dog-fight and the spin that had followed it.

Franz Meyerhofer was the first to reach me, clapping me on the shoulder.

'Well Prohaska old man, back in one piece I see. Did you get your holiday snaps?'

I smiled. 'Yes, thank you very much,' I said, signing the motor-cyclist's receipt for the photographs against the side of the fuselage. 'Mission accomplished exactly as per orders. But that wasn't all: Toth here shot down an Italian two-seater on the way home.' A cheer went up from the ground crew and, smiling self-deprecatingly, Toth was hoisted on to their shoulders to be carried across the field in triumph. They would have done the same to me, but the gulf between officers and rankers in the k.u.k. Armee was too great for them to feel confident about such horseplay, so I followed behind the triumphal progress.

'But what's happened to Schraffl and Jahudka?' I asked. 'Are they back yet? We saw them go into a cloud somewhere this side of Palmanova, but then the Italians came after us and we had other things to think about. I'd have expected them to have got home ahead of us.'

'Don't worry about it: they've probably had an engine failure or got lost or something and landed at another field. It happens all the time. Bad pennies always turn up somehow. Anyway, you'd better go and get a bite to eat. Kraliczek's working on his monthly returns, so he can't see you just yet.'

'Can Toth come with us for a drink in the mess?'

Meyerhofer suddenly looked doubtful. 'No, no, I think not: better not risk it. Herr Kommandant wouldn't like it – against regulations, thin end of the wedge and all that. But Toth can entertain you in the NCOs' mess if he wants; can't see anything against that.' So I shook my faithful coachman's hand in farewell and made my way to my tent.

I managed about an hour's much-needed nap before Petrescu shook me awake, obediently reporting that Herr Kommandant Kraliczek wished to see me now. I rinsed my face hurriedly at the canvas washbasin – I was still grimy from exhaust smoke – ran a comb through my hair and set off to meet him in his office.

As I stepped up to salute and report the success of our mission I could see at first glance that Hauptmann Kraliczek was not pleased. He returned my salute in perfunctory fashion, then bade me sit down. He however remained standing; in fact stalked around the office throughout the interview with his hands behind his back, addressing his remarks to the corners of the room so that I had to keep swivelling my neck around to listen to him. His first question emerged only after some moments of evident inner struggle.

'Pray tell me, how many kilometres did you fly today, Herr Linienschiffsleutnant?'

'Forgive me, Herr Kommandant, but I have no real idea. It's about fifty kilometres from here to Palmanova as the crow flies, but we took a more circuitous route to get there, over Görz, and we flew some way to west of our target so as to be able to come at it from the direction of Venice. Meanwhile, as for our return journey, I can't say exactly where we flew since we were engaged with the enemy for part of the way.'

'So you mean to say, in other words, that you are an officer-observer, but you have no real idea of how far you flew in total? Some might consider that a grave dereliction of duty.'

'But Herr Kommandant,' I protested, 'surely the precise distance we flew is of no great importance? The point is that we reached our target, carried out our mission and returned unharmed to our base, having accounted for one enemy aeroplane on the way and successfully dodged another. Exactly how much ground we covered in the process is surely quite irrelevant.'

'Not in the least, Herr Linienschiffsleutnant, not in the least. The success of this unit depends, like the success of all military operations, upon minute precison and the scrupulous maintenance of records. In future I shall require your written combat reports and attendant forms to contain a clear statement, accurate to the nearest hundred metres, of the distance flown, so that this can be compared with the stated consumption of fuel for the flight.

However . . .' he turned to address his remarks to a different corner of the room, 'I have to say that there are other serious matters to discuss with you concerning your verbal report of this mission, at least as it was related to me a few minutes ago by Oberleutnant Meyerhofer. It appears that you shot down an Italian aeroplane?'

'I have the honour and satisfaction to report that we did – or rather, Zugsführer Toth did.'

'I see. Of what kind?'

'Herr Kommandant, I really cannot say. It was a two-seater certainly, with a rotary engine, possibly of the Nieuport family. I cannot say for sure. Certainly it was not a type that I remember from my study of the recognition handbooks. If Corps Air Intelligence want a rough sketch I am sure . . .'

'So you really have no idea what aircraft it was?' he snapped.

'Not really. All that concerned me at the time was that it was manoeuvring under our tail to try and shoot us down.'

'And have you any tangible evidence of having destroyed it? Standing orders from Fliegertruppe headquarters are that positive identification of crashed enemy aircraft and their crews is to be secured wherever possible.'

It was some time before I could answer, the breath having been taken out of me by the stark idiocy of this question; by its total incomprehension of the conditions of fighting in the air.

'I regret, Herr Kommandant, but it somehow slipped my mind in the tension of the moment to follow them down and perhaps snatch off the pilot's shoulder-straps as we passed. I'm afraid that having just narrowly escaped being shot down ourselves, with another enemy aeroplane closing upon us, twenty kilometres behind enemy lines, we thought it best to put our nose down and head for home without any further delay. Perhaps we could go back and get their names and addresses?'

'Spare me your facetiousness, Prohaska: I am not amused. Nor am I amused by the fact that your wanton engagement of enemy aircraft – clean outside the scope of your orders, I might add, since they made no mention of aerial combat – has led to extensive damage to yet another of this unit's aircraft. In fact, following Oberleutnant Rieger's writing-off of a machine the day before yesterday . . .'

'. . . Not to speak of Oberleutnant Rieger's writing-off of himself.'

'Be silent. As I was saying, following the loss of our machine just back from repair, and following Feldpilot Toth's recent criminal mistreatment of yet another aeroplane, the effective establishment of Fliegerkompagnie 19F is now reduced from six aircraft to four: two Hansa-Brandenburg CIs and two Lloyd CIIIs. And I wish to leave you in no doubt that I regard this as highly unsatisfactory. I gather from the Technical Officer that your own aeroplane, number 26.74, is likely to be under repairs for at least a fortnight, so please comprehend if you will . . .' he tapped a graph with a little ebony pointer like that used by orchestral conductors, '. . . please comprehend exactly what it is that you have done. The graph line for Effective Against Reserve Aircraft for the month of August should have gone—so. Now it will have to go here.'

'Herr Kommandant, with respect, we may have damaged an aeroplane, but we brought it home intact. And not only that but we carried out our mission successfully and destroyed an enemy aeroplane in the process. Surely that should more than make up for some minor damage to one of the unit's aircraft? After all, this is a war we are engaged in, not a statistical exercise . . .' I stopped: this last remark had clearly brought Kraliczek to that condition which, in any normal person, would manifest itself as bellowing purple-faced apoplectic rage and flinging the inkstand at the head of his interlocutor. That is to say, he grew even paler than usual and pursed his thin lips.

'What? How dare you question the value of statistics! Perfect knowledge of what is going on will win this war for us. If it were not so then why do you imagine that at my own expense – my own expense mark you! – I have designed and had printed a series of return forms to supplement those used by the War Ministry? That, Herr Linienschiffsleutnant, is how deeply I care for the efficiency of this unit: why I slave here in this office into the small hours of each morning without even an adjutant to help me, collating information for Army Headquarters. Anyway . . .' he looked at me triumphantly over his spectacles, as if producing an argument to stop all further debate, 'anyway, as regards your mission this morning, your Italian aeroplane shot down is of no consequence whatever. Flik 19F is a long-range reconnaissance and bombing unit, so there are no statistical returns emanating from here as regards enemy aircraft destroyed, and will not be until such time as I have devised an appropriate record form. The aeroplane which you say you have shot down may be claimed by you as a personal victory – unconfirmed by the way – if you wish; that is entirely your own affair. But as far as my reports are concerned no mention will be made of it. Such anomalies do not lie within my purview, I am afraid.'

'Herr Kommandant, you may call it an anomaly if you wish, and there may, as you say, not yet be any suitable piece of paper on which to record it. But I feel compelled to point out that the victory took place, and that it was not mine but entirely the work of Zugsführer Toth. It was his flying and marksmanship that brought the Italian down.'

He turned to look at me again, smiling a curious little self-satisfied smirk. 'Ah, Herr Linienschiffsleutnant, there I am afraid that I have to correct you: the victory, if it is credited to anyone, must be credited to you as commander of the aeroplane.'

'But all the shots were fired by Feldpilot Toth, from the forward machine gun. I did not fire the rear weapon once.'

'Perhaps so; perhaps not. Altitude and the confusion of combat cause people to make mistakes. My reports after you landed were that you had fired the shots.'

'But this cannot be. I can show you if you wish.'

Kraliczek rolled up his eyes in a look of weary patience such as one reserves for dealing with tiresome and confused elderly relatives. He sighed.

'Very well, if you insist I shall accompany you to look. But I cannot take long: I am a very busy man with only two clerks to assist me and the end of the reporting month is drawing near.'

76

So we strode out – Kraliczek with an insufferable and quite uncharacteristic air of jauntiness – to the Brandenburger being serviced by Feldwebel Prokesch and the rest of the ground crew. They put down their work and stood to attention as we approached.

'Feldwebel,' said Kraliczek, 'show us the machine guns from this aircraft.' The two weapons had been dismounted and laid out on a trestle bench for cleaning by the armourers. 'Open the breech of the forward gun.' Prokesch slid the breech block back as instructed. It revealed a firing-chamber as shiny-clean as if the gun had never been fired in its entire life. 'Now the observer's weapon.' The breech slid back to disclose a barrel clogged with the characteristic greyish-black grime of the cordite residue. 'There.' He turned to me, smiling. 'What did I tell you? Don't worry: an understandable mistake. You had better get to bed early tonight. As for that Italian aeroplane of yours, you had better claim it in a separate report to Army Headquarters . . .'

'With respect, Herr Kommandant, I have no wish to claim it as a victory since it was none of my doing.'

'Oh well, that's all right then. If you don't want to claim it then no one gets it and it didn't happen: much the best thing if you ask me. Such miscellaneous entries make nonsense of orderly compilation. Only by ruthless excision of such statistical irrelevances can we hope to see the greater picture and achieve that organisational perfection which will bring us victory. Now, if you will excuse me, I have wasted enough time already this morning on these trifling matters. I must be getting back.'

'Herr Kommandant?'

'Yes?' He turned to look back at me.

'By your leave, I have what I think may be a useful suggestion to make.'

'And what might that be?'

'If we were to regard all the separate events of this world war as statistical irrelevances, as you call them, then perhaps we would find that the war had never happened at all. In which case we could all stop killing one another and go home.'

He thought this over for some moments, then smiled at me. 'Yes, yes, Herr Linienschiffsleutnant: very amusing, most droll. Now, perhaps if you will excuse me at last? Some of us have better things to do than to waste our time composing witty epigrams. Myself, as a professional soldier, I would have considered that war was too serious a business for jokes.'

I noticed that throughout this exchange Sergeant Prokesch and the ground crewmen had been busy about their work, backs turned to us, rather than standing about with ears cocked relishing every word and storing it up to be recounted in the mess that evening. I sensed that the men were embarrassed by the scene they had just witnessed. Although they had acted under orders in swapping the barrels of the two machine guns, they doubtless felt that they had been made accomplices to a shabby piece of knavery and were correspondingly ashamed of themselves. I served in the armed forces for over half my life, and one of the things that I learnt was that a sense of honour is by no means the exclusive property of the commissioned ranks.

As for myself, I wandered back towards the mess tent in a state of some depression. In my sixteen years as a career officer of the Noble House of Austria it had been my lot to serve under some notable blockheads. But in all that time I had never met one, however tyrannical, stupid or plain incompetent he might have been, who would knowingly have told a lie or practised sleight of hand either on a brother-officer or upon the lowliest ranker. For the first time it struck me what disaster had fallen upon Old Austria now that creatures as abject as Hauptmann Kraliczek were creeping into positions of command. As I passed the Kanzlei hut I saw Meyerhofer descending the steps. I was about to speak with him concerning my recent conversation with our commanding officer. But he spoke first.

'It's Schraffl and Jahudka. We've just had a telephone call from Vertoiba. They've crash-landed in a field near by.'

'Are they all right?'

'Jahudka's dead. Schraffl's unhurt it seems but in a bad state of nervous shock. They're bringing him along by motor car. They should be here any minute.'

'What happened?'

'So far as I can make out from talking to Schraffl they lost contact with you in the clouds east of Palmanova, then saw an aeroplane falling out of the sky a few minutes later. They thought that it must be you and Toth, so they gave full throttle to get back across the lines. I gather that they crossed near Gradisca at about four thousand metres to avoid the flak – and had a Nieuport single-seater drop on them out of the sun. The first burst knocked the engine out and put a bullet through Jahudka's neck. They fell about a thousand metres with petrol pouring all over them from the fuel tank before Schraffl managed to drag Jahudka out of the pilot's seat and pull them level again. The poor devil was already near-dead – severed artery by the sound of it – so all Schraffl could do was to glide them down into a field on our side of the lines. It was a miracle they weren't set alight. With the propeller wind-milling the magneto must have been sparking all the way down, a good ten minutes or so. The people at Vertoiba say that when they reached the wreck they found Schraffl still in the pilot's seat, sitting up to his ankles in a pool of petrol and staring into space. A pretty impressive piece of flying though by the sound of it, bringing down a dead machine with a dying man on board and the cockpit awash with petrol. Rather him than me though, all the same. The poor sod's had a rough enough war of it already by all accounts. He got blown up by a shell at Sanok, even before he stopped that bullet in the knee, and they say he's never been quite the same since.' We turned. It was the sound of a motor-car horn. A large dun-coloured staff car was lurching up the trackway from the Haidenschaft road. It drew up, and the pas-senger door was opened for Schraffl, dazed and grey-faced, to be set down, half carried between two medical orderlies. He was still wearing the jacket of his leather flying overalls, but I saw that his breeches and puttees were saturated in blood like the garments of a butcher. They led him past us to undress him and lay him out on the folding bed in our shared tent. As they left, one of the orderlies spoke with Meyerhofer.

'The Medical Officer thinks he'll be all right after a while, Herr

Leutnant. He's given him an injection to make him sleep, and says if there's any further trouble to telephone the hospital in Haidenschaft. It's acute nervous prostration, but the MO says he should get over it once he's had a spell of leave.'

Schraffl did not get over it, and he never managed to go on leave. He got up that evening and ate a little, saying nothing to any of us, then went back to bed and slept heavily until mid-morning of the next day, when our servant Petrescu came running to me out on the field.

'Herr Leutnant, Herr Leutnant, you will come quick please! Herr Oberleutnant Schraffl not well.' I made my way to the tent while Petrescu ran to fetch Meyerhofer. I lifted the tent flap – and was greeted by an awful farmyard stench. Schraffl was lying curled up on the camp-bed, arms crossed tightly over his head, crying to himself like a small child. He had fouled his breeches. Flies buzzed about us as Meyerhofer and I tried to get him to speak. He seemed not to see us, only stared and blubbed uncontrollably in great uncouth sobs. In the end the two of us had to lift him bodily, still curled up with his knees against his chest, and load him on to the stretcher as the motor ambulance from Haidenschaft pulled up outside. The ambulance doors closed, and we never saw him again: only learnt later that he had been diagnosed as suffering from complete mental breakdown and confined to a ward for acute shell-shock cases in the Steinhof Mental Hospital outside Vienna. To my certain knowledge he was still there in 1930 – and quite possibly ten years later, when the SS began its programme of 'merciful release' for the incurable mental cases left over from the previous war; incidentally clearing the beds needed for the new intake.

5

CIVIL POPULACE

The result, then, of my first airborne mission over enemy lines was credit – thirty aerial photographs successfully taken and one enemy aeroplane shot down – against debit: one of our own aeroplanes moderately damaged and another destroyed, since Schraffl's Brandenburger had been so badly knocked about by its crash-landing at Vertoiba that in the end it had been written off by the inspectors: 'totalhavariert', to use that characteristic Austrian official formulation. This brought Flik 19F's operational aircraft park at the end of July 1916 down to three aeroplanes – not to speak of putting Meyerhofer and myself hors de combat for the next three days or so filling in crash reports and damage return forms, now that Hauptmann Kraliczek's dreaded 'end of the reporting month' was upon us.

Not that there was much that I could have done anyway in the flying line. As Toth and I had watched our dismantled *Zośka* being loaded on to a flat-bed wagon at Haidenschaft railway station the Repair Officer had told us that she would be away at the Fliegeretappenpark in Marburg for a fortnight at least. A largely peasant country, the Danubian Monarchy had never been too flush with skilled craftsmen at the best of times, and the policy of recklessly drafting every man in sight in 1914 for the war that was to have been over by Christmas had not helped matters, now that a high proportion of Austria-Hungary's potential airframe fitters and engine mechanics were either fully occupied building railways in Siberia or lying picked clean by the crows in the fields of Poland. The Monarchy's aircraft-repair parks were desperately short of hands. Seventy- and even eighty-year-old retired cabinet-makers were being conscripted into the factories to build airframes. Two years into the war it seemed that only the bureaucracy of the rear areas was able to meet its manning levels. Despite the ever-swelling number of procurement agencies and their insatiable demand for people to staff them, there was as yet no visible shortage of manpower in the ministries and in the munitions factory administrations – one of which was already known as 'the House of Lords' because of the number of sons of the aristocracy who had been safely tucked away there for the duration.

But even if the k.u.k. Fliegertruppe on the South-West Front had been up to complement in men and aircraft, our strength would still have been inadequate for the trials that loomed ahead of us that summer of 1916. For as July turned to August we stood on the brink of one of the most haunting, if most obscure, tragedies of the twentieth century: the battles of the Isonzo. I say 'battles' because there were in fact no less than eleven of them between the summer of 1915 and October 1917, when the Italian lines finally collapsed at Caporetto. That last battle would take place further up the river though, along the stretch that ran through the mountains between Flitsch and Tolmein. The previous ten battles had been fought for two blood-soaked years on one of the tiniest battlefronts of the entire First World War – the mere thirty kilometres or so between Görz and the sea – a front so minute that a man with powerful binoculars, standing on Monte Sabotino at one end of it, could clearly see men moving on the hills above Monfalcone at the other.

Looking back on those dreadful, now almost forgotten events, I suppose that there was never a clearer illustration – not even Verdun or Passchendaele – of the aphorism that for its first three months or so the generals ran the First World War, after which the war ran the generals. Certainly, when the Kingdom of Italy changed sides in May 1915 and declared war on its former Austrian ally, its politicians and people had expected an easy and rapid victory against our sclerotic old empire, already engaged in desperate and not very successful campaigns against Russia and Serbia. A 'jolly little stroll to Laibach' – even to Vienna itself – was confidently predicted in the Italian newspapers. But before they embarked upon this adventure the Italian politicians might have been advised to look elsewhere in Europe and see that, if nothing else, barbed wire and the machine gun had put an end once and for all to jolly little strolls, whether to Vienna, Berlin, Paris or anywhere else.

They might also have done well to consult their maps, because the fact is that in the summer of 1915 Italy was quite exceptionally ill-placed for a war against Austria. Everywhere along that four-hundred-kilometre frontier, from Switzerland to the Adriatic, topography favoured the defenders and hindered the attackers. As for the High Alps west of Lake Garda, forget it: in the entire three and a half years this awesome wilderness of peaks and glaciers never saw anything more serious than belts of barbed wire staked across the great silent snowfields, or ski patrols exchanging shots down the echoing ice-valleys. Nor was the terrain much more favourable among the mountains east of the Adige. The fighting of 1916–17 in the Dolomites was certainly bitter as the two armies grappled with one another for control of that chain of fantastically shaped mountain peaks east of the Marmolada. Sappers tunnelled through the rock for months on end to lay mines which permanently altered the shape of several mountain-tops. Men fought and died by the thousand in those savage battles above the clouds to capture ridges about which, before the war, even the most intrepid of rock climbers would have thought twice before scaling. Probably as many perished from avalanches and frostbite as from enemy action. But, for all its epic qualities, the war in the mountains of the South Tyrol was still a small-scale business; for even if the Italians had succeeded by some stupendous effort in dislodging our armies from the first ridge of the Alps, they would only have found themselves facing a second, even higher ridge, with nothing beyond it more vital to the Central Powers than the shuttered-up tourist hotels of Innsbruck.

That left the easternmost sector of the Austro-Italian Front: the stretch along the valley of the Isonzo from the Carnic Alps southwards to the Adriatic, along the western edge of what is now

Yugoslavia. So it was that a lonely, picturesque, fast-flowing mountain river which hardly anyone had ever heard of became to all intents and purposes the entire Austro-Italian Front: a miserable little parody of the more grandiose destruction taking place on the Western Front, a winding ribbon of smashed villages and silent forests of pine and chestnut reduced to vistas of blackened stumps. Eighty kilometres it ran, winding down from the Alps at Malborgeth through Flitsch and Caporetto and Tolmein to reach the Adriatic at Monfalcone where, in the summer of 1916, the trench lines ran across the Cantieri Navale shipyard and the rusting, bullet-pocked hulk of a half-finished ocean liner still sat forlornly on the slipways, stranded in the middle of no man's land.

By the time I arrived there in July 1916, the Isonzo Front had already claimed perhaps three hundred thousand lives in five successive battles. Yet the worst was still to come. True, the Julian Alps were not quite as high as the Dolomites. But the mountains through which the Isonzo wound its way north of Görz were every bit as difficult and unprofitable for an attacking army. So that left only the somewhat lower-lying country to the south of Görz: the twenty or so kilometres between the Vippaco valley and the sea, where the river curves westward then south around the edge of the Carso plateau. Even this was murderously difficult terrain for an attack (as events were to show), but it had something which—from the Italian point of view—no other sector of the front possessed: a worthwhile objective. For only twenty or so kilometres down the Adriatic shore from Monfalcone lay the city of Trieste: largest commercial port of the Austro-Hungarian Empire, home to 120,000 ethnic Italians and, ever since the 1870s, largest single item on the shopping-list of Italia irredenta.

Thus, like your own Sir Douglas Haig on the Somme that fateful summer, the Italian Commander-in-Chief Cadorna was presented with a fait accompli, locked into a situation not of his choosing: he had to attack somewhere, and the lower Isonzo happened to be both the only place where he could attack and the only one where there was some worthwhile strategic reason for doing so. His own stubborn and self-opinionated temperament did the rest. So for the next fourteen blood-soaked months, like a man compelled to keep picking at the same infected scab, Cadorna battered away obsessively at that tiny front, throwing men's lives at it by the hundred thousand and then, when they were all dead, flinging a hundred thousand more. It was the same dismal, pitiful story as on the Western Front in those years: gains measured in metres and losses measured in tens of thousands; endless reinforcement of failure; blind stupidity mistaken for determination; utter strategic bankruptcy. In the years since, I have often heard people in this country mock the Italian Army for running away at Caporetto. To me though, who saw something of what they suffered in offensive after grinding, futile offensive, the wonder is that they stuck it as long as they did, division after division of peasant soldiers herded forward to their deaths, always without adequate artillery support, usually ill-fed and often without proper gas masks or wire cutters or even decent boots on their feet.

Individual obsession on the part of one military commander is destructive enough; but on the Isonzo Cadorna's manic insistence on attack was mirrored in a sort of military folie à deux by his Austrian counterpart, General-Oberst Svetozar Boroević, Freiherr von Bojna, commander of the 5th Army's sector on the lower Isonzo. Old Boroević was by no means the classic Habsburg military dolt: he had the reputation of being an able staff officer and was one of the very few Austrian generals to have emerged with any credit from the Galician campaign in the autumn of 1914. But he too was a remarkably stubborn man. Known to his officers as 'der Bosco', his long-suffering troops characterised him less flatteringly as 'der Kroatische Dickschädel' – 'the Croatian Numbskull'. The trouble with Boroević was that whereas Cadorna had a thing about attack, he himself suffered from an equal and opposite mania for defence. Not a centimetre of ground was to be given willingly, be it never so worthless or costly to hold. And if the Italians took ground from us, why, then we were to counter-attack immediately, regardless of cost, to recapture it. It was a recipe for disaster: a long-drawn-out, miserable, grinding disaster which in the end claimed the lives (I imagine) of nearly a million men.

I suppose that for connoisseurs of human destructiveness the Isonzo Front could never quite rival the baroque horror of Verdun or the Ypres Salient; Austria and Italy were not major industrial powers, so neither was ever able to run to the extravaganzas of high explosive that were being staged in France: millions of shells raining down for months on end until the very tops of the hills were blasted down to bare rock. Likewise the two armies involved were not quite as combative as their more northerly neighbours; that is to say, while a German or French infantry battalion in 1916 would still fight on after losing nine men out of ten, its Italian and Austro-Hungarian equivalents might give up after suffering a mere seventy-five per cent casualties. Even so, for two armies conventionally dismissed by military historians as 'moderate', they contrived to do one another frightful damage.

But then, for the k.u.k. Armee the Italian Front was special: the only one where, right up until November 1918, troops from all the nationalities of the Monarchy – even ethnic Italians – would fight with equal enthusiasm against the despised 'Wellischen'. Elsewhere, one could be confident that German-Austrian troops would fight pretty well on any front. As for the rest though, the Magyars would fight with some enthusiasm on the Serbian or Romanian Fronts, against their own national rivals, but showed little interest in shooting at the Russians. Likewise the Poles were only too glad to fight the hated Muscovites, but had little concern with the Balkans. Czech and Ruthene regiments were liable to be wobbly on most fronts. But in Italy all nationalities fought, if not outstandingly well, then at least with a measure of enthusiasm.

It sounds perhaps a little strange now, to speak of men being enthusiastic about the prospect of getting themselves killed. But please try to understand that it was a different, less questioning world that we lived in then. Even in the year 1916 it was scarcely possible for those of us who had been through the cadet colleges of the old Monarchy so much as hear to the word 'Italien' without suddenly seeing a vision of black and yellow; without hearing the blare of bugles and the 'Sommacampagna March' and the steady tramp of boots on the dusty summer roads; Novara and Custozza; Mantua-Peschiera-Verona-Legnago; 'Graf Radetzky, Edler degen, schwur's sein' Kaisers Feind zu fegen aus der falschen Lombardei . . .' It was still an enticing prospectus, and one in which (naturally) the carnage at Magenta and Solferino tended to be somewhat played down; as did the fact that since 1849 every Austrian campaign in Italy had ended ultimately in defeat and loss of territory, even when the Whitecoats had won on the battlefield.

In those last days of July the storm was clearly about to break. The incessant banging of artillery in the distance had turned to a constant steady, air-trembling rumble as the Italian guns poured shells down upon our trenches, from Monte Sabotino across the Isonzo valley in front of Görz, then from Monte San Michele around the western rim of the Carso to the coastal marches at Monfalcone. The gun-flashes which lit the night sky to westward had now merged into a constant flickering like that of a failing electric light bulb. Yet for us at Fliegerfeld Caprovizza it was a time of profound idleness. Apart from a few requests from Army HQ in Marburg for photo reconnaissance on the other side of the lines, Flik 19F sat twiddling its thumbs, condemned to inactivity by lack of aircraft. On the last day of the month 5th Army Staff sent a request for a long-range bombing-raid on the railway junction at Udine, the Friulian provincial capital, in the hope – highly optimistic, we all felt – of interrupting the flow of troops and munitions to the Front. A Brandenburger had just come back from repairs at the Flieger-etappenpark in Marburg; so Leutnant Szuborits and Fähnrich Teltzel and their pilots were hastily detailed to set off on a night raid. It was a fiasco, their bombs falling harmlessly in open country. They had got lost, searchlights and flak had put them off their aim when they at last found their target, and in the end the townspeople of Udine had refused to succumb to mass panic and rush out and drown themselves like lemmings in the river. Only Szuborits made it back to file a report. Teltzel and his pilot failed to return and were posted missing, a state in which (I learnt many years later) they remained until 1928, when wood-cutters discovered the wreckage of an aeroplane and a jumble of bones deep in a pine forest amid the hills north of Cormóns.

As for myself, sans aeroplane, I was left to kick my heels and try to pass the time as best as I could. This was no easy task I can assure you at k.u.k. Fliegerfeld Caprovizza in the summer of 1916. The flying field itself was just that: a field used the previous year for growing barley, and now used for flying military aircraft, with no modification other than getting an infantry battalion to march up and down it for an afternoon to flatten out the worst of the ruts and hummocks. Amenities there were none; not even a proper canteen for the men. Our sole luxury, compared with Flik 19 at Haidenschaft, was that we were on the banks of the Vippaco. True, the river was low in the summer drought, but in the baking August heat and dust of that valley it was pleasant to be able to bathe in what remained of it, even if the water barely reached knee level. I was particularly glad of this I must say, because I was still condemned to wear my navy-blue serge jacket, my field-grey summer tunic having gone astray in the post on its way up from Cattaro. But in wartime an officer cannot reasonably bathe more than twice a day, and my tent was insufferably hot, and I had soon run out of books to read; so when I was not on duty or filling in Kraliczek's endless forms I had no choice but to go off exploring.

In truth, there was little enough to explore in the immediate neighbourhood of Haidenschaft. Before the war this part of the world – the Gefürstete Grafschaft Görz und Gradiska, to give it its official title – had been an obscure and seldom-visited region: a strange little corner of Europe where the Teutonic, Latin and Slav worlds met and overlapped. The Vippaco valley was moderately fertile, but the stony Carso region to southwards had long been one of the most poverty-stricken parts of the entire Monarchy, fit to stand comparison with Eastern Galicia or the backwoods of Transylvania as an area where most of the men called up for the Army each year were sent home as being too weak and ill-nourished to stand the rigours of military service: some of them with voices that had still not broken at nineteen years of age.

Once upon a time – perhaps back in the fourteenth century or thereabouts – the municipality of Haidenschaft (or Aidussina or Ajdovščina) had evidently been a place of some note, at least to judge from what remained of the town walls that had once surrounded it. In fact I have a vague recollection lurking at the back of my mind that 'Count of Haidenschaft' figured somewhere about number fifty-seven among the sixty-odd titles read out at Imperial coronations. But perhaps I am wrong about that: perhaps by the time I arrived there the place had been in decline for so long that not even Habsburg court protocol took cognisance of it any longer. Certainly the town was situated picturesquely enough, nestling beneath the limestone crags of the Selva di Ternova which towered above it to the north and east. But otherwise there was little to remark upon. In fact I am not really sure that, whatever its former status, the appellation 'town' fairly describes Haidenschaft in the year 1916. It was one of those seedy, sleepy little settlements, scattered in their thousand across the Dual Monarchy, that were not quite large enough to be towns but still too large to be villages, places whose sole reason for existence seemed to be the Habsburg state's mania for scribbling on sheets of Kanzlei-Doppel paper. Apart from the ochre-painted government offices – the town's largest building as always – there were two streets and a half-dozen shops, a small town square, the usual miniature corso with its row of chestnut trees, a gendarmery post – and very little else. The houses were Italian-looking, with their crumbling stucco and wide eaves and slatted wooden shutters. But the red roof tiles were still weighted down Slovene-fashion with chunks of limestone to stop them becoming airborne in the bora, while the town's two peasant-baroque churches, though they had Venetian-style campaniles, both wore on top of these the octagonal onion-domes which are the hallmark of Central Europe. The war had brought airfields and supply dumps and a makeshift hospital in wooden huts just outside the town. But off-duty entertainments were still basic, consisting of two cafés, packed solid now with field grey; a makeshift cinema under awnings rigged against the town wall; and two military brothels: the 'Offizierspuff' and the 'Mannschaftspuff'.

Ever since losing my virginity in such an establishment in the Brazilian port of Pernambuco in 1902 I had never again set foot in a maison-close except on service business. And even if I had not recently married a delightful woman whom I loved to distraction, I would still certainly have found the commissioned-ranks bordello intensely unappetising: a business (no doubt) of fake champagne and twenty-year-old newly commissioned Herr Leutnants trying to swagger like hard-bitten soldiers of fortune in front of the bored-looking girls. But as for the establishment provided by the War Ministry for the common soldier, as I walked past it it struck me as one of the least alluring suburbs of that peculiar twentieth-century version of hell known as the Front.

Over the years, in the course of my duties as a junior officer leading naval police pickets, I had seen many such places in the sea-ports of the Mediterranean. But what I remembered of them, I have to admit, was not so much their sleaziness as the rather jolly atmosphere of roistering debauchery that surrounded them: sailors and marines of all nationalities laughing and hitting one another in the street outside among the pimps and accordion players in that seafarer's elysium still known (I remember) in the Edwardian Royal Navy as 'Fiddler's Green', or in the French fleet as the 'Rue d'Alger'. Here though I was struck by the utter sadness of it all: dead-eyed soldiery on a few hours' leave from the trenches, queuing patiently two-by-two under the supervision of the Provost NCOs, waiting their turn to exchange five kronen for a two-minute embrace on an oilcloth-covered couch, then trousers on and out into the street again. There they waited in their dust- matted grey uniforms, like animals in the layerage pen at a slaughterhouse; standing as patiently as they would soon queue in the trenches, laden down with stick-grenades and equipment, waiting for the whistles to blow and the ladders to go up against the parapet. It seemed to me that not the least of the horrors of machine-age warfare was the way in which it had brought the assembly-line system even to the time-hallowed business of military fornication.

No doubt the townsfolk of Haidenschaft were doing well enough out of the the war, standing up or lying down. But there would have been little disaffection in these parts anyway. Beneath a thin Austro-Italian veneer the people of this region were mostly Slovenes, and the Slovenes had every reason to support Habsburg Austria because the alternative was so much worse. The Italians claimed this whole area as their own territory – in fact had been secretly promised it by Britain and France once the war was over – and it was widely feared that if they ever managed to lay hands upon it they would soon set about Italianising the inhabitants. The anxieties of the local people were well grounded as it turned out, for in 1920 Italy annexed this whole region and embarked upon a vigorous campaign against the Slovene language and customs, making liberal use of castor oil and rubber truncheons to persuade the natives of the superiority of Italian culture.

For its part Vienna had always tended to look down upon the Slovenes as a 'Dienervolk', a peasant people without a culture or literature or educated class of its own. Yet of all the Habsburg peoples in those years I suppose that none fought as bravely or as long in the service of Old Austria. Ethnographers used to say in those days that the Slovenes were the original stock from which all the Slav peoples sprang, preserved in their purity by centuries of isolation in their mountain valleys. I have no idea what truth there was in that theory: probably like most 'racial science' it was complete twaddle. But certainly the Slovenes had a characteristic look about them: a squarish, fair-haired people with strong, regular, wide-mouthed faces and long straight-bridged noses and grey-blue eyes. Even in 1916 the country people still wore what would now be described as 'folk costume' – wide-brimmed felt hats, embroidered waistcoats and wide breeches for the men; bodices and brightly striped flounced skirts for the women – for the simple reason that they had never worn anything else. Relations between these villagers and the k.u.k. Fliegertruppe were very cordial, despite the odd haystack demolished by a forced landing. Many a crashed Austrian airman in those years would return to his flying field lying in the straw of a peasant cart, accompanied by the entire village with the priest at its head and surrounded by baskets of hard-boiled eggs and curd cakes to sustain him during his stay in hospital.

Relations were also warm at a more personal level, as I was to discover one evening early in August. I had been out for a stroll from the flying field that afternoon, having nothing else to do. I had smashed my right shin in a flying accident in 1913 and although the surgeons had done an exemplary job on me, I still had to use a stick sometimes and found that the leg tended to stiffen unless I walked a good deal. I was returning along the single, dusty street of the hamlet of Caprovizza—or Koprivijca, as the local people called it—when I saw coming towards me my pilot Zugsführer Zoltan Toth. And on his arm was a quite delightful village girl of about eighteen or nineteen, flax-blonde and dressed in the flower-embroidered bodice and flared, red-blue-green-striped skirt of the locality. Toth had just been awarded the Silver Bravery Medal for his exploits in the spring—much to Hauptmann Kraliczek's disgust—and this now clanked gallantly against the Truppenkreuz on the breast of his best tunic (we still wore medals on our service dress in those days, ribbons folded into triangles as laid down by regulations). I must say that he looked very dapper, and he saluted me with only a trace of irony as we passed, the girl on his arm smiling winsomely and bidding me good-evening in German. Funny, I thought as I walked on: strange what the company of a pretty woman will do for even the ugliest of men; the fellow normally looks like a mentally retarded ape, but put a handsome country girl on his arm and her radiance seems to reflect from him. Probably just a village pick-up, I supposed: a local doxy prepared to roll with him behind a hayrick for a few kronen and a little diversion from the embraces of the village youths. But even so, Toth had certainly done pretty well for himself in the doxy line. Perhaps he possessed that most unaccountable of skills, a way with women.

As it turned out I could not have been more wrong about the girl and Toth's attachment to her, or have felt more ashamed of myself for having even imagined such farmyard goings-on. For the next morning, while bicycling through Caprovizza to post a letter to my wife at Haidenschaft post office, I nearly ran into the same girl coming around a corner with a basket of eggs on her arm. She curtsied prettily and dimpled, and enquired after my health in accented but still perfectly creditable German. I replied in Slovene, which I knew quite well since it is very similar to my native Czech. This delighted her. I learnt that her name was Magdalena Lončarec and that she was the daughter of the village blacksmith, who also ran a bicycle shop and farm-machinery repair business. She had been to convent school in Görz, she told me, and had been training to be a schoolmistress when the war and the approach of the Front had shut the college. She had met Toth in May when he had come into her father's shop to have a loop spliced in the end of a snapped bracing-wire. The two had fallen for one another at first sight – God alone knows how, since my first instinct on seeing Toth, had I been a young woman, would have been to scream and run for my life – and now they were inseparable. Curious, I asked how they managed to communicate. After all, Toth's German was almost non-existent, so far as I knew he spoke no Slovene, and I doubted very much whether she spoke Magyar.

'Oh,' she said, 'in Latin. I studied it to the sixth grade and I speak Italian anyway, so it's no problem for me. As for Zolli, Herr Leutnant, he's such a clever man you'd never believe: ever so well-read and so kind and considerate as well. I don't think there's anyone in the whole world like him. He trained in a seminary before the war, you know, and wanted to be a priest. But he's given that up now. When the war's over we're going to get married and take over my father's business with my brother, when he comes back from Russia; and we're making plans to set up an air mail-delivery service – Zolli says that there'll be lots of aeroplanes being sold off cheap once it's all over. He's full of good ideas like that and he knows so many things. Really, Herr Leutnant, you don't know how lucky you are to have such a clever man flying you around.' She grasped my arm and gazed at me with her great, long-lashed blue eyes, so that despite myself my knees suddenly felt unsteady. 'Please, Herr Leutnant, *please* promise me that you'll look after him and see that he comes to no harm. Don't let him do anything dangerous.' I mumbled something to the effect that I would do my best to fulfil her wishes, and kissed her hand as we parted. I was not sure about this afterwards: Old Austria had very definite ideas concerning what courtesies could be paid by whom to whom, and an officer kissing the hand of a Slovene village girl was something that was certainly well outside the accepted codes of conduct. Yet this Magdalena seemed so unlike any village maiden that I had ever met: so modest and unaffected, yet so poised and graceful and ladylike. But courting in Latin though: 'O cara amatrix mea, convenire cum mihi hora septis ante tabernam . . .' No, no, it was all too much.

At last, on 2 August, Toth and I received orders to make ready for a flying mission the next morning. In the temporary absence of our usual mount we were to take up one of the Flik's Lloyd CII biplanes. Our task, it appeared, was to be artillery-spotting with the aid of wireless. But this was to be no ordinary observation for a common-or-garden field-artillery battery. Instead we would be spotting for a single gun in an extremely difficult operation far away from our usual sector of the Front: an operation so delicate and vital that 5th Army Headquarters was anxious that the observer should be an experienced gunnery officer with a sound command of Morse code. For that reason the choice had fallen on me: I had indeed been a gunnery officer – though aboard a battleship long before the war – while as a sailor my command of Morse, though not quite as good as that of a full-time telegraphist, was still quite good enough for what was required.

It was plain at first sight that the Lloyd CII was an aeroplane of a somewhat earlier vintage than the sturdy Hansa-Brandenburg: a pre-war design in fact, marked by long, narrow, swept-back wings and by a much sharper nose and more fish-like fuselage than that of the Brandenburger. I understand that it got its curious name because the factory which built it in Budapest had been part-owned by the Austro-Lloyd shipping line. Certainly it had taken many twists and random convolutions of events over the years to get the name of a seventeenth-century London-Welsh coffee-house proprietor attached to an Austro-Hungarian warplane. For me, one lasting consequence was that I was never able to see the sign 'Lloyd's Bank' in Ealing Broadway without having a sudden faint odour of petrol and cellulose dope wafted to me from all those years ago.

The Lloyd CII had been chosen for this particular mission because although it was somewhat slower than the Brandenburger in level flight, and a good deal less manoeuvrable, its payload was larger and its performance at high altitudes marginally better (one of them had in fact taken the world altitude record in the summer of 1914). This ability to carry loads to great heights was going to be very necessary, I learnt as a staff officer briefed me for the flight, because we were to be flying over the Julian Alps – over Monte Nero, to be precise: 2,245 metres above sea level, which was not far short of the effective ceiling for a two-seater aeroplane in those days, especially when it would also be carrying the full weight of an airborne wireless transmitter.

So far in 1916 there had been little fighting in the mountainous sectors of the Isonzo Front north of Tolmein. There had been some sharp encounters here in late 1915, as their initial ardour carried the Italians across the Isonzo to capture some of the mountain ridges beyond. But, as in the Alps proper, the lie of the land – that is to say, most of it standing on end – had allowed us to hold it against them with only a handful of defenders. Most of the time in fact all that we had to do was to roll boulders over the edge of thousand-metre precipices on to the Italians below. The furthest that the Italians had got, after heavy losses, was to cross the river and work their way up a few mountain ridges on the other side; most notably the one called the Polovnik, which swells up from the bend of the river at Zersoccia to become Monte Nero. And there the two armies had left matters for the past year, outposts often within ear-shot of one another, but separated by dense belts of barbed wire on picket stakes cemented into the rock-faces. Both sides made life as unpleasant as possible for the other by sniping and trench-mortar-ing and patrol skirmishes, but no large-scale action was considered by the generals to be either possible or necessary.

In this stalemate, artillery work tended to turn into virtual duels of battery against battery: exchanges lasting for months in which ingenuity and ant-like persistence counted for as much as any practical effect. Whole weeks were sometimes spent in hoisting field guns piece by piece up sheer rock-faces so that they could lob a few shells into the next valley before being hastily lowered back again. In places tunnels were even bored through the rock of mountain ridges so that the gunners could fire at otherwise hidden targets. And several weeks before, one such exercise in levitation had enabled the Italians to lug three or four heavy howitzers – 24cm calibre at least—up a steep, narrow, wooded valley on the western face of Monte Nero, above the village of Caporetto, so that they could fire over the ridge of the mountain. The beauty of it was that thanks to the bulk of the mountain they were completely hidden from our outposts on the summit 1,500 metres above. Likewise there was not a single gun on the Austrian side that could reach them: all had either too little range or too flat a trajectory to lob shells over the mountain into the valleys on its western face.

For two weeks past, the Italian battery had been making life extremely difficult for the trains of mules and the human porters who carried supplies and ammunition up the trackways to our front line. The Italian outposts, though lower down the ridge than ours, gave an excellent field of view over the country to the east of Monte Nero and were doubtless connected by telephone to the battery to give fire direction. At any rate, even after the convoys had taken to moving up to the line only by night, the shells would still come howling over, screaming down to excavate craters the size of a house and – more often than not – blow some panic-stricken team of animals and their drivers to oblivion. Before long the trees alongside the mountain trackways to the east of Monte Nero were festooned with blackening rags of mule-flesh and tatters of grey uniform cloth, often with an arm hanging out of a torn-off sleeve or a head wedged in a crook of the boughs. Carrying-parties were already getting extremely nervous of making the journey, even at night, and were turning back at the first sound of a shell coming over. If this went on (the staff officer told me) the k.u.k. Armee might no longer be able to hold the summit of the mountain. Something had to be done. Attempts at bombing from the air had proved futile, so stronger measures would now be taken.

Even as the Italians shelled the other side of the mountain, those stronger measures were being made ready by shifts working around the clock in the Skoda Armaments Works at Pilsen. In 1913 Skoda had already built a giant gun: the 30.5cm howitzer called (with the nauseating coyness that seems obligatory in these cases) 'Schlanke Emma', or 'Slim Emma'. A battery of those monsters had been loaned to the German Army in August 1914 to deal with the forts at Liège, which were holding up the German advance through Belgium. They had proved gruesomely efficient in that task, and a larger 38cm version had been built in 1915. Now, in July 1916, a 42cm howitzer, the very non plus ultra of Austrian artillery, was nearing completion and looking for a suitable proving-ground. And what field trial could be more conclusive than here in the Julian Alps, dealing with the Italian howitzer battery so frustratingly beyond reach in its valley on the other side of the mountain?

The great steel monster was made ready and loaded on to a special strengthened railway wagon for transport to Feistritz, the nearest point on the railway to Monte Nero. Then, unloaded after dark in strictest secrecy, the tarpaulin-shrouded colossus had begun its slow journey up into the mountains, broken down into three loads – barrel, carriage and mounting – each drawn by its own motor tractor and riding on wheels surrounded by pivoting steel feet. The villages on the way had been evacuated for secrecy, and when the procession finally reached a point where the specially made trackway was too steep for the tractors alone, teams of horses and motor winches had been brought up to assist. The last kilometre of the journey had taken two entire days, with thousands of soldiers and Russian PoWs sweating at drag-ropes and cursing as their boots slipped in the mud, to drag the thing to its final firing position in a shallow valley just below the treeline on the east side of the mountain. There it had been assembled, and concreted into its emplacement: another two days of labour. A small railway was laid to bring up its shells, each of which weighed just over a tonne, and once that and a few other trifles had been installed – like a concrete bunker to protect the firing crew from the concussion – the brute was ready to teach the insolent Wellischers that the Austrian artillery was still a force to be reckoned with.

But it was still a blind monster as it squatted there among the pine forest, surrounded by camouflage netting. Our part in this exercise, Toth and I, would be to provide it with eyes. Visibility permitting, firing would commence at 0830 on the morning of 2 August, as soon as the sun had risen sufficiently for any mist to clear and the western face of the mountain to come out of the shadow. We were to circle above the Italian battery at about three thousand metres and use the wireless to provide spotting for the gunners. It would not be a leisurely task, I was told: the Italian howitzers were not quite in the same league of destructiveness as our mighty gun, but there were four of them and they could fire faster: about one shot every three minutes as against five minutes for the Skoda weapon, which had to have its shells loaded into the breech by a small crane. Once our gun fired it would betray its position to the Italians up on the ridge; so when the duel commenced it would be a matter of which side could fire the faster and whose spotting was the more accurate. Once one side had got the other's range and location it would all be over, the losers faced with an ignominious choice of abandoning their guns or of being blown to bits when a shell finally found them.

It became clear as we made our preparations at Caprovizza that afternoon that it was not going to be anywhere near as simple as it had sounded. The first problem was the sheer weight of the wireless apparatus. The guts of the system was a marvellously archaic contraption called a spark-generator. This worked by creating an arc through the teeth of a brass cog-wheel spinning against an electrode. Every time a tooth passed the electrode a spark jumped across the gap, and in this way, when connected to the aerial, it would produce a hideous, rasping crackle – barbed wire made audible – like that which one gets nowadays from a wireless set when there is a badly adjusted switch near by. The principle of signalling was that the operator worked a Morse key to turn this excruciating noise into a signal: a long crackle for a dash and a short one for a dot.

That part of the wireless alone weighed about thirty kilograms. But there were all the other accoutrements that went with it. Power was provided by a dynamo fixed on to a bracket under the aeroplane's nose and driven by a leather belt from a pulley-wheel on the propeller shaft: that weighed about seven kilograms. Then there was the aerial: twenty metres of wire with a lead weight at one end to trail behind us in flight, plus a cable reel to wind it in when not in use: about ten kilograms' worth in all. Other accessories comprised a signal amplifier, a tuning coil, an emergency battery, an ammeter, a set of signal rockets plus pistol and a repair kit. Altogether the wireless apparatus – which could only transmit, mind you, not receive – weighed about 110 kilograms. Or to put it another way, the weight of a very fat man as a third crew member.

With all that in mind you will perhaps understand my trepidation as I examined a relief-map of the Julian Alps. Laden down like that I was very doubtful that the Lloyd would be able to reach its advertised ceiling of 4,500 metres. In fact three thousand seemed to be expecting a great deal, and that was uncomfortably close to the height of some of the loftier peaks. In that aerial war over the Alps many a machine came to grief by running out of altitude, its engine labouring desperately in the thin, cold air as its pilot struggled in vain to lift it over a mountain ridge.

Another worrying consequence of the weight of our wireless set was that we would be flying unarmed: there was simply not enough lift to carry a machine gun, nor enough space left in the cockpit to work it if we had. Toth and I would have only our pistols to defend ourselves. However, some cover would be provided against the possibility of the Italians sending a Nieuport up after us. One of the k.u.k. Fliegertruppe's impressive total of three fighter aircraft – a German-supplied Fokker Eindecker – would be detached from

Flik 4 at Wippach and sent to the field at Veldes, from where it would fly to escort us over Monte Nero. I must say that I was none too happy about this arrangement: the previous week I had been talking with our senior ranker-pilot, Stabsfeldwebel Zwierzkowski. He had recently been able to test-fly a newly delivered Eindecker against an Italian Nieuport which had run out of petrol over our lines some weeks before and landed at Prosecco. No comparison, he had reported: the German aeroplane's only good point was its machine gun firing through the propeller arc. Otherwise he had found it to be slow and unresponsive, with a poor rate of climb, restricted downward vision because of the wings and a disturbingly flimsy feel about it. But the Nieuport though, that was a real lady, 'eine echte Dame': climbed like an electric lift and as agile as a cat. The only thing he had not much liked was the machine gun mounted above the top wing – difficult to reload in flight and the magazine held only fifty or so rounds. But in view of the Nieuport's other virtues, he said, he doubted whether as many as fifty rounds would be required for it to do its work.

6

DUEL OVER THE MOUNTAIN

I think that I have seldom been struck so forcibly as on that August morning by the sheer fortuity of human existence; by the contrast between the serene majesty of the natural creation and the puny bellicosity of men. As we flew northwards along the valley of the Isonzo the pin-point flashes of the early-morning fire-fight crackled over the mountain slopes below. Then the sun came up at last over the looming mass of the Julian Alps ahead of us, turning the patchy summer snow on the triple summit of Triglav to a blaze of pink and orange. It seemed so absurd, so blasphemous almost, to be fighting for possession of these indifferent mountains, as if two rival strains of microbe should be disputing ownership of a granite boulder. Perhaps the intrinsic craziness of war was less obvious on the plains of Galicia, where a marching soldier was usually higher than anything within sight.

But there: if the absurdity of it all was so plain to me, seated safely up here in the whistling cockpit of an aeroplane two thousand or so metres above suffering humanity, I doubted whether my philosophical reflections would bring much solace to the poor devils down there in the trenches and battery positions. I tried to make out the main features on the map as we flew northwards over Tolmein. Hauptmann Kraliczek's form giving us our detailed orders for the mission had specified, for reasons known only to himself, that we were to cross the trench lines at Monte Sabotino, just across the river from Görz, then turn northwards to fly over Italian-held territory until we crossed the lines once more near Tolmein. But I was damned if I was going to have any of that. One of the first and most important things a career military officer learns is just how far he can go in ignoring orders, and I was little inclined to take Kraliczek's flying instructions too seriously. We had flown down the Vippaco to Görz, round the edge of the Selva di Ternova and the Bainsizza Plateau, then turned sharp starboard to follow the Isonzo up to Tolmein, staying safely on our own side of the deep valley for most of the way. Not the least of the hazards of flying an aeroplane in that war in the Alps was that ground fire was liable to come at you not only from below but from either side as well, and on occasion (though mercifully it never happened to me) from above.

In any case, 'lines' was altogether too grand a description for the string of outposts and belts of barbed wire which straggled up and down the mountain ridges around Tolmein. I could just make out where they climbed up from the valley at Vollaria to the peak of Mrzli Vrh, then up to just beneath the summit of Monte Nero ahead of us. I had intended that we should turn north-west over Tolmein to take us towards Monte Nero, but as I saw tracer fire coming up at us from Mrzli I changed my mind and decided to veer away to the east. But how was I to communicate this change of flight plan to Toth? There was no point in shouting in his ear in the roaring wind, and he barely understood German in any case. Then suddenly a thought struck me. Why not? I reached for my note-pad and pencil, and scrawled 'Verte ad orientem XX grada – altitudiem sustine.' I tapped Toth on the shoulder and showed him the message. He looked mildly surprised – then nodded and turned the steering wheel to bank us away; just in time, as it happened, since a flak shell burst to port of us with a bright orange flash and a cloud of black smoke. I was pleased to have avoided that little unpleasantness, but I was even more delighted that Toth and I seemed to have established communication at last, even if by such unconventional means.

We arrived over Schlanke Emma at 0825 as arranged. The weather was good and the mist was lifting rapidly in the valley on the other side of the mountain. It looked as if shooting would commence as planned. I reached down to flick the switch for powering up the transmitter, saw that the blue spark was flickering across the gap as the toothed wheel began to spin, then leant over the side to fire a white rocket: the signal to the battery wireless operators that I had started transmitting. I gazed at the jumble of forest and bare rock below. Even though I knew from the map where it was hidden, there was no visible sign of the Skoda howitzer lurking among the pine trees: the camouflage experts had done their job too well for that. I tapped out the pre-arranged letters 'K-U-K' on the Morse key, and saw a white flare arch up from among the trees to signal that they were receiving us. There was a pause as we circled above. Surely something had gone wrong – no, there was the green rocket, the signal for us to begin our work. The enormous gun was loaded and ready to fire. Our task now was to find its target.

That, I had realised from the outset, would not be easy. The Italians were no fools and had done a thorough job themselves of camouflaging their howitzer battery in its mountain valley, even hanging up screens of wire mesh to break up the noise of firing and prevent us from using sound-location to get a cross-bearing on them. I also knew perfectly well that as soon as an aeroplane appeared above them they would cease firing until it had gone. So in the event it was an extraordinary piece of luck that one of the howitzers should just have fired its first ranging shell of the day as we came over the ridge of the mountain. I missed the flash, but my binoculars caught the remains of the brown puff of cordite smoke that it left behind. Hastily I fumbled with the pencil in my thick flying gloves to mark the position on the map, then tapped out its co-ordinates on the Morse key as Toth banked us around to the south. That should give our gunners an area a kilometre square to range upon. Once they were hitting that I would use a crude system of letter-and-number signals to correct their shooting: 'U' then so many metres for 'Overshoot', 'K' – 'Kurz' – for 'Undershoot', 'L' for 'Too far left' and 'R' for 'Too far right'. The aim was to signal the conclusion of the process by a single letter: 'V' for 'Volltreffer' – 'Direct hit'. From what I knew of the Skoda 42cm howitzer I doubted very much whether more than one 'V' would be necessary. The thing spoke but seldom, I understood, but when it did its arguments were of impressive finality.

We had only just circled back across the ridge when the Skoda howitzer fired its first shot. Even from a thousand metres above it was a spectacle of brute explosive violence that remains with me to this day. I had seen heavy guns fire before, of course: I had been a battleship gunnery officer before the war and still had impaired hearing in the upper registers to prove it. But I had never seen anything quite so big fired before – or been looking almost down the barrel as it did so. It astonished me to see that the shock waves were actually visible, spreading out like ripples on a pond around the great gout of orange and brown which suddenly erupted from the dark forest, making the trees about it flex and thrash as if some localised hurricane had struck them. A few seconds later the blast hit our flimsy aeroplane, making it skip and bounce suddenly like a mountain goat. The enormous shell was just visible for a moment or two as it reached the apex of its flight above the mountain ridge, losing speed before toppling over to plummet down towards its target. I was able to imagine – though with no particular relish – the feelings of the Italian gunners as the express-train roar came rushing down upon them to announce the arrival of the mighty projectile.

It landed on the mountain slope some way above their position. Seen from where I was it looked like the sudden birth of a volcano: a disc of rock and forest floor about fifty metres across, suddenly heaving itself into the air as though a giant mole were stirring beneath it, then belching forth a great cloud of yellowish smoke as full-grown pines flew into the air like so many matchsticks. When the smoke cleared I saw that a hole the size of a small quarry had been excavated in the valley side, surrounded by a chaos of fallen trees and a circle of shattered rock. I marked the crater on my map and signalled 'K200 L300' to indicate that the shot had fallen two hundred metres too short and about three hundred metres too far left of the target. Meanwhile the slopes below me broke out into a rash of flashes and smoke clouds as the Italians recovered from their shock and, realising what was afoot, let fly with every gun available to try and find the perpetrator of this outrage. The telephone lines down from the ridge of the mountain must be glowing red, I thought, as the Italian spotters signalled back the position of the muzzle-flash from our gun.

They began to make it uncomfortably hot for us, now that they had realised what we were up to flying in slow circles over the mountain. A desultory spatter of rifle fire had greeted our first appearance – Italian infantrymen in their rocky trenches relieving the boredom of yet another day in the line by loosing off a few shots at a passing aeroplane. But now the shooting began in earnest: machine guns coming into action, then a flak battery in the valley sending shells up at us. I signalled to Toth to take us higher. Meanwhile the Italian howitzer battery fired a salvo. The shots were well short of our gun, and loosely grouped, but the line was worryingly accurate. By now the Italian outposts up on the ridge must be taking compass bearings to fix the hidden Skoda's position. Like us, they knew that down there among the trees men were cursing and sweating as they struggled to hoist the enormous shell into the still-hot breech, then swinging the ponderous breech block into place and locking it shut before cranking furiously at the elevation wheels to raise the mighty barrel skywards once more.

Our second shot fell even further short than the first, dropping right into the bed of the torrent that ran down the mountain valley. I suppose that there must still be a miniature lake there, interrupting the course of the stream and providing puzzlement for the area's natural historians. I like to think that, now the trees have grown back around it, the village children from Caporetto go up there to fish and to swim on summer afternoons, unaware of the events that took place in that quiet valley when their great-grandfathers were young. I signalled back 'K300' as we banked away once more to await the Italian reply. Neither contender could move of course: the Italian howitzers, though (we understood) mounted on wheels, would have taken several hours to dig out of their emplacements and haul away. As for our Skoda weapon, it was concreted into its emplacement and could only be released with the aid of blasting charges and pneumatic drills. Neither contender could do anything more than await the enemy's riposte. It was like watching some bizarre medieval duel to the death, prescribed perhaps in a fable to establish which suitor would have the hand of the princess; the two opponents with their feet set in tubs of mortar and taking turns to lunge at one another through a paper screen, their thrusts guided only by the calls of the spectators in the gallery.

The Italians fired a second salvo after three minutes or so, just as we were coming back over them. It was more closely grouped this time, and it landed only four hundred metres or so from our gun. Meanwhile our third shot went wide again: two hundred metres over and one hundred too far right. Damn them, what was wrong with our gunners this morning? Heavy artillery shooting was never an exact science: shot falls varied because of wind and air density and the precise chemistry of each propellant charge – and by 1916 Austrian cordite was becoming very uneven in quality. But even so their shooting was not up to the usually high standards of the Imperial and Royal Artillery. Did they realise what peril they were in? At this rate it was more than likely that the Italian battery would find them before they found the Italians.

Watched from my position, four hundred metres up in the singing cold air, there was something dreadfully, sickeningly fascinating about observing this duel of monsters taking place below us: watching the great flashes that shook the trees and the sudden plumes of smoke, feeling the aeroplane shudder around us as the shock waves reached it. Sitting there like some indifferent god, tapping the Morse key and pencilling crosses on the map, it was only too easy to forget that in a few minutes one battery or the other would be reduced to a smoking pile of twisted steel, smeared with the blood and entrails of perhaps fifty of my fellow-men. What would happen if the wireless broke down, or if the Italian flak gunners managed to knock us out of the sky? We had been at this for some ten minutes now. The Italians were well up in wireless and might soon contrive to jam our signal. The terrible iron logic of war had taken over. Down there was a large number of young Italian soldiers who had never done me the slightest harm and whom I would cheerfully greet as friends if I met them in some café. Yet here I was, bending all my efforts to secure their deaths as if we had always been the most mortal of enemies. Sitting here in an armchair it sounds completely insane; but up there that morning a lifetime ago it made chilling sense.

In the end it was them and not us. The Skoda gun's fifth shell landed just on the edge of the hundred-metre circle within which I judged a shellburst would put the battery out of action. After that, things happened with bewildering rapidity. The smoke dispersed in the breeze to reveal a patch of devastated forest. But then a confused series of flashes and spurts of fire began to spread through the still standing trees. I suppose that it was the usual story: that in his haste to load and fire the battery commander had allowed too many propellant charges to accumulate on the lines, so that the flash of one catching fire set off the next in a powder-train which finally led back to the ammunition dump. I hope that some of the Italians survived, crouching terrified in their slit-trenches as the world exploded about them. But somehow I doubt it: not when I saw the entire ponderous carriage of one of the howitzers being tossed into the air as casually as a child's toy. Within a few seconds a vast ochre-coloured cloud of smoke was boiling into the summer sky like some obscene toadstool. By the time we were safely back over our side of Monte Nero it must have been visible to the Austrian gunners down in their emplacement, deafened and dazed with muzzle-blast despite their padded helmets. I tapped the signal 'V' on the Morse key, then followed it in a fit of patriotic exultation with a display of white and red rockets and the message 'V-I-V-A-T'. Our mission had been accomplished.

Our orders were that once firing had ceased we were to make for the flying field of Flik 2 at Veldes. Our route would take us over the long, narrow Wocheiner Lake which lay in a deep trough of the mountains below the Triglav massif, about ten kilometres to the east. I shut down the transmitter and scribbled another note in Latin to direct Toth to Veldes, where we would land and rest awhile before refuelling and heading back to Caprovizza – once more over the Italian side of the lines, if we took any notice of Kraliczek's mysterious orders. The only thing that puzzled me was where that damned Eindecker of ours had got to. It should have been waiting over Monte Nero for us when we arrived, but I had seen no sign of it. Engine trouble? Muddled instructions from the Air Liaison Officer at Marburg? Probably the latter, I thought: none of us had much of an opinion of staff officers. Anyway, it scarcely mattered now that we were on our way home.

I first saw the speck in the sky to the north-east as we came within sight of the Wocheinersee. Must be the Eindecker, I thought, and peered at it more out of curiosity than anything else. It was a rather disturbing sensation to find as I tried to steady my binoculars on the cockpit edge that instead of the expected monoplane front-view of an Eindecker, I was looking at what was quite unmistakably a small, rotary-engined biplane with its lower wings markedly shorter than the upper and with a machine gun mounted on the top wing.

I dropped the binoculars and scrawled a note for Toth: 'Festina – hostis insequitur nobis!' He turned around and nodded, but did nothing. I thumped him on the back and wrote 'Accelera, inepte!' so fiercely that the point of my pencil snapped off. The Nieuport was gaining on us fast we ambled along, seemingly unconcerned. What was the matter with this Hungarian imbecile? Did he want us to die? Before long the Italian was only about twenty metres astern, jockeying on our tail some way above us now that he had seen that we carried no machine gun. No doubt he was congratu-lating himself on having surprised two such dim-witted Austrians, and was not in too much of a hurry to despatch us, much as a cat will play for a while with a sparrow before biting its head off. I turned to shake my pilot and urge him to give full throttle – and saw the Italian pilot laugh as he watched his victims now apparently fighting one another. I drew my Steyr pistol from its holster, intent on making even a futile attempt to defend ourselves. As for Toth though, he merely looked over his shoulder at the Italian single-seater. His face wore the malicious half-smile of an idiot child. Then he put our nose down a little and opened the throttle. The Italian brought his nose down too to take aim, evidently thinking that we were going to try diving away from him.

He had come so close that I could see his tongue clenched in concentration between his white teeth. He would lower his nose until we were in his sights – an unmissable target at less than fifteen metres – and a sudden flickering orange flash would obscure the gun muzzle above his upper wing. That would probably be my last sight in this world. Yet despite the imminence of death, I found that sight of the Nieuport intensely interesting, as I suppose the closeness of danger sharpens all the senses. It was such a pretty little machine I thought, so delicately French: painted a smart silver-grey with black edges to the wings and with the Italian red-white-green tricolour on the rudder. So pleasing to look at, yet so deadly, like a poisonous snake.

I was sure that he was just about to fire when Toth pushed the throttle forward and put our nose down a little more (he had a motor-car mirror fixed above the windshield and had been watching the Italian intently all the time with one eye). The Italian laughed, and brought his nose down as well to regain his aim. Toth replied by making our dive a little steeper. The Italian followed: if we expected to escape him by diving away then we were even greater buffoons than we had seemed at first. His nose came down, and he fired a burst which cracked over our upper wing, snicking the fabric in places. With magisterial calm, Toth merely increased our angle of dive and eased the throttle forward to full speed. We were screaming down at forty-five degrees now as the cobalt-blue lake rushed up towards us. The Italian fired another burst, which just missed. It was certain death for us now, either from bullets or from diving into the lake. I looked about me in terror as the wind howled past. I saw that the fabric on our wings was beginning to ripple and surge as the airframe creaked ominously above the roar of the engine. Then I looked back at the Italian above us, still trying to take aim. We had only a few seconds now to pull out of our dive, and when we did we would come into his sights and be shot to tatters.

It began as a slight flexing of his lower wings, starting at the wingtips and spreading inward to the roots. He tried to pull back the stick, but it was too late: with a great shudder the upper wing of the Nieuport shook itself, then broke away to fly astern, turning over and over in the air like a giant sycamore seed. He hurtled past us out of control and breaking up as Toth lugged at the column to pull us out of our own plunge, only metres above the waters of the lake. I thought that our own airframe was going to break up under the strain, but somehow we managed to level out, then bank away to port to come back to the place where we had parted company with our pursuer. It was a flower-sprinkled Alpine meadow between two pine woods at the head of the lake. Toth brought us in to land on the lush grass while a herd of cows rushed away in panic, bells clunking wildly. We jumped out as the Lloyd came to a halt and set out to look for the wreck as soldiers camped in the next field came running over to join us.

I had never expected that such a flimsy thing as an aeroplane could embed itself so deeply in the ground. Only the shattered wings and part of the tailplane had been left on the surface. As for the pilot, there was no sign of him. We entered the cool, dark silent glade of pine trees, the carpet of needles deadening our footsteps. Toth stopped and seized my arm. 'Vide,' he said, and pointed. It was a windless morning, but one of the pine trees was shuddering slightly. We looked up. Blood was dripping slowly through the branches from thirty metres above. In the end we had to borrow a two-handed saw from a pioneer battalion camped near by, and cut down the tree before we could remove him. His identity disc proclaimed him as Sergente-Pilota Antonio Patinelli, aged twenty-three, from Ferrara. We stayed at Althammer for his funeral and saw that everything was fittingly done: guard of honour, flag over the coffin and the Italian anthem played by special permission of the local corps commander. It was the least we could do for an enemy whose tenacity had been greater than the structural strength of his machine. We felt sure that he and his comrades would have done the same for us, had the positions been reversed.

When my nerves had calmed down sufficiently from the morning's excitements I took Toth aside for a confessional session in a mixture of Latin and Service German. I found that he spoke

Latin well, though with a marked Magyar accent and often having to grope for a while (as I did also) to find words to describe things unknown to the ancients. I was keen to question him because that morning's reckless adventure had set my mind working about events a few days earlier over Palmanova.

'Di mihi, O Toth,' I said, 'how on earth did you get us out of that spin?' I was extremely curious to know how he had done it. An English airman, Major Hawker, was reported to have pulled out of a spin in the summer of 1914, but the outbreak of the war had prevented us from asking him how he had done it. Now Toth had performed the same feat, and I suspected that it was not by sheer good luck. Toth considered for a while, then spoke.

'Res facilis est,' he said, grinning that disturbing smile of his. 'I slow down, then start to spin . . . so.' He held out his arms then dropped to one side suddenly. 'Gemein Flieger – aviator vulgarus – try to bring his wing up, so. But his wing is already stalled, so it only makes worse. Nihil bonum est.' He shook his head. 'But I allow the aeroplane to spin a few times, make the controls central, then work the rudder: gubernaculum dexter sinister dexter, so. Then no more spin.' He grinned broadly.

'I see,' I said, 'and did you discover this yourself?'

'Gehorsamstmelde jawohl, Herr Leutnant. Inveniego ipse. Zugsführer Toth Magyarus est . . .' He tapped the side of his head. 'He has good brain – cerebrum bonum habet, nicht wahr?'

I considered this for a while, then called over a Hungarian sergeant who was working on our aeroplane. I was far from sure how much German Toth understood, since he spoke it so villainously, and I wanted there to be no ambiguity about what I said. I also admit that sixteen years after leaving school I had no great confidence in my own ability to compose impromptu Latin orations. The sergeant agreed to act as our interpreter, so I was able to have my say in German.

'Very good, Toth. It is my considered opinion, after having flown with you twice, and after what you have just told me, that you are a dangerous madman and perhaps more of a threat to the k.u.k. Fliegertruppe than to the enemy. You have just hazarded our lives and one of the King of Hungary's aircraft by wantonly engaging an enemy single-seater in direct disobedience to my orders, while a few days before, on your own admission, you tried to kill the pair of us by deliberately putting us into a spin. I could have you court-martialled on both counts if I were so minded. However, it seems to me as a qualified pilot myself that you are an exceptionally talented flier, and that the system of my telling you how to fly the aeroplane is a remarkably poor one, regardless of whether I give the orders in Latin, German, Magyar or colloquial Hottentot. Therefore I have decided that from now on, as long as we fly together, I shall leave you in effective command of the aeroplane while we are in the air. I shall give you only general instructions beforehand as to where we are to go, and I shall leave it entirely to your own best judgement how we get there. I know that I could be court-martialled for suggesting this, since I am still technically in command of the aeroplane, but I feel that the present system cannot work on active service, and that we must therefore move with the times. However, I will impose two conditions. The first is that you should never breathe a word to anyone about this understanding of ours; the second is that if you feel an overwhelming urge to kill yourself coming upon you, you will be so kind as to tell me first so that I can get out at the next stop. If you really wish to die and leave that charming girl of yours alone in the world then I would suggest either placing a pistol to your head or asking to be posted back to the trenches. Both methods will be cheaper and will not involve me in making out official reports. Now, would you like these remarks of mine in Latin as well? Perhaps on vellum with my official seal attached?'

He grinned, and nodded to signify that everything was perfectly clear as it was. So from that day onwards a historic compromise was struck. Aboard at least one of His Imperial Royal and Apostolic Majesty's aeroplanes, regardless of what the regulations might say, the man in the pilot's seat would be the man in charge.

*

We had to remain at Veldes for the rest of that day while minor repairs were carried out to the Lloyd. The airframe was badly out of joint after our headlong dive and the engine sounded like a chaff-cutter, but Flik 2's mechanics assured us that they could patch it up sufficiently to get us back home. While we were there, that same afternoon, we received a personal telegram from General Boroević. He congratulated the two of us in the warmest terms for having made possible the destruction of the Italian battery that had plagued our men for so long.

We landed at Caprovizza early next morning. Hauptmann Kraliczek was waiting for us as we came to a stop and Toth switched off the engine. Our commanding officer was clearly not in a benign mood: in fact he even went so far as to put his foot in the stirrup in the fuselage side and hoist himself up to confront me still sitting in the cockpit. His pallid bespectacled face glowered at me as I removed my flying helmet. I saluted.

'Good morning, Herr Kommandant. Up early I see. And in what may I perhaps be of service to you?'

'Prohaska, I want to know the meaning of this.'

I smiled. 'Of what, Herr Kommandant?'

'You know perfectly well what I'm talking about: your damned disobedience to orders.'

'Begging your pardon, to what disobedience can you possibly be referring, Herr Kommandant? Zügsfuhrer Toth and I carried out our assignments to the letter . . .'

'Damn and blast you both, I could have you court-matrialled and shot for cowardice! Your orders were to proceed to the scene of action over the enemy side of the lines and to return by the same route, not skulk in safety behind our lines. You are guilty of avoiding contact with the enemy, that's the truth of it.'

I breathed deeply and tried to count up to ten: the temptation to use violence against a brother-officer was overwhelming.

'Herr Kommandant, I choose to ignore your accusations of cowardice: so far as I understand the term, skulking is something that one does in Kanzlei huts, not in the air. As to your orders for us to proceed to Monte Nero to the west of the lines, they were not

113

clearly expressed and I chose to interpret them as seemed most sensible at the time. If you care to examine this map you will see that the most direct route from here to the operational area keeps us well to the east of the trench lines almost all the way. I could see no point whatever in risking our mission by flying unarmed over Italian territory.' He fairly exploded at this, spluttering with all the fury of a damp firework.

'Not see any sense in it? Who are you to question orders, you degenerate! The whole point of a long-range reconnaissance unit is to fly as many kilometres as possible over enemy territory. You would have added at least a hundred kilometres to our total for August!'

'I see. Might I obediently enquire, then, whether we could bring forward some kilometres on account from September? Or perhaps borrow some unused kilometres from another unit if it helps balance the books? I know for a fact that Flik 4 at Wippach have been grounded for most of July. Surely they would help us out if we asked nicely . . .'

'Be quiet! And there's the matter of your shooting down an Italian aeroplane, clean contrary to your orders not to engage the enemy . . .'

'. . . By your leave, Herr Kommandant, the enemy engaged us, not we him. And incidentally, we didn't shoot him down: he tried to follow us into a dive and broke up in mid-air.'

This information seemed merely to enrage Kraliczek even further — so far as I could gather on the grounds that destroying enemy aircraft without the aid of bullets would make nonsense of his monthly returns for expenditure of ammunition. At last he recovered himself sufficiently to speak.

'Herr Linienschiffsleutnant, you are henceforth sentenced by me as your commanding officer to a week's confinement to this airfield. As to your pilot here — five days' solitary arrest on bread and water! Abtreten sofort.'

He turned to leave. I called after him.

'Oh, Herr Kommandant.'

He turned back irritably. 'What do you want?'

'I thought that you might like to see this.' I rummaged inside the breast of my flying jacket. 'It's a telegram of congratulation to us from a fellow who claims to be commanding the 5th Army, a chap called Boroević or something like that. I thought that you might perhaps care to read it out to the assembled ranks on parade this morning.'

He snatched the telegram – and tore it up into tiny pieces before striding back to his office. The fragments fluttered among the grass blades on the field. As I climbed out of the aeroplane I saw the assembled ground crew grinning among themselves in delight. Any old soldier will tell you that, for an enlisted man, being spectator to an exchange of insults between two officers of equal rank is one of the very sweetest pleasures that military life affords.

7

THE GREATER REICH

I suppose that if I had been minded to do so I could have dug out my manual of military law and contested my sentence of five days' confinement to base. But in the event I was no more troubled by it than Toth was by his own summary condemnation to five days' close arrest on bread and water. They would have needed to transfer him to Army HQ in Marburg for this anyway, since we had no lock-up ourselves and the Provost Major of the local infantry division had stood firm on regulations and refused to lend Flik 19F the use of a prison cell. And anyway, there were more important things to think about that week, for the next day, 4 August, after an intense nine-hour bombardment, the Italian 3rd Army began its long-awaited offensive: the Sixth Battle of the Isonzo, which merged with the Seventh, Eighth and Ninth Battles into a conflict which was to rage on until the onset of winter.

The Italians captured Monte Sabotino across the river from Görz after two days of bitter fighting. By the 8th our positions on either side of the town were collapsing under the ferocious barrage, and that night the 5th Army Command decided to pull back the line for fear of being outflanked. So on the morning of 9 August the Italian Army marched triumphantly into the deserted but still largely undamaged town of Görz: by far the most worthwhile Allied gain of that whole blood-saturated year. With Görz taken, the action shifted to the south and the approaches to Trieste. The battle for the Carso Plateau had begun, and with it one of the most terrible episodes even of that four-year catalogue of butchery.

I think that one of the hallmarks of the twentieth century must be the way in which the names of the most humdrum and obscure places on the whole of God's earth have become synonyms for horror, so that the very words themselves seem to twist and buckle under the weight of misery piled upon them. When I was a small boy I remember how we used to pay visits to my grandparents, decayed Polish gentry living in a small manor house on a hard-up country estate some way west of the city of Cracow: how we would get off the train at a typically small, sordid Polish provincial town and hire its one shabby fiacre; and how we would creak and sway the five kilometres or so along the rutted road across the flat fields by the Vistula and pass as we did so a small military-clothing depot built on land that my grandfather had sold to the War Ministry about 1880. It was barely worth noticing, I remember: five or six wooden huts surrounded by a decrepit fence, and with a black-and-yellow-striped gate which the bored sentry would open from time to time to admit a cartload of tunics and trousers from the Jewish sweatshops in Bielsko-Biala. This was k.u.k. Militär-bekleidungs Depot No. 107 Oswięcim – or Auschwitz, to give it its German name. The collection of huts would pass in 1919 to the Polish Army, who would enlarge it a little; then in 1940 to new and more purposeful owners, who would expand it a great deal and really put the place on the map, so to speak.

It was the same on that dreary limestone plateau east of the Isonzo in the summer of 1916: places that no one had ever heard of – San Martino and Doberdo and Monte Hermada – suddenly turned into field fortresses around which titanic battles raged; lives squandered by the hundred thousand for places which were just names on a local map – and sometimes not even that, so that the hills for which entire divisions perished had to be denoted by their map-height above sea level. So it was at Verdun that summer. I saw some photographs in a colour supplement a few months ago: the Meuse battlefields seventy years after. It appears that even today large areas are still derelict, that the incessant shelling and gassing so blasted away the topsoil and poisoned the earth that the landscape is still a semi-desert of exposed rock and old craters, covered (where anything grows at all) by a thin scrub.

The chief difference, I suppose, between Verdun now and the

Carso then is that, so far as I could make out, the Carso had always looked like that: a landscape reminiscent of Breughel's 'Triumph of Death' even before the armies got to work on it. Indeed I think that the whole of Europe could scarcely have contained a piece of ground intrinsically less worth fighting over than the Carso – or the 'Krst' as its few mostly Slovene inhabitants called it, as if the place was too poor even to afford vowels. It was an undulating, worn-down plateau of low limestone hills devoid of trees, grass or any vegetation whatever except for a few meagre patches of willow and gorse which had managed to get roots down into the fissures in the rock. What little soil there was had collected by some freak of nature into puddle-like hollows in the rock, called 'dolinas', and was bright red in colour, like pools of fresh blood. What little rain water there was had a way of disappearing as if bewitched into pot-holes in the rock, to reappear perversely a dozen kilometres away where an underground stream came out into the open. Baked by the sun all summer and swept by freezing winds all winter, the Carso was scourged in between times by the notorious bora, the sudden, violent north wind of the Adriatic coastline which would work itself up in these parts to near-hurricane force in the space of a few minutes, and had been known to blow over trains of goods wagons on the more exposed stretches of the Vienna–Trieste railway line.

At the best of times the Carso was a place such as even an early-Christian hermit might have thought twice about inhabiting. But as a battlefield it was a hell all of its own: a howling grey-brown desolation of broken rock spattered with dried blood and the dirty yellowish residue of TNT. The peculiar horror of the Carso fighting – the local speciality that distinguished it from the other great abattoirs of those years – was the enormous number of the wounded who lost their eyesight; small wonder, when every shellburst would send knife-sharp splinters of rock whining in all directions. Before long every last stone, every pulverised village of this wilderness would be stained with agony: places like the ruined market square in Sagrado, where a thousand or so Italians had staggered back from the trenches to die, remains of a brigade which had just been gassed with phosgene; or the little valley leading up on to the plateau from the hamlet of Selz, known as 'the Cemetery of the Hungarians' after an entire Honvéd battalion had blundered into it in the smoke and confusion of a counter-attack and had been wiped out to a man by the Italian machine guns.

Before the war, if it had been mine to sell, I would cheerfully have sold you the entire Carso Plateau for a gulden. Yet now whole armies would immolate themselves for it as if it contained all the riches of the world. Before the war the eroded hills of Fajtji Hrib and Cosich and Debeli Vrh had been unvisited, known only to a few Slovene shepherds. Now their barren slopes and gullies would become the graveyards of a generation. When your great dramatist wrote of a little patch of ground that is not tomb or continent enough to bury the slain, I think that he must have had the Carso in mind. That summer of 1916, they lay everywhere, visible through any trench periscope: the sad, sunken bundles of rags tumbled among the rocks or sprawled across the thickets of barbed wire where they had fallen, their only passing-bells the frenzied jangling of the tin cans which our men used to hang from the wire as alarm signals. Even a thousand metres above the battlefields that August one could detect the sinister, sweetish taint of decay. By some black joke on the part of biochemistry, it had (for my nose at any rate) a faint hint of overripe strawberries to it. Many years later my second wife Edith bought a lipstick perfumed with just such a synthetic strawberry scent. It brought back so many disturbing memories that I had to ask her to stop using it.

Yes, I speak as though I saw it all. But then I did, as near as makes no difference. The Carso front was tiny – perhaps ten kilometres in total – so we fliers could see pretty well the whole of it as we flew above that terrible greyish-dun landscape: the shallow valleys below us boiling with smoke suffused with orange flame; then coming down sometimes when the murk parted to see the lines of tiny human specks scurrying forward among the shell-bursts; the evil greenish-yellow clouds of poison gas and the sudden white puffs of grenades and the boiling black-fiery squirts of flame-throwers; men rushing forward to kill and maim one another with grenades and entrenching tools so as to gain or regain another few square metres of this ghastly desolation. The memory haunts me to this day: the sheer crushing lunacy of it all. Why did we do it? Why did we allow them to do it to us? I was there and you were not, so I wonder if you could tell me why. Because I was there to see it, yet sometimes I think that I perhaps understand it less than you who were not.

The battle raged to westward of us throughout that second week of August. The Italians had captured Görz, and they were now attacking the hills of Monte San Michele on the north edge and Debeli Vrh on the southern edge of the Carso escarpment, trying to fight their way on to the plateau above. Our men in the front line were suffering atrociously in their rock-bound trenches, shelled day and night so that it was impossible either to bring up food and water or to evacuate the wounded. Rationed sometimes to a cup of water a day in the summer heat and dust, plagued by great corpse-fattened blowflies, they hung on as best they could, counter-attacked when ordered to do so and died in their anonymous thousands for their distant Emperor and King. Yet while this whole dismal tragedy was being played out a few kilometres away, Flik 19F sat idly on the field at Caprovizza and chewed the ends of its collective moustache with boredom and frustration. We were on standby – which is why Toth and I were not much affected in practice by our sentence of arrest – but otherwise little happened. We were short of aircraft of course: one Brandenburger had arrived back from repair, but the Lloyd which we had flown on the Monte Nero artillery-spotting operation was out of action. Toth had let the revs build up during our dive to a degree where the cylinder liners had been irretrievably damaged, so the machine was now standing in a hangar waiting for a replacement engine. This left us with three effective aircraft – two Brandenburgers and a Lloyd. Yet we felt that there was still work that we could do to support our hard-pressed comrades in the trenches. Flik 19 at Haidenschaft had been heavily engaged from the first day. Its aircraft would often return, badly shot-up, to deposit yet another blanket-shrouded bundle on the handbarrow, and add one more to the rapidly extending line of propeller-crosses in the cemetery.

It galled us all beyond measure, sitting there waiting for the telephone to ring. We were under the command of 5th Army HQ, not the local division, and it seemed as if Marburg had entirely forgotten our existence. At last, on the Saturday after Görz fell, it all became too much: the entire officer strength of the unit – except for myself, who was confined to base – elbowed the protesting Kraliczek aside and marched down the road to Haidenschaft to offer their services to Flik 19. Heyrowsky was not able to see them – he was in the air over Gradisca that afternoon, where he shot down a Nieuport with his hunting rifle – but when he got back he sent a curt reply to the effect that Flik 19 was a front-line fighting unit and would only use the services of (as he put it) 'fashion photographers and killers of civilians' when its last able-bodied flier was dead. When they got back Kraliczek had thrown a fit and threatened to have everyone court-martialled for mutiny. In the end Oberleutnant Meyerhofer, standing in temporarily as Chefpilot, had called everyone together in the mess tent and composed a round robin (as I believe you call it) to General-Oberst Boroević. It protested our undying loyalty to the Noble House of Austria and offered our lives as pledges of our devotion, if not in the air then (if need be) in the front-line trenches, where we would fight to our last breath come shot, shell, bayonet, flame-thrower or poison gas. We all signed, even the wretched Kraliczek, whom we dragged out of his office and whose reaction, when shown the document, had been that of someone in the early stages of rabies confronted with a glass of water. His hand shook visibly as he signed, with the rest of us standing around him wearing our swords and black-and-yellow belts to offer moral support. The General's reply next day thanked us for our loyalty to our Emperor and King, but said that trained airmen were in short supply and must not have their lives squandered without

121

thought for the future. Boroević concluded by promising us all the fighting we wanted, and more besides, in the weeks to come.

So the early part of August passed peacefully enough for us at Caprovizza, as the guns thundered in the west and the wind sometimes brought us the faint smell of TNT fumes, mingled (as the hot days wore by) with a hint of something even less pleasant. We often saw Italian aircraft overhead, but were prevented by our orders from doing anything about it; that is, until one day when Meyerhofer had gone up with Stabsfeldwebel Zwierzkowski to test-fly a Brandenburger just back from repair. They were away for an hour or so, and when they returned they were preceded by a large, clumsy-looking pusher-engined biplane. It was an Italian Farman SP2 artillery spotter which they had sighted over Doberdo and engaged.

The SP2 was an awful aeroplane by all accounts: a pre-war French design – outdated even in 1914 – which the Italians had licence-built in huge numbers as part of an emergency programme to create an air force out of nothing. It was a mistake which I believe Lord Beaverbrook was to make a generation later: tooling up the aircraft factories to turn out vast numbers of obsolete machines. The Italians were now trying to use up stocks. But in so doing they were also using up the lives of their airmen at a fine old rate, because the SP2 was simply a death trap: too slow to run away, unable to climb out of trouble, too clumsy to dodge and with so restricted a field of fire for the observer's machine gun in the front cockpit that the thing was effectively a flying blind spot. Meyerhofer and Zwierzkowski had made a first pass at it with the forward machine gun and shot it about a little, had allowed the Italian observer to fire back at them as much as honour required, and had then stood off to observe events. Seeing that their line of retreat across their own lines was cut off and that they were done for if they resisted further, the observer had finally stood up in his cockpit and held up his hands in surrender; very sensibly too, we all agreed. The Italians were escorted over to meet us and shook hands with us all: Tenente Balboni and Caporale-Pilota Scaranza. Their feelings were as mixed as one might have expected:

downcast at their capture and the prospect of a long spell behind the wire, but glad to have come out of it alive – which was not the usual fate of Farman aircrew. We commiserated with them as we looked over their bullet-peppered machine, and all said (I was interpreting for the rest, being fluent in Italian) that it was a shame that men should be sent up to die in such miserable contraptions.

'You know what "SP2" stands for, Tenente?' the observer said to me. ' "Seppultoro per due" – "the Sepulchre for Two".'

'No, no,' added his pilot, laughing, 'it means "Siamo perduti" – "We are lost"!' We entertained them to dinner that evening, and waved them goodbye the next morning as the staff car came to take them away to the prison camp. In the end the only dissatisfied party was Kraliczek, whose returns for August had been upset on three counts: (a) that yet another machine had been brought down by a unit which was not supposed to engage the enemy; (b) that the Italian had been forced down by an aeroplane which officially did not exist, since it had been signed off the books at the Fliegeretappenpark but had not yet been accepted back on to the strength of Flik 19F; and (c) – gravest dereliction of all – it had been brought down by an officer who was not on the combat flying strength of the unit. We learnt later that rather than deal with the administrative nightmares thus caused, Kraliczek had proposed letting the Italians get back into their aeroplane and fly home under a safe-conduct.

Thus the days passed idly, sitting on that sun-scorched field trying to find what shade we could as the hot, irritating Carso wind scurried straw and dust along the ground and rattled the tent-sides. There were few diversions for us except reading and playing cards – and listening to Leutnant Szuborits' gramophone in the tent next to mine.

He had a rather nice wind-up portable gramophone which his mother had bought him; but records were in short supply in Austria by 1916 (the blockade had stopped the importation of the shellac from which they were made and no substitute had been found), and anyway the Leutnant's musical tastes were limited. So it was constant, maddening repetition of the duet 'Sport und immer Sport' from a failed Lehár operetta of 1914 or thereabouts – called *Endlich Allein* if I remember rightly – with Hubert Marischka and Mizzi Günther squawking away like an egg-bound hen. It was an intensely irritating piece of music: one of those maddeningly catchy marschlieder so beloved of Viennese light-music composers about 1913–14, when the sudden Europe-wide vogue for deep breathing and general outdoor heartiness had spread to affect even dingy, sedentary old Austria. It was to turn up again many years later (I recall) as 'Frei und Jung Dabei' when Lehár tried reviving his old operetta, only to see it sink once more to well-merited oblivion after a couple of nights.

Records in those days tended to wear out very quickly, but this one seemed to be made of tungsten carbide: just went on and on and on playing until I was tearing my hair out in tufts and trying not to look at my pistol in its holster hanging on the tentpole. And that is how I remember the summer of 1916 on the Isonzo Front: the sun's glare and the nagging moan of the wind and the sound of aircraft engines; the fretful flapping of tent canvas and Mizzi Günther warbling scratchily through 'Sport und immer Sport', accompanied by the ever-present rumbling orchestra of high explosive to westwards.

Apart from the affair of the captured SP2, the only diversion of those early days of August was the arrival of a new Chefpilot to replace poor Rieger. He arrived by staff car one morning just after breakfast. I was the only one around to meet him, and as he stepped down with his bags I thought that he was surely one of the pleasantest-looking men I had ever seen: in his early twenties, of medium height, gracefully formed, with fine light brown hair and gentle, rather melancholy blue eyes such as a poet or composer might possess. He gazed at me sideways, smiled politely in greeting and saluted. Then he turned his head slightly – and I saw that most of the left side of his face had gone, cheekbone and temple replaced by a tortured confusion of lumps and puckered scar tissue surrounding an eyeball which looked to be in danger of tumbling out on to his cheek. Despite myself I winced slightly and tried not to look. My wife Elisabeth had worked for the past two years in a specialist facial-injuries unit at the Vienna Medical School, and she had shown me a good many spine-crawling photographs of 'before'. Well, this was clearly one of the 'after' cases: one of those less severely damaged casualties whose face the surgeons had managed to rebuild sufficiently for an army medical board to class him once more as 'dienstauglich'. He shook my hand – no doubt noticing that, like everyone else he met, I was trying not to look at his face – and introduced himself as Oberleutnant-Feldpilot Svetozar von Potocznik.

I got to talk with Potocznik that evening and over the next few days, and I must say that I found him at first to be one of the more engaging people I had so far encountered: tactful, humorous, modest, and endowed with great precision and sensitivity of expression. He was also quite remarkably intelligent. Little by little I learnt his story. He had been born in 1894 in the small town of Pravnitz on the southern edge of Carinthia, where his father was chemistry master of the local grammar school. And of course, the gymnasium at Pravnitz in the 1900s had become a cause célèbre throughout the Austro-Hungarian Monarchy because of a bitter dispute over the language of instruction in the school, now that the local Slovene population were demanding equality with German-speakers. This wretched dispute had dragged on for years, with the school closed down for long periods because of riots and boycotts and blockades, punctuated by outbreaks of pandemonium in the Vienna Reichsrat as the German and Slovene deputies from Carinthia hurled inkpots at one another. At least three k.k. Ministers for Education had resigned because of the Pravnitz gymnasium affair. At last, in 1908, to the inexpressible disgust of German Nationalists throughout the entire Monarchy, Vienna had given in and made the school officially bilingual.

But while this nonsense had been going on, events had been moving for the Potocznik family in another direction. Always an ingenious man, Herr Doktor von Potocznik had used his long spells of enforced leave to perfect a revolutionary new process for synthesis of ammonia. In the end he had managed to patent it and sell it to the CIVAG syndicate, who made it a condition of purchase that he should move to Germany to supervise the setting-up of the first process line. So in 1909 the family had sold up and moved to Mannheim, bidding a not very affectionate farewell to the decrepit old Austrian Monarchy which had given in so easily to the insolent demands of its lower races.

Thus young Potocznik had grown up in Germany. An outstanding pupil and talented poet, he had excelled at music, though his interests had turned towards theology and moral philosophy. He had also, about 1910, become involved with the Wandervögel, the curious movement among the idealistic German young which rejected the horsechair-stuffed values of the Wilhelmine Reich and instead set out in search of the authentic and the natural: birdsong in the forest, church bells in the Alpine valleys, rucksacks and lederhosen and guitars around campfires, running barefoot in the morning dew and all the rest of the nonsense which (I must confess) made me thankful for a youth spent playing billiards in the smoke-filled ambience of Austrian provincial coffee-houses.

Potocznik had been due to enter Göttingen University in 1914 to study philosophy. But the war had got there first. Like millions of other German adolescents, he had rushed to the colours filled with a burning desire for self-sacrifice in this war, which (they believed) was not about territory or dynastic claims but about power and youth and the force of the spirit; a near-religious crusade to give Germany her rightful place in the world and break the shackles forged for her by the old nations. There had been official reservations about his nationality of course: he was still technically an Austrian subject. But he was eventually given permission to join the German Army, 'pending an administrative decision'. He enlisted in the Academic Legion and was flung almost immediately, after the sketchiest of training, into the fighting at Ypres, given the task of storming the village of Langemarck. Eighteen thousand of them had set out across the water meadows that morning, singing Beethoven's 'Ode to Joy' as

126

they advanced. Less than two thousand were to come back. 'The Massacre of the Innocents', they called it. A patrol had found Potocznik next day among the stacks of corpses, the left side of his face smashed by a rifle bullet.

He had spent the next six months in hospital in Germany, and had then been transferred to the specialist facial-injuries unit being set up by Professor Kirschbaum and his colleagues at Vienna University. My wife Elisabeth had been one of the sisters on his ward. They had patched him up after a fashion, rebuilding his cheekbone with bone-grafts and creating a metal bridge for his upper jaw. But plastic surgery was a primitive business in those still-experimental days before antibiotics, and the surgeons had in the end only been able to restore function, not appearance. But another unpleasant surprise awaited him in mid-1915: the Imperial German Minister for War – having probably concluded that someone with a name like Svetozar von Potocznik was not an acceptable soldier of the Reich – had not been pleased to grant his application to serve in the German armed forces. To my surprise, though, I found him not to be too upset about this.

'Of course,' he had said to me in the mess tent after supper, 'it was a let-down not to be able to serve in the German Army, especially after I started getting interested in flying. Their air force is about five years ahead of ours in every respect. But quite frankly it doesn't make a lot of difference to me now. We're all fighting for the Greater German Reich, and wearing an Austrian cap badge signifies as little for me as wearing that of Bavaria or Saxony. Germany and Austria are being welded together now into a single billet of steel under the blows of the enemy, tempered in the forge of war into a weapon such as the world has not yet seen. True, I'd have more fun flying on the Western Front against the Britishers and the French. But there: I think we'll have sport enough here on the South-West Front before long, once the Americans come into this war. And anyway, I'm glad in a way to be defending this region.'

'What, the Kustenland?'

'No, Carinthia, my home province: defending the southern

marches of Germany against the Latins and Slavs. That was something I could never convince them of in north Germany: that we Germans who live on the frontiers of the Reich have a far keener awareness of what it means to be German than those who sit comfortably in Darmstadt and Mannheim and never look into the eyes of the wolf-packs that surround us.'

'You seem to have a very clear idea of what you are fighting for,' I remarked.

'I certainly have. But what are you fighting for, Prohaska, if I might ask?'

'Me? I can't say that I've ever thought much about it. I just fight for the House of Austria because that's my job and it's what I swore on oath to do. Anyway, my time's been so taken up thinking about how to do it these past two years that I've never wondered a great deal about why. I'm just a career naval officer; things like that are for the politicians to decide.'

'Precisely. That's the trouble, if you'll excuse my saying so: you professional officers always fight bravely, but sadly you lack any very deep appreciation of what this war is about. Probably I'd have been the same if I had grown up in this corpse-empire of ours and been through a cadet school. But as it was I saw the future in Germany – the factories, the cities, the laboratories. And I also had time to read a great deal when I was laid up in hospital: Nietzsche, Darwin, Treitschke, Bernhardi, the lot. It was then that I first fully understood why I was lying in bed with half my face missing; and I swore to dedicate my life to Greater Germany. Our German revolution is being created in this war. Nothing can stop it now – not even defeat – and it'll turn the world upside-down before it's finished.'

'You sound like a socialist to me.' He smiled, his mouth twisted to one side by his rebuilt jaw. I could see how sweet his smile would have been before his face was wrecked. His eyes were not those of a crazed fanatic but of a seer; a dreamer of dreams.

'Perhaps I am, my dear Prohaska. But a German socialist second and a German warrior first.' It may have been ill-natured of me, but I could not help interjecting at this point that some might consider 'Svetozar von Potocznik' a pretty odd sort of name for a warrior of the Greater German Reich. But he had obviously been asked that question before. He laughed, and answered me with his usual calm earnestness. 'We all have to have a name, Prohaska, and names are landed down in the male line except, I believe, in a few odd little countries in Africa. The "Svetozar" bit is rather awful, I agree: my mother was greatly addicted to romantic novels when I was born and she thought that it went better with "Potocznik" than "Willibald" or "Englebert", which were my father's choices. As to the "Potocznik", it doesn't argue for any but the tiniest element of Slav blood. Tell me Prohaska, how long do you think people in Europe have been using surnames?'

'I really couldn't say. Since the fifteenth century perhaps? Up in the Tyrol I believe they still give people names according to their occupation.'

'Good, the fifteenth century: say twenty generations ago to be on the safe side?' I nodded my assent. 'Well then, I worked it out recently and that gives me a theoretical possibility of something over two million ancestors. Only one of those needed to have the name "Potocznik" to have passed it on to me. And anyway, there's no certainty that he was a Slav: he could have been a German kidnapped in a border raid and taken into serfdom by the Croats. No, there is not the slightest doubt in my mind that I am of purely Germanic stock.'

'I see. So where precisely does that leave me in this crusade for the Greater German Reich? After all, I'm a Czech on my father's side and a Pole on my mother's, and as you can hear I still speak German with an accent.'

'Well, since you ask me I would have said that by becoming an Austrian officer you have automatically cast your vote for Germanic culture.'

'I see. And will you let me in?'

'Of course: to be a German is not only a matter of blood and soil but of culture. The Romans – who were the earliest Germans by the way: I read a book about it recently – never had anything against barbarians becoming Roman citizens, after they had given sufficient proof of their loyalty. The border peoples like the Czechs and the Poles will be offered a choice after this war: either become part of the German Reich or become German protectorates outside it – or if you don't want either of those alternatives then clear off to join your Slav brothers beyond the Urals.'

'And do you think that they'll accept that choice willingly?'

'I don't doubt it: look at all the Czechs in the k.u.k. Armee who've been voting for Russia lately by raising both hands. As for the rest, I don't imagine that they'll have much choice. Did the Britishers ever ask the people of India whether they wanted to be part of their empire? The mark of a truly vigorous nation is that it has a way of resolving these matters without the need for ballot boxes. The British and French only became interested in democracy once they had taken as much of the world as they wanted by force.'

'But surely, Potocznik, haven't you noticed that in this pan-German crusade some of our best fighters are Slavs? Look at the Bosnians for instance. Or the Slovenes: I doubt whether you'd find a braver and more loyal people in the entire Monarchy.'

He snorted. 'Brave and loyal: you certainly wouldn't have found them very brave and loyal if you'd seen them back in Pravnitz during the gymnasium affair. The sheer colossal impudence of it: a silly little ethnographic relic of a people with no literature and no history and no culture of their own, challenging the rights of a major world nation. It's just too absurd. There's no such people as the Slovenes, and their language is a fraud: a monkey-jabber made to look like a proper language by a German-speaking bishop – a Jewish convert, by the way – to create enemies for Germany and keep it under the thumb of Rome. The Slovene Nation, indeed – not a million of them, and nothing but a lot of illiterate yokels in felt hats and silly costumes. For them to claim equality with the nation of Goethe and Schiller and Beethoven is like a sparrow claiming equality with an eagle. Darwin proved that there is no such thing as equality in nature, only the stronger and the weaker.'

'Do I take it, then, that you propose shooting all the Slovenes once we win this war? It seems pretty shabby thanks after the way they've fought for us.'

'Of course not: the so-called Slovene people would continue to exist for as long as it wished to. But with no equality in German-speaking areas, that's for sure, and with German as a compulsory subject in all their schools from the lowest level up.'

'Do you think that they'd take kindly to that? You make it sound like running a colony in Africa.'

'Perhaps it is rather like that. If they are eventually absorbed into Germany, then frankly we would be doing them a kindness. Honestly, Prohaska, there's no future in these little peoples now: the Slovenes and Czechs and the rest. They only survived this long because the Habsburg state has somehow managed to stagger a century too far. From now on it'll be the big nations who count; this war demostrates that if nothing else. Cruel to absorb them into Greater Germany? We'd be far crueller to them in the long run if we didn't, with the Italians waiting out there to swallow them up. We're bringing them into the modern world, making them catch up with the rest of Europe after a thousand years of slumber. That's our Germanic mission: to force these fossil peoples into the twentieth century. "Deutsche Wesen soll die Welt genesen." '

The next morning the telephone rang at last in the Kanzlei at Caprovizza airfield. We were to make ready for a fresh experiment in wireless artillery direction from the air. The news of our success at Monte Nero at the beginning of August had spread as far as the High Command, and a new operation was being planned to try and take some of the pressure off our troops on the Carso. The elderly coast-defence battleship S.M.S. *Prag* was lying at Pola and would steam up to the Gulf of Trieste on 14 August to shell a large group of ammunition dumps which had just been revealed by aerial photography in a wood near the railway line between Sagrado and Ronchi. The ship would anchor off Sistiana and her battery of four 24cm guns would fire at maximum elevation to try and hit the dumps, hoping to set off a general and demoralising explosion since (our artillery experts said) the Italians had stacked the shells far too close together for safety. It would need wireless spotting to do the job – the target was twelve kilometres inland and hidden from our spotters by the edge of the Carso escarpment – and it would also require an officer-observer used to naval signalling and gunnery practice. The choice was obvious, so Toth and I were ordered to get ready to fly the next morning.

We would be flying a Lloyd once again, since the fuselage of the Brandenburger was still not quite roomy enough for all the paraphernalia of a wireless station. Likewise we would once again be flying unarmed, for reasons of weight-saving. I was none too happy about this after our encounter with the Nieuport over Monte Nero, so I was determined this time to take along something more powerful than a Steyr pistol by way of protection. A Mannlicher cavalry carbine was not a great improvement, it is true, but it might give us some chance if we could let the enemy get close enough.

As to the wireless station, we learnt that we would not be carrying the clumsy spark transmitter which we had used at Monte Nero. Instead we would be provided with the very latest in German wireless technology: a Siemens-Halske valve set. This apparatus was (we were told) more fragile than the spark set, and almost as heavy, but it could be tuned more precisely and, above all, would allow us not only to transmit but also to receive signals, thus doing away with the previous rigmarole of white and red and green rockets.

That part at least was reasonably simple, installing the wireless set that afternoon and going up to run a few test-exchanges of signals with a ground station at Haidenschaft airfield. The fun started when we landed and found a naval liaison officer waiting for us so that we could co-ordinate our plans for tomorrow. The first thing we discovered was that the naval charts did not extend as far inland as our target, and that the k.u.k. Armee's maps of the area were not only on a different scale but used an entirely different grid system. In the end I had to make up an 'oleat': a sheet of transparent paper with a naval grid marked on it so that we could superimpose it on the army map.

That problem was simple enough to solve; far trickier was the difference in gunnery signalling practice between the Army and the k.u.k. Kriegsmarine. This would make it necessary for the *Prag* to carry a major of artillery as a liaison officer. However, the officer in question did not know Morse code, so it would be necessary to asign him a naval telegraphist. But at this point questions of inter-service etiquette began to arise. The Navy's self-esteem would not permit an army officer to give direct orders to the crew of a battleship while at sea, so a naval Korvetten-kapitän would have to be detailed to transmit instructions from the Major to the ship's Wireless Operator. Likewise the army officer would not be permitted to give orders direct to the *Prag*'s turret captains. Instead (it was eventually decided) he would give the necessary bearing and elevations to the ship's Gunnery Officer as 'recommendations', and the latter would then transmit them to the turrets as orders. Likewise the order 'Fire!' would be respectfully suggested to the naval Liaison Officer, who would give it to the Gunnery Officer, who would then convey it to the turret-commanders. Furthermore, it was decided that in case things went wrong and the two services started blaming one another, all orders were to be duplicated in writing. In fact I suspect that it was only because I was a naval officer myself that I escaped having a petty officer telegraphist squeezed into the aeroplane cockpit with me to relay my signals to the ship. As it was it involved a chain of no less than seven persons in converting my aerial observations into a shell issuing from the muzzle of a gun. It was a fire-control system such as only Habsburg Austria could have devised.

Another drawback to this operation, from our point of view at least, was that our Siemens-Halske wireless set was ultra-top-secret. In fact at first Kraliczek was going to forbid it to be carried across the lines for fear of its being captured. It was only after we had spent a hour or so explaining, with the aid of diagrams, that there is not a great deal of sense in artillery-spotting on one's own side of the lines that he had relented on this – but only on condition that we flew with a large demolition charge attached to the set so that it would blow up the apparatus, and us, if we crashed. Thus it was that, a generation before the Japanese kamikazes, Toth and I found ourselves flying in an aeroplane containing a two-kilogram slab of Ekrasit, the Austrian brand of TNT, attached to the wireless with surgical tape and wired up to explode if we hit the ground. It was all most reassuring.

In the event, though, our fine new wireless set was barely used that day. Our take-off from Caprovizza was delayed until mid-morning by fog over the target (the lower end of the Isonzo is notoriously foggy, even in summer). So it was not until nearly 1100 hours that we crossed the lines near Görz and made our way southwards in a half-circle over Gradisca and Sagrado to approach our target from the landward side. It was evidently going to be a rough ride: flak shells banged around us at intervals from Görz onwards, and once the mist cleared from their airfields there would be Italian single-seaters coming up to chase us. Better get the job done as quickly as possible and make for home, I thought: flying unarmed over enemy territory in broad daylight with a slab of explosive next to me did not appeal to me in the least.

We arrived over the target at two thousand metres amid a desultory peppering of flak bursts – only to find that the target was no more. There could be no doubt about it as we circled overhead and I scanned the forest clearing with my binoculars: the shell-dump had almost gone. When I compared the scene with an aerial photograph from two days before I could see where the tarpaulin-covered stacks had been – pale oblong patches on the grass of the clearing – but nearly all of them had gone now. As I watched, a beetle-like chain of motor lorries bumped along the forest trackway, carrying the shells forward to the hungry battery positions. I flicked the wireless set switch to 'Transmit' and put on the headphones, then tapped out the message 'Shells gone – query what now?' There was an acknowledge signal from the *Prag*, a distant grey shape out on the blue shining expanse of the Adriatic, but nothing more. Meanwhile we circled fretfully, dodging the flak shells. I could imagine the scratching of heads and confusion that reigned inside the conning tower of the old battleship. But that was scarcely any consolation to us now, flying around in slow circles to provide target practice for the Italian flak battery crews. I was just wondering whether to take matters into my own hands and head us for home when Toth turned and tugged at my sleeve excitedly. He pointed away to southward.

I could scarcely believe my eyes. Here indeed was something far more worthy of our attention than the place where a target had once been. Toth needed no order from me to turn and give full throttle. It was an Italian airship, strolling towards the lines above Monfalcone. It was about six kilometres away, and (I thought) about a thousand metres above us. That would mean at least eight minutes of climbing around in circles before we could reach him, not to speak of closing the distance. Still, it seemed worth a try. Airships were a matter of some interest to me that summer. I had won my Maria Theresa in part for having shot down just such an Italian semi-rigid, south of Venice in July. They were not very large airships as such contraptions go: certainly nothing to compare with the German Zeppelins. The gasbag was a single, soft envelope and rigidity was given by a long V-sectioned keel of aluminium girders from which the engines and control gondolas were suspended. The Italians had built quite a number of these airships – the larger ones had a crew of nine or ten – and had been trying for the past year to use them on bombing-raids, with conspicuous lack of success. And here was one of them now, insolently flaunting its toad-like, pale-yellow bulk over the countryside in broad daylight. Such effrontery could not go unanswered.

The only trouble was, I realised as we climbed up towards the airship, that apart from my Mannlicher carbine and five clips of ammunition we had no means of attacking the airship short of ramming it. As for the Italians, they were quite well equipped to defend themselves. There seemed to be a machine gun in each of the crew gondolas, to judge by the streams of tracer that sprayed out at us like water from a garden hose each time we tried to manoeuvre within range. The one great advantage of an airship over an aeroplane in those days was the former's ability to climb. An aeroplane had to labour round in cirlces for six or seven minutes to gain a thousand metres, whereas all that an airship had to do was to release water ballast and whee!, up it would go like a witch on a broomstick. But for some reason which I shall never understand the Italians neglected to escape that way, only continued at the same height and allowed us to climb above them –where we saw to our delight that there was no machine-gun position on the top of the gasbag.

So we circled for a while, like Red Indians around a settler's wagon, as I fired off our entire stock of ammunition into the airship's envelope. It had no visible effect though. I suppose that, like me that morning, you have some mental picture of the airship going pop! at the first hit, like a child's balloon pricked with a pin. Well, forget it: the pressure of the gas in an airship's envelope is not in fact much above that of the surrounding air, and the seepage of hydrogen from a few puny rifle-bullet holes could probably have gone on for days before the thing even began to lose its shape. As we climbed away from our last futile pass, followed by a valedictory spatter of fire from the forward gondola, I looked around desperately for some other means of attack. Then an idea struck me: the wireless set. It weighed forty kilograms and, although it left much to be desired from an aerodynamic point of view, it had lots of jagged edges and sharp corners. Feverishly I got to work wrenching out wires and disconnecting the demolition charge as Toth turned to make another pass at the airship. He seemed to sense what I wanted, and took us roaring in a shallow dive along the airship's swelling, pig-like back.

I almost ruptured myself as I lugged the wireless set on to the cockpit coaming, struggling to hold it steady in the howling slipstream, then heaved it into space at what I judged to be the correct moment. The aeroplane skipped and lurched, relieved suddenly of the weight, and it was several seconds before Toth could steady her enough for us to come around and survey the results – if any – of our unorthodox bombing attack. We saw that the wireless set had almost missed the airship as it plummeted past. Almost, but not quite: a large rent about two metres long had been torn in the fabric about a third of the way forward from the tail. The envelope was already beginning to sag and billow slightly as we watched, circling above. As for the Italians, they had clearly realised that something was wrong and were trying to turn around and get back across their own lines before they crashed. But to no avail: a rapidly deflating airship is almost impossible to steer, and in any case a south-west breeze had sprung up. Try as they might, they were being blown deeper and deeper into Austrian territory, losing height as they went. Meanwhile we circled above like a buzzard, waiting to see where our victim would come down.

In the end, twenty minutes later, the airship hit the ground way behind the lines, some distance outside the hamlet of Logavec, a Carso settlement so remote that no one had even bothered to transliterate its name into Italian. The crash was a prolonged and untidy business. The airship draggled along the ground like a wounded partridge for a good kilometre, leaving bits behind on stone walls and thickets, before what was left of it fetched up among the buildings of a farm, the envelope and broken keel finally draping themselves across the roof of a stone cottage. We circled above, looking for somewhere to land. A larger-than-usual dolina lay near by, about two hundred metres long and level from years of culivation. So we decided to chance a landing, despite the demolition charge which we were still carrying. Toth brought the Lloyd to a stop only a couple of metres in front of the steep, rocky end of the hollow and we leapt out to scramble towards the farm, intent on capturing the survivors before they could sort themselves out after the crash.

I carried the empty carbine and Toth his Steyr pistol. They were not a great deal of use, but at least I thought that we might menace the Italians into surrendering quietly if they were still disentangling themselves from the wreckage. But we were too late. I stuck my head up over a drystone wall to get a look at the wreck – and was obliged to pull it down again smartly as a burst of machine-gun fire rattled and whined off the rocks. The Italians had barricaded themselves into a stone outbuilding, carrying the airship's weapons with them. No doubt they hoped to hold out until nightfall and then slip away unobserved. The front to northwards of Görz, among the forests of the Bainsizza, was much less densely manned than the Carso sector, and anyway there were more than enough ethnic Italians in these parts to provide them with shelter and civilian clothes. Troops would reach us eventually – the entire Isonzo Front must have watched the airship coming down – but they would take time to find us. Clearly, our task was to hold the Italians where they were until reinforcements arrived.

I crept round as close as I dared to the outbuilding where the airmen were hiding and called out to them. Lucky, I thought, that four years at the k.u.k. Marine Akademie had made me fluent in Italian. The reply was another short burst of fire, aimed at random as far as I could make out. I tried again.

'Friends . . .' I paused, awaiting more shots. But none came. I went on, 'Friends, Italian aviators, we mean you no harm.' There was a single shot, but I went on regardless. 'Please see sense: you are now deep in Austrian territory after being brought down in a fair combat with no dishonour to yourselves. You have done everything that your country could reasonably expect of you and you must not sacrifice your lives in so futile a fashion after surviving a crash. You are now surrounded and heavily out-numbered. . .' (I have to add that I choked a little at this whopper), 'so please be reasonable and surrender. You will be treated with every courtesy and in strict accordance with the Hague Convention and the laws of war: I myself promise you this upon my honour as an officer of the House of Austria.'

There was a long silence, then a voice answered. The accent was Piedmontese, I noticed.

'Do you have Ungheresi with you, or Bosniaci?'

Biting my tongue, I assured the invisible speaker that I had only one Hungarian among my men, and no Bosnians whatever. 'But why do you ask?' I called.

'Because it is well known that the Hungarians carry bill-hooks with which they scalp their prisoners. While as for your Bosnians, they are Mohammeddan bandits and make eunuchs of their captives in order to sell them to the Sultan of Turkey for guarding his harem. This much is common knowledge: I read it myself only the other day in the *Corriere*.' I answered that, to the best of my knowledge, our own single Hungarian had never so much as owned a bill-hook in his life, let alone scalped anyone with it; while as for the Bosnian eunuch dealers, whether Muslim or of any other religion, I had no such people under my command (I might have added that from what I had heard of the Bosnians they very rarely took any prisoners; but this would have been extremely tactless in the circumstances).

When I had finished, the voice still seemed unconvinced. Meanwhile, from within the stone cottage on top of which the airship had landed, there had issued for the past five minutes or so the sounds of a woman having hysterics in Slovene, pausing every now and then to implore the aid of each of the saints in the Church's calendar, starting with St Anna the Mother of Our Lady. She was already on the line to SS Cyril and Methodius, Apostles to the Slavs, and the shrieks in between were growing louder by the minute. At that moment one of the numerous goats browsing the scrub around the farmstead was bold enough to climb up a drystone wall and peer over the top – only to fall back a second or two later riddled with machine-gun-bullets. It was clear that our Italians still required some persuasion as to the hopelessness of their case. I felt a sudden tug at my sleeve. It was Toth, creeping along in the lee of the wall, pistol in hand.

'Magnum fragorem face – boom! – auxilio Ekrasito.' I stared at him for a moment in bewilderment, then realised what he meant. Of course: the slab of TNT. We scrambled back along the wall and ran to the Lloyd, which was standing out of sight of the Italians in the sunken dolina. Toth seized the block of Ekrasit and its detonators while I ripped out the aerial wire and the wireless set's emergency battery. Then we ran back to the lee of the outbuilding and heaped up rocks from the wall on top of the explosive charge. When all was ready we clambered over a wall, trailing the wires behind us, and took cover. I looked at Toth and he nodded back. I was far from sure that this would work . . . I touched the two ends of the wire to the battery terminals.

It did work. There was a most impressive bang, and Toth and I had to huddle up to the wall for shelter as stones rained from the sky around us. The flock of goats was scattering in all directions, bleating in panic as the rocks showered down among them. From within the cottage there came a piercing scream, followed by frenzied calls for St Blasius of Ragusa to orare pro nobis. I crept up to the outbuilding and called out:

'Come out and surrender. Your position is hopeless. Our artillery has these buildings ranged now. That was a warning shot. I have only to signal to them and the next one will land among you.'

The moral effect upon the airship crew was much as I had hoped: before long a man in leather flying overalls came out of the outbuilding bearing a white handkerchief fixed to a stick. There were ten of them in all, largely unharmed by the crash, apart from a mechanic who had fallen out of an engine gondola as they hit the ground and broken his leg. Toth gave him morphine from the aeroplane's first-aid kit as I parleyed with the airship's commander, an army Capitano in his late twenties. He marched up and saluted me stiffly, then, seeing with some surprise that I was wearing naval uniform (I had cast aside my flying jacket in the heat), demanded to speak with the local troop commander. I answered that so far as he was concerned I was in command of the troops in the immediate area – which happened to be perfectly true, since there was only one of them. Where were the rest of them then, he demanded? I intimated as politely as I could that this was none of his business. He persisted: it was my duty to provide a proper prisoners' escort at once, as laid down in the relevant international conventions on the treatment of prisoners of war; and in any case he was not going to surrender either his crew or the wreck of his airship – for which he demanded a signed receipt, by the way – to anyone of a rank less than his own. I replied that I was an Austro-Hungarian Linienschiffsleutnant, and that so far as I was aware that rank was equivalent to Capitano in the Italian Army; at any rate, it was equal to a Hauptmann in ours. With this he changed tack and said that as an officer in an Italian cavalry regiment – and a rather grand one too by the sound of him – he could not agree to present his formal surrender to a naval officer: the honour of the Army would not allow it. I sympathised, but said that I thought that with things as they were he was in no position to lay down terms.

And all the while this pantomime was going on I was thinking, damn them, where are they? They must have seen the airship come down. When would help reach us? For I sensed from the way the conversation was drifting that if our Italian captives realised that there were only two of us, they might seriously reconsider their earlier intention to surrender. I could even foresee a possibility that the tables might be turned, and that Toth and I would end up by being dragged back across the lines with them into captivity. And as if that were not enough to worry about, I now had the farmer and his wife to deal with as well. She had at last overcome her fright enough to be able to come out of the cottage. Even today I still think that she was one of the fattest women I have ever seen: like a walking fairground tent in the striped dress of the locality. The airship envelope was billowing flaccidly above the cottage, the remaining gas having collected inside the nose section; but the farmer's wife still almost managed to upstage it as regards bulk. Her husband was a whiskery-chinned, peg-toothed Slovene peasant with a white walrus moustache. He stood before me with the limp, riddled carcass of the goat in his arms, like Our Lady with the dead Christ.

'Kompensat,' he wheezed toothlessly, 'koza mea e ganz kaput –capria moja ist finito – totalverlust, capisco?' He rubbed finger and thumb together, then pointed to the devastated thatch of his cottage. 'Casa mea je auch havariert! Pagare – geld – penezy!'

I answered in Slovene as best I could. 'In a moment, Gospodar . . . the War Damage Assessment Officer will be notified and will deal with your claim in due course, you may rest assured of that . . . Now, if you will excuse me . . .'

The airship captain was by now asking me a number of rather impertinent questions about how exactly the Austriaci had brought down his airship: the *Città di Piacenza*, we later learnt. He had evidently not seen Toth and me land nearby after the crash and did not associate us with the aeroplane that had attacked him. I was beginning to suspect that he was looking around for an excuse—having been unfairly shot down or something—that would allow him to square his earlier word as an officer and gentlemen with his present intention of overpowering us and making a run for it . . . Then, at last, to my intense relief, I heard the sound of a motor lorry coming up the trackway. It was a party of soldiers. As they got down and came to join us I saw with some dismay that they were Hungarian Honvéds, and that several of them had hanging at their belts the wicked-looking bill-hook or 'fokos' which was much favoured by the Magyars as a trench-fighting weapon. The Capitano saw this as well and grew pale—then turned to me with a most reproachful look, marking me down for future reference as a trickster and a man devoid of honour. With that, we left things to the Army. The Italians climbed on to the lorry peaceably enough, and an ambulance was sent for to take the injured man to hospital. They waved to us in farewell as they bumped away down the track. I could see that, whatever their commander might think, the crew were mightily relieved to have come out of it all alive and unhurt. Hydrogen-filled airships were extremely inflammable and very few people ever survived being shot down in one.

And that was the end of the matter as far as we were concerned. I signed a few slips of paper for the farmer and his wife, who had by now stopped screaming and invoking the saints, for want of breath. Then Toth and I went back to our aeroplane to take off for Caprovizza airfield. So that, if you please, is how I came to achieve what I suppose must be my one claim to singularity in the course of something over a hundred years of earthly existence: that of being the only man – so far as I know – ever to have brought down two airships.

8

IL CARSO SQUALLIDO

There was a wondrous row about it all when I made my report to Hauptmann Kraliczek that evening, back at Fliegerfeld Caprovizza. Not only had I brought down a lighter-than-air machine when there was no appropriate form on which to report the fact; I had made a complete nonsense of his graphic projections for the entire month of August, no less. Fliegertruppe standing orders clearly stated that for the purposes of computing pilots' aerial victories, one airship would be regarded as equivalent to five heavier-than-air machines; and this meant that Kraliczek's new, reluctantly introduced line for Enemy Aircraft Destroyed climbed so abruptly when it reached the month of August that not even the airship itself could have gained altitude with such speed. In the end Kraliczek had to paste an extension-piece of squared paper above the main graph to accommodate the line. That was bad enough, but when I told him how we had done it – bombing the airship with a wireless set – his normally pallid features took on the livid white hue of a fish's underbelly.

'You . . . you . . . what?' he stammered, aghast.

'Obediently report that I dropped the wireless set on it. I had fired five clips of ammunition into the thing to no effect and there was nothing else that we could do, short of ramming it. But where's the problem? Surely an enemy airship destroyed is worth a wireless set at any rate of exchange?'

'What do you mean, worth a wireless set, you maniac! That wireless apparatus was a top-secret item of equipment, of inestimable value to the enemy. And now you've gone and dropped the thing on their side of the lines! Du lieber Gott . . . Do

143

you realise that you could be court-martialled for betraying military secrets to the enemy?' I tried to persuade him that after a fall of something like three thousand metres a fragile item like a wireless set would have virtually exploded on impact, transforming itself into a thousand unrecognisable fragments. But he was unpersuaded: unfortunately he remembered the freakish incident in May when Toth's observer, the ill-fated Leutnant Rosenbaum, had fallen from about the same height to land inside a convent greenhouse in Görz, stone dead but with hardly a mark on him. He was silent for some time, staring at me reproachfully from behind his spectacles. At last a faint smirk of self-satisfaction returned some colour to his features.

'Herr Linienschiffsleutnant,' he said in his most solemn tones, 'oh my dear Herr Linienschiffsleutnant, it is my duty to inform you that you are in the very deepest trouble. There is only one course of action open to you. I shall delay making my report on this disgraceful incident on condition that you and Zugsführer Toth fly out at the earliest opportunity to try and find the remains of the wireless set. If you can bring it back – even in pieces – then the War Ministry may – I say only may – be content with charging you its cost of, er, let me see . . . 7,580 kronen. If you are unable to find it then I am afraid that my report of its loss will go to 5th Army Headquarters by tomorrow evening at the latest. Is that clear?'

I protested that this was a ludicrous assignment; that quite apart from the hazards of landing close behind the enemy lines, I had no real idea of where I had dropped the thing to the nearest square kilometre or so, and that even if I had, it would either have smashed into innumerable fragments on the rocks of the Carso edge or buried itself deep in the Isonzo marshes.

However, war is war, and an order from one's commanding officer is an order – especially when backed by a threat of immediate court martial. So at first light the next morning Toth and I took off from Caprovizza airfield on what looked set to be the most hazardous mission of my entire three-week career as an officer-observer.

*

By comparing our own recollections of the previous day's events and by checking them against the map, we had eventually narrowed our area of search down to a two-kilometre square of marshland and pasture between the town of Monfalcone and the River Isonzo, south of the Cervignano road. We had managed to contact a number of front-line observation posts by telephone and they more or less confirmed this, as did the look-outs of the battleship *Prag*, who had taken bearings as they saw us close with the airship. Even so I was not at all hopeful of finding anything other than death or captivity as we set off that morning. The search area was only a couple of kilometres behind the Italian lines and would doubtless be stiff with troops and guns. The best that we could hope for was that the sheer bare-faced effrontery of our mission – flying at tree-top height over enemy territory in broad daylight – would so dumbfound the Italians that they would be put off their aim.

We crossed the lines east of Gradisca, taking advantage of early-morning mist, then flew the Lloyd in a wide half-circle to land on a stretch of pasture in a thinly populated region of marshland south of Cervignano. We waited there until about 1000, by which time the sun was clearing the last rags of mist from the flatlands, then took off again to approach Monfalcone from the west, flying low and hoping to be taken for an Italian aeroplane if anyone noticed us. Then the fun began. The first two passes over the area of search went well – except that I saw not a sign of the wireless set as I scanned the ground beneath through my binoculars. But on the third sweep, heading south this time, we passed over a tented encampment and some sentry noticed the black crosses beneath our wings. There was a sudden outbreak of bright little flashes among the tents as they opened fire. Machine-gun posts joined in, sending streams of tracer up at us, and before long the flash-puffs of anti-aircraft fire were following us as we flew –then bursting above and ahead of us as they found the range, kicking us about as urchins kick a tin can in the street. Then I saw it, in the middle of a field: a battered, splayed-out metal box of about the right size and shape for our wireless set. I signalled to Toth to turn us round and land.

It was a magnificent piece of flying, even by Toth's high standards: to bring an aeroplane about and put it down under fire on a space pehaps a hundred metres square. I can only assume that we survived either because the Italian gunners thought that we had been hit, or perhaps because they thought that we had gone mad. At any rate, their fire slackened for just long enough to enable me to scramble out of the cockpit and run to the metal box. Sure enough, it was the remains of the wireless set. The box had burst open on impact and its contents had been distributed over a good fifty metres' radius. I saw a valve lying near by, miraculously intact, and the metal base of another. I knew enough about wireless to know that the valves were what would really be of interest to an enemy intelligence officer, so I gathered them up, then ran back to the Lloyd, which was standing by with its engine idling. Just as I reached it the first Italian soldiers appeared at the field's edge. They shouted, then began to fire. Breathless and too confused by it all to be frightened, I quickly cocked the Schwarzlose and fired a couple of bursts at them to keep them at their distance while Toth turned the aeroplane's nose into the breeze and pushed the throttle forward. Bullets cracked around us as we wobbled into the air. Against all the odds we had done it: found the remains of the wireless set and secured enough of it to convince even the most obdurate security officer that the thing had smashed on impact to a degree where no one would ever be able to deduce how it had worked.

That, it soon became clear, had been the easy part of our exploit. We were no sooner into the air and heading over the Lisert Marshes than the Italian flak gunners found our range again. They were not going to let us escape this time. Shells were bursting all round us as we climbed over the roofless, gutted buildings of Monfalcone, heading for the rim of the Carso and the safety of our own lines among the hills to the north-east of the town. Then the inevitable happened: there was a flash and a deafening concussion to starboard, and something hit my shoulder. As I regained my senses and Toth brought the aeroplane level again I saw that the starboard lower wing had been reduced

146

to a fluttering jumble of smashed ribs and trailing rags of fabric; also that the fuselage and wings had been riddled by shell splinters, one of which (I later discovered) had gone through the shoulder of my flying jacket and grazed the skin beneath, leaving a faint brown burn-scar which I carry to this day. But that was not the worst: the engine was faltering as steam and boiling water hissed from the radiator above the upper wing. We ducked to avoid the scalding spray as Toth struggled to keep the aeroplane up. I looked ahead, and saw a low, bare, rat-coloured ridge of limestone looming ahead of us as we lost height. Its slopes were pocked with shell craters and streaked with the dark smudges of wire-belts. We were approaching the notorious ridge of the Švinjak.

The Švinjak – more or less 'the Hill of the Pig' in Slovene – did indeed rather resemble a sleeping sow. Not that anyone would have given it a second glance before the war: it was merely a barren, eroded limestone ridge exactly like a hundred other such limestone ridges on the Carso Plateau; an arid jumble of rocks and scrub barely capable of providing a living for a herd of scrawny goats. But since the start of 1916 it had been one of the most ferociously contested parts of the Austro-Italian Front, constantly bombarded and fought over as the lines swayed up and down its desolate slopes. The Austrian strongpoint at the northern edge of the Carso, Monte San Michele, had been taken the week before, but the southern bastion here on the edge of the Adriatic had held firm, much to the dissatisfaction of General Cadorna, who clearly intended to capture our positions here – Hill 144 and the Švinjak and Debeli Vrh – and turn the Austrian flank. So Toth and I now found ourselves descending into one of the hotspots of European civilisation in the year 1916. The only question now was: would we be able to keep the Lloyd airborne long enough to be able to come down on our own side of the lines?

As it turned out the answer was: nearly but not quite. The engine failed as we crossed the Italian forward trenches, and we finally hit the ground about two-thirds of the way across no man's land, just in front of our own first belt of wire. At first I thought that it would make little difference to us, hearing the fearful tearing crunch as the aeroplane's undercarriage smashed and the belly skidded along the confusion of rocks that passed for ground in these parts. I think in fact that what saved us was hitting an outer line of barbed wire, which brought us to a halt like the arrester-wire on the deck of an aircraft carrier before we had skidded far enough for the aeroplane to break up around us. All I remember at any rate is a violent jolt as we came to a stop, then distentangling myself from Toth in the front of the cockpit and the two of us scrambling over the side, cut and bruised and shaken but otherwise unhurt, to dive for cover in a nearby shell hole as the first bullets whined around us.

My first instinct on tumbling into the crater was to tumble out again as quickly as possible and never mind the shots cracking overhead. Even with a hail of lead buzzing a couple of metres above our heads it was a shock to find that the hole was occupied already. As for the tenant, he seemed not to mind our intrusion; only grinned in welcome. It was evident at first glance that he had been here for quite some time. Still, it is remarkable, I have always found, how quickly one can grow accustomed to things which, in other circumstances, would make one's flesh creep with revulsion; and this is doubly true when (as on this occasion) lifting one's head above the lip of the crater to look for other accommodation would certainly mean having it blown off. Toth and I quickly reached the conclusion that, on balance, the dead are less threat than the living, and settled down to make the best of things, trying not to look at our silent companion lying on his back against the other side of the crater and gazing with empty eye sockets into the cloudless blue sky. I think that he had been an Italian, but I was not sure. Both armies wore grey, but if ours had a somewhat bluer tint and theirs a somewhat greener, months of sun and rain and dust had long since faded away such distinctions. I was not concerned anyway to carry out a post mortem: the dead have about them a silent finality that makes mock of such petty considerations as nationality.

I took stock of our position. We two had survived the crash

intact, and if we were pinned down by the enemy's fire for the rest of the the hours of daylight, I supposed that the Italians further down the hill would be similarly pinned down by our people and would not come bothering us. A small shell had landed near by just as we had scrambled into the crater, but there had been nothing since, so I concluded that the enemy would wait until dark, then send out a patrol to remove anything of interest from the wreck. My intention was that we should have left by then, after setting it alight.

So for the time being it just meant lying here in a shell crater under the blistering sun with a corpse for company, counting the hours until sundown. I looked at my wristwatch: 1135. That meant another ten hours grilling here before it would be dark enough to make a run for it. My mouth was already parched from excitement and exertion. It was going to be a long wait. Toth and I sought what shade we could, arranging our flying jackets into a crude awning across a couple of strands of barbed wire strung over a shattered rifle which we had found in the bottom of the hole. We settled down to wait, trying to ignore the huge blowflies which had already located us and were beginning to gather into a swarm. It puzzled me that with so many other items of interest in the area – as could readily be detected by the least sensitive nose – these insects should still pay such attention to the living.

Quite apart from the stench, the other feature of this wasteland that impressed itself upon me as we lay there that August morning was the unspeakable noise. This was what I supposed would be called 'a quiet spell' on the Švinjak – which is to say that the two armies had temporarily exhausted themselves fighting over it. But even so the shells moaned and rumbled overhead incessantly, looking for the trackways and communication trenches behind the lines and the sweating ration parties trudging along them. Rifle fire crackled constantly along the line, like dry twigs in a stubble fire after harvest. It seemed that it needed only one shot in a sector to cause a blaze-up of musketry which would take several minutes to subside, much as one village dog barking in the night will set off all the other dogs in the district until they grow tired of it. If this was a quiet spell, I thought, what must a noisy one be like? Yet amid all this din one could sometimes make out curiously ordinary domestic sounds, like a latrine bucket clanking in a nearby trench, or someone chopping up ration boxes for firewood, or a man whistling: noises that reminded us that this bleak hillside, which only two years before had doubtless been as deserted as the Arctic tundra, was now as crowded with humanity as a city street.

Around midday the noise of firing died down sufficiently for me to listen incredulously to the sounds drifting faintly down from our front line, about two hundred metres up the ridge. It was a violinist, playing the tune 'In Prater blühn wieder die Bäume', which was all the rage that summer of 1916. Quite apart from the bizarre effect of its syrupy harmonies in this charnel-house of a place, I must say that the music itself rather set my teeth on edge. While I enjoyed most operattas I had never cared too much for this glutinous Schrammel-quartet stuff, which for me always conjured up visions of fat civil servants weeping into their half-litre wine mugs in Viennese Heurige-gardens of a Sunday afternoon. In any case, I could hear even at this range that the player was not very good: probably more of a trial to his comrades than even the stench and the flies. Then there was a heavy thump somewhere down the hill. A few seconds later, looking up into the sky above us, we saw an object like a beer barrel with fins flying through the air and trailing sparks behind it. It vanished from sight – and a moment later the whole hillside shook to an enormous blast like a miniature earthquake; so powerful that the back-draught made our eardrums pop and caused the wreck of our aeroplane (which I could just see over the edge of the crater) to lift momentarily into the air. It was a trench-mine, thrown by one of the 'bombardi' which the Italians had been making lately in large numbers: about two hundred kilograms of TNT mixed with bits of scrap metal and packed into a barrel. As our hearing returned I heard a bugle away in our trenches sound the call 'Stretcher bearers'. More routine wastage, I thought; the battalion diarist would make a laconic entry that evening: 'Quiet day in the line: nothing to report. Four men killed by trench-mortar mine.' As for the violinist, he had given up for the while, having no doubt dived for cover in the nearest dug-out when he heard the mine coming over. I had often suffered in the past from amateur musicians, who are a plague aboard naval vessels, but on balance I considered that dropping oil drums full of high explosive on them was going rather too far by way of showing disapproval.

We lay like that until about two in the afternoon, enduring the glare of the sun and the thirst and the flies and the fetid reek of the battlefield. Then, suddenly, Toth gripped my arm and pointed. The crater was on a hill-slope, so the lip on the downhill side was lower than the uphill edge. I could see only sky, unless I wished to lose the top of my skull to a sniper. But as I watched, puzzled, the vivid summer blue was obscured by mist. At first I thought that it was the top of a fog-bank rolling in from the Gulf of Trieste: unusual at this time of year but by no means impossible. Then I saw to my horror that the mist had a sinister yellow hue and that it was rolling uphill towards us on the slight breeze. It was a poison gas cloud, and we were directly in its path!

The same idea seemed to occur to us at the same instant. It was a sickening task, and one that only the threat of imminent death could have nerved us to perform. We nearly gave up, when the body came to pieces as we tried to lift it by its rotted clothing. But we clutched handkerchiefs to our faces and tried not to look, and eventually found what we were searching for among the decaying equipment: a canvas haversack with something resilient inside it. In the event we were only just in time, pulling out the mask just as the first curling wisps of gas came pouring into our hole. The next few minutes were not exactly the pleasantest that I have ever spent, taking turns to inhale through the face piece of a perished gas mask, foul with the smell of decay and of heaven alone knew what efficacy after months of lying out in the open. To this day I have no idea what sort of gas it was; only that it had a cloying sugary smell rather like that of a rotting pineapple, and that it made our eyes burn as well as causing a most painful tightness of the chest. We tried to sit as still as possible, so as to avoid getting more of it into our bloodstreams than we could help, and crawled up on to the crater edge on the assumption that, whatever it was, it was heavier than air and would collect in the bottom of the shell hole.

We ducked back into our refuge as the cloud began to thin. Dim figures were rushing past in the tail end of the cloud, and a great deal of shouting and confused firing was taking place further up the hill. We lay down and hoped to be taken for dead if anyone noticed us. Dear God, when would darkness fall? I did not care in the least for this game of soldiers. After about five minutes, just as the last of the gas cloud was passing, there were two explosions away towards our lines, then a further burst of shooting. I decided to chance a peep over the edge of the crater towards our trenches. Perhaps help was coming. I heard shouts – then saw the tops of steel helmets bobbing among the craters. They were the new German coal-scuttle helmets, so that (I knew) meant Austrian assault troops. Despite the enormous number of head-wounds in the Isonzo fighting, the War Ministry was still only thinking about manufacturing an Austro-Hungarian steel helmet – in fact would not get around to it until the war was in its final months. In the mean time a few thousand steel helmets had been purchased from our German allies, but so far they had only been issued to the 'Stosstruppen', the teams of specialist trench-fighters who were now being given the most difficult and dangerous tasks in the front line. Anyway, that meant we would soon be found and escorted back, even if we still had to wait until nightfall. Had they perhaps got water canteens with them, I wondered? I shouted, 'We're over here!' as loudly as I could above the din, then scrambled back down into the hole.

That shout was very nearly my last words. There was a sudden scratter of stones as something landed in the hole with us. I stared at it, paralysed. It was a stick-grenade, lying and hissing faintly as the fuse burnt down. If it had been left to me we would both have been dead men; but with a true pilot's reflexes Toth leapt across, seized it and flung it over the edge, ducking as he did so. It exploded just as it cleared the lip, sending vicious fragments of hot metal rattling off the rocks. I was still too afraid to move. But that was not the end of the matter. A moment later I was knocked to the ground as someone fell on top of me. The next thing I was lying with a hand grasping my throat, looking into the face of a creature so obscene that the mere sight of it took my remaining strength away: something that combined grasshopper and pig and horse's skull into the features of a devil from a medieval doom-painting. Its arm was raised above me with a club in its hand, poised to dash my brains out. 'Stop!' I yelled, hoarse from thirst and gas. The arm stayed poised – then was lowered slowly as its owner got off my chest. He knelt back, and removed the steel helmet so that he could lower the hideous can-snouted mask with its two huge, flat black eyepieces. It revealed a sweaty, rather florid face of unmistakably Germanic cast, with fair short-cropped hair and glaucous pale-blue eyes. He wiped his face with his tunic sleeve before replacing the helmet. His two companions released Toth and then removed their gas masks as well.

'Good thing that you shouted in German,' he said, 'otherwise I'd have smashed your head in for you. Did you chuck that grenade back out again?'

'No, he did.' I pointed to Toth, crouched near by. The Stosstruppen leader smiled.

'Not bad, not bad at all. Can I interest you in joining my storm-company perhaps? We could use people with reflexes as quick as yours.' He turned back to me. I noticed that although he had the Edelweiss collar badges of the élite Tyrolean Alpine troops, the Landeschützen, he spoke with a marked Sudetenland accent. 'Anyway, let me introduce myself,' he said. 'Oskar Friml, Oberleutnant in the 2nd Landeschützen Regiment; currently leading the 28th Storm-Troop Company attached to infantry regiment No. 4, Hoch-and-Deutschmeister. Pleased to make your acquaintance.'

I thought this display of courtesy rather forced, coming from someone who not a minute before had nearly killed us both. However I said nothing, but merely shook hands and introduced

Toth and myself, then thanked him and his men for coming out to rescue us. He smiled: a rather nervous, evasive smile I thought.

'Not a bit of it. We didn't know you were here. Our look-outs saw your plane come down and we thought you were either dead or taken prisoner by the Wellischers. We came out after that raid to see if we could cut some of them off as they tried to get back. Our people killed quite a lot of them and cleared the rest out of the trenches.'

'Were there many of them?'

'About a hundred I reckon.'

'Is it usual then for the Stosstruppen to take on the enemy at odds of three against a hundred?'

'Oh, not unusual at all. Moral force and quickness on your feet is what counts in this sort of warfare. In the trenches a dozen real soldiers can see off a thousand conscripts – or perhaps two thousand if they're Italians. Cowardly rabble: no stomach for fighting at all – except for a few of their own storm-troops that is, the "Arditi". Some of them are quite good I understand, but they wear body armour, which isn't much use and weighs a man down too much. We believe in fighting light, as you see.'

He was quite right about that: he and his men had no rifles or equipment, only a haversack full of stick-grenades slung over one shoulder, a gas-mask canister over the other and a short, vicious-looking spiked cosh. Friml smiled as he showed me his own version of this weapon. It consisted of a wooden handle with a short length of tight-coiled steel spring and, on the end of that, a steel ball studded with hobnails. I noticed that the handle bore rows of filed notches.

'There, how do you like it?' he enquired. 'I had it made specially. Much better than the standard issue. Here, look . . .' He bent down and picked up a battered, rusty Italian steel helmet which I supposed had once belonged to the dead soldier: the French 'poilu' type, with a raised comb along the crown. He placed it on a stone, then dealt it a sudden blow with his cosh. The helmet-top caved in like an eggshell. 'Not bad, eh? And it's pretty well silent too. Most of them never know what hit them. I've killed at least fifty men with it, but I haven't kept a close account lately. I did for twenty of them at least that afternoon at San Martino. We had about two hundred trapped in a bombshelter. They tried to surrender, but we just squirted flame-throwers in through the air vents. You should have heard them howl in there. I had a wonderful time of it: stood by the entrance knocking them off one by one as they tried to get out with their hair on fire. Half-trained conscript refuse the lot of them: there wasn't one of them over twenty.' He smiled as if at some idyllic memory.

'How old are you, Herr Leutnant?' I enquired. To me he looked about thirty-five.

'Twenty-three last birthday.'

'And do you expect to see twenty-four at this rate?' To my surprise he seemed not to be at all put out at this question.

'That all depends,' he replied, smiling. 'It's my belief that bullets find out the cowards and weaklings, so I may come through. I've been wounded nine times, but nothing serious so far. Anyway, whether I live or not scarcely matters. The thing that the Front has taught me above all else is that in this century the "we" will be everything and the "I" nothing. So what if I do die? The blood and the nation will live on after me as they lived before me. We are the aristocracy of mankind, we trench-fighters: the steel panthers, the very finest specimens that the human race has ever produced, without fear and without pity. The devil take the rest of them, the conscript herd corrupted by town-living and Jew-culture. They're good for nothing but following up an attack and occupying ground already taken. It's the front-fighters who bear mankind forward with them in the attack.'

I ventured the view – diffidently, eyeing the spring-loaded cosh as I did so – that at the present rate of losses, if the Stosstruppen were indeed the vanguard of the human species then by about 1924 we would have regressed to the early Stone Age.

'A typical peacetime soldier's view,' he replied. 'The reason why people like you can't cope with this war – and most regular officers can't in my opinion – is that you regard this sort of war, total war, as an aberration. Well, it isn't, the Front *is* the future:

155

permanent war; the Darwinian battle for survival in which only the strongest and those of the purest blood will survive.'

So this was the modern age, I thought to myself: less than two decades into the Century of Scientific Progress and Rationality and here are men fighting in this dreadful wilderness with weapons and ideas more appropriate to the Dark Ages.

'Anyway,' I said at last, 'do you want us to come back with you now or shall we wait until dark? Sunbathing out here with a corpse for company is not really my idea of a pleasant afternoon.'

Friml looked puzzled for a moment, then regarded the remains of the dead Italian as if he had just noticed them.

'What, this one here?' He laughed. 'You'll pretty soon get used to sights like that once you've been here at the Front for a while: that and much worse. It's nothing really: just a quantity of decaying tissue returning to the soil from which it grew . . .' At that moment there was a tremendous crash nearby which knocked the breath from our lungs and sent stone fragments shrieking over our heads. As we picked ourselves up I put my fingers into my ears in an attempt to stop the ringing in my dislodged eardrums. Friml was much amused by this.

'War music, Herr Leutnant, the orchestra of battle. That was a 20cm by the sound of it. You'll get used to it after a while, so that you hardly notice it any longer . . .' He paused, alert. 'Quiet,' he whispered, 'what's that? . . .'

As my ears began to function once more I realised that what I had taken to be the ringing left by the blast was in fact voices nearby: voices talking quite loudly in Italian. We all listened intently. There seemed to be two of them, in a crater near the aeroplane wreck: two soldiers left behind by the raiders to guard it until nightfall and the arrival of the salvage party. By the sound of their voices they seemed to be an older man and a youth. Whoever they were, they were certainly very unwise to be conversing so loudly in broad daylight when predators like Friml and his men were roaming the battlefield. Friml crouched, intent as a cat stalking a bird. Slowly, he drew a stick-grenade out of his haversack, tugged the toggle at the base of the handle, waited poised for what seemed like hours, but could only have been a couple of seconds – then threw it in a graceful arc to land somewhere out of sight. There was a muffled explosion and a puff of white smoke, then silence for a while. Then the wailing began. It was frightful to listen to. The older man seemed to have been killed outright, but the younger was still alive – just. If you see people in films spinning around and falling and lying still, do not imagine for one moment that this represents anything other than Hollywood's deodorised idea of death in action. In reality sixty or seventy kilograms of muscle, blood and bone have a great deal of life left in them even when they have been blasted and scorched and shot through with a hundred slivers of red-hot metal. It began with invocations to the Holy Virgin, then to God and Jesus and the saints, then to his mother. A second grenade served only to make the screams louder, until at last they subsided into a moan, then ceased altogether.

'Right,' said Friml, 'we'd better get back now. I didn't want to use that second grenade. The Italians'll soon be calling down artillery on us if they've spotted the smoke-puffs. Let's go. Just get out when I say and follow me.'

The Italians had indeed seen the grenade bursts: we left the crater just as their first shell arrived. After that I have only a very hazy recollection of events as we scrambled crazily from hole to hole with shells dropping all around us. We fell into an old trench and half ran, half crawled along that for some way, tumbling as we did so over dimly glanced things which I was heartily thankful not to have time to examine properly. At last we found the entrance to the tunnel in the wire from which Friml and his companions used to sally forth on their raids, and squirmed our way along it on our bellies like rabbits in a gorse thicket. What seemed like several hours later, we heard at last the challenge of an Austrian sentry. We were safe.

Our hosts were the ninth battalion of Imperial and Royal Infantry Regiment No. 4, 'Hoch-und-Deutschmeister'; the city of Vienna's local regiment. I had seen the old Deutschmeisters back in 1913, swinging proudly along the Ringstrasse in the great parade to mark the centenary of the battle of Leipzig. That had been a different world, and they had been different men. The old k.u.k. Armee was odd among the armies of Europe in having no foot-guards regiments. However, among the Emperor of Austria's soldiers it was generally recognised that the four Tiroler Kaiserjäger regiments were the élite, and that after them the Deutschmeisters were the premier line-infantry regiment, allocated the finest-looking of cach year's crop of recruits. They were all long since gone, dead in Poland and Serbia. The ranks had been refilled several times already, and the Deutschmeisters of 1916 were sorry specimens in comparison with their predecessors of only two years before: undersized, ill-nourished and pathetically young conscripts from the grey slum tenements of Vienna's outer districts. Clad in shoddy wartime ersatz uniforms, they looked a woebegone lot, even after making allowance for the effects of a prolonged sojourn in the Carso trenches. Not the least of the disturbing effects of service in the front line, I observed, was that it made everyone look alike: lifeless, drawn faces and eyes sunk deep into their sockets. It seemed that the battalion had already been holding this sector without relief since early August, its losses made up by sending new drafts forward into the line by night, or whenever the shelling eased up. Those who had been here since the beginning of the Sixth Battle – perhaps a third of the battalion now – already had that characteristic glazed look that resulted from a long stay at the Front. My second wife Edith had been a nurse in Flanders in 1917, and she told me of the extreme shell-shock cases, the ones whose minds had completely given way, like poor Schraffl's. But myself, from what I saw during that brief spell in the trenches on the Švinjak, I think that everyone who survived the front line in that war must have come out of it at least mildly deranged. Quite apart from anything else there was the awful brain-jarring noise. At least in France I suppose that some of the noise from exploding shells was muffled by the soil. Here on the Carso they had only rock to burst on, and they would go off with a bright yellow flash and a vicious, jarring crash which seemed to make one's skull ring like a bell in sympathy. It was maddening; unendurable except (I suppose) by switching one's brain off and going through it all on reflexes alone.

The Adjutant of the Deutschmeister battalion was very courteous to us, once Friml had handed us over. He greeted me before I recognised him. He was a young officer called Max Weinberger, the son of the Viennese music publisher. We had met one evening late in 1913 at one of my Aunt Aleksia's literary evenings, but I had failed to recognise him now under the dust and grey exhaustion of the Front. He was now the only other survivor from the ninth battalion's officer strength at the start of August, he said. But he still found time to make arrangements for our transfer to the rear, along with a batch of prisoners captured after the recent trench raid. I noticed that he was very solicitous of their welfare and had appointed three sentries to watch over them in their dugout. I thought this excessive, since they showed no inclination whatever to escape; in fact seemed only too pleased to be getting out of the war.

'They're not there to stop them escaping,' he confided in me. 'They're there to protect the poor bastards against Friml and his gang. The day before yesterday we were holding twenty of them in a dug-out, waiting to get them back when the barrage lifted, and one of Friml's men tossed a grenade in among them for fun. The swine was grinning all over his face: said that he'd dropped it by accident. I was going to have him arrested but Friml kicked up a row and said that line officers have no authority over the Stosstruppen. . .' he smiled, '. . . and all the more so when they're dirty Jews like myself.'

'From what you tell me Oberleutnant Friml sounds a difficult guest.'

'Difficult? I tell you, the man's completely mad, more of a danger to us than to the Italians. Everywhere he goes he stirs up trouble, then leaves us to dodge the mortar bombs they send over. Every time he goes out we hope he'll get it, but always he comes back. He's not right in the head and half his men would have ended up on the gallows as common murderers but for this rotten war. Do you know what he makes them do to qualify for his

159

storm-company? They have to pull the toggle on a stick bomb, then balance it on top of their helmet and stand to attention until it goes off. He must have killed dozens with that trick. And now I hear they're putting him up for the Maria Theresa. I tell you, if I were a Maria-Theresien Ritter and they made that criminal one as well, I'd send them their medal back by the next post.'

Toth and I made our way back along the communication trench that evening. We were shaken, and torn by barbed wire, and my chest ached from the effects of the gas, but otherwise we were none the worse for our crash landing in no man's land – and I still had the valves from the wireless sets tucked inside my flying jacket. There were about thirty of us in the party: a guide, Toth and me, the Italian prisoners, plus three badly wounded men on stretchers and two corpses, whom we made the Italians carry. The dead were both victims of the trench-mortar mine about midday: two blanket-covered forms and two pairs of dust-clogged boots joggling lifelessly as we manhandled the stretchers across heaps of broken rock and squeezed against the trench-walls to let ration parties go by. Alongside one of the bundles on the stretcher were the smashed remains of a crude violin made from a petrol can. I saw it, and suddenly felt very ashamed of myself for my flippant thoughts that morning about amateur musicians.

Once we were over the brow of the Švinjak and in the dead ground on the other side, out of view of the enemy, I was able stand up straight and look back at the fantastic jumble of dug-outs and shelters on the reverse slope. Made promiscuously from the local stone and from sandbags and cement and timber and corrugated iron, the whole crazy troglodyte town sprawled along the safe side of the bleak limestone ridge, like a lost city of the Incas high in the Andes, or the rock tombs of some long-forgotten civilisation in the Arabian desert. What an odd world we live in, I thought; once we buried old men because they were dead, and now young men have to bury themselves in order to stay alive.

The need for this impressed itself upon me very forcibly as we came out of the protective lee of the Švinjak. The Italians might not be able to see us, but their artillery could still throw shells over the ridge. Almost before we could think they were howling down to burst on the rock all about us, sending more splinters and fragments of hot metal rattling viciously along the trench walls. Our guide motioned us all into a bomb shelter cut into the side of the rock trench and roofed with railway sleepers. We scrambled in, leaving only the dead outside. The guide was a battalion message-runner, a Viennese lad of about nineteen selected not for his physique – he was an under-nourished product of the slum tenements – but for his agility and cunning in dodging shells. We crouched there for the next half-hour until the shelling stopped. Our guide seemed not to be unduly concerned. Cigarettes were passed around by one of the Italians, and he lit his up as calmly as if he had been waiting for a tram on the Mariahilferstrasse.

'Hot this evening,' I ventured as a shell crashed near by, showering us with dust and debris.

He considered for a moment, exhaling the smoke with an expression of intense pleasure: it was months since we had been able to get cigarettes free of dried horse manure.

'Obediently report that it's not too bad today, Herr Leutnant. They dropped a heavy right in among a relief party here last week: scraping them up with spoons we were.' I saw that he was not exaggerating: I had suddenly noticed a blackening human finger lying below the duckboards of the shelter. 'No,' he went on, drawing on his cigarette, 'most days it's worse than this.'

'How do you stand it out here, week after week?'

He laughed at this. 'Oh, we get by, Herr Leutnant, we get by somehow. All depends what you're used to I suppose. I grew up in Ottakring, eight of us in one room and my dad out of work for three years, so I suppose this isn't too bad really. The smell's about the same, the food's better and the meals are more regular if the ration parties don't get blown up on the way; and there's about the same amount of space to lie down in our dug-out. So overall it's not too bad a life if you don't think more than twenty seconds ahead. I've got a brother with the 11th Army in the Alps and he says its like a holiday camp up there – except that the Wellischers send a shell over every now and then and someone gets killed. He hopes the war'll go on until he retires, he says.'

I found that our Italians were also realists about the war. Peasants from Basilicata with sad, honest brown faces and lugubrious black moustaches, they had the look of men who never expected life to be much fun – and who have not been disappointed in this expectation. I could barely understand what they were saying with my Venetian Austro-Italian. But from what I could grasp I gathered that they were less than totally filled with eroismo ardente. I asked one of them, a man rather older than the rest, where they were supposed to be going with this offensive of theirs. He replied that he had no idea and cared less; knew only that the signori ufficiali and the military police would take a poor view of them if they didn't go forward when the whistles blew.

'Pah! La guerra – cosa di padroni!' he spat. His companions all spat as well and cursed the whims of the bosses, which had torn them from their families and smallholdings and sent them to fight for the Carso Plateau – 'il Carso squallido', as they called it, with a great deal of spitting and obscene gestures. Then they fell to reviling the politicians and journalists who had got them into this mess.

'Politics,' they said, 'dirty business. Where we live Italy is an express train: it only stops around election time. All we see of it in between is the tax collector and the recruiting sergeant.'

'And what about your oppressed brothers in Trieste, groaning under the Austrian yoke? At least, that's what the newspapers tell you.'

'We don't read the newspapers,' replied the older man with great dignity, 'because we are illiterate. But as for the Triestini, we couldn't care a farthing. Would the Triestini come and rescue us when the landlords and the money lenders tip us off our land to beg? I tell you, Tenente, I care as much about fighting for Trieste as I do for New York.'

A younger soldier interrupted him. 'No, Beppo, fair's fair. Myself, I'd much rather fight for New York than for Trieste: I've

got a brother living in Brooklyn and he sends us money orders.'
Everyone laughed, and thought this a very apt remark.

'Well,' I asked, 'if you are so fed up with the war why do you go on fighting?'

They found this hugely amusing. One of them levelled a finger and traversed it around slowly, squinting along it as he did so:

'. . . Sette, otto, nove – PAFF! . . . diciasette, diciaotto, diciannove – PAFF!'

From this I gathered that, if nothing else, the Kingdom of Italy, self-proclaimed heir to ancient Rome, had borrowed from its ancestor a number of practices in the area of military discipline.

Some weeks after these events I happened to mention Oberleutnant Friml to Flik 19F's Technical Officer Franz Meyerhofer, who was also a Sudetenlander.

'Oh, that thug?' he said, ' "the Death-Angel of the Isonzo Front", as the papers are calling him? Funny thing, but we were at school together in Eger. He was about six years below me, but my brother was in the same class.'

'What was he like then?'

'Rather a weed, my brother said: always being picked on, and wouldn't go skating and playing football like the rest. He left school after his Matura and became a life-insurance salesman. It's strange really what the war brings out in people.'

I happened to meet Friml again on the last day of 1916, at a New Year's party in Vienna. He had recently won the Maria Theresa, but he was clearly in a very bad way: nerves completely gone to pieces. He was killed a few weeks after he got back to the trenches: by snake bite, I understand. It was a very odd business I remember, from the reports that I heard of the enquiry. He took his boots off and got into the bunk in his dug-out after a raid, and was bitten by a horn-nosed viper hiding under the blankets. His men said that the snake must have been hibernating there, but they called in a snake expert who said that horn-nosed vipers don't hibernate. So they changed tack and said that it must have hidden there from fright during a bombardment. In which case, said the expert, it must have been a very frightened reptile indeed, and very disorientated, because horn-nosed vipers are unknown north of the Dinara Mountains, about three hundred kilometres further south. The military procurators tried pinning it on a Croat soldier in Friml's storm-company, but the rest of the men closed ranks and they could never get enough evidence for a charge of murder. I suppose that it was better in a way that he died: I would have hated to think of him back in civilian clothes, reduced to selling life insurance on the streets of Eger with his spring-loaded cosh in one hand and a briefcase in the other. The 'trincera-crazies', the Italians called them. Europe's tragedy was not the Oberleutnant Frimls who died, I think; it was the ones who came back.

9

HOME FRONT

We arrived back at Fliegerfeld Caprovizza early next morning to find that we had been posted missing. Observation posts on the ridge of Debeli Vrh had seen a Lloyd two-seater hit by anti-aircraft fire over Monfalcone and had watched it come down in no man's land on the Švinjak. I also discovered to my fury that my commanding officer Hauptmann Kraliczek had gone a step further and reported us both dead in action, in consequence of which a telegram had already been sent to my wife in Vienna. So it was necessary for me to leap straight away on to a bicycle, still in my tattered flying overalls, bone-weary and covered in trench grime, and rush to Haidenschaft telegraph office to send a telegram telling her that I was all right. Then it was back to Caprovizza, muttering curses against my commanding officer, and to bed for a few hours' much-needed sleep, my head still ringing from shell bursts and my lungs aching from the after-effects of gas.

I was woken up by my batman Petrescu a few hours later, still feeling rather seedy. A staff officer was waiting to see me outside my tent. I came out, unshaven and blinking in the sunlight, and had my hand warmly shaken by an Oberst, the Air Liaison Officer from 5th Army Headquarters, who had motored down from Marburg to meet me. He congratulated me on my extraordinary feat in bringing down the airship *Città di Piacenza* the previous day, and requested that I should please to present myself with my pilot in Haidenschaft that afternoon to be introduced to the Heir-Apparent, the young Archduke Karl, who was visiting the troops in the area and had expressed the wish to meet us. I mentioned the missing wireless set, and obediently reported that we had managed to retrieve some parts of it the previous day even if we had lost an aeroplane and almost lost our own lives in doing so. He seemed surprised.

'Top-secret? Not to my knowledge. I'll speak with the Corps Technical Officer, but so far as I'm aware those valve sets came off the secret list last month. There must have been a clerical slip-up somewhere. Anyway, don't worry about it: your commanding officer was probably misinformed.'

So we washed and shaved and spruced ourselves up, Toth and I, and got into a staff car to be driven to the town square in Haidenschaft to meet our future Emperor as he reviewed a guard of honour. A sizeable crowd had gathered in the little square to greet the Archduke and his entourage. As he drew up in his grey-green Daimler I got my first good look at the man who must surely become our ruler before much longer. He was a slight young man with an amiable if rather weak face, wearing the tunic – the austere field-grey 'Karlbluse' – which he had made his trademark and which had been widely adopted of late as a mark of loyalty by front-officers of the more Kaisertreu variety. I noticed however, once I had had the chance to inspect this garment close-up, that it was well cut and of noticeably finer material than the increasingly shoddy wartime cloth that the rest of us wore.

The young Archduke shook my hand: a curious palm-downwards handshake in which I had been schooled beforehand by an ADC and which involved me extending my own hand palm upwards as if soliciting a tip. He made the usual small talk – how long I had been an officer, where I came from etc. etc.? Then he questioned me on every detail of our attack on the Italian airship, and also on our exploit the previous day in landing behind enemy lines to retrieve the fragments of the wireless set. As to our experience in the front line, I must admit that I glossed over certain incidents: like that of our rummaging beneath a decomposing corpse in our desperate search for a gas mask. I suspected that members of the Imperial House were even more solicitously protected than the general public from the gruesome realities of life and death in the trenches, and I felt that he would find this story – like the murderous exploits of Oberleutnant Friml – too distressing to be borne. I took good care though to say a great deal about Toth's courage and quick-wittedness in flinging a hand grenade out of our shell hole – omitting only to mention that it was one of our side who had thrown it in the first place.

The Heir-Apparent enquired why I had left the submarine service to take up flying? And I, for my part, was preparing to give him the expected answers: looking for ever more dangerous ways of winning honour for the Noble House of Austria and so on and so forth. But then I thought, why should I? Perhaps it was the shaking-up administered to my brain by shell fire the previous day, but a sudden wild thought came into my head: why not tell him the truth for once? There are more than enough lies and half-lies in this venerable Monarchy of ours, I thought, and more than enough court flunkeys to filter reality; and anyway, who needs the truth more than this young man, who will soon be ruling over fifty-five million people? So I told him that in fact I had not volunteered for the Flying Service, but had been volunteered for it by my superiors to get them off the hook with the Germans over their sunken U-Boat; and that while I had no objection to risking my neck each day as an officer-observer in the k.u.k. Flieger-truppe, I felt that my talents might still be more profitably employed back in my own trade at sea. He listened sympathetic-ally, nodding as he did so and intoning, 'Yes, yes.' He seemed to have had a look of concern built into his face in his mother's womb. He concluded the conversation by remarking that so far as he could see an injustice had been done, then shook my hand in farewell and moved on to speak with Zugsführer Toth.

I knew now that I would henceforth be a marked man among the Habsburg officer corps for the rest of my days. In military life there are few offences against service propriety more heinous than that of going over the head of one's immediate superior and complaining to his superiors. It is something which can occasion-ally be done, but only in the direst extremities and in the knowledge that one will be regarded with suspicion ever after. And now I, a junior naval officer, had committed the ultimate solecism by going to the man very near the top. Short of complaining to the Emperor himself I could scarcely have committed a greater outrage. And all for nothing: for I knew perfectly well from my experience of royalty that he would probably have forgotten about it already.

The Heir-Apparent made a great deal of talking with Toth in Magyar. I asked him afterwards in Latin what the Archduke had said to him. He replied that he had not the faintest idea: he thought that the man was trying to speak Magyar, but that he was by no means sure.

But at least there was some brightness in that dismal little square in Haidenschaft that afternoon. Our orders for the presentation had said that, if we wished, we might bring family members along to watch. Well, I had no family members nearer than Vienna. But not so Zugsführer Toth: his Slovene girlfriend, the delightful Magdalena, had come along with him. And very fine she looked as well, wearing the gala version of the local costume: her best frock and bodice with the addition of a lace-trimmed headband and coloured ribbons in her hair. The written orders had said 'Ladies: promenade toilette or national costume', and as I looked at her I was profoundly glad that she had chosen the latter, making herself a glorious splash of gaiety and colour amid the field-grey wartime drabness of the square, like a kingfisher amid a flock of town-sparrows. She was presented to the Heir-Apparent afterwards, curtsied most prettily and answered his questions intelligently and confidently in German.

The Archduke passed on to someone else – and his place was immediately taken by a gangling and achingly aristocratic young ADC with a toothbrush moustache and a foolish grin: General stabshauptmann the Prince von and zu Steyer-Würmischgarten and Rothenfels, or something like that. He completely ignored Toth, who as a ranker had to stand rigidly to attention before him. But he seemed very interested indeed in young Magdalena, even proposed taking her for a ride in his motor car, with perhaps a spot of supper afterwards at a hotel he knew in Marburg? I held my breath and watched Toth: assaulting an officer in wartime was a death-penalty offence. But I need not have worried; Magdalena smiled graciously and announced in her clear voice, 'It is true, Your Serene Highness, that I am only a simple village girl and that you are a prince. But I'm afraid that Your Serene Highness has been watching too many operattas: we simple village girls aren't anything like as simple as we used to be. However, if Your Serene Highness is desirous of the company of local young ladies I can supply him with the address of some very nice ones indeed.' The prince looked disappointed. But like a true soldier he seemed to recognise failure when he saw it and to be prepared to accept second-best. So the address was duly noted down in his pocket book before he bowed and left us. When he was out of earshot I asked her:

'Gnädiges Fräulein, what was the address you gave him, if I might ask?'

She giggled deliciously. 'The back entrance of the Other Ranks' knocking-shop on the Via Gorizia. There should be quite a stir among the townsfolk when his car draws up there. I hope he enjoys himself.'

She turned to Toth and took him by the arm, digging him in the ribs with her elbow. 'Quod dices, O Zolli? Princeps maxime fatuus est, non verum?'

I must say that I was rather shocked by this, even if filled with a certain admiration. I would not have expected convent-educated Slovene village maidens to know that such things as military bordellos even existed, let alone their address.

After the presentation Toth and I went to see the Medical Officer in Haidenschaft. We were both suffering from chest pains and nausea. Our eyes were sore and red and Toth was developing a fine inflamed rash around his neck. The Medical Officer diagnosed the after-effects of poison gas and wrote us each out a note authorising us to go and take two weeks' immediate leave somewhere with clear air. He said that we would soon get over it – he thought that it sounded like a phosgene derivative, and apparently one needed to inhale quite a lot of phosgene to be permanently injured by it – but he recommended us both to get well away from the Front for a while. 'Nervous tension: all the fliers get it before long. Too much altitude and excitement and inhaling petrol fumes. Yes, yes, I know the poor devils in the trenches have a much worse time of it; but for them it's largely a matter of endurance, and they've got their comrades around them all the time to support them. Up in the air you fellows are completely on your own and, believe me, the strain begins to show very quickly.'

So a telegram was sent to Elisabeth at her hospital in Vienna, and that evening I boarded the train at Divacca. She had been due for leave for quite some time now, and in any case she would soon be tendering her resignation on grounds of pregnancy. However, we wanted to be alone together and I doubted whether we would be allowed that in the capital, so I told her to pack her bags for a holiday in my home town of Hirschendorf in northern Moravia. She had never met my father, so here was a wonderful opportunity to combine convalescent leave with filial duty.

We met early the next morning on the platform at the Franz Josephs Bahnhof. It was not quite a month since I had last seen her, but still her beauty struck me as forcibly as it had the first time I had met her, in Budapest the previous year. Beauty in women, I have always found, is far more a matter of personality than of looks. True, Elisabeth was certainly well provided for in the latter department, as are many Hungarian women (though in her case she counted Romanians, Italians, Russians and even Scots among her ancestors). But her dark-green eyes and dark-brown, almost black hair and fine-boned oval face would have been nothing without the gaiety and intelligence and grace of manner that illuminated them from within. She rushed over to meet me as I climbed down from the fiacre which had carried me from the Südbahnhof. She was wearing a summer frock and hat and carried a parasol, since military nurses were allowed to wear civilian clothes off-duty. She flung her arms around me and kissed me, then stood back to look at me.

'Well, still alive I see after all. Whose idea was it to send me that telegram?'

'Yes, I know. They could have waited. It was only a minor accident and they might at least have contacted the unit holding the sector where we came down. It was my commanding officer I'm afraid. I'd have wrung his neck for him but he was out when I got back to the airfield. Did it upset you very much?'

She smiled faintly. 'I can't say that it gave me a very agreeable sensation in the pit of my stomach when I opened it – until I looked at the date. Luckily it seems to have been delayed and I'd opened yours first. But your commanding officer – Kralik or whatever his name is – he sounds a first-class rotter. "It is my sad but proud duty to announce to you that your husband has died a glorious flier's death on the field of eternal honour . . ." I mean, who in their right mind writes stuff like that two years into a world war? He sounded almost glad that you'd been killed – as if I ought to send a telegram back thanking the Army for making me a widow second time around.'

'Did you think that they had?'

'Not really: in my heart I knew that you'd be all right. I just knew – woman's intuition I suppose.'

'Flying's a dangerous business, you know? I never wrote to you about how many men and machines we've lost these past few weeks, or the scrapes I've had.'

'I knew that perfectly well. We've had a lot of burnt and smashed-up airmen coming into the hospital recently. But I still knew that you'd be all right. Don't ask me why, I just knew. I've got a little picture of the Blessed Virgin on my bedside table next to your photograph and I pray to that each morning and evening to keep you safe.'

'I thought that you didn't believe in all that sort of thing?'

'I don't. But it's like the man who went around Messina a few years ago after the earthquake selling anti-earthquake pills. When the police arrested him he asked them, "Well, what else do you suggest?" I think that my prayers keep you up in the air and turn aside the bullets by force of will. I know it sounds crazy but I'm sure that it works. And anyway, there's nothing else that I can do for you. I tried to talk you into deserting when we were up in the

171

mountains in Transylvania – even arranged you somewhere to hide until the war was over – but you wouldn't hear of it: the Honour of the House of Austria and your duty to your men and so on. So I'm afraid that whatever protection that I can give you now is only second-best.'

'And I'm sure that it'll see me through.'

She smiled. 'Well, let's look on the bright side of things. You've got this far without a scratch, so I imagine you must be quite good at flying. And anyway, every day's a day nearer the end of the war. Surely it can't go on much longer. The papers say that the French have lost half a million men at Verdun; so you can be pretty sure the Germans have lost even more. At this rate there's not going to be anyone left before long. The k.u.k. Armee's sending men back into the line now after their fourth or fifth wound, barely out of hospital. It can't last much longer – and between us the Virgin Mary and I are going to make damned well sure that you see the end of it.'

I was silent for a while, pressing her warm body against me. I was thinking of the dying Italian soldier sobbing and moaning after Friml had tossed the stick-bomb into his shell crater. Doubtless his family and sweetheart had been praying for his safety and lighting candles even as he pumped his life blood out into that dismal hole. And a lot of good it had done him. Like most men who emerged from that war, such vestiges of religious faith as I had once possessed were finally blasted away by the barrages. The mind-numbing enormity of it all so outraged imagination, so transgressed normal experience, that all the comfortable little formulations of the bishops and theologians have sounded to me since like the empty jangling of the tin cans on the wire after an attack.

The train was crowded, shabby and slow, drawn by a locomotive with badly worn axle bearings and burning lignite, which gave about as much heat as damp newspaper. It took us most of the day to crawl miserably across the Moravian countryside, through

172

Lindenberg and Prerau. The day was grey and close; not August weather at all. It had been a dismal summer north of the Alps and one did not need to be a country-town boy like myself to see as we trundled along that the harvest this year would be a poor one. In fact the most obtuse of city dwellers would have noticed the ground visible between the stalks of rye in the fields, and the fact that the harvesters were mostly old people and women and children with the occasional soldier on leave and a few parties of Russian prisoners. Elisabeth and I talked little as we clanked along. The compartment was crowded, the corridor was packed with soldiers going on leave, we were both tired out and anyway, it was quite sufficient for us to be near one another: two insignificant specks of dust clinging together for a while as the whirlwind bowled us along.

We arrived at Hirschendorf Station early that evening – only to find to my utter dismay that the town band and a welcoming committee were waiting for us. There were cheers and speeches, and I was invited to appear next day, 18 August, in the town square at the festivities to mark the Emperor's eighty-sixth birthday. I groaned inside, but I could hardly refuse. Ever since anyone could remember the Kaisersgeburtstag had been one of the fixed points of the Austrian year, by now (it seemed) as immutable a date on the calendar as Christmas and All Souls' Day. As the town of Hirschendorf's most famous son—a Maria-Theresien Ritter no less—it would clearly be impossible for me to refuse my attendance. Already reporters from the *Hirschendorfer Nachrichten* were buttonholing me to arrange interviews, and someone was asking me something about opening a war exhibition. It was beginning to look as if we might as well have stayed in Vienna after all.

The town where I was born and grew up was not much of a place really—little more than a scaled-up version of Haidenschaft: a typical small Austrian provincial town of the late nineteenth century with a cobbled square, a large baroque church with onion domes and a government office block in that curious heavy neo-Italianate style – invariably painted a darkish yellow ochre – which

173

distinguished all the public buildings of the Dual Monarchy. Like all such provincial towns, its life before the war had been inseparably bound up with the countryside around it. In my childhood one always knew which way the wind was blowing by the smell: the warm sweet smell of malt when the south wind was blowing from the brewery; the sharp, clean tang of resin when the east wind was blowing from the sawmills; and that peculiar, sour, dungheap-and-treacle odour of beet when the west wind was blowing across the sugar factory. All that had changed now, as we approached the third year of the war. True, the sawmills were still at their old occupation – in fact working three shifts a day to convert the thousands of trees hacked wantonly from the Silesian forests into boards and timbers for dug-out roofs and ammunition wagons. As for the beet factory though, it had been turned over to the manufacture of artillery shells, lathes screeching day and night like the souls of the damned to produce the cases which would then be taken to a rickety sprawl of huts a few kilometres outside the town to be filled with explosive. Most of the town's remaining able-bodied population – that is to say, its women – were now working in the munitions factories and could readily be distinguished by the butter-yellow complexions which came from inhaling TNT fumes all day. The wages were good, they said, but they were paid in paper and steel money which brought less and less each week.

As for the brewery, it was still in business; more or less. But the once powerful and highly esteemed Hirschendorfer lager beer with its stag's-head label had now become a sorry fluid for lack of barley: a pale straw colour with a froth like soap scum, and barely strong enough to crawl from the tap into the mug now that most of its remaining alcohol content was being extracted for the munitions industry. It made me wonder why on earth anyone bothered drinking the stuff any more. But then, I suppose that there was not a great deal else on offer either in the late summer of 1916. Rubber and copper were distant memories. The parish church of St Johann Nepomuk had voluntarily donated its bells to the war effort by government order the previous year. Even leather for shoes was becoming hard to find now, so that the women wore clacking canvas monstrosities with wooden soles once their pre-war footwear had fallen to pieces. As for clothing, wool was reserved for military uniforms and cotton was unobtainable because of the blockade, so that left linen (which was now in increasing demand for covering aircraft) or, failing that, hemp, nettle fibre or spun paper, which had a disturbing way of coming to pieces in the rain.

Elisabeth told me that for some months past she and her fellow-nurses had been obliged to spend a large part of each day washing cotton bandages – except that the bandages were now dropping to pieces from constant reuse and were being replaced by crêpe paper, or a substitute fibre made from the inner bark of the willow tree: 'superior in every respect to cotton', a journalist had written in the *Reichspost*. Elisabeth's eyes had blazed up with fury when I showed her this cheerful little article, and she had uttered certain words in Magyar which, although I could not understand them, certainly sounded not to be the sort of expression that nice convent-educated girls ought to know.

Until now, I was told, food had not been too difficult out here in the countryside, even if groceries like coffee and tea and chocolate and soap had all long since carried the loathsome qualifications 'ersatz' and 'surrogat' and 'kriegs'. But now butter and milk and meat were in short supply, and before long (it was said) even barley and potatoes might be scarce. I talked with old Josef Jindrich the forester, husband of my childhood nurse Hanuška.

'Yes, young master Ottokar,' he said, rubbing his bony old chin as we sat in the parlour of their cottage, 'it's a bad business and no mistake, this war of theirs. I fought with the old 54th Regiment back in '66, and that was bad enough; but at least we lost after six weeks and it was all over. Who'd have thought this war would go on so long? Mark my words, we're in for a bad harvest this year. They say it's the British blockade, but that's eyewash if you ask me. It's all the men and horses they've taken off the land, that's what. And Vienna and their war prices. They've set them so low that the country-people aren't growing to sell any more, just

175

enough for themselves and some for the black market. Yes, my young sir, if you want my opinion that old fool at Schönbrunn's declared one war too many this time . . .' he grinned, '. . . and if you like you can bring a gendarme along here to arrest me for saying so. I'll just show him my old army paybook and the wound I got at Trautenau.'

I found though that the changes wrought by the war in the material circumstances of life in that small town were as nothing compared to the alteration in its people, as if the human spirit was also in short supply and being replaced by an ersatz version. I had not been home a great deal in recent years. I had gone to the Imperial and Royal Naval Academy in Fiume in 1900, my mother had died two years later and my brother Anton had entered the Army as an Aspirant in 1903. My father had remained in Hirschendorf, immersed in his duties as k.k. Deputy District Superintendent of Posts and Telegraphs and (after hours) in his activities as one of the leading luminaries of the local Pan-German Nationalist movement. I had been home to see him from time to time over the years, even though my home town – in so far as a sailor can ever have one – was now Pola. But this was largely a duty performed out of filial piety. My father had never been an easy man to get on with, so the visits had become less and less frequent with the years.

We had last met in Vienna back in July, when he was invited to my investiture as a Maria-Theresien Ritter, and also to my wedding two days later. In the event the wedding had been cancelled – or rather, much reduced in scale and moved to a suburban registry office – and the old man had been cabled not to bother coming. Not that he had minded a great deal: he disapproved of the marriage on eugenic principle – mingling good Germanic blood with that of a Magyar-Romanian minor aristocrat from Transylvania, even though it was patently obvious that both he and I were solid square-faced Slav peasants. Remarks had been made about 'the degenerate mongrel aristocracy of the Habsburg corpse-empire; the sweepings of Europe gathered up by Vienna and set to rule over the solid fair-haired peasants and burghers of

176

the Germanic borderlands'. In fact he had not been too keen on the Cross of Maria Theresa either: 'a piece of worthless Habsburg tinware manufactured in the Jew-shops of Vienna' was how he had chosen to characterise the Old Monarchy's highest military honour. I believe that he bore no particular animus against Elisabeth as a person – after all, being a degenerate mongrel aristocrat was not her fault – but there was no warmth either. Before he had turned to German Nationalism my father had once been a Czech liberal nationalist, and he still retained a Czech democrat's somewhat less than total admiration for countesses, even where (as in this case) the countess had renounced her title and was about as devoid of snobbery as it is possible for anyone to be.

In any case, the old boy had more important things on his mind at present than his son's new wife: he had just become the local organiser of the recently formed Deutscher Volksbund in this part of Moravia. It was a mark, I suppose, of how far the Habsburg state had fallen into senile decay by the year 1916 that it could now look through its fingers when a quite high-ranking provincial civil servant became a part-time functionary of an extreme German nationalist organisation which, if not exactly a political party, was not far off being one. In days gone by Vienna had been intensely mistrustful of any nationalist activity, German quite as much as any other sort, and would not have tolerated it for one moment in a civil servant. The old doctrine was that whoever entered the service of the House of Austria ceased to have a nationality. And to be fair to them, nearly everyone lived up to that high ideal. But now it seemed that after two years of war and a humiliating chain of defeats rectified only by German troops and German brains, the Dual Monarchy was fast becoming a spiritual colony of the Greater German Reich, which already extended from Flanders to the marshes of the Tigris.

The Deutscher Volksbund claimed to be nothing more than a patriotic organisation of German-speakers within the Austro-Hungarian Empire. But you would certainly have been hard put to it to see any sign of that in our house on the Olmutzergasse. It had

177

been turned into a shrine to the Goddess Germania, with more than a hint of Wotan-worship. Portraits of Hindenburg and Ludendorff hung on the walls, draped in black-red-gold banners. A smaller portrait of the German Kaiser hung below them. Garlands in the black-white-red of Prussia bedecked a full-length portrait of Oberleutnant Brandys, the spike-helmeted hero who was supposed to have captured Fort Douanmont at Verdun virtually single-handed. Everywhere, posters for the German Flottenverein and the 7th War Loan and the German Women's League; posters exhorting Gott to straff Engeland and for people to give their Gold in exchange for Eisen. A vast map of Europe covered the whole of one wall. On it the German and Austro-Hungarian Empires had been merged with most of Belgium and sizeable chunk of northern France into one dingy uniform expanse of field grey surrounded by barbed wire and with its borders bristling with bayonets. Beneath it was a legend in Gothic script: IT HAS COME AT LAST, NEVER TO PERISH – THE REICH OF NINETY MILLIONS. In the alcove in the hallway, where once the family's statue of the Madonna had stood, was now a wooden pedestal bearing a German steel helmet – the kind Oberleutnant Friml and his marauders had been wearing a few days before – with a slot cut in the top for coins. A plaque fixed to the pedestal proclaimed: THE MOST SUBLIME SHAPE OUR CENTURY HAS YET PRODUCED: NOT THE WORK OF AN ARTIST'S STUDIO, BUT FORGED FROM THE UNION OF THE GERMAN SPIRIT WITH GERMAN STEEL. It was all intensely depressing.

Worse was to come that first evening as I took Elisabeth for a stroll around the town. The atmosphere of the place was oppressive in the extreme. It had never been a particularly friendly place as I remembered it: like many towns and cities in the Old Monarchy, it had been disputed territory between two nationalities, or in this case, between three of them – German, Czech and Polish – who each had their own name for the place and each claimed it as their own exclusive property. In the years before the war the heavy presence of official Austria, in the shape of its gendarmes and civil servants – and in extremis, its soldiers in the barracks on the Troppau road – had preserved an uneasy quiet in

Hirschendorf, broken only by the occasional riot. But now that Austria-Hungary was at war in alliance with Imperial Germany, the German faction in Hirschendorf was letting it be known in no uncertain manner that they were on top and intended staying there. In pre-war Austria the Germans had felt themselves an increasingly threatened minority in a country that they had once regarded as their rightful property. But now the tables had been turned: the Czechs and Poles and Slovenes and all the rest of the impudent riff-raff were now themselves minorities – and small ones at that – in a Greater German Reich of ninety million people.

Certainly no opportunity was being missed in Hirschendorf in the summer of 1916 to ram that message down the throats of the non-Germans. The town's Czech newspaper had been closed down under emergency powers and a number of Czech nationalists had been arrested by the military and interned. The local Polish organisations had been forbidden to hold meetings and were being watched by the police. Also the statue 'The Spirit of Austria' had been removed from the public gardens in the middle of the town square.

The statue had never been much of a success. It had been put up at Vienna's behest in 1908 to mark the Emperor's sixtieth jubilee and to try and promote some nebulous concept described as 'the Austrian Idea' among the Monarchy's quarrelling subjects. Commissioned from the studios of the sculptor Engelbrecht, it represented a willowy young female nude in characteristically flowing Wiener Sezession style, holding aloft a very clumsy-looking broadsword, hilt-uppermost, as if someone had absent-mindedly left it on a tram and she was calling after them to attract their attention. It was an innocent enough piece of statuary, in fact quite graceful and pleasing to look at, even if no one could ever quite work out what naked young women holding swords had to do with Old Austria. But somehow, far from promoting a spirit of unity and mutual tolerance, it had managed only to provoke the warring factions into an even more bilious passion. Each nationality became obsessed with the idea of claiming the statue for themselves, and the favoured method was to creep up in the dead of night with paint pots and adorn the young woman with a striped bathing costume: either black-red-gold if it was the Germans, or red-white-blue if it was the Czechs, or simple red and white if it was the Poles. The municipal cleansing department must have spent thousands of kronen over the years in paint removers and wire brushes.

But now 'the Spirit of Austria' was no more. Both she and the square's other statue, Imperial General Prince Lazarus von Regnitz – 'noted in the wars against the Turk' – had been melted down to make driving-bands for artillery shells, and her place had been taken by a monstrous wooden 'Denksäule': a hideous commemorative column with a bust of Field Marshal von Hindenburg on top and with medallions of Ludendorff, the Kaiser, Frederick the Great, Bismarck, Wagner and other German heroes around the sides. It was studded with iron nails driven in by those who had donated money to the War Loan and other such patriotic funds. Stupid and dodderingly oppressive as it might have been, the Old Austrian Monarchy was a state conceived on a human scale, and had undeniably displayed a certain taste in artistic matters. Now it seemed that we were being engulfed by the very grossest sort of Greater German vulgarity: the bloated blood-and-iron bombast; the increasingly crazed gigantism; the total lack of any sense of proportion.

And around this idol to the Germanic war-god set up in Hirschendorf town square there limped its human votaries: the soldiers in shabby field grey enjoying what might be their last leave; the women in black whose husbands and sons had already had their last leave; the overworked housewives and their ill-nourished children; and the men in the hideous blue uniforms of the wounded, some with empty sleeves, many with dark glasses and white sticks, some on crutches or (in one case) legless and pushing himself along on a little wheeled trolley. As Elisabeth and I sat on the terrace of the café-hotel 'Zum Weissen Löwe' and drank our raspberry-leaf tea, we saw a proclamation being posted up on the side of the government offices on the other side of the square. It announced the hanging in Olmutz jail the previous day of five local men who had deserted to the Russians in 1915 and then been recaptured in Volhynia wearing the uniform of the Czech Legion. The proclamation was only what the law required, I suppose, and would have been pasted up even before the war. But now it was accompanied by five photographs in close-up, each showing a black-faced man dangling by his crooked neck from a gallows.

The proclamation was taken down the next day so as not to add a sour note to the celebrations of the Emperor's birthday. I had to turn up of course, in best Flottenrock complete with sword-belt and the Cross of Maria Theresa prominently displayed on my chest.

It was a sultry, overcast afternoon with thunder in the air. The crowd, I saw, was much smaller than usual for the Emperor's birthday. Because of the war the local garrison had been able to provide only a military band made up of pensioners – one of whom suffered a stroke while playing the 'Prinz Eugen March' and had to be carried away on a stretcher. Likewise the usual gathering of local notables seemed to be very thin. In fact it was made up almost entirely of the town's Jewish worthies: Dr Litzmann from the local hospital, Herr Birnbaum the notary and my old childhood friend Herr Zinower, the bookseller and secretary of the natural history society. As for the German nationalist bigwigs like my father, they had all absented themselves on one pretext or another.

All in all it was a pretty miserable and spiritless occasion. The congratulatory addresses to our venerable monarch lacked conviction. Everyone present seemed listless and merely to be going through the motions of loyalty. At last the band struck up the Imperial anthem, Haydn's beautiful old 'Gott Erhalte'. As was customary on these occasions, a choir had been provided by the local schools to lead the singing. But after the first few bars I sensed that something had gone wrong. Dr Litzmann standing next to me on the platform stopped singing and looked about the square in alarm. Choir and crowd were not singing 'Gott erhalte unsern Kaiser, Gott beschütze unsern Land . . .' Instead several hundred throats were bellowing, 'Deutschland, Deutschland über alles, über alles in der Welt . . .'

Dinner that evening was potatoes with some thin sauerkraut and slices of an evil-tasting sawdust briquette which my father's house-keeper said was made from processed wood-mushrooms. After we had finished, Elisabeth and I left my father sticking little coloured flags into a map to mark the advance of the German armies in the Baltic provinces and went out for a walk along the Olmutz road to get some fresh air: one of the few commodities which had not so far been replaced by a substitute version. We had things to discuss.

'When will you hand in your resignation at the hospital?' I asked her.

'Next month, I think. By then my belly should be swelling to a point where I can't hide it any more, even under those awful white overalls we have to wear. Here,' she placed my hand on her abdomen below her belt, 'here, you can just feel it now. It hasn't started sticking out yet but you can feel something hard in there.' She laughed, 'I wonder what it's going to be: a boy or a girl. I say though, isn't it exciting?'

'It would be, I suppose, if it weren't for the war. This isn't much of a time for bringing children into the world. The poor kid may never see its father. What a mess.'

'Oh don't be such an old misery, Otto. There never was a good time to bring children into the world ever since the world began. What better time could there be than now, when the human race is doing its best to wipe itself out? Having babies spits in the eye of the Ludendorffs and Kaiser Wilhelms and the Krupps and all the other deathmongers who'd kill the lot of us if they could.'

'Why, are you anxious to bear children to be more cannon fodder for the front in the next war?'

'No, to have children who'll perhaps have more sense than we had, and pull the war lords down from their horses one day. I don't care: long live motherhood – it's the only hope we've got for a better world.'

'Do you want motherhood even if I'm killed?'

'Especially if you're killed: at least some of you will live on to remind me of what you were like.'

'Well, that's comforting to know I suppose. But what happens now to your career in medicine? Babies are said to be very time-consuming and nursemaids are not easy to find these days, what with all the women who are going into the munitions factories.'

'Oh, I'll manage, once the war's over. My foster-parents disinherited me when I married you, but I'm still not short of money. My father set up a trust fund in Zurich for me and my brother before he died, and now Ferencz is dead it all comes to me. We'll manage, don't worry. Anyway, perhaps after the war you'll leave the Navy and take up an honest trade in engineering or something. You're a clever man and your talents are being wasted making a lot of Croat fisherman scrub their hammocks and polish brasswork. You can even sit at home and rock the cradle for me if you like.'

'Will you go back to the hospital after the baby's born? My aunt says that you're welcome to stay with her on the Josefsgasse, and Franzi's said to be very good with children. The poor girl's so soft in the head they've refused to employ her in a shell factory. And Professor Kirschbaum told me that he'd keep your job open for you.'

She was silent for a while, gazing out over the stubble fields.

'No. No, I'm not going back to the hospital: not as a nurse and not while the war's on. I've had enough.'

'You always told me that your patients came first.'

'I've changed my mind since then.'

'Why? You were always so dedicated before.'

'A number of reasons, really. Above all because I've realised what we're really doing there in a military hospital.' She turned to look at me, her deep-green eyes gazing into mine. 'Don't believe all that rot you read about us nurses in the papers: "the Angels in White" and so on, nursing our wounded young heroes back to health. It's not like that any more – if indeed it ever was. What we're doing is cobbling them back together to a degree where they're fit to be sent back to the trenches and blown up again, that's all. I tell you, what we're doing now isn't medicine, it's veterinary surgery. The only wonder is that we aren't shooting the worst ones with a captive-bolt pistol yet – though according to Dr Navratil that's what they're doing in some of the field hospitals: giving the difficult cases a double injection of morphine and leaving them out all night.'

I was incredulous.

'Send them back into the trenches? Even the patients you have to look after? I don't believe it.'

'It's a fact: even the ones I have to look after. They're all severe head-wounds – mostly facial reconstruction – and the authorities have realised that once they've been patched up to a degree where their brains no longer dribble out of their ears, they can still usually fire a rifle. In fact I think that the War Ministry is actually anxious to get the worst face-wound cases out of the way once they're discharged. At least if they're in the war zone they can't go around alarming the public.' A tear began to glisten in the corner of her eye. 'There was one boy on my ward in the spring, called Emil Breitenfeld. He'd been a Fähnrich with the Kaiserjägers in Poland and had half his lower jaw shot away. We spent the best part of a year rebuilding his face, Professor Kirschbaum and the dentists. They had to build in a metal bridge, but it never really took and gave him a great deal of pain. Anyway, in June the War Ministry Inspection Board people came around and told us not to waste any more time on him: that he was perfectly dienstauglich and wasn't going to get any better and was taking up a bed; and anyway they were desperately short of officers at the Front. So out he went: recalled to active service on the Russian Front. We sent him off with a bottle of painkiller pills in his greatcoat pocket.'

'What happened to him?'

'He was killed a month later. He wrote me a letter just before and said that he couldn't care any longer whether he lived or died – in fact he'd rather die if he had to go around after the war with half his jaw missing. His men looked after him as best they could – even mashed his food up for him like a baby so that he wouldn't have to chew it – but he stopped a bullet in the end. His sergeant wrote to tell me. He was only twenty-two. And just before I left there was a secret War Ministry directive came around. It seems that in future we are not to devote scarce resources to treating the really severe cases but instead concentrate our efforts on "those military personnel likely to be of further use to the war effort". May they all rot in hell for it. Another couple of years of this and we'll have an army entirely made up of cripples and men half crazy with shell-shock.' She paused, thinking. 'But then, I suppose that's the best idea really: have your war fought for you by people who've got nothing left to lose.'

As we walked homewards, evening shadows streaming along the dusty white country road, a sudden thought struck me.

'I say, Liserl, did you ever have a fellow called Svetozar von Potocznik on your ward? He was wounded in the face when he was with the Germans in Flanders in 1914 and spent some time with Professor Kirschbaum in Vienna I believe.'

She stopped suddenly. 'Potocznik? How did you know about him?'

'When he was discharged he joined the k.u.k. Fliegertruppe and he's now Chief Pilot with Flik 19F at Caprovizza. I haven't spoken with him much, but he seems a decent enough sort, even if he has got Greater Germany on the brain. He's very bright, and he would have been very good-looking too if he hadn't lost one side of his face.'

She was silent for a while.

'Yes, yes. I knew him quite well. In fact before I met you last summer we might have got engaged. I liked him very much at first – but less and less as I got to know him better.'

'What's the matter with him?'

'I couldn't really say. He's very intelligent, as you say, and beautifully spoken, and very sweet and courteous when he wants to be. But there's something off about him. In fact I came to the conclusion in the end that he was quite cracked. Perhaps it was the head-wound; perhaps he was like that before, I really don't know.'

'Were you serious about each other?'

'Oh yes. At least, I was quite taken with him at first. Patients falling in love with you is an occupational hazard in my trade: I used to get at least three proposals a week before I married you and got this ring safely on my finger. But he was different for me. It's just that he had reservations about me in the end, not the other way round.'

'How did you find that out?'

'It was one evening in the gardens. He was up and about by then, back in uniform instead of a dressing-gown. I'd just come off duty and we were sitting together talking about this and that. And after a while it got around to getting engaged. Not that I think we had any burning passion for each other; just that we rather liked one another, and if he was a little odd I put it down to what he'd been through and I thought that I might be able to spend my life with him. We got on to marriage, and what we wanted to do after the war, and I thought he was going to ask a certain question. Then he asked me . . . something else.' She stopped.

'What did he say?'

'Oh, it was so stupid, it embarrasses me to tell you . . . don't ask me, please.'

'What was it?'

'Really something so absurd that I don't think even now . . . Oh there, you've made me get the giggles just thinking about it.' I was fascinated now, devoured with curiosity.

'Please tell me Liserl, what did he ask you? I'll never rest now until I know. There shouldn't be secrets between man and wife. I've told you about all my old affairs when you've asked.'

'Oh well then, if you have to know . . .' She was almost choking now as she tried to suppress her merriment. '. . . The silly idiot asked me what colour my nipples were. There, look, you've made me blush even now just with telling you about it.'

'For God's ask, why did he ask you that?'

'I must say I was a bit puzzled myself at the time. In fact I couldn't answer him for a while I was so embarrassed. "Silly boy," I said once I'd managed to stop giggling, "you really mustn't ask nice well-brought-up girls questions like that. But why on earth do

186

you want to know?" I said, "Is it a hobby of yours? And anyway, what do you mean by colour? Most women's are more or less pink I believe, so I can't see that the exact shade matters a lot." But he wouldn't give up: sat there staring into my eyes, ever so solemn, and asked me, "Yes, but are they dark pink or light pink?" '

'What on earth was he getting at?'

'Yes, I wondered that as well, In fact I was about to call for help in case he went completely loopy and started attacking me. But once I'd got my breath back he asked me again, so I told him that although I'd never had a great deal of opportunity to make comparisons – at convent we had to bathe wearing linen gowns – if he really had to know I thought that mine were quite dark, what with being half-Romanian and fairly brown-skinned. And that did it: the silly fool just sat back and nodded to himself as if to say "Yes, just as I thought," then announced to me that we could never marry. "Why not?" I said. "Because science has shown that dark nipples in a woman are a sign at least of Latin and possibly even of Jewish ancestry. No true German of pure racial stock can ever think of diluting the blood by miscegenation with those of other races. Women of pure Nordic race invariably have rose-pink nipples." '

'I see what you mean. And what did you have to say to that?'

'I didn't cry. Once I'd got over my surprise I just laughed and told him he was either joking or completely mad, and that either way I didn't want anything to do with someone who sorts the human race into bloodlines like a racehorse breeder. In fact I told him that if he wanted a nice Germanic brood mare with a backside on her like the side of a house and blond plaits hanging down over her rose-pink nipples he'd better go putting advertisements in the local papers in the Salzkammergutt. The impertinent sod! And what's wrong with Jewish ancestry anyway? I don't know whether I've got any, but the de Bratianus have got a bit of just about everything else, so I'd be surprised if they didn't have that as well.'

I considered all this for a while. 'Yes, I suppose that it does sound a bit odd really, Liserl. But that isn't conclusive proof of insanity. We're all of us a little mad about something, and I've often seen that even the most reasonable people can have a potty opinion about something or other. When I was a cadet on my first voyage my old captain Slawetz von Löwenhausen was as fine a sailor as you could hope to meet – we'd all have followed him to the ends of the earth. But he had a thing about the crew shaving the hair off their legs: tried to make us do it each month because he believed it prevented malaria.'

'Yes, I know. But I still say he's completely cracked. It's just that there are so many cranks in Germany nowadays – weltpolitikers and machtpolitikers and Wotanists and sun-worshippers and vegetarians and racial hygienists – that you don't notice it any more. But believe me, if someone as bright as Svetozar von Potocznik can seriously believe that the worth of human beings is determined by the colour of their nipples, then there's no hope for any of us. He's mad I tell you: I'd suspected as much before then but ignored my instinct. It was a good thing I found out when I did – and that I met you the following week.' She turned to me. 'You don't care what colour my nipples are, do you Otto? And I'll bet you've had more opportunity than most for making comparisons.'

'My dearest love, if they're yours then for all I care they might as well be viridian or cobalt blue.'

She cuddled up to me as we walked. 'You are sweet. I thought you'd say something like that.'

We set off to return to Vienna on the last day of August. We had agreed that Elisabeth would hand in her month's notice when she got back to the hospital, and would then move to live with my Aunt Aleksia in her flat on the Josefsgasse. For my part I would return to my flying duties and hope that somehow, Zugsführer Toth, *Zośka* and the Blessed Virgin between them would contrive to keep us airborne. So we bade my father farewell. He hardly noticed our departure since he was leaning over a world-map on the dining-room table, engrossed in a pamphlet concerning German plans for building a giant ship canal through the Caucasus and Hindu Kush to the head waters of the Ganges, so that ships would be able to steam overland from Rotterdam to Calcutta. He had asked my professional opinion upon the project as a naval officer, and had not been at all pleased when I had commented that it seemed an expensive way of avoiding seasickness. We took a fiacre to the station, and caught the local stopping train to get us to Oderberg junction so that we could board the Cracow–Vienna express.

We were only a couple of minutes out of the station at Grüssbach when the train suddenly came to a shuddering, clanking halt in the middle of a pine forest. For some time there was no sound except the hissing of steam. Then there were shots in the wood, and the unmistakable crash of a stick-grenade. We waited uneasily. After a few minutes we heard the sound of voices and the crunch of boots on the trackside ballast. It was a party of five or six yellow-helmeted gendarmes with rifles slung at their shoulders, leading a captive. He was about nineteen or twenty I should think: tousle-haired, unshaven and with his face streaked with blood. He was wearing a tattered army greatcoat. His hands were tied behind his back and they were pulling him along by a halter around his neck, kicking him to his feet each time he stumbled and fell. They disappeared and the train started to move once more. The conductor came into our compartment.

'What on earth was all that about?' I asked him as he clipped my rail warrant.

'Nothing really, Herr Leutnant, just some trouble further up the line.'

'Trouble with whom?'

'With bandits, Herr Leutnant.' He lowered his voice. 'At least, that's what we're supposed to say. Everyone knows it's really deserters.'

'Deserters? Surely not around here, this far from the Front.'

'Deserters sure enough: men who came home on leave and didn't bother reporting back. There's a lot of them in these forests now. They live by robbing the farms – though from what I hear there's more than enough of the villagers who'll give them food and hide them in their barns. Dirty rotten Czechs – the Böhmes all want shooting if you ask me. There's not one of them wouldn't run away if you gave them the chance.'

10

PAPER AEROPLANES

I returned to Fliegerfeld Haidenschaft-Caprovizza on the first day of September 1916. It appeared that not a great deal had happened during my fortnight's absence. The Sixth Battle of the Isonzo had fizzled out around 20 August, as the Italians ran low on artillery shells. In those two weeks they had captured the town of Görz and had then pushed on to the Carso Plateau to a maximum depth of about five kilometres, leaving them now with a more or less straight front line some ten kilometres in length, running from Görz down the shallow depression called the Vallone to reach the sea a little to the east of Monfalcone. It had cost them something over sixty thousand lives to gain, and us about the same number to lose. Both sides were now gathering their breath and preparing for the next round.

Flik 19F had flown a number of reconnaissance flights when requested by Army Headquarters, and had also done a little long-range bombing, losing one Brandenburger along with Fähnrich Baltassari and Corporal Indrak in an attempt to bomb the rail junction at Treviso. Otherwise there was little to report in the first couple of weeks after my return to the unit. Zugsführer Toth had been home on leave to visit his parents in Hungary. I would dearly have loved to have been able to question him more closely about this, since Toth having parents was a concept that I found quite fascinating, giving rise to visions of creatures sitting around a fire on the floor of a cave gnawing the bones of an aurochs. But my Latin was not quite up to the task; and anyway Toth, though impeccably 'korrekt' in his relations with officers – at least when not tipping them out of aeroplanes – was someone who would not willingly discuss his private life with strangers.

The weather was beginning to close in now, autumn approaching a good deal earlier than usual, which (so the local countryfolk said) presaged a hard winter. Morning fog and low cloud made flying impossible for much of the time – 'Fliegerwetter' the ranker-pilots used to call it, since they did not wear the black-and-yellow sword-belt and were thus under no obligation to pretend that they were anxious to get themselves killed. But the fog and cloud began to clear around mid-month as the bora season set in.

I did once understand the precise mechanism of the bora, eighty-five years ago when I was studying meteorology at the k.u.k. Marine Akademie. As I remember it, it works rather like the syphon in a lavatory cistern: that cold air accumulates behind the mountain ranges of the Balkans until some of it overflows down a mountain pass, and that this initial flow brings the rest rushing down after it. The danger signs, I remember, were clear air and a low, white cap of cloud over the distant mountain peaks. There would be a few hours' stillness and an uneasy feeling in the air, then whoosh!, suddenly a howling gale would be shaking the tents and scurrying loose gear across the flying field as the ground crews struggled to wheel the aircraft into the shelter of their log-and-earth bora pens. The bora would make flying impossible for the next day or two, even though the air was as clear as could be and the sun shining brightly. We knew that. But so, unfortunately, did the Italians. The bora rarely blows west of the Isonzo, so they could take off and land as they pleased while we were firmly grounded. Likewise the bora is a curious wind in that, although it blows with extreme fury, it only blows near to ground level, up to about a thousand metres or so.

We at Flik 19F made this discovery one morning in mid-September just after breakfast. We had woken to find our tents flapping wildly as the wind screamed down a side valley from the Selva di Ternova. But the meteorologists at Army HQ had warned us the previous evening, so everything had been securely pegged down and the aeroplanes moved into shelter. It seemed a pity not to be able to fly on a day of such perfect visibility, but there we were: man proposes, God disposes. I held my jacket closed with one hand and my cap on my head with the other and struggled across the field in the face of the gale to enter the heaving mess tent. Breakfast was the usual meagre affair of ersatz coffee and kreigsbrot, the only matter for comment being the proportion of sawdust in the latter. I read in the *Triester Anzeiger* that the Western Front was holding firm in the face of massive and costly British assaults: what you called the Battle of the Somme and we called the Battle of the Ancre. I finished my breakfast, and Meyerhofer and I set off for the workshops to inspect our Hansa-Brandenburg *Zośka*, which had arrived back from the repair workshops the previous evening. As we walked out of the tent into the blustering gale Meyerhofer stopped and held his hand to his ear, listening.

'What is it?' I asked, shouting to be heard above the wind.

'Funny thing,' he replied, 'I could have sworn I heard engines. Surely not in this wind though. Can you hear anything, Prohaska?'

I listened. Sure enough, above the buffeting of the bora I could now hear aircraft engines: not one or two engines but a great many of them.

'Look!' he shouted, pointing down the valley towards Görz. 'I don't believe it – not in this weather!' It was a formation of eight or nine aeroplanes high above the valley, perhaps three or four thousand metres up. They were plainly not ours. They were large biplanes with twin-boom fuselages and three engines: Italian Caproni heavy bombers. We dived for cover in a slit-trench as the first bombs came crashing down on the airfield, throwing up fountains of rock and earth. We had anti-aircraft machine-gun nests placed around the airfield, but they were only to deal with low-flying attacks. They loosed off belts of ammunition into the sky: to no effect whatever. Two figures leapt into the trench beside us as we peered out at the destruction going on all around. It was Potocznik and Zwierzkowski, both in flying kit.

'Come on!' Potocznik yelled above the din, 'come and help us get after them!'

We scrambled out and ran to a bora shelter where a dozen or so soldiers were struggling to wheel out a Brandenburger into the shrieking wind. Somehow we all managed to hold it steady as Feldwebel Prokesch swung the propeller and Potocznik scrambled into the observer's seat. 'Glück auf!' we all shouted as the engine roared and the aeroplane started to lurch crazily across the field with five or six men hanging on to each wing, staggering forward then sideways then forward again like a drunkard as the wind snatched at it. It was not to be: directly the ground crew let go of the wings a vicious gust of wind got beneath the fragile contraption and flicked it contemptuously to one side. The next thing we knew it was lying upside-down, smashed against one of the wooden hangars. We ran over to it and dragged the two men from the wreckage, both shaken but fortunately unhurt. The drone of engines was now submerged once more beneath the blasting of the wind as the attackers turned away towards Trieste and home, mission accomplished. We looked sadly about us. Only one man had been killed, but a hangar had been wrecked, along with our remaining Lloyd CII inside it, while still-smoking bomb craters peppered the airfield as reminders of our impotence. It was all intensely humiliating.

Still, as your proverb remarks, it is an ill wind that blows nobody some good. A bomb had landed at the end of the officers' tent lines and had destroyed the tent next to mine. Leutnant Szuborits's gramophone was found intact among the debris, but a bomb-splinter had gone through his box of records. And, to my inexpressible joy, 'Sport und immer Sport' had been among the casualties. A blissful silence descended upon Fliegerfeld Caprovizza now that Mizzi Günther would squawk no more. I almost felt moved to write a letter to the Italian Air Corps to thank them for enabling me to keep my sanity.

Then came the autumn rains, as the fighting flared up again on 17 September: the start of the so-called Seventh Battle of the Isonzo. And if the bora is one of the two great natural freaks of the Carso region, its drainage pattern is the other. A whole hidden world of caverns and grottoes and underground rivers lay beneath that dreary plateau; something which only began to be appreciated in 1916, as the excavation of trenches and dug-outs revealed a hitherto unsuspected network of caves and passages in the limestone. As the human insects fought and died in their swarms up on the surface, the patient stalactites dripped as they had dripped for the past ten thousand years: steady; calm; patient in their purpose; totally indifferent to empires, kingdoms and generals sticking flags into maps.

Yet this hidden world would occasionally make its presence known. Rain would pour down in torrents for weeks on end in the Carso autumn, turning the churned-up trackways to troughs of rust-red mud in which the men and mules would flounder and curse as they struggled forward under their loads. Yet on the bare rock, most of the rainwater would disappear as if it had never been, seeming scarcely to dampen the arid surface. Then one morning, we woke up at Fliegerfeld Caprovizza to find the field a gleaming sheet of water. The mysterious underground lakes which feed the tributaries of the Vippaco had filled up at last, and were now decanting their excess water down the valley like an overflow pipe.

We flew infrequently in those early weeks of September: a little photo reconnaissance work when holes opened in the clouds, or some artillery-spotting over the battlefields when Army Headquarters requested it. We also flew a series of desultory bombing-raids into the Italian hinterland by night, in an attempt to disrupt supplies to the Front by damaging this or that or the other rail junction. They had a magic all of their own, those night-time raids: the charm of the mystery rail outings of my childhood, in which one bought a ticket and perhaps ended up for the day in Olmutz or Trenčin, or even in Prague for long enough to consume a lemonade and a couple of frankfurters at the station buffet. They were largely without danger to us – the Italians had no more idea of night fighting in the air at that stage of the war than anyone else – but by the same token they posed very little threat indeed to the enemy.

Quite apart from navigational problems, not the least of the reasons for the basic harmlessness of these raids was that about the middle of the month, gazing in despair at his graph line Total Weight of Bombs Dropped, which had nose-dived during early September because of bad weather, Hauptmann Kraliczek had been struck by a sudden thunderbolt of inspiration: he would rectify the situation by drawing the graph in future, not according to the weight of bombs dropped on enemy territory each day, but according to their number! In this way (he explained to us), if an aeroplane took off on a raid carrying – say – four 20kg bombs instead of two 40kg, the statistical efficacy of the raid would be doubled at a stroke and the graph line would immediately climb like a rocket. We all came away from his lecture feeling very depressed, knowing as we did that a telegram had already gone to the munitions depot in Marburg requesting them to supply us with the smallest aerial bombs they had in stock. These were old 5kg and 10kg models which had lain there since 1915 because they were pretty well useless, the accuracy of a bomb generally being a function of its weight. Meyerhofer did his best with the Marburg people over the telephone, pleading with them to dump their old stock in the nearest river and tell Kraliczek that they had nothing smaller than 20kg. But it was too late, and anyway it was plain that the Ordnance Officer in charge of the depot was only too happy to unload surplus munitions on to those idiots at Caprovizza rather than having to keep entering it on his own monthly stock inventory. A red-painted ammunition wagon arrived at Haidenschaft Station the next day. From now on the only thought with which we could comfort ourselves as we risked our lives on bombing-raids over Italy was that no one on the ground was likely to come to any harm. Our only chance of influencing the outcome of the war, Meyerhofer said ruefully, was if one of our puny bombs happened to hit Cadorna on the head.

The first of my own night-time excursions took place in the third week of September, lurching away into the sunset from Caprovizza airfield with eight 10kg Carbonit bombs stowed on the cockpit floor beneath my feet. Our objective was the town of Gemona in the Alpine foothills, and our task was to bomb the

196

railway station, incidentally (though this was not explicitly stated in our orders) causing alarm and despondency in the Italian rear, panic on the Milan stockmarket, the soil to ooze blood, the moon to be obscured and cows to give birth to two-headed calves across the whole of Lombardy-Venetia. The only problem was that, like most people in 1916, we had no experience whatever of night flying and no equipment for it beyond the aeroplane's dubious magnetic compass and a pair of spirit-levels for judging our attitude and angle of bank. I had made some experiments a few days before in using a nautical sextant to find our way by the stars; but, experienced sea navigator though I was, I had found it to be a hopeless task with no visible horizon to work to and nothing but the ponderous Nautical Ephemerids to do the calculations with. The bubble sextant and look-up tables would not be available for another twenty years – and quite frankly would not be a lot of use even then.

There was no moon that night, so in the end the best that Toth and I could do was to fly west until we found the River Tagliamento, its tangled channels gleaming dully below us in the starlight like a half-unwound skein of silver thread. We then turned to follow the river up through the forests and hills until it began to bend to westward. It is a curiously hypnotic state, to be flying in an open-cockpit biplane at night over enemy territory. The absence of any sensations but the steady roar of the engine, the rushing of the cold wind and the flickering pulse of flame from the engine's six stub-exhausts all conspired to produce (I must admit) a rather drowsy state in which it was far from easy to concentrate on navigational landmarks. I made a point of prodding Toth's shoulder every five minutes to keep him alert. With a single-engined aeroplane in those days it was all too easy for even an experienced pilot to lose his sense of balance, especially if the night was overcast, and for propeller torque to tip the aeroplane gradually over to port until it would be flying along on one ear, dropping out of the sky as it did so.

The Italians had enough experience of air-raids now to be careful about black-out, so it was only by the unmistakable glow of a railway engine's firebox and some lights in a goods yard that we managed to find Gemona. Numb and stiff with cold despite layers of clothing, I struggled to lug the first bomb on to the cockpit edge. Then suddenly I was struck blind by an amazing glare of light. The Italians had searchlights below. The first flak shells flashed around us as Toth banked away to starboard and I lost my grip on the bomb. I suppose that the searchlight crew must have heard it whistling down, because it was quite extraordinary to see how smartly they turned off the light. I saw the bomb flash red below as Toth brought us back round to repeat the compliment. I tipped the remaining bombs overboard one after another. As we climbed away at full throttle into the night sky with the searchlight beams criss-crossing vainly behind us, I saw that we had set a building on fire: a wooden goods shed, to judge by the sparks boiling up into the sky.

It was a tricky landing back at Caprovizza, coming down on to a rough field only by the uncertain light of a few flares made out of petrol tins half-filled with sump oil and with wicks of rag. We both went to get a few hours' sleep before I wrote out and filed my report on the raid. I then strolled over to the hangars, where the Brandenburger was being serviced after our flight. Feldwebel Prokesch saluted, then said that I might care to see something. He pointed silently to the aeroplane's plywood fuselage. The sides bore two holes the size of my hand exactly opposite each other athwart the observer's seat. A piece of shrapnel had gone clean through the aeroplane when the flak shell burst near by. If I had not been standing up to hoist the first bomb on to the cockpit edge it would undoubtedly have passed through me on the way, at about kidney level.

Because he was busy with his compilations I was not able to make my verbal report to Hauptmann Kraliczek until nearly midday. I found him to be in an even more peevish mood than usual.

'Well, Prohaska, a fine mess you have landed us in this time.'

'In what respect, Herr Kommandant?'

'It wasn't Gemona that you bombed, it was Tolmezzo. And it wasn't a railway station, it was a brickworks.'

'Permit me to ask, Herr Kommandant, what difference does it make? Where bombing-raids are concerned one Italian town is much the same as any other I should think; while as for the target, it was unfortunate that we didn't hit the railway station as intended, but I imagine that bricks are necessary for the Italian war effort as well.'

'Difference? My form giving you your orders for the raid had "Gemona" clearly written in the box "Primary objective" and "To attack railway station" in the box "Purpose of mission". It said nothing whatever about either brickyards or Tolmezzo. If you had said that you were diverted by heavy fire over the target and flew on to bomb somewhere else that would have been acceptable, though a matter for regret. But in your report – which has now been forwarded without my approval to Army Headquarters – you stated categorically that you attacked Gemona when in fact you bombed Tolmezzo. I have it here in black and white on this form which you filled in when you landed. I regard this as a serious breach of discipline.'

'But Herr Komandant, navigating an aeroplane by night is a very hit-or-miss business, everyone knows that . . .'

'Not in Flik 19F it isn't: your targets are given to you, and I shall expect you in future either to reach them or to give a very good reason why you were not able to do so: "Unable to find the target" will simply not be acceptable, do you understand? Precision in reporting is the essence of operational effectiveness. But quite apart from that, I gather from Army Headquarters that your attack on the brickworks has caused us serious problems.'

'Permit me to ask how that can be?'

'A railway station is state property, and attacks upon it are permitted by the 1907 Hague Convention. A brickyard is private property, and is therefore immune to attack under the provisions of the same convention. But what makes it all far, far more serious in this case is the fact' (he adjusted his spectacles) 'that the brickworks in question now turns out to have been the property of an Austrian national: one Herr Wranitzky of the Südkarntner Ziegelkombinat AG in Klagenfurt. The factory manager telephoned him this morning via Switzerland to tell him of the attack, and I gather that the insurers are refusing to pay on the grounds that his policy excludes acts of war committed by the forces of his own country. He has already been to visit the War Ministry to complain, and is talking, I understand, of suing you in person for damages.'

So after that I took good care on all such night-time raids to unload our bombs over open country near the target. I also evolved an infallible system for precision bombing at night. We would be given a form specifying our target – say Latisana – before we took off. Usually we would be quite unable to find Latisana, or at most would end up dropping our bombs near somewhere that looked as if it might conceivably be Latisana. We would return from the raid, and I would go to my tent and sleep a few hours before writing out my report in longhand, leaving blank spaces for the name of the place attacked. I would then go back to bed until about midday, and when I woke up, send my batman Petrescu down into Haidenschaft on the station bicycle to buy the midday edition of the *Triester Anzeiger*. This would usually contain a report received via Reuters in Zurich and entitled 'Our Heroic Fliers Bomb the Town of Pordenone' – or Udine, or Portogruaro or somewhere similar: usually anywhere but Latisana. I would dismiss Petrescu with a tip of a few kreuzers, and then fill in a name – perhaps 'Pordenone' – and maybe add a few convincing details gleaned from the article before handing it over to the Kanzlei to be typed out. I would then fill in Kraliczek's report form, entering 'Unable to attack primary objective because of heavy flak fire' or something like that against Latisana, and writing 'Pordenone' in the box 'Secondary target chosen'. It worked splendidly. In fact before long I had received a special mention from 5th Army Headquarters complimenting me on the extraordinary precision of my bombing-missions. I was fast becoming an accomplished practitioner of the art of retrospective aerial navigation: that is to say, not of getting from where one is to where one wants to be, but rather from where one was to where one ought to have been. But

I was lost to shame now and cared about it no longer. So far as Toth and I were concerned, precision bombing at night meant hitting the right country.

All things considered though, it was perhaps no bad thing that we could do so little flying in the early part of September, for the Italians were now stationing a number of specialist single-seater squadrons along the Isonzo Front. These fighter squadrons were very much a new idea in 1916. When the Germans had brought out their revolutionary Fokker Eindecker on the Western Front at the end of 1915 they had been content to operate them singly, each aeroplane prowling like a peregrine falcon above a specified sector of the front and pouncing on any Allied aeroplane that tried to cross. But in the skies above Verdun that summer the French had finally dealt with the Eindecker by forming special squadrons of single-seat fighters: the famous Escadrilles de Chasse, led by pilots like Nungesser and Fonck. Always quick to see which way the wind was blowing, the Germans had followed suit, forming their own specialised fighter units – the Jagdstaffeln – which would make up for the German Air Force's inferiority in numbers by moving about the Front to wherever the High Command was planning something, and then simply sweeping the enemy out of the sky for a fortnight or so.

And now, in the autumn of 1916, the Italian Air Corps had also taken up this idea. Special squadrons of Nieuport single-seaters were being formed under leaders like Barracca and Ruffo di Calabria. The cult of the fighter ace was reaching now even to the remote and little-regarded Austro-Italian Front. But as yet, only to one side of it. The official doctrine on our side of the lines was an aeroplane worthy of the name ought to be able to carry out any front-flying task demanded of it, even if the result was that it did them all more or less poorly. We were told the General Uzelac had been moving heaven and earth in Vienna to get a budget allocation for an Austro-Hungarian single-seater capable of taking on the Nieuport. But so far nothing had emerged. Aircraft procurement was the business of the k.u.k. Fliegerarsenal, not the pilots at the Front. While we fought and cursed and died amid the stink of cordite and petrol and burning bodies, the desk-aviators sat in their offices at the War Ministry, floating serene and godlike above the suffering of mankind, and exchanged memoranda and aides-memoire with their fellow-bureaucrats at Fischamend. It was only by removing themselves (they said) as far as possible from the vulgar brawl – 'dcr Kricgskrawalle' – taking place on the Isonzo that they could arrive at considered and administratively correct decisions on how best to spend the taxpayer's money.

So for the time being it looked as if we must go on trying to do our duty in our unwieldly Brandenburg two-seaters. It had been a hazardous business even when the Italians had been operating their Nieuports in ones and twos. But now that they would be going around in gangs, our life expectancy would be quite dramatically reduced, to a point where even Oberleutnant Friml would decline to quote us a premium. Our own strength in single-seat fighter aircraft consisted of precisely three aircraft: Fokker Eindeckers reluctantly sold to us by the Germans and grounded for most of the time at their base at Wippach because Flik 4 could no longer obtain the castor oil used as a lubricant in their rotary engines. Not that they would have been much use however, even if they could have got airborne more often. The Eindecker had not been a brilliant aircraft even in 1915, and it stood little chance now in single combat with a Nieuport flown by a half-way competent pilot. In any case, the Eindeckers were forbidden to operate west of the front line. The Germans were still worried that the Allies would capture and copy the secret mechanism that allowed the Eindecker's gun to fire through the propeller arc, so they had only agreed to sell them to us on strict condition that they always stayed on our side of the lines.

The wretched early-autumn weather and our lack of serviceable aircraft put paid to flying for most of the third week of September. It also gave a marked downward trend to nearly all the lines on nearly all of the graphs that decorated the walls of Hauptmann Kraliczek's office: particularly to the all-important red line

Kilometres Flown over Enemy Territory, which, for our commanding officer, was the touchstone of Flik 19F's efficiency as a fighting unit. At last, on 20 September, three days after the resumption of large-scale fighting on the Carso, Kraliczek was able to bear the strain no longer. Perhaps because they could no longer be bothered organising them when the results were so meagre, 5th Army Command had given the commander of Flik 19F a completely free hand in planning long-range bombing operations: in future he would be able to go and bomb whatever he pleased, provided that he submitted his plans first for approval by the High Command and provided that his aeroplanes were not required elsewhere for photo-reconnaissance. The result was a daring plan; so daring in fact that it was plain at first sight that whoever had conceived of it was confident that someone else would have the job of turning it into reality. The next day Flik 19F's entire effective strength of four Hansa-Brandenburgs would take off to fly on a raid to the very limit of their range: to the city of Verona, some 250 kilometres behind the Italian lines.

For our commanding officer, what we were to do when – and if – we reached Verona was of quite secondary importance. Photographs of the railway junction and a barracks were cursorily indicated at our briefing session that afternoon; but even if we managed to get that far and identify them, there was not going to be a great deal that we would be able to do to them. The raid would be in daylight, so each aeroplane would have to carry an observer and machine gun for defence, while at that range our bombload would be limited to two 10kg bombs each. So far as we could make out, Hauptmann Kraliczek had selected Verona as a target and chosen to send four aircraft against it purely on the grounds that $4 \times 250\text{km} \times 2 = 2{,}000\text{km}$, which would suffice to pull the Kilometres Flown line back up to where it had been at the beginning of August. My polite enquiry, whether we might just send up one aeroplane four nights running with instructions to fly around in circles until its tank was empty, was met with a baffled stare from behind the round spectacles. That is the trouble with people of Kraliczek's cast of mind, I have always found: sarcasm is quite wasted upon them, since their brains can only proceed from A to B and from B to C.

None of us was at all confident as we made our preparations that we would even complete the hundred-kilometre round trip, let alone do anything worthwhile on the way. No one cared to say as much, but we all knew that intelligence reports had revealed the presence of a new Italian single-seater squadron recently arrived at San Vito airfield, just east of Palmanova and directly under our planned flight path. It was the recently formed Squadriglia 64^a, led by the legendary Major Oreste di Carraciolo.

I suppose that, along with the tank, the fighter aces were the year 1916's great innovation in the field of warfare. Or perhaps it was all just public relations, I cannot say. At any rate, they fulfilled a deep public need. The grey, anonymous infantry might be perishing by the million, gassed, blown up and burnt alive with as little compunction as rats in their burrows. But up in the air above this frightful massacre – as if to give the public's numbed imagination something that it could grasp – the flying aces were fast acquiring the status of opera singers. Even this early, in the summer of 1916, cigarette cards and books of salon photographs and the first ghost-written autobiographies were being produced to feed the public's hunger for heroes to worship in this, the most monstrously unheroic war the world had ever seen. Fonck, Guynemer, Boelcke, Immelmann: even in tradition-encrusted old Austria the naval fighter pilot Godfrey Banfield was already being styled by the newspapers as 'the Eagle of Trieste'.

It was against this background that one morning early in September we officers at Caprovizza had circulated among us at breakfast a cutting from a Swiss newspaper. It carried a photograph of a shortish, thick-set man in the uniform of an Italian army officer, standing against the side of a Nieuport fighter. The aeroplane bore the emblem of a rampant black cat, claws extended, and the article was entitled 'Italy's Black Cat: Ready to Pounce on the Austrians'. It appeared from the text of the article that a journalist from a Berne newspaper had managed to obtain an interview with Major Oreste di Carraciolo: sculptor, explorer, duellist, racing driver and aviator.

The Major, we learnt, though not a career army officer and although well past forty years of age, had volunteered for the Italian Air Corps in 1915. Since then he had made a spectacular career as a flier, with ten kills to his credit already, including one of our Fokker Eindeckers and a Halberstadt single-seater from a German squadron that had operated briefly from Veldes. But by all accounts this extraordinary turn to his career was something that might well have been expected; for Major di Carraciolo was clearly a character in the mould of the condottieri of the Italian Renaissance.

His early life had mostly been spent as a sculptor, helping found the Futurist movement and leaving a few score writhing monuments in white marble in the squares of Italian towns and cities, as well as enjoying the friendship and patronage of Rodin. His 'Monument to the Heroes of Adowa' had been particularly praised: to a degree where it had almost overshadowed the fact that Adowa was a battle in which an entire Italian army had been wiped out by the Emperor Menelik's barefooted Abyssinians. But he had managed to take time off from hammer and chisel to live the life of the literary salons; and to enjoy the favours of a great many salon hostesses; and to fight a great many duels – sometimes victorious, sometimes not – with their husbands. It was one of these complications (the article said) that had obliged him to go and live for several years in the wild mountain fringes of the Italian colony of Eritrea. During his time in Africa he had discovered a major lake in the Rift Valley; had been mauled almost to death by a dying lioness; and had later rescued the lioness's cub, which he had brought up in his household and which now followed him about like a pet dog. He had driven racing cars, had taught himself to fly about 1910, and had then flown in the Italian war against Turkey, where he claimed to have been the first man to drop a bomb from an aeroplane: on a Turkish steamer in Benghazi harbour.

It appeared also that in 1914 he and a gang of like-minded

desperadoes had tried to force the hand of the dithering Italian government by provoking a war with Austria. They had hired a ship and arms and had been about to sail from Rimini to attack the island of Cherso when the carabinieri had arrived and arrested them. Carraciolo had received a sentence of five years, but in the event he had served only a few months, since Italy had declared war on Austria in May 1915. He had then organised a similar expedition against an Adriatic islet off Lissa: an expedition which I myself had unwittingly frustrated the previous July, when my submarine *U8* had torpedoed the Italian cruiser leading the force.

All in all, it looked quite an impressive curriculum vitae. Major di Carraciolo was now (he said) ablaze with a passionate desire to clear the Habsburg eagle out of the remnants of Italia irredenta in Trieste and Dalmatia and the South Tyrol. He had no personal animus against us, he assured the Swiss journalist: 'The Austrian is a brave and determined fighter,' he said, 'but he is also ill-organised and not very well equipped and now outnumbered into the bargain. I think that I can promise him a hot time of it once Squadriglia 64ª gets into action.' Some of our younger officers dismissed the article as empty Latin bragging; but for myself I had little doubt that the Major would be as good as his word. I hoped that so long as I was flying a Brandenburger we would never meet him in the air.

We were to meet, though, and a good deal sooner than I had anticipated. 21 September dawned sunny after a week of mist and drizzle, though with some patchy cloud coming from the west. Laden down with fuel and bombs, the four Brandenburgers had squelched across the water-logged flying field at Caprovizza and lumbered heavily into the air. We were all climbing slowly, the aeroplanes not only heavy-laden but themselves damp-soaked and sluggish after weeks of standing around in the rain and fog on the airfield. It was not until we were almost over the trench lines east of Görz, still climbing, that we finally got into formation. We would fly in a diamond shape, perhaps fifty metres apart. The leading aeroplane would be flown by Oberleutnant Potocznik, Toth and I would fly on the starboard flank, while a new officer called Leutnant Donhanyi would take the port flank. The rear aeroplane would be flown by Stabsfeldwebel Zwierzkowski with Leutnant Szuborits as observer. The idea of the diamond formation was to guard against aeroplanes wandering off and getting lost. We also hoped that we might be able to give one another supporting fire if the Italians came up after us.

In the event they had no need to come up after us: they were already waiting as we crossed the lines, circling a thousand metres above and positioned to make the best use of the sun. Everything just happened so fast: six or seven black specks hurtling down upon us out of the glare as our shadows skimmed phantom-like across a white field of cloud about five hundred metres below. Outnumbered, our only hope of survival lay inside the cloud. I turned as I cocked the machine gun and saw Potocznik's aeroplane waggling its wings to tell us to follow, then putting his nose down to head into the white fluff. But the Nieuports were upon us before we could hide ourselves, two of them edging beneath us to shoot us down if we tried to dive. Donhanyi's aeroplane was the first victim. I swung around and fired a hurriedly aimed burst or two in an attempt to knock out the Nieuport manoeuvring under his tail. Then the Schwarzlose jammed. I opened the breech and fumbled in my thick gloves to clear the blockage. I cleared it, but I was too late to be of any help to Donhanyi: orange flame burst suddenly from behind the Brandenburger's engine mantle, and there was nothing more to be done except watch helpless as the aeroplane curved away to port and down into the cloud, ablaze and leaving a plume of greasy black smoke floating in the air. But there was no time to stand watching, only swing the gun around to fire at an Italian coming at us from the starboard side. He was firing at us as he came. Somehow Toth managed to flick us sideways and down into the cloud – just as our engine coughed and missed fire.

I suspected a bullet through the fuel pump, but it scarcely mattered as we drifted down through the clinging damp murk with the engine spluttering to a standstill. By the time we emerged from the underside of the cloud a half-minute later, the engine was gone for good, the wind singing eerily in the bracing-wires as the propeller windmilled idly in the slipstream. In the sudden, intense silence I was aware for the first time of the noise of other aeroplane engines and the dry rattle of firing above us.

I looked about us fearfully as we emerged into the sunshine once more. No one was to be seen for the moment. The Italians were presumably off chasing Potocznik and Szuborits. I looked below, trying to get my bearings. The first thing that I saw was the familiar outline of Görz below me. Well, I thought to myself, if the Italians had jumped upon us as we crossed the lines, this did at least mean that the cripples might have some chance of limping home. I signalled to Toth to turn us around towards our lines, then lugged our two bombs up on to the edge of the cockpit and tipped them overboard. Provided that we could escape the attentions of Italian fighters and flak batteries, we might still make it back. We were still about three thousand metres up and our lines were perhaps five kilometres to the east. The aeroplanes of 1916 might have been primitive, slow, flimsy contraptions, but they could at least glide well.

I stood behind the machine gun, scanning the sky about us. We might just escape unobserved . . . Then I saw the shape swooping on us out of the cloud. I ground my teeth and traversed the gun around – more out of a feeling of honour than from any hope of beating off our attacker. A two-seater would stand little enough chance against a Nieuport even under full power. Gliding along like this, though, we were the most pitiful of sitting targets, incapable of doing anything more than drift gently downwards in a straight line at about half our maximum speed. The Italian came along behind us, manoeuvring for the fatal burst. Then to my surprise the little grey aeroplane turned away to port and throttled back to fly alongside us. As the pilot waved to me I saw that the aeroplane bore the familiar emblem of the pouncing black cat painted on its side. It was the famous Major di Carraciolo in person. As he raised his gauntleted hand and pointed down I grasped that he was signalling us to fly on towards our own side of the lines – with himself as our escort.

Quaint as it might sound now, such chivalrous behaviour was by no means uncommon in those days. By 1916, war in the air had become a fairly murderous business: not at all the gentlemanly jousting of legend. Even so, men had been flying then for something not much over a decade. The very act of taking to the sky was still something only marginally less dangerous than fighting in it, so it is scarcely surprising that we aviators were still bound together in some degree by a fellow-feeling that crossed the battle lines. I believe that even in the last months of 1918 in France, where the air battles had long since turned from duels into vast, ruthless engagements involving hundreds of aircraft on each side, there was still a general disposition to leave obviously broken-down aircraft to their fate rather than simply shoot them out of the sky. In any event, Major di Carraciolo shepherded us down until we were within reach of our lines, and on the way headed off another Nieuport which was moving in to attack us. As we crossed the lines he waved in farewell and turned away, leaving us to glide down and land on a level stretch of pasture near the village of Biglia, suffering nothing worse than a burst tyre in the process. When we got the engine panels off we found that it was not battle damage that had forced us down but a blocked fuel filter.

We sat dolefully in the mess tent that evening back at Caprovizza. Kraliczek's Verona raid had been a costly fiasco. Toth and I had got back with little more than a few bullet holes, but the others had fared a good deal worse. Potocznik had managed to limp home with a badly shot-up aeroplane and a dying observer. But at least he had sent down one of the attacking Nieuports in the process. As for Szuborits and Zwierzkowski, they had crashed near Ranziano as they tried to get home. Szuborits was all right except for a few cuts and bruises, but Zwierzkowski had a suspected fractured pelvis, while the aeroplane was a wreck. As for young Donhanyi and his pilot, there was no point whatever in speculating about their fate: in 1916 one did not usually survive a fall from four thousand metres in a burning aeroplane.

Even in the k.u.k. Armee there were certain limits beyond which incompetence would not be allowed to run, and with the virtual elimination of an entire squadron those limits had been reached. Hauptmann Kraliczek was summoned that same evening to Marburg to explain himself to the 5th Army's Air Liaison Officer and to General Uzelac himself. He duly set off in the staff car next morning, wearing his best General Staff officer's salon trousers and shiny dress-shako, and with a thick folder of statistical abstracts under his arm in order to demonstrate how, despite losing nine aircraft and five crew over the past eight weeks for negligible gains, Flik 19F was still the most meticulously administered unit in the entire Imperial and Royal Flying Service. In the mean time the rest of us were left orphan-like at Fliegerfeld Caprovizza, suspended in a sort of administrative limbo while it was decided what to do with us: whether to rebuild the unit with new aircraft and fliers or whether – as Hauptmann Heyrowsky at Flik 19 wanted – to reabsorb us into the parent unit. Among us remaining officers, feelings on the matter were mixed.

'It always was a stupid idea,' said Potocznik in the mess that evening, downing a double schnapps to steady hands that were still trembling after the morning's battle. 'Long-range bombing in daylight's a complete waste of time. If you're going to drop bombs on cities, then do it at night and do it unexpectedly with everything you've got instead of sending out four aeroplanes with a couple of jam-tin bombs each.'

'I agree,' I said, 'but the trouble with night bombing is that if they can't see you, you can't see them either. Showering bombs about at random means that innocent civilians are liable to get hurt. Bomb-aiming's an uncertain enough business in daylight.'

He looked at me steadily, turning the destroyed side of his face away from me as was his custom. A curious look had come into his normally rather dreamy eyes.

'There's no such thing as an innocent civilian. This is war, not a game of croquet. The civilian behind the lines is every bit as much our enemy as the soldier in the trenches, and just as legitimate a target.'

'But that's monstrous . . . The Hague Convention clearly lays down . . .'

'To hell with the Hague Convention and all the rest of the laws imposed on us by the Latins and the Anglo-Saxons. This is a twentieth-century war we're fighting, not one of Louis XIV's little summer campaigns in Flanders where the ladies come out to watch the battle from a grandstand. And we're not civilised fighters but Germanic warriors, descendants of the tribesmen who wiped out a Roman legion in the Teutoberger Wald and then sacrificed every last survivor to their gods. I only wish that I could convince our suet-brained generals of that, what with their permitted targets and their laws of war. Just look at the way we handed Görz over to the Wellischers: a whole town given to them intact "so as to spare it from further damage". I tell you, the German Army wouldn't have stood for it: the Italians might have taken the site of Görz, but not one stone would have been standing on another when they got there. Every house would have been blown up, every tree sawn down, every well poisoned and every cellar booby-trapped.'

'For heaven's sake Potocznik, why are we fighting then? If we had to win the war by such means than frankly I'd rather we lost it a hundred times over.'

'And we will lose it too, I know that in my bones. There are too many against us already and the Americans are going to come in before long. But I promise you this, Germany will lose this war only to rise next time and win. That's the war I'm planning for now, not this miserable abortion: the war when we'll have got rid of the Kaisers and the Kraliczeks and the rest of the desk-warriors and be able to fight it according to our own rules.'

'Do you mean then that you're fighting this war now without any hope of our winning?'

He smiled: the old, agreeable Potocznik smile. 'Between ourselves, quite without any hope, my dear Prohaska. I realised back in the winter of 1914 when I was lying in hospital that Germany had already lost. The mistakes we made at the beginning were simply too great for us to overcome them. It may take us two years, perhaps even three to lose, but for the time being our enemies are too strong for us. The German High Command tries everything a little; flame-throwers, poison gas, U-Boats and so forth. But it always fails.'

'From my experience of poison gas, we deserve to lose for having used such filthy stuff.'

'The trouble, Prohaska, is not that we used such filthy stuff but that we used it half-heartedly. Just like aerial bombing: we do it too little, and piecemeal, without any sort of plan.' He leant across to stare into my eyes. 'Personally I couldn't give a hoot about poison gas, or about bombing hospitals or orphanages. In fact if it were left to me I'd aim for them specially, and use poison-gas bombs on cities too, if it did the job more efficiently. Terror is a weapon like any other, and civilians are as fit a target for it as anyone else. Only, if we're going to use it, we must use it for maximum effect; not pinpricks with four or five aircraft against cities of a hundred thousand people, but raids with a hundred or even a thousand aircraft against towns of ten thousand people: arrive out of a blue sky and fly away five minutes later leaving the place a blazing cemetery. And leave them guessing which town will be on the menu for tomorrow. That's war as I understand it: strike ruthlessly and hard, at random, without warning. If thine enemy offend thee – then go one night and blow his house up and cut the throats of his wife and children and poison his dog. That way he'll leave you alone in future.'

I was silent for some time. I had always considered Potocznik to be slightly odd, a dreaming German poet-philosopher perhaps with some rather strange opinions, but at base a decent enough person. But now here he was preaching this murderous lunacy with the conviction of a dogmatic vegetarian or a convert to Christian Science. It was rather as if next door's pedigree spaniel, always so playful and gentle, should suddenly appear in front of you with a crazed light in its eyes and a child's torn-off arm dripping in its mouth. I suddenly understood Elisabeth's remark (which I had previously taken to be flippant) about calling for help when he started questioning her about the shade of her nipples.

'I see,' I said, 'so you are an enthusiast for long-range bombing after all. Are you planning to use it on a large scale in your second world war?'

'Not in the least. I consider that strategic bombing may have some place in modern warfare, but not a major one except as a terror weapon. Do it regularly, night after night, and the enemy will have time to build up defences and get used to it, like our famous preparatory barrages which last for weeks and merely serve to let the enemy move up his reserves in readiness. No, the sort of air power I'm interested in is completely different: massive and overwhelming air power, but used as close to the Front as possible in direct support of the armies – battlefield flying carried out by an air force specially designed for that purpose; fleets of aircraft in contact with the ground troops by wireless and used to smash any strong points ahead of an advance.'

'The wireless sets are going to be rather heavy for the ground troops to carry, don't you think?'

'Not in my German army of the future. The British have been using armoured caterpillar tractors on the Ancre, I read in this week's "Corps Intelligence Summary". Only the complacent idiots who write it are dismissing them as "mechanical toys of no lasting signficance". Not if I know anything about it they won't be. That's the war of the future: columns of armoured motor cars with wireless and with fleets of aeroplanes to call up as flying artillery. No more of your nine-day bombardments and twenty thousand lives to capture a square kilometre. We'll win by speed and ruthlessness – and we'll keep what we've conquered by the same means. It's Latin, but it's still a good motto: "Let them hate us so long as they fear us".'

'Are you going to lead Germany in person in this war of yours, then?'

'No, not me. Nor Ludendorff nor Kaiser Wilhelm nor the House of Hohenzollern. No: in ten, twenty, even thirty years a kaiser will arise from among the German people to lead us to our final victory. But I'll tell you something: I think that he won't be a German from the fat, complacent beer-swilling heart of Germany, but someone from the borderlands like myself, where we know what it really means to be a German.'

213

I returned to my tent that evening feeling rather depressed. Was the entire world going mad? Terror bombing and women's nipple-colour and Volkskaisers – it was as if everyone had mild shell-shock now. As I reached the door of my tent I met Leutnant Szuborits, who had just been brought back by staff car. He had a bandaged hand, but otherwise seemed very pleased with himself. I congratulated him on his escape and asked how Zwierzkowski was doing. He smiled that fat, rather self-satisfied little smile of his.

'Oh, he's fine. They took him to a civilian hospital in Trieste. I went in the ambulance with him to see him in. Here . . .' he rummaged in a paper bag, 'here, I had a couple of hours to spare afterwards before they could get a car to bring me back here. I went into a music shop and found this. It was the last one in stock.'

The record gleamed black in the twilight. I looked at the label with sinking heart. It was Mizzi Günther and Hubert Marischka singing the duet 'Sport und immer Sport' from the operetta *Endlich Allein* by Franz Lehár.

11

THE SPIDER AND THE BLACK CAT

If the continuing existence of Fliegerkompagnie 19F might have been a matter of some uncertainty in the last week of September 1916, the continuation of the war most certainly was not. The fighting had broken out again on the Carso on 17 September, as the Italians once again felt strong enough to continue their blood-soaked, metre-by-metre push towards Trieste. The weather had cleared for a while, so the two remaining serviceable aircraft with Flik 19F were assigned on 25 September to fly a very important photo reconnaissance mission.

The mission involved photographing a wood near Gradisca which was known to be concealing a large naval gun mounted on a railway carriage. This weapon – at least 30cm according to intelligence reports – had been brought up the previous week and was now causing a great deal of grief to our troops on the Carso. Known popularly as 'Waldschani' – Viennese dialect for 'Johnny-in-the-Wood' – it had been sending shells over at the rate of one every three minutes or so, day and night, to crash down on the trackways behind Fajtji Hrib amid the supply columns of men and mules struggling in the red mud. It was not known how they were aiming the guns – secret wireless messages from spies had been spoken of – but the Italians were certainly finding their targets now with depressing frequency. Normally this would not have weighed much in the counsels of the generals: being blown to bits by half-tonne shells wailing down out of the darkness was what common soldiers were for. But the previous day 'Waldschani' had succeeded in dropping a shell alongside the farmhouse near the village of Vojscica which served as headquarters for the 9th

Infantry Division. Its commander the Archduke Joseph had not been injured when the roof fell in on him, only shaken and covered in soot from the chimney. But insults of that kind – a direct threat to the safety and well-being of staff officers, no less – could not be tolerated; especially when one of the officers in question was a member of the Imperial House. An order had gone out that all possible measures must be taken immediately to put an end to Waldschani's destructive career.

A heavy bombing-raid would have to be laid on, since no Austrian gun on the Carso Front had enough range to reach Grandisca. The first requisite for this, though, would be to find out exactly where the gun was firing from, since we had now lost the heights along the rim of the Carso and no kite-balloon could get high enough to peer over the edge. Photo reconnaissance by aeroplane would be called for. But it would not be an easy task. The Italians would be expecting photographers and would certainly have ringed the site with flak batteries as well as detailing fighter aircraft to cover it. The best that we could do was to aim for surprise – after all, even Nieuports could not hover in the air all day long – and provide an escort for the two-seater taking the photographs. However, the mission was of the utmost importance, we were told, so not one but two Brandenburgers would be used – Potocznik's and mine. It would also mark the operational début of Austria-Hungary's first single-seat fighter aeroplane, the Hansa-Brandenburg KD – the 'Kampfdoppeldecker' or 'fighting biplane'.

The fighter escort had been a last-minute decision on Vienna's part, made possible by the fact that the first four Brandenburg KDs had been delivered from Berlin to the aircraft park at Marburg the previous day. So you may imagine that we were fairly dancing with anticipation that evening of 24 September as we received the telephone call and rushed out to watch the tiny specks materialise in the distance above the mountains, coming in to land at Caprovizza flying field. Only Meyerhofer remained in the Kanzlei hut, to speak with the Air Liaison Officer at the other end of the line. But we had been promised four aircraft, he said. And now Oberleutnant Potocznik was standing by him to report that only three aeroplanes could be seen. Yes, said Air Liaison; there had been . . . er . . . an unfortunate mishap on take-off from Marburg, so it would now be only three aircraft. However, that should be more than sufficient for our needs tomorrow. Meyerhofer put down the receiver and rushed out to join us on the field just as the aeroplanes were lining up to land.

'Lining up' is scarcely an accurate term for what was going on: the three aeroplanes were swaying and weaving through the air like a flight of drunken gnats. The first two managed untidy, bouncing landings on the field, but the third had no sooner touched its wheels to the ground than it promptly nosed over, seemed to stand still with its wheels like a recalcitrant mule, and stood on its head, then did a sort of forward somersault to end up lying on its back with a smashed propeller and a badly bent undercarriage. We all ran over to the wreck to find the pilot alive but badly concussed, hanging upside-down by his seat straps. We got him down and wheeled him to the ambulance on the hand barrow used for the injured. Then we went to look at the aeroplanes that had survived the journey, standing now under camouflage netting in the bora shelters. We all stood gazing for some time in silence.

Bear in mind if you will that in the year 1916 aeroplanes had not been flying for very long. Szuborits was the youngest of us, little more than an adolescent still, but even he had been at junior school in 1903 when the Wright brothers had made their first flight. Since that time every possible layout had been designed, built and (usually) crashed by aspiring designers: tractors, pushers, monoplanes, biplanes, triplanes, sesquiplanes, canards and deltas. There was as yet no settled notion of what an aeroplane ought to look like. Yet even so, standing there that evening, we all realised that there was something not quite right about the Hansa-Brandenburg Kampfdoppeldecker. It was as if the plans for an aeroplane had mistakenly been posted to a manufacturer of agricultural machinery.

True, it was a conventional enough aircraft in layout: a small single-engined tractor biplane with a propeller at one end and a tailplane and rudder at the other. It was just that compared with the pretty little Nieuport, which was as delightful to look at as it was dangerous to engage, something seemed to have gone badly wrong with the Brandenburg KD's proportions, as if we were looking at a normal aeroplane in a fairground distorting mirror. It seemed so inordinately high off the ground in relation to its length and wing span. The fuselage was a deep, narrow mahogany trunk of an affair with an Austro-Daimler engine completely blocking the forward vision, so that the pilot had to look along the recessed sides past the cylinder block (as with many of his other designs, Herr Heinkel seemed to consider forward view an unnecessary luxury). The rudder was tiny, a mere comma-shaped flap hung on the knife-edge sternpost of the fuselage. The short wings were squared-off and of equal width, so that the pilot had a badly restricted view downwards. Likewise his upward view was not too good, through a cut-out in the trailing edge of the upper wing. But the most bizarre thing about the whole contraption was the struts holding the wings apart: not pairs of sticks as in a normal aeroplane, but an arrangement of pyramids held together in the middle by a star-shaped metal bracket, rather like the four legs of a canvas field-washbasin.

And to crown all these eccentricities, making an already high aeroplane look higher still, like a dwarf wearing a top hat, was a curious wood-and-aluminium fairing structure atop the upper wing. This, we learnt, housed the aeroplane's armament of a single Schwarzlose machine gun. It appeared that when he had designed the aeroplane for the k.u.k. Fliegertruppe Heinkel had assumed that he would be able to have a machine gun firing through the propeller arc as in all the latest German machines. Not a bit of it though: the German War Ministry had refused to sell Fokker interrupter gear to Austria and had in fact even refused to license the patent to us. The machine gun on top of the wing was an afterthought, and the fairing – universally known as 'the Baby's Coffin' – was a desperate attempt to reduce the drag. Not only did it do next to nothing to help the aeroplane's speed, it made it completely impossible – as we would soon find out – to clear a machine-gun stoppage in flight. In the years since, I have heard it said that we used to call the Brandenburg KD 'the Flying Coffin'. I cannot say that I remember that nickname being used, even though I suppose looking back on it that it was quite apt, and that the varnished mahogany fuselage did look rather like a burial casket. The only name I ever remember being used for it – and that but seldom – was the 'Spinne', or 'Spider'. Nicknames, after all, are usually reserved for people and things for which we feel a glimmer of affection, and certainly no one who flew the KD could ever feel that.

We made our way back to the mess tent in silence. The two delivery pilots were already there, being plied with drinks by the orderlies like two unhurt but still intensely shocked survivors of a train crash. One was a Hungarian called Terszetanyi, if I remember rightly, the other a Pole called Romanowicz. The latter was still chalk-faced as he poured himself yet another schnapps with a trembling hand.

'Holy Mother of God,' he said, 'I'm volunteering for the trenches tomorrow. Anything: storm-battalion, flame-thrower company, gas, burying corpses – I don't care.'

'Was it that bad?'

'Bad? Jesus Christ I've never flown anything like it. Not even the Aviatik Rocking-Chair. The thing's a disaster. The first time I took it up was yesterday afternoon, and it got me into a spin at two thousand metres. I managed to pull out just above the ground, God alone knows how. It wanders from side to side like a snake, while as for landing the thing, I don't know how I managed not to tip over on my head like poor old Belounek. We took off from Marburg well enough – the pig climbs quite decently if nothing else – but we were hardly out of sight of the airfield when Metzger's plane went into a spin for no reason at all.'

'I suppose that must have been Air Liaison's "problems on take-off"?'

Romanowicz smiled grimly and gulped his drink. 'Yes, I suppose you could call it that. Only for Metzger it's the end of his problems for ever. The poor bugger dived straight into the ground and went up like a firework: "strengthened the ranks of the angels", as we say back home.'

'Why didn't you turn back?'

'No choice, old man: orders and all that. Terszetanyi and I were with Flik 14 in the Ukraine, you see. We had some trouble there earlier this year over another flying abortion, the Aviatik BIII of blessed memory, commonly known as "the Rocking-Chair" or "the Fairground Swingboat". The thing killed so many of our chaps that in the end we had a little mutiny – "mass refusal of duty" is the polite term among officers, I believe – and said that we weren't going to fly it any more. So they broke up the unit and moved us all to other Fliks. We were officers and not rankers so they couldn't shoot us all or stick us into a penal battalion. But I tell you, we're marked men. One more refusal of duty and we're for the high jump and no mistake.'

'What do you think the KD will be like as a fighting machine?' asked Potocznik. Romanowicz found this immensely amusing.

'A machine that will rapidly carve for itself a lasting niche in the brief annals of aerial warfare, if you ask me: the Italians will either think we've all gone mad and stop fighting or crash into the ground following us down. Here . . .' he rummaged inside his tunic. 'Here's my will, made out ready and signed. Be a good chap and leave it in the Kanzlei safe, will you? As for my personal effects, you can auction them here among yourselves to save you the bother of sending them back to Marburg.'

The mist was clearing from the valley the next morning as the remnants of Flik 19F took off from Caprovizza airfield, accompanied by their two ungainly escorts. I was in the leading aeroplane with Toth as pilot, while Potocznik and Leutnant Szuborits followed in the unit's other serviceable Brandenburger. Low cloud lay over the Vippaco valley, but the Meteorological Officer had assured us by telephone that it was clearing rapidly west of the Isonzo and giving way to bright autumn sunshine: ideal conditions for photography. We droned around in circles to gain height, entering the cloud at about a thousand metres and emerging at two thousand to form up with our escorts. We watched the two KDs pop up from the fleecy white carpet, then got into line with them on either side of us and about fifty metres above. I watched them anxiously from my place behind the machine gun. They seemed a little unsteady to be sure. I supposed that Terszetanyi and Romanowicz were sitting in the cockpits, knuckles white with gripping the control column and waiting for the first tell-tale lurch that would presage the fatal spin down to disaster. Not for the first time I was glad that, whatever the hazards of front-line aviation, at least the Brandenburg two-seater was an easy and gentle old bus to fly, with no conspicuous vices; sturdily built and tolerant of wayward piloting.

I waved to them, but they did not wave back: mainly (I suppose) because they were too frightened to take a hand off the controls. At least they seemed to be managing the aircraft a little better than on the previous day. Perhaps it was just that the KD took some getting used to for pilots who had previously flown only two-seaters. It certainly seemed to have adequate speed. We were flying at seven-cighths throttle to gain height, but the two KDs seemed to be ambling along at only about three-quarters to judge by the exhaust smoke, which used to turn black at high revs. Perhaps things would not work out so badly after all.

We met with a little ill-directed flak as we crossed the Monte Cosbana ridge north of Görz. As agreed, we then made a wide circle over the town of Cormóns and approached Gradisca from the rear. So far there was no sign of any hostile aircraft. We flew over the target at three thousand metres; Toth and I first, then Potocznik. We were covering the same area with our cameras, but the whole operation was judged so important that it had been decided to have two aeroplanes carry it out in case one failed to return. Try as I might I could see no sign of the railway gun on its carriage in the wood below, only the spur of railway track leading off the main line into the trees. But that was not my affair: my job was to work the camera, get the twenty or so plates back to

Haidenschaft and then leave it to the intelligence experts with their magnifying-glasses and stereoscopic viewers to detect where exactly Waldschani was lurking. After about two minutes of ambling over the area as instructed, I fired a green signal rocket to indicate that we were finished. Potocznik waggled his wings in answer, and we all turned to give full throttle and run for home, the two Brandenburgers and their escorts who had been circling overhead. We had got away with it so far, but surely the Italians must be coming up after us by now. Being of a naturally rather suspicious cast of mind, it worried me more than a little that we had been allowed to fly over the target, quite obviously engaged in photography, without attracting so much as a single flak shell from below.

We found out as we crossed the Isonzo that it had indeed all been too good to be true: three Nieuports fell upon us out of a patch of cloud. I abandoned the camera and stood behind the Schwarzlose, ready and hoping that the ammunition feed would not seize up like last time. Remember, I thought, don't fire too soon: rely on Toth to fly the aeroplane and just fire defensively when a target presents itself. Our real hope of salvation lay in getting up enough speed in a shallow dive to outrun the Italians. We were not far from our own lines after all. Weaving and jinking to throw them off their aim before it was absolutely necessary would only lose us speed and make us easier to catch. The Italians needed to close to thirty metres or less to be sure of hitting, and their gun magazines only held about fifty rounds . . . It was with thoughts such as these that I tried to hearten myself as the three familiar shapes closed with us. Yet when all is said and done, no thoughts are really cheering enough to console a man who will shortly be required to stand up full-length with only a thin plywood sheet for protection, three thousand metres above the ground, and face an assailant armed with a machine gun at a range less than the length of most people's back gardens.

The thing about aerial combat, as opposed to making a U-Boat attack, is that everything happens so fast. I always found it rather like going under anaesthetic for an operation, when the last thought that one takes in is also the first thought as one comes out, the intervening couple of hours having somehow got lost. It was very like that over the Isonzo that morning: a desperate, savage, confused bout of wheeling and shooting which perhaps lasted no more than a minute. Our first concern was to keep formation and support one another as the Italians tried to break us up, seeking to fasten on to an aeroplane and worry it to death, as wolves will detach a stag from the herd and then run it down. A Nieuport flashed past us some way above with a KD – Terszetanyi's as it turned out – on his tail trying to take aim. I think that I saw Terszetanyi fire a few times, but then I suppose that his gun must have jammed. At any rate, as he wheeled back into view below us I saw that he had broken off the attack and was now kneeling half out of his cockpit, steering with one foot and hammering at the gun fairing with his fist in an effort to pull it off and get at the gun. He did not succeed. Horror-struck, I watched as his aeroplane suddenly slipped sideways into a spin. My last sight of him is still branded into my mind's eye seventy years later: of his arms and legs flailing wildly as he fell to his death on the Carso rocks three thousand metres below.

There was no time to mourn him, only to try and save ourselves as a Nieuport came at us out of the sun. Blinded by the glare, I swung the gun around and felt it jolt and clatter in my hands as I pressed the thumb triggers. Bullets spacked through the fuselage as he aimed for the black Maltese cross on our side. But we lived; the Nieuport shot past under our tail as I gave him another burst. He came up on the other side and I fired again. He was visible just long enough for me to make out the black-cat emblem on the side of his fuselage. Then it was hidden by a stream of smoke and a sudden bright tail of red and yellow flames. The Nieuport banked away and span downwards, leaving a curving trail of smoke behind it as the fire licked around the wing roots and spread towards the tail. It dawned upon me belatedly that I had just shot down Major Oreste di Carraciolo, the Black Cat of Italy.

All this happened in an instant, though I see it still with the vivid clarity of a dream. But we had not the leisure to congratulate ourselves on our victory. We could only thank our lucky stars and run for home as best we could. In the end Potocznik and I crossed the lines circling around Romanowicz's KD like lapwings protecting a fledgeling from hawks: a ludicrous state of affairs in which the escorted ended up escorting back the aeroplane which was supposed to have been escorting them. The Nieuports only left us in peace after we had reached Dornberg and the protection of our own flak batteries.

It was not until then, skimming down towards Caprovizza flying field, that I had time at last for the luxury of thought. The whole of the previous ten minutes or so had been conducted largely by instinct, on spinal cord alone. But now the sun was shining and it was peaceful once more, and apart from that constant throbbing of the air the war might never have existed. Only a smoke-grimed face and bullet holes letting the sunlight shine through the fuselage – and a hot machine-gun barrel burnt blue with excessive firing – served to remind me that the recent events had not been some kind of brief but intense nightmare. I looked down at the camera. Good, it was intact still. We had lost one aeroplane but we had accomplished our mission. Oh yes, and we had also shot down Major di Carraciolo.

I suddenly remembered this with surprise – then with a flooding sense of dismay, as I recalled how I had last seen him, spinning down on fire. War was war, and I had far rather that it had been him than us; but all the same it seemed to me a scurvy thing to repay a chivalrous enemy for his generosity by burning him alive. I hoped that he might already have been dead as the Nieuport began its plunge, perhaps killed by a bullet of mine through the head. But I knew enough of aerial warfare to doubt it. Had he perished with his skin bubbling and sizzling as he struggled to bring the aeroplane down? Or had he managed to release his seat straps and fling himself out, to endure perhaps a minute of stark terror as he plummeted down to burst like a blood bomb on the pitiless rocks? Either way it seemed a wretched end. Death by fire was the secret dread of us all in those days before parachutes. Like most fliers, I carried a pistol; not for defence, but with a view to my own deliverance if I should ever find myself trapped in a burning aeroplane. I hoped that di Carraciolo had been able to use his, if that was what it had come to.

We landed at Caprovizza around midday. The boxes of photographic plates were handed over, we made our verbal reports and I then went straight to my tent to lie down. It never ceased to amaze me how fighting in the air, though it usually lasted only a few seconds, seemed to drain reserves of nervous energy that would normally suffice for several months. As I was taking off my flying overalls Petrescu stuck his head around the tent flap and respectfully reported that there was a telephone call for me in the Kanzlei hut. I got up wearily from my camp-bed. What on earth did they want now? Couldn't the idiots leave me in peace for an hour at least? When I picked up the receiver from the Adjutant's desk I found that it was a staff officer from 7th Corps Headquarters at Oppachiasella.

'I say, are you the fellow who shot down that Italian single-seater over Fajtji Hrib about an hour ago?' I answered that so far as I knew I had that melancholy honour. I was expecting to be told where the aeroplane had come down and to be offered some fire-blackened fragment as a souvenir – a trophy for which I must say I had no desire whatever. What came next was a complete surprise. 'Well, the pilot's here with us at Corps Headquarters: chap called Major Carraciolo or something – quite famous, I understand.'

'I'm sorry . . . I just don't understand. The aeroplane was ablaze when I saw it go down . . .'

'Quite so. I understand that your Major Whatshisname climbed out of his cockpit and stood on the wing, steering the thing by leaning over the edge. Apparently he managed to slide it sideways to blow the flames away from the petrol tank, then brought the thing down in a field next to one of our batteries. Our fellows said they'd never seen flying like it – the Italian ought to be a circus performer.'

'Is he badly hurt?'

'Not in the least: dislocated shoulder and a few bruises and a bit singed, but that's about it. The Medical Officer's patching him up at the moment and when he's finished we'll send him over to you. I believe that he's Flik 19F's prisoner. You can have the aeroplane too, for what it's worth. We've posted a sentry by the wreck to keep the village brats away, but frankly there's not a lot of it left except ashes.'

Major Oreste di Carraciolo arrived in some state at Caprovizza flying field about an hour later, seated in the back of a large drab-coloured staff car. A sentry with rifle and fixed bayonet sat on each side of him and in the front seat was a staff colonel. The door was opened and he stepped down from the running-board to meet us. He wore a bandage about his head and had his left arm in a sling, but otherwise seemed undamaged except that his eyebrows and moustache and neat pointed beard were a little scorched. He wore the grey-green uniform of the Italian Air Corps and a leather flying coat, unbuttoned in the afternoon heat; also a pair of smart, and evidently very expensive, high lace-up boots.

I have perhaps made the man sound a trifle foppish. It is true that he was trim and not very tall; but his powerful shoulders and hands were clearly those of a sculptor. He stepped up grim-faced and saluted with his good hand, giving us a glare of intense hatred as he did so. I stepped forward and saluted in return, then held out my hand. Any remaining doubts about the Major's powerful build were immediately dispelled as the bones in my hand were crushed against one another. Trying not to betray my pain I welcomed him to Fliegerfeld Caprovizza in Italian, rearranging the bones of my hand as I did so. He glowered at me, his intense black eyes boring into mine – then broke into a radiant smile.

'Ah, Herr Leutnant, was it then you who . . .?'

'Yes,' I answered, 'I have the honour to be the one who shot you down this morning. But believe me, my dear Major, it gives me a thousand times more pleasure to see that you are alive and unharmed. I apologise. But you will understand, I hope, that war is a ruthless business.'

'Ah, my dear Tenente, please do not reproach yourself, I beg you. You were only doing your duty – and you may comfort yourself with the fact that you will be able one day to tell your grandchildren that it was you who brought to an end the career of Major di Carraciolo . . .' He smiled, '. . . Or perhaps I should rather say, caused a temporary interruption in the career of Major di Carraciolo, until such time as he escapes from prison and returns to fight again for his country.'

'Your confinement need not be close, Major, if you gave your word not to escape. You are now in your forties, I understand, and might easily be repatriated on parole.'

'I would never give it. In an ordinary war such things might be permissible, but a patriot fighting for the final liberation of his people has a sacred duty to escape and fight once more, so long as there is breath left in his body.'

'Very well. But you must at least be the guest of honour in our mess this evening. I and my brother-officers insist upon it. Surely you can give your word not to try to escape just for these few hours.'

He smiled broadly. 'Then you may consider it given, and I shall be delighted to accept your hospitality. I have always considered myself to be fighting against the Austrian Monarchy and not against the Austrians, whom I regard as an intelligent and artistic people like ourselves.'

'Splendid. But tell me one thing if you will, Major. How exactly did I manage to shoot you down? The sun was in my eyes and I was quite unable to take aim, and I fired only a few shots anyway. You had us in your sights and could hardly have missed, yet you veered away at the last moment. What went wrong? I ask as one aviator to another.'

'It is the fortunes of war, my dear . . . er . . .?'

'Prohaska. Otto Prohaska. Lieutenant of the Imperial and Royal Navy.'

'Ah yes, Prohaska. Well, as I attacked I knew that you could not aim at me because of the sun, and also that your Schwarzlose gun is as much use as a garden syringe. But there, even random shots sometimes find their mark. One of your bullets severed an oil-feed

227

pipe and hot oil sprayed back in my face. By the time I had regained my sight I was flying past your tail and you were shooting at me again. Then I saw fire coming at me from the engine cowling – and after that I lost all interest in you, as I think you will understand. But the rest of the story I believe you already know?'

'Yes, the Intelligence Officer at Oppachiasella told me all about it. You are to be congratulated by all accounts on a magnificent piece of flying. But, dear Major, I am doubly glad to meet you because it was you who escorted us back across the lines a few days ago when our engine failed.'

He looked puzzled for a moment – then laughed loudly and slapped my shoulder.

'So it was you? I remember now: your Brandenburg *Zośka* if my memory serves me right? Then we are acquaintances already. My sergeant wanted to shoot you down but I headed him away from you. "Why did you let the Austrian pigs escape, Maggiore?" he asked me later. No, I said, to spare the life of an enemy in distress will bring us luck. And who knows? he may well do the same for us one day. Well, you certainly brought me luck.'

It was as convivial an evening in the mess as our increasingly meagre rations would allow. The food might have been poor, but the local wine flowed freely and we were entertained by Flik 19F's gypsy orchestra, drawn from its Hungarian ground crewmen; also by Potocznik, who played a good deal of Schubert very well indeed on the mess piano. Even Hauptmann Kraliczek was there, looking as unhappy as an owl forced into daylight, and only present because Meyerhofer and Potoznik and I had arm-locked him into attending. As for Major di Carraciolo, he provided us with magnificent entertainment of his own. He spoke German tolerably well, and I was able to help him out in Italian when needed, so the evening was one long succession of anecdotes about his days in Africa. His time there, it appeared, when he was not discovering lakes or being mauled by lionesses, had been spent mostly in the arms of a succession of Eritrean mistresses who had their teeth filed to points and who chewed qhat leaves. And when the African reminiscences failed there was always his career as a sculptor, adulterer, duellist and racing driver to fall back upon. All in all he seemed to have lived enough lives for a roomful of people. He was a flamboyant and theatrical character it is true, but I found myself not at all irritated by it. The Major loved to entertain people, while as to the truth of his stories I had not the slightest doubt that most of them had really happened – or at least almost happened. Only Potocznik made a rather disapproving face. I asked him afterwards what was the matter.

'That insufferable Wellischer and his greasy lies. And a lot of Hungarian gypsies scraping fiddles. And that Levantine Meyerhofer into the bargain. It's enough to make anyone sick. This is supposed to be a German-speaking empire, not some filthy bazaar in Constantinople.'

'Oh come on: Carraciolo's a bit of a boaster but I don't doubt most of it's true.'

'A typical degenerate Latin – would laugh in your face while he's sticking a knife in your back. I tell you the bastard uses scent like a woman! We should have shot him when he landed and had done with it.'

Apart from this drop of acid, all went splendidly until about 2300, when I heard a motor lorry draw up outside and the noise of soldiers' boots crunching on the cinder pathway. Thinking that it was the liberty-lorry bringing the drunkards back from Haidenschaft I went out to tell them to quieten down – and found myself confronting a Provost major and a squad of soldiers with rifles and fixed bayonets. From their grim faces it was clear at first glance that they were here on official business.

'Excuse me,' I said, 'but I think that there must be some mistake. This is a k.u.k. Fliegertruppe flying field and this tent is the officers' mess.'

'I know that. Kindly stand aside.'

'What do you mean . . .?'

'What I said. We're here to make an arrest.' He shouldered me aside to enter the mess tent, followed by his men. I heard the sudden silence inside, and made my way in. Everyone had frozen in his place and was staring at the intruders, some swaying slightly.

229

No one spoke. Di Carraciolo still sat between Meyerhofer and Potocznik behind the long trestle table, one hand raised with a glass in it. In the pale, flaring light and deep shadows of the petrol lamps the scene put me irresistibly in mind of the Caravaggio 'Last Supper': distant memories perhaps of all those Easter Thursday masses when I was a child. Kraliczek was the first to recover from his surprise.

'Herr Major, might I enquire what is the meaning of this intrusion?'

'Herr Kommandant, do you have here an Italian prisoner by the name of . . .' he examined the slip of paper in his hand, 'by the name of Oreste Carlo Borromeo di Carraciolo, currently serving as a major in the Italian Air Corps?'

'We do. But he is our guest for this evening and will be transferred to a prisoner-of-war camp tomorrow morning. This is the custom . . .' He looked around him, suddenly uncertain. 'Er . . . at any rate, my officers here inform me that this is the custom in the Fliegertruppe.'

'I couldn't give a farthing about your customs.' He turned to address di Carraciolo. 'Are you Oreste Carlo Borromeo di Carraciolo?'

Our prisoner answered calmly, in German. 'I am.'

'I have here a warrant for your arrest on a charge of high treason and desertion from the armed forces of His Imperial Majesty. You will come with us. Feldwebel – put the handcuffs on him.'

'But this is monstrous,' Meyerhofer spluttered as we moved to close ranks about our guest. 'This man is a major in the Italian Air Corps and a prisoner of war, shot down this morning by one of our aeroplanes . . .'

'For all I care he could be a Chinese station master. As far as the k.u.k. Armee is concerned the man is an Austrian subject who has evaded military service to fight against his Emperor in the armed forces of a hostile state. If you don't believe me you can examine the warrant. Come with us if you please now, my Signor di Carraciolo. We'll give you a nice cell of your own in the Caserne Grande and an interview tomorrow with Herr Major Baumann. I don't envy you one bit. Take him to the lorry, Corporal.'

We all moved to defend our guest-captive: to all right-thinking front-soldiers in every army on earth the military police are objects of instinctive dislike. But in the end there was nothing much that we could do. The arrest warrant was unarguable, bearing as it did the signature of Major Baumann, the Governor of Trieste's aide in charge of security. Baumann was a functionary of the notorious KUA, the Kriegsüberwachungsamt, which had been set up to govern the Austrian war zones under martial law. He had not been long in Trieste, but he had already acquired a grim reputation for his ungentle ways in dealing with political suspects.

In the end we had to let them lead Major Carraciolo away in handcuffs and bundle him on to the lorry. All that we could do was to assure him as they drove away that we would see to it that he was decently looked after in prison and treated according to international law as a legitimate prisoner of war.

We did not have much success in fulfilling either of these promises. In fact when we saw the Trieste newspapers the next morning we knew beyond a shadow of doubt that it was curtains for our late guest. We read that although he had been resident in Italy since 1891 he had been born and brought up in the city of Fiume and had never renounced Austrian nationality. We also learnt that when called up for military service in that year he had simply done what thousands of other young Austrians would do, one Adolf Hitler among them: that is to say, simply ignored the letter instructing them to report for medical examination and left the country instead. Tens of thousands had done it over the years, and it had been over twenty-five years ago now, but it still made him in theory an army deserter. And now he had been captured in Italian uniform after a series of newspaper articles in which he had proclaimed his undying hostility to the Austro-Hungarian Monarchy. It was going to be a fair trial and a fair hanging.

The trial four days later before the k.u.k. Militärhofgericht in Trieste was correct enough in the legal sense I suppose: at least the outward forms were preserved throughout the entire fifteen minutes that it lasted. A counsel for the defence was present, and

Meyerhofer and I were there for the k.u.k. Fliegertruppe, but otherwise it was Old Austria at its most unappealing: a harsh, crashing military puppet-show in the worst traditions of General Haynau. The verdict had been announced by the Trieste German-language papers the day before. But it could not really have been otherwise. Di Carraciolo did not deny any of the charges against him: only said that he had done what he did for Italy and that he would regard it as a singular honour to die as a martyr for the final redemption of his people. I sensed that he was already assuming the heroic pose of one of his own statues. He had quite plainly not been well treated in prison: his face was bruised, his hair and beard had been savagely cropped and to increase his humiliation he had been stripped of his own clothes and given the worn-out grey fatigues of an Austrian private about twice his own height, so that he had to stand in the dock holding his trousers up while two stone-faced sentries stood behind him with fixed bayonets. He finished his remarks. The bored-looking judge-president looked up from his crossword and enquired, 'Is that all?' in a listless voice. It was.

'Very well then. Oreste Carlo Borromeo di Carraciolo, you have been found guilty by this court of high treason and desertion as defined by the Austrian Criminal Code, by the Military Penal Code and by the Articles of War. You are hereby condemned to death by shooting, the sentence to be carried out within twenty-four hours. Next case, please.'

Back at Fliegerfeld Caprovizza that afternoon a hurried officers' conference took place in the privacy of a stores hut. All of us – even Potocznik, oddly enough – were incensed at this high-handed treatment of a guest of the unit, who was now to be shot next morning, on tenuous moral and legal grounds, as an example to the thousands of other ex-Austrians currently serving the King of Italy. 'Judicial murder' was one of the politer phrases used. We decided that something must be done, if for no other reason than to save the honour of Flik 19F and to assert the solidarity of fliers of every nationality. In the end Meyerhofer and I – the two uncles of the unit – were detailed to make the necessary arrangements. I requisitioned the station motor cycle to go to Trieste while, towards dusk, Oberleutnant Meyerhofer took off into the sunset in a lone Hansa-Brandenburg with a white cloth fluttering from each wingtip. There was not much time. We were all involved now up to the eyebrows in what I suppose, looking back on it, must have been one of the strangest episodes in the entire history of the Habsburg officer corps: a business which, had it come to light, could easily have landed us all in front of a firing squad along with Major di Carraciolo.

12

DUE PROCESS OF LAW

The next morning dawned cloudy but calm. The place appointed for the execution was the military Exerzierplatz between Villa Opocina and Trebiciano, up on the arid comb of the karst ridge that towers above the city of Trieste: a bleak, windswept expanse of roughly levelled ground among the thin pine trees, worn bare of vegetation by generations of tramping soldiers' boots and the bellowing of countless drill sergeants. I was relieved by this: as I had suspected, the original plan had been to shoot di Carraciolo against the wall of the Citadel in the centre of the city, but in the end it had been decided to carry out the grisly ceremony up here on the ridge for fear of unrest and perhaps demonstrations among the city's Italians. There was a small, overgrown cemetery near by, used once for burying smallpox victims from the city below. After the execution the body would be discreetly interred here in an unmarked grave. Old Austria had centuries of experience at this sort of thing and knew that patriots would be less inclined to keep laying wreaths if they had to trudge all the way up from Trieste to do it.

Meyerhofer and I arrived at first light in the Flik's staff car. Neither of us spoke much. Inside us our stomachs were already knotted with apprehension. Suppose that someone got nervous and talked? We stood waiting in the early-morning chill of autumn as the sky began to lighten over Lipizza. It had not been easy for us to get permission to attend. Myself, I had had a very trying interview with the Naval District Defence Commander, Rear-Admiral the Freiherr von Koudelka, to explain exactly why I thought that I ought to be present at the execution to represent the k.u.k. Kriegsmarine. In the end I had been reduced to arguing that since Fiume came within Military District No. 72, which was a naval recruitment area, di Carraciolo might technically speaking be a deserter from the Imperial and Royal Fleet. The Admiral had given me a very strange look, perhaps wondering whether I collected leather straps and manacles as a hobby.

'Hmmm. Why are you so anxious to attend this execution, Prohaska? Interested in that sort of thing are you? I've always tried to avoid it myself, ever since I was a lieutenant on a torpedo-boat and had to attend as a witness when they hanged one of my crew for stabbing a tram conductor in Zara. Leave that kind of business to the provost's department if you'll take my advice: they have a taste for it.'

'I obediently report that I have no interest in executions, Herr Admiral. It's just that my brother-officers and I are . . . er . . . outraged by this man's dastardly treachery towards his Emperor and King and his base disloyalty towards the Noble House of Austria.'

'You're *what*?'

'Outraged by his disloyalty, Herr Admiral. We feel strongly that now the swine is getting his just deserts there should be representatives there from both armed services to see justice done.'

'But Prohaska, for God's sake: from what I can see of it this Italian chap of yours is an Austrian subject only in the most technical sense of the word. Damn it all man, if we shot everyone who'd dodged service in the k.u.k. Armee and left the country these past thirty years we'd have all the ammunition factories working overtime to meet the demand. At a guess I'd say that about two-thirds of the United States Army must be technically Austrian subjects. No: in my official capacity as local naval commander I have to agree that the fellow deserves shooting, but as a sailor and a fighting soldier of the House of Austria I have to say that it stinks. If you ask me the military are looking for victims to frighten the rest, and frankly I'm surprised that you young fellows should wish to have any part in this wretched charade. This

235

cursed war's destroying everything we used to value. Even the junior officers are turning into prigs and informers now – no better than a bunch of Prussians. Frankly I'd have expected better of a Maria-Theresien Ritter. But there you are . . .' He scribbled something contemptuously on a slip of paper. 'There's your damned permission and may you choke on it. Once you've seen some poor devil tied to a post and shot you won't be so keen for a second showing.'

So we waited there on the exercise ground, fortified only by a swig from Meyerhofer's hipflask. I looked at my watch: 6.10 a.m. We had said 6.30. Would they arrive late even if they arrived at all? What would happen if they arrived before the execution party? It had always been a dictum in the tactics lectures back at the Marine Academy that in military operations, at least seventy-five per cent should be planning and no more than twenty-five per cent left to the vagaries of chance. I was beginning now to suspect, as I shivered in the early-morning chill, that we had pretty well reversed those proportions.

At last we heard the clashing and grinding of gears as a motor lorry laboured up the last steep stretch of the road that zigzagged up from Trieste. It contained the firing squad: a party of ten young and very sick-looking soldiers led by an Oberleutnant whose face expressed an intense desire to be anywhere else on earth but this particular place on this particular morning. The lorry was followed by a motor car containing the notorious Major Baumann – who always liked to be present at the execution of his victims – and a captain from the staff of the Militärhofgericht. They were accompanied by a military chaplain with two gold stripes on the cuffs of his soutane and by an army doctor with a black bag: to certify death I supposed. A working party out on the exercise ground had just finished driving a post into the stony soil and painting a whitewash line on the ground about ten paces in front of it.

Finally there arrived a second lorry, some way behind the rest of the procession. It lumbered to a halt and two soldiers with rifles and fixed bayonets got out to let down the tailboard. The lorry contained the star performer in this entertainment, handcuffed and escorted by four more soldiers. He was helped down none too gently from the lorry. He looked pale and exhausted: clearly Baumann and his assistants had still gone through their accustomed procedures even though the accused had admitted to everything from the very beginning. But I considered that, even with his hair cropped almost to disappearance and dressed in a patched infantry uniform several sizes too large for him, Major di Carraciolo still managed to comport himself with the dignity and bearing of a true officer. I glanced again at my watch. It was 6.17 already. Meyerhofer and I were straining our ears to catch any unusual noise, but so far we had been able to hear only the sounds of the city below awaking to yet another day of the war: the whistles of engines in the goods yards and the sirens of the factories. And of course the constant dull rumble of gunfire away on the Carso.

The rituals of justice now commenced. I had been present at an execution once before: my own, at a fort in the Arabian desert early in 1915, when the Turks had taken it into their heads to hang me as a spy. But this was the first time I had seen these procedures as a witness, and the whole business only served to reinforce my intense dislike of capital punishment. To kill a man in battle is not much: I had done as much several times already and would do so a number of times again. In those circumstances there is usually no time to think about it or to devise any better reason for doing it than that your victim will undoubtedly kill you if you do not kill him first. What I found obscene about this whole rigmarole as I saw it there that morning was the cold-blooded deliberation of it all: a thousand times more horrible and despicable than the lowest villain who sticks a knife into a café landlord in a brawl.

First the firing squad was marched up and sent forward one by one to pick up a loaded rifle from the ten weapons leaning against the lorry. Two of the ten had been loaded with blanks so that the young conscripts might console themselves afterwards by thinking that they had not after all fired a bullet into a defenceless man: a feeble pretence in fact, because anyone who has ever fired an army rifle will at once recognise the difference in recoil between

237

ball-cartridge and blank. That part of the performance completed, the prisoner was led forward and bound to the post. Then, to my surprise, the doctor came up with his black bag and produced a stethoscope as di Carraciolo's tunic was unbuttoned. He applied the instrument to the condemned man's chest, then felt his pulse.

'What's he doing?' I whispered to Meyerhofer.

'Making sure that the poor sod's fit to undergo capital punishment.'

'What happens if he isn't?'

'I suppose they just take him to the prison hospital, then bring him back here and shoot him when he's feeling better.'

The medical profession having done its bit for the victim's well-being, it was the turn of the Catholic Church, as embodied in the young Feldkurat, complete now with crucifix and purple penitential stole. This appeared to be causing problems. Baumann strode over, then the chaplain signalled to me to join them. Di Carraciolo was being awkward and refusing to speak German.

'Tenente,' he said to me, smiling, 'I'm afraid that the mental stress of preparing to be shot has caused me to forget how to speak German. Would you be so good as to tell these people that I'm an agnostic and a Freemason, and that I certainly don't require the ministrations of this reactionary black-frock.' I translated these remarks for the benefit of the chaplain and Major Baumann. It looked for a moment as if the latter was going to explode. A large, red-faced man who always carried his head jutting forward like a bullock, his eyes bulged and he turned purple with rage.

'How dare you, you grovelling miserable Italian serpent! You're under military law now and if I say you'll get benediction you'll damned well get it! Is that clear? Herr Feldkurat, absolve this bastard and give him the last rites at once so that we can get on with shooting him.'

'But Herr Oberst, the prisoner refuses to make confession . . .'

'DO AS YOU'RE DAMNED WELL TOLD!'

So di Carraciolo was hastily absolved and smeared with unction in nomine patris et filii et spiritu sancti. Then the chaplain was curtly dismissed to make way for a sergeant bearing a metal disc on a loop of string. It was the top of a ration tin. He hung it around the Major's neck so that it lay over his heart as an aiming-point for the firing squad. Our fellows should have been in the air a good quarter-hour already, to draw away the hunt. Where were they? Meyerhofer said that they had certainly seen the message canister as he dropped it.

My thoughts were suddenly interrupted.

'Herr Leutnant, Herr Major, if you please. It's the prisoner again: he wants to speak with you both.' I walked over once more to di Carraciolo, tied to the stake but still unblindfolded. Baumann stalked along beside me, head lowered and spluttering with rage.

'What is it now, damn and blast you? Herr Leutnant, tell this insubordinate Italian swine to stop wasting my time and to stand to attention when he addresses me.'

I conveyed these remarks to di Carraciolo.

'Please tell the Maggiore,' he said, 'that I have not been granted a last request.' I relayed this to Baumann. The response was an immediate and vicious slap around the face for the condemned man.

'Himmeldonnerwetter! Last request, you miserable horse turd . . . By God I'll have you shot . . . I mean, damn your eyes you greasy Wellischer bastard . . . '

'I only asked to be granted a last request. It is the custom I believe for condemned prisoners . . .'

I felt at this point that things were getting out of hand: Baumann was loosening his sabre in its scabbard and might soon use it. I beckoned Meyerhofer across to give me moral support. 'Herr Major, we respectfully suggest that this man should be granted a last request. It is the custom in all civilised countries.'

'There's nothing about it in military regulations.'

'No, Herr Major, but it is still the custom. Oberleutnant Meyerhofer and I are here to represent the k.u.k. Fliegertruppe and the Imperial Navy respectively, and we feel that it would be unfortunate if our reports on these events had to make reference to such an omission.'

'Oh very well then, damn you. Give the bugger his request, but quick about it: I've got prisoners waiting to be questioned back at the barracks. What does he want?'

'To make a last speech if you please, Herr Major.'

'Speech? Speech be damned: I won't allow it . . .'

'But Oberleutnant Meyerhofer and I must respectfully insist, Herr Major. It is also the custom that a condemned man should be allowed a speech from the gallows – or from the stake in this case. So if he can combine that with his last request time will be saved and everyone will be happy.'

Baumann rolled up his eyes, appealing to heaven. 'Oh all right then. What language does the scum want to speak in?'

'In Italian I think, Herr Major.' Carraciolo nodded his assent.

'Herr Oberleutnant,' Baumann called to the officer commanding the firing squad, 'do any of your men know Italian?'

'Obediently report that no, Herr Major. They're all Ruthenes.'

'Carry on then. But make it snappy, and no sedition, do you understand?'

So, lashed tightly to his post, di Carraciolo proceeded to make his last oration. Of those present I suppose that only I understood the full import of the ringing phrases as they resounded across that barren, empty plateau high up there on the ridge of the karst, as the young soldiers of the firing squad fidgeted uneasily and the waking birds twittered among the pine trees: la Patria; Italia; il Risorgimento; the sacred flame of patriotism; the liberation of the last unredeemed fragments of Italy from under the rule of Francisco Giuseppe – 'that blubber-lipped old hangman', as the Major was pleased to describe him. By now Major Baumann was tapping his boot on the ground with impatience and looking at his watch. But Carraciolo was in full spate now on the glorious privilege of shedding his blood for his nation in these last days of struggle 'to choke the life for ever from the two-headed Austrian vulture'. Future generations, he predicted, would hold sacred this spot where he had spilt his heart's blood in the holy cause of freedom. Then he turned his attentions to me. 'But what shall we say . . . si orrible, si perfido . . . of those vipers whose miserable

240

lives I once spared, but who now come to gloat over my death. Yes my Austrian friend: you were unable to get the better of me in fair combat in the air, so now you have come to watch them shoot me, helpless and bound to a post like a dog. Be thankful that they will blindfold me, so that my eyes may not look into the depths of your black soul.'

If only you knew, I thought; if only you knew. But keep on, my Italian friend: the longer you spout the more time there'll be. But where have they got to, damn them? It's nearly 6.40 already. Suddenly Baumann barked:

'All right, that's enough of that now, do you hear? You've had your say and breakfast'll be getting cold.'

'But Herr Major . . .' I protested.

'Shut up. Feldwebel – tie on the blindfold and let's get on with it.'

My heart was pounding. No time left now: two minutes at the most. As the blindfold was being bound about his eyes Carraciolo burst into song: the 'Chorus of the Hebrew Slaves' from Verdi's *Nabucco*. Even after making allowance for the distressing circumstances, I considered that as an opera singer he was quite a good sculptor. At last everything was ready.

'Execution party, load and make safe!' The bolts of ten rifles rattled.

'Execution party, safety catches off – take aim!' The rifles were levelled as the Oberleutnant stood with his sabre raised. I could see that his hand was shaking. Then a car horn honked from the edge of the exercise ground. It was a motor lorry lurching up the road with as much speed as a motor lorry could manage in those days when laden with soldiers. It stopped as the Oberleutnant hesitantly lowered his sabre and signalled to his men to order arms.

'Oh God, what is it now?' said Baumann.

As the officer marched up from the lorry and saluted I saw that he and his men were wearing the peakless high-fronted forage caps of a Hungarian cavalry unit. 'Herr Major,' said the young Hauptmann in his sing-song Magyar-German, 'I fear that I must respectfully ask you to move your firing party aside and allow my men to execute this criminal.'

'On what grounds, damn you?'

'It has come to light that since this man in a native of Fiume he is a subject of Ferencz Josef, Apostolic King of Hungary, and not of Franz Joseph, Emperor of Austria, and therefore falls under the jurisdiction of the Royal Hungarian military authorities.'

'I don't believe this,' Baumann muttered weakly, 'does that mean that you want to retry him?'

'Respectfully no: the royal Hungarian government in Budapest is quite content with the verdict of the Militärhofgericht here in Trieste. But it is also anxious that he should be shot by Hungarian troops. The matter has been referred to Prime Minister Tisza and he is quite emphatic on the point. I have the telegram here with me if you would like to see it.'

'But this is monstrous . . . outrageous. The court was assured that the man is an Austrian subject.'

'If he comes from Fiume then, by your leave, this cannot be. Fiume has been Hungarian territory since the Ausgleich of 1867.'

'But not all of it . . .'

'The suburbs perhaps not. But the main part of the city is ruled from Budapest.'

'I refuse to accept that: the court established that the man was born in the commune of Cantrida, which is Austrian territory . . .'

'. . . But with respect, his birth certificate was made out in the district of Bergudi, which is Hungarian territory . . .'

'. . . But he was later resident in the commune of Pilizza . . .'

'. . . Which became in part Hungarian territory in 1887 when the city boundary was extended.' The Hungarian captain turned to his sergeant and said something in Magyar. The man hurried across to the lorry and returned with a map. 'Here, Herr Major. May I obediently suggest that we settle the matter by asking the condemned man on which street he lived before he left for Italy?'

So di Carraciolo's blindfold was removed and, with me as interpreter, he was politely asked to indicate exactly where he had lived a quarter-century before, so that it could be decided whether

Austrian or Hungarian troops would have the the honour of shooting him. This delighted him.

'Tenente,' he gasped, 'please tell these buffoons to hurry up and shoot me, because if they don't I think that I'm going to choke myself to death with laughing.'

In the end no decision was reached as to the precise nationality of the condemned man. Baumann thereupon settled the matter in his usual manner.

'Herr Oberleutnant, clear these greasy Magyar reptiles out of the way and shoot this man.'

'Herr Major, I must protest . . . My government will take a very serious . . .'

'Stuff your protests up your arse, you Levantine gyppo. Firing party – make ready! . . .'

But the firing party was otherwise occupied. The Honvéds had moved up to the white line and attempted to elbow them out of the way. A scuffle had broken out and rifle butts were being used by the time the two officers restored some semblance of order. In the end an agreement of sorts was reached: the ten-man firing party would be made up of five Austrian and five Hungarian soldiers. However, the problem then arose of who would give the order to fire, and in what language. It was finally agreed that both officers would stand with raised sabres, and that the fatal order would be given in French. Thus it came about that the k.u.k. Militärexezier-platz above Trieste early one autumn morning in the year 1916 witnessed the bizarre spectacle of ten Austro-Hungarian soldiers standing for several minutes chanting, 'Tirez bedeutet Feuer, Tirez bedeutet Feuer . . .'

They were still busy sorting themselves out when I heard it: the first droning in the distance. Meyerhofer and I turned to gaze into the sky to north-west. There were five of them. As they drew closer we could make out four Nieuports and a two-seater which looked like a Savoia-Pomilio. As for Baumann and the inter-national execution squad, they were too preoccupied with French imperative verbs to notice anything amiss, almost until the first bullets were whining off the rocks as the leading single-seaters dived to attack. A few men tried to stand and return the fire, but most just scrambled for cover behind the lorries and among the boulders, contenting themselves with only the odd snap-shot as the two-seater came in to land on the other side of the exercise ground.

Meyerhofer and I scrambled from cover and ran to where di Carraciolo was standing, bound to the post, still blindfolded and (I should imagine) extremely bewildered by the sudden turn of events. When we were being questioned later we said that he had already cut himself free and that we grappled with him as he was about to make his escape. The reality though was rather different. Meyerhofer tore off the blindfold as I hacked at the cords with my pocket-knife. Bullets were singing about us in all directions now that the exchange between the soldiers and the circling fighters had been joined by the pilot of the Italian two-seater, who was firing bursts from his machine gun above our heads to harass the soldiers behind the lorries. I fear that even when he was free Major di Carraciolo was a troublesome customer. He had evidently been working himself up for martyrdom for several days past and was now finding it difficult to accept the sudden and dramatic change in his fortunes. I had judged at our first meeting that he was a powerfully built man, and I now had the opportunity to test that observation as he landed me a thump which knocked me clean over. In the end Meyerhofer and I had to overpower him between us, then practically frog-march him over to the aeroplane and fling him bodily into the cockpit before lying down flat as the pilot pushed the throttle forward and the aircraft began to bounce away across the stony field, followed by a spatter of farewell shots from behind the lorries. The last we saw of them they were climbing away into the autumn sky above the Gulf of Trieste, surrounded by their escorts. It was all over – at least, as far as Major di Carraciolo was concerned. The rest of us would now have to clear up the mess as best we could.

As you might expect, there was the devil's own row about it: a condemned political prisoner impudently snatched in broad daylight from under the very noses of his executioners on the outskirts of one of the principal cities of the Dual Monarchy. Meyerhofer and I both underwent prolonged and detailed questioning by the Military Procurator's department, who plainly detected a strong smell of rodents. We perjured ourselves energetically, and since we had all agreed our story beforehand they were not able – for the time being at any rate – to garner sufficient evidence to prosecute: even though Major di Carraciolo was found to have severed the ropes that bound him with an Austrian-made pocket-knife picked up on the scene afterwards and clearly marked with the initials o.p. My story that he must have picked this from my pocket before being bound to the stake sounded lame in the extreme and I knew it. I was dismissed for the moment, but was left in no doubt that investigations would continue.

As for Major Oreste di Carraciolo, he returned home to find himself a national hero. The Italians had little enough to celebrate that autumn, after a summer of appalling carnage on the Isonzo for minimal gains, so here was a wonderful opportunity for whipping up the flagging enthusiasm of the public. He was promoted to Colonel, given a new squadron of the most modern aircraft to lead, sent to tour the United States and generally lionised wherever he went. He also wrote a book about his adventures. This came out early in 1917 and a copy was procured via Switzerland and sent to me at Cattaro, where I was back commanding a U-Boat. It was all highly entertaining, I have to admit – grand opera rendered into prose – but quite marvellously inaccurate on a number of points: notably on how the Major had smuggled a message to his squadron from his dungeon in the Trieste Citadel – conveyed, needless to say, by a jailer's daughter who had fallen in love with him – and on how his oration from the scaffold (in his version they had been going to hang him) had so moved the Hungarian soldiery present that they had turned their rifles upon their Austrian oppressors with a cry of 'Viva la libertà d'Ungheria! A basso la tiranneria Austriaca!', then set him free. I got only a walk-on part in all this I am afraid: as an Austrian naval officer of Polish extraction called Brodaski whose slumbering national conscience had been so pricked by the Major's call to freedom that he had finally cast off the yoke of an Old Austria and thrown himself upon his own sword by way of expiation. Major di Carraciolo averred with complete confidence that it was his escape that had finally broken the heart of our old Emperor, whose dying words (it was reliably reported) had been: 'O Carraciolo, questo diavolo incarnato!'

There was also the condemned man's last letter to be disposed of, handed to the official of the Military Procurator's department, on the morning of the execution. Normally this would have been forwarded unopened to the dead man's relatives: even in 1916 Austria still had enough decency left to observe the proprieties in these matters. But now, since the condemned man had not been shot after all, it was felt proper to open the fat, triple-sealed envelope. It was found to contain detailed drawings for Carraciolo's memorial, to be erected after the war on the site of his execution on the ridge above Trieste. Meticulously drawn during his last days in prison, it would certainly have been a most impressive sight if it had ever been built: a sort of wedding-cake structure of naked figures – mostly young women – in white marble with the top tier bearing a statue of the man himself in his death agony, radiant as Our Lord arising from the tomb, while his Austrian tormentors fell back blinded and confounded on every side. The inscription was to have read 'Giovenezza, Giovanezza, Sacra Primavera di Bellezza!' – 'Youth, Youth, Sacred Springtime of Beauty!' – which I thought frankly was a bit thick, coming from a man who was nearing forty-five at the time of these events.

That was not in fact the last that I saw of Major Oreste di Carraciolo, that September morning as his aeroplane climbed away into the Adriatic sky. It was in the year 1934 I remember, when Polish naval business took me once again to the port of Fiume to visit the former Ganz-Danubius shipyard at Bergudi, now rechristened the Cantieri Navale di something-or-other. There had been many changes since I had last seen the city where I

246

had once been a pupil for fours years at the Imperial and Royal Naval Academy. I was now a grey-haired commodore approaching my half-century, charged with the task of organising the Polish Navy's infant submarine service. As for Fiume, it was now at the very easternmost edge of Mussolini's Italy. The years had not been particularly kind to either of us; but on balance I considered that Fiume had come off worst, as I surveyed the shabby streets of this once busy city. From being the principal – indeed only – seaport of the Kingdom of Hungary, Fiume had been reduced to the status of a ghost town, straddling the bitterly disputed frontier with Yugoslavia and split in two by a hideous rusting fence of barbed wire and corrugated iron.

Politics had done most of it, and the Great Depression had done the rest. My business in the town was to inspect the old Danubius shipyard, which was tendering to supply a number of submarines to the Polish Navy. I had concluded that in just about every conceivable respect the other tenderer, the Fijenoord yard at Rotterdam, offered the best bargain to the Polish taxpayer. So, having written out my report in my room at the old Lloyd-Palazzo Hotel on the waterfront – and having thereby added my two-pennyworth to Fiume's decline – I went out for a stroll since I had half a day to kill before I caught the Vienna train.

'Never go back' is a sound rule for life, I have always found. The prosperous city where I had spent four happy years in my youth was now a poor bedraggled ghost of what it had once been: a living graveyard where grass grew in the streets and mangy dogs scavenged among the rubbish; a necropolis peopled by cripples and beggars and imbeciles of a horror equal to any port in Italy or the Levant, but still perversely stuck on to the fringe of Central Europe: the slums of Naples without the gaiety. Increasingly depressed, I returned from the old Marine Academy – now a tumbledown 'public hospital' of the kind that serves only as a sorting-house for the cemeteries – and stopped for a drink in a café that I had once known on the Riva Szapáry, now rechristened the Via Vittorio Emmanuele or something. As I stood at the bar I heard a voice from behind me.

247

'Tenente, non si me ricorda?' I turned around. I was quite unable to recognise him at first, this wretched creature with the eyepatch and the missing teeth, sitting at a table over a stagnant coffee with a crutch resting beside him. 'Tenente, surely you remember me: your old enemy Oreste di Carraciolo, whom you helped escape that morning from under the rifles of the firing squad.'

I bought him a grappa, since he was quite clearly in great poverty. He gulped it greedily, then began to tell me what had happened in the years since we last met.

He had served with distinction for the rest of the war, he told me, scoring another eight victories, and had then returned to the studio after the Armistice, doing a wonderful trade for some time as the cities and towns of Italy vied with one another in the splendour of their war memorials. However, a measure of boredom had set in, and he had entered politics. He had returned to Fiume in 1919 with the poet-aviator Gabriele d'Annunzio and had played a leading part over the next year in that brief, bizarre episode in Europe's history the proto-Fascist 'Regency of Fiume', when d'Annunzio and his desperadoes – mostly half-deranged survivors of the Isonzo trenches – had run the place as an independent city-state on messianic, near-lunatic principles. Parades and public circuses had been a major part of the Regency – especially when the bread ran out – and the Major had been appointed as a sort of artistic director for the whole ludicrous spectacle. In the end the League of Nations had moved in, but di Carraciolo had simply returned to Italy and taken part in Mussolini's march on Rome.

This had advanced his career as a sculptor no end: for five or six years he had been effectively artist-in-residence to Il Duce. But then, in the early 1930s, as the residual wartime idealism was replaced in the Fascist movement by blackjacks and castor oil, he had quarrelled with the leadership and finally been thrown out of the party. He had refused to be quiet, so in 1932 he had been summarily arrested by the Blackshirts and so savagely beaten up that he had lost an eye and been permanently lamed. Six months later they had released him, tipping what was left of him back on to the street. Since then he had been a non-person, avoided by

248

everyone who cared for their health and deprived of all pensions and royalties. By a nice irony, his only source of income was a small monthly payment from the Austrian Republic, which had expropriated some family property in 1919 and was now paying compensation. He was understandably bitter about it all.

'Before the war,' he said, 'our slogan here in Fiume was "Give us Italy or death".' He swallowed at his drink. 'And now do you know what we have? Italy *and* death.'

That was the last I ever saw of him. I read many years later that he had not let up in his denunciations of Mussolini and his followers, whom he believed had stolen and misdirected the Fascist movement. In the end they lost patience altogether. In 1942 I understand that he was arrested one night and taken to the concentration camp on the Adriatic island of Molata. Very few people ever came back from that dreadful place, and di Carraciolo was not among those who did.

Often I think that perhaps it would have been better if we had let them shoot him there that morning. His marvellous white-marble monument would have been built, and each generation of Italian schoolchildren would now be taught about him as a great artist and patriot who died nobly for his people, not as a great artist and patriot who died miserably at the hands of his own people, after having helped bring to birth the cause which eventually devoured him.

13

LA SERENISSIMA

Hauptmann Rudolf Kraliczek was not a happy man in those early days of October 1916. Not only had the flying unit he commanded been reduced from a total establishment of eight aircraft to two, but he himself was being held responsible by his superiors both for these losses and for the fact that nothing had been achieved in return – except, that is, for a prodigious output of paper. And now, as if this were not enough, several of his officers were under investigation by the Military Procurator on suspicion of having aided and abetted the escape of an Italian prisoner.

It was all getting to be too much, and had become extremely disruptive of the form-filling and statistical compilation that was Kraliczek's reason for military existence. Something bold had to be done. Drastic measures were called for. Leadership must be asserted in the strongest possible terms. So Hauptmann Kraliczek took a sheaf of Kanzlei-Doppel paper, a pencil and a ruler, and sat down to plan a desperate last throw of the dice; an operation so daring that it would entirely vindicate the concept of long-range bombing and perhaps (with any luck) keep him safely seated behind an office desk; a project in which other men would risk their lives in a last attempt to change the direction of all those relentlessly plunging red and black and green and blue lines drawn on sheets of squared paper. In the end he must have frightened even himself by his own audacity, for the remaining two aircraft of Flik 19F were to attempt no less a feat of arms than a daylight bombing-raid on the city of Venice.

There were two main obstacles to this scheme. The first and lesser of the two was that for our Hansa-Brandenburg CIs to carry any worthwhile bombload such a distance we would have to fly to Venice with the prevailing east wind of autumn, then turn north to try and reach the nearest Austrian flying field, in the foothills of the Alps. The second – and by far the greater – of the objections was that in the whole embattled continent of Europe in the year 1916 it is doubtful if there was another city more formidably protected against air attack than Venice. A major naval port and the site of several munitions factories, the island city was protected against air-raids by layer after layer of defences: first a line of watch vessels and patrolling airships out in the Gulf of Venice, then the fighter airfield 'La Serenissima' at the Lido and the powerful flak batteries at Forts Alberone, Malamocco and Sabbioni, then further belts of flak artillery mounted on barges, then lines of tethered kite-balloons. The flying-boats of the Imperial and Royal Navy had been carrying out bombing-raids against Venice practically each day since the war with Italy began, but the defences forced them now to attack at night and flying above three thousand metres, which – given the primitive bomb-sights of those days – meant that most of their bombs had no other effect than flinging up spouts of muddy water in the lagoons.

In Hauptmann Kraliczek's master plan the problem of range was to be overcome by making the flight from Caprovizza to Venice merely one leg of a four-cornered journey. The two aircraft – Potocznik and Feldwebel Maybauer in their Branden-burger and Toth and myself in *Zośka* – would carry two of the new 100kg bombs each, slung on electrically operated bomb racks beneath the centre section, and would fly to Venice with a tail wind. We would drop our bombs, then – in the event of our still being airborne after all this – would head northwards to cross the lines north of Vicenza and land to refuel at Fliegerfeld Pergine, among the mountains near Trient. We would then take off again and fly behind the lines along the crest of the Alps as far as Villach, where we would refuel once more before flying south on the final leg of our journey, through the Julian Alps to Caprovizza. Altogether the round trip would take about two days, weather and the enemy permitting.

251

Normally, in all such missions conceived on paper by Hauptmann Kraliczek, the hostile purpose of the operation seemed very much to take second place to the business of accumulating Kilometres Flown. But this time our commander had selected a really grandiose aim for us: no less an undertaking than severing Venice's connection with the rest of Italy, by destroying the causeway-bridge that carried the road and railway line across the lagoon to the mainland. It was of little concern to Kraliczek that the entire well-equipped Imperial and Royal Navy Flying Service had been trying without success to do precisely that for a year or more: as far as he was concerned, no one had ever thought of the idea before, and anyone who dared to suggest that the Italians might have thought of it first and taken precautions was dismissed out of hand as a niggling defeatist. But there we were: orders are orders, however crazy and ill-conceived they may seem to be to the poor devils who are given the task of translating them into reality. The General Staff and the 5th Army Command had been told of the scheme and had given their approval, so who were mere lieutenants to demur? As officers of the House of Habsburg, had we not sworn to do our duty or die in the attempt?

Once again we checked our maps and made our preparations. The two aeroplanes would head out over the Gulf of Trieste just after dawn on the morning of 13 October, and, if they avoided the flak batteries and fighter aircraft off Sdobba, would make landfall some way west of the former Austrian seaside resort of Grado, then head inland and follow the railway line through Portogruaro and San Dona di Piave until they reached Mestre. We would then fly across the lagoons to attack the bridge from the east, hoping in this way to get in between the defences that protected Venice to seaward and the balloon lines and anti-aircraft batteries that guarded it against attack from the north.

It would be a hazardous business, the crossing of the Gulf of Trieste nearly as dangerous in its way as the attempt to penetrate the defences of Venice. But in between those two danger zones I did not expect too much trouble. In those days before radar, aircraft in ones and twos usually had little trouble in wandering about over open countryside. Biplanes look much alike from the ground, telephones were few in the Italian countryside in those days, and anyway, people's vision had not yet become adjusted to looking up into the sky all the time. For this reason, and in order to save weight, we decided to do without the forward-firing machine guns. On this flight we would have only the observer's Schwarzlose to protect us.

Toth and I made our final checks that October evening by the light of the petrol lamps in our hangar. Flying suits, maps, compasses, pistols, emergency rations; also razors, towels, soap and two blankets, since we expected to be away overnight and knew that such things were now in so short a supply that host flying fields expected visitors to bring their own with them. We completed our preparations and while I had a few final words with Feldwebel Prokesch and the mechanics – the ignition had been giving trouble lately – Toth went down to the village to see Magdalena.

Quite a number of our men had taken up with village girls of late. Only the day before, Kraliczek had received his first formal request for permission to marry a local girl – and had promptly set to work devising a suitable wad of printed application forms. There had already been a number of paternity suits filed against enlisted men. It astonished me how quickly our men – drawn from every province of our vast empire and totally ignorant of either Italian or Slovene – had managed to put down roots in the locality. Not for the first time it occurred to me that one of the few good things to be said about war is that it does at least do something to prevent inbreeding, which must once have been a serious problem in an out-of-the-way place like the Vippaco Valley. On the contrary, to judge by the noises I had heard among the haycocks on evening walks that summer, the men were doing everything in their power to make breeding an outdoor activity.

I went for a walk as dusk fell, and met Toth and his belle walking up the lane arm-in-arm and chatting in the curious modified Latin that they used to exchange endearments. Magdalena bade me good-evening as graciously as always; really a quite extraordinarily confident and poised young woman, I thought, considering that she was only a village girl and only nineteen years old.

'Well, Herr Leutnant, I hear that you're off tomorrow on another long-distance flight.'

'Indeed? I hope that Zugsführer Toth here has not been compromising field security by telling you where?'

'No, Zolli here is being tighter-lipped than usual and won't tell me a thing; but I hope that doesn't mean that it's going to be somewhere dangerous?'

'No, my dear young lady, nowhere in the least bit dangerous,' I said, hoping that my patent insincerity would not show through the smile. 'Please don't worry yourself in the slightest on our account. I expect in fact that it will all be rather tedious. But we shall be gone for two days at least.'

'Oh all right then. But make sure that he behaves himself and doesn't get into any scrapes. We're planning to get engaged at Christmas; sooner perhaps, if the war's over by then.'

I made my way back to my tent to turn in. It was autumn now and getting too cold to sleep under canvas in the blustering Carso wind. Still the promised wooden barrack huts had not arrived. 'If the war's over by then . . .' Some hopes: the war had been going to be over in three months ever since August 1914; but now it had been going on for so long that it was getting to seem as though it had always been with us and always would be. It was about that autumn, I remember, that the first signs became visible of that war-weariness which would eventually bring our venerable Monarchy tottering to its final collapse. The harvest had been wretched that year, as old Josef the forester had predicted. But that I suppose was at least bearable, the common lot of populations under siege. What was more disturbing was the way in which the shortages were now beginning to affect our ability to fight. Copper and brass had been unobtainable for a year or more, now that all of Central Europe's pre-war coinage and most of its church bells, statues, doorknobs and curtain rails had been requisitioned and melted down. Engine exhausts which should have been made of copper were now fabricated from thinly galvanised steel sheet. A number of Fliegertruppe pilots had already been injured by corroded exhaust stubs snapping off and flying back to hit them in the face. Steel tube radiators constantly sprang leaks.

But far worse was the shortage of rubber. Our German allies were commandeering every last scrap of the rubber smuggled in through the blockade via Holland. So the Austro-Hungarian aircraft factories were left to make do with a loathsome substitute called 'gummiregenerat' – more usually known as 'gummi-degenerat' – confected from old motor tyres, galoshes and ladies' mackintoshes shredded and dissolved in ether to form an evil-smelling, sticky substance that tore like paper and would not vulcanise. This was used for engine hoses and inner tubes. Aeroplane tyres were still made from proper rubber, but we were under strict orders to save them from unnecessary wear. The aeroplane could only run on its own wheels at take-off and landing: at all other times it was to be dragged around with a sledge fitted beneath its axles, and when an aeroplane was sent for repair to a Fliegerettapenpark we were instructed to remove its tyres and store them under lock and key in the Kanzlei safe for fear that they would be stolen in transit by other units. To judge by the number of orders on the subject that we had recently received at Caprovizza, it now appeared that the aeroplane was merely an accessory to its tyres.

But even when we had retrieved our tyres from the Kanzlei safe, discarded our skids and got airborne, things were not much better. The supply of aviation petrol had lately been 'rationalised', which in k.u.k. terms meant that still came from the same refineries, but that a thousand-strong supply agency had been set up to administer its distribution – with the inevitable result that it became much harder to get and was now of poorer quality, so that aeroplanes could rarely reach their stated speeds or service ceilings. Things were in a mess.

Still the war went on, and showed no signs whatever of ending. They said that some of the more elaborate dug-outs up on the Carso already had electric light and stoves and armchairs; even wallpaper, according to some sources. We were still due for wooden barrack huts at Caprovizza, but Flik 19 at Haidenschaft had received theirs some weeks before. Perhaps the war had now become such a fixed feature of the national economies of Europe, and the fronts so immobile, that in a few years we would be living in permanent bases behind the lines, complete with married quarters, and travelling to the trenches each day by tram.

During the summer my own ground crew had laid down a vegetable garden behind the main hangar and were now spending a large part of their off-duty hours hoeing, weeding and watering. I was quite content that they should do so: it augmented their increasingly miserable rations and even gave them a surplus to sell for tobacco-money in Haidenschaft market. I was beginning to feel though that Feldwebel Prokesch's runner beans were fast coming to eclipse the war in importance, and wondered at what point I ought to mention it at morning parade; particularly when the men dropped their work and ran out with buckets and shovels whenever a horse-drawn artillery train passed along the road. But they were still a conscientious and devoted ground crew, so I was happy to let it go on for the time being. Only Oberleutnant Potocznik looked down his nose at the whole business. After all, a warrior for the Greater German Reich could hardly be expected to approve of such distractions. What would Siegfried have said if the Nibelungs had started to grow lettuces?

The next morning was overcast, with a light north-east wind. It was still dark as Toth and I made our way out on to the field and climbed into the cockpit of our aeroplane. We made the regulation pre-flight checks, and when everything was in order called, 'Ready!' to Potocznik, seated in the cockpit of his Brandenburger parked alongside us. Potocznik called back, 'Ready!' in reply, and the process of starting the engines began, Toth cranking the starter magneto as the mechanic swung the propeller. The two engines snorted into life almost at the same instant, pouring out grey smoke and occasional gouts of blue and yellow flame as they warmed up. At last Potocznik waved to me to signal that they were about to move off. The mechanics pulled the wheel chocks away and the aeroplane began to trundle forward, lumbering heavily under the weight of two 100kg bombs slung beneath its belly. I watched apprehensively as the machine waddled slowly to the far end of the field. With two of the heaviest bombs available, plus two men and a full load of fuel, a Brandenburger was dangerously near its maximum permissible load – in fact well over it, if one took the most prudent view of that rather hypothetical figure. In order to get into the air we were going to need the longest possible take-off run, and even so I was still far from certain that the airframe would not collapse under the strain as we lifted off. Selfish as it might sound, I was more than happy to let Potocznik and Maybauer try it first.

In the event they did manage to stagger into the air, engine roaring at full throttle and the whole airframe wobbling most alarmingly under the load. Then it was our turn. We went about into the breeze at the end of the airfield. With my heart fluttering wildly I slapped Toth on the shoulder and called 'Ite nunc – celere!' Toth pushed the throttle lever forward through its gate latch and black smoke belched from the stub-exhausts as we began to creak and lurch forward. I thought that we had had it as the wheels left the ground: the wings gave a tortured groan and bounced visibly as they took the weight. But Toth was a good pilot. Somehow he managed to sweat and coax our protesting lattice of wood and piano wire up into the air, climbing ponderously to join Potocznik, who was making a circuit of the airfield – with the sedateness of an old lady in a bath chair, for fear that the strain of banking too tightly would leave the wings behind. We formed up in line ahead, Potocznik leading, and then began the slow, tedious business of climbing as we flew south-east up the Vippaco valley, gaining height at barely ten metres per thousand, a rate of climb that would have been unimpressive in a goods train.

It was not until we were above Niedendorf at the head of the valley that we had enough altitude to turn east over Sesana and fly across the karst ridge above Trieste. It was just getting light as we flew over the steep scarp-edge at Villa Opicina and saw the city spread out below us, with the still dark expanse of the Adriatic beyond. It was now just light enough to make out the white turrets of the Schloss Miramare on its headland above the sea. I hoped that this would not be an ill omen for what was already a hazardous enough enterprise: Miramare had been the residence of the unfortunate Archduke Ferdinand Max, who had ended his days in front of a Mexican firing squad. Legend had it that the castle had since brought misfortune and a violent end to all who had anything to do with the place.

When we were a couple of kilometres out to sea I noticed that we were slowly overtaking Potocznik's aeroplane: also that his engine was giving out fitful puffs and coughs of bluish smoke and leaving a strong smell of burning oil in its wake. Before long they were starting to lose height. I watched as Maybauer in the observer's seat conferred with Potocznik, then turned to me and shrugged his shoulders, shaking his head in an exaggerated pantomime. They were turning back to land at Prosecco airfield – a broken piston-ring, we learnt later. I wondered for a moment what we should do. But no, our orders were specific on the point: if one aeroplane fell out the other must press on regardless. We were on our own now.

Though only about twenty kilometres in all, the crossing of the Gulf of Trieste was likely to be the most hazardous part of our flight until we reached the outer defence lines of Venice. We had chosen to fly over the sea, in order to dodge the flak batteries on the Isonzo; but even so it was a dangerous business. The gulf was now little more than a salt-water no man's land, thickly sown with minefields and fought over day and night by seaplanes and motor-boats. If we ditched in the sea and managed to avoid drowning, then in all probability it would be at the cost of being fished out and taken prisoner by an Italian MAS boat.

As it turned out, our crossing was surprisingly uneventful. The k.u.k. Kriegsmarine's flying-boats were already at work harassing the Italian batteries at Sdobba, so I suppose that must have diverted their attention. An Italian seaplane tried to climb up after us as we made landfall at Porto Buso, west of Grado, but we were were too high up for him and a providential patch of low cloud allowed us to give him the slip while he was still climbing round in circles. After that there was not a great deal to remark upon, flying along at 120 kilometres per hour three thousand metres above the monotonous green and brown coastal marshes of the Veneto. Winter was setting in early, and I constantly readjusted my scarf to try and block out the nagging chill that kept creeping down the collar of my flying jacket. I would have huddled down behind Toth and out of the wind, but I was the officer and the job of officers was to navigate.

Not that there was a great deal of navigating to do. In fact all the help that we required in that line was provided by the gleaming railway tracks running dead-straight across the marshy fields and meadows below us. The countryside here was thinly populated, and in those days still malarial in places. I checked the few towns as we flew across them – Portogruaro and Latisana and San Dona – and also the rivers that ran down from the Alps, already swollen with the autumn rains: Tagliamento, Ausa, Livenza and Piave. I interrupted my map-reading from time to time in order to scan the sky about us for enemy aircraft. All that I saw however in the whole journey was a lone biplane in the far distance. It turned away and disappeared when it saw us: quite possibly one of our own.

The plan was that we would turn sharp south just short of the town of Mestre and then drop down to attack the bridge at low level from the landward side. But it was not until we emerged from a patch of thin, low cloud west of San Dona that I realised that – as usual – my wayward pilot had other ideas. As we sliced through the last thinning tendrils of cloud into the pallid, watery sunshine of a Venetian autumn morning I saw that below us there lay not a further expanse of wet farmland, but the vast dull pewter expanse of the lagoons east of Venice, intricately fern-leaf-patterned with a million creeks and rivulets and dotted with dark islands of reed and sedge. I was not going to stand for this: I scribbled, 'Quo vademus?' on my notepad and shoved it under Toth's arm. He glanced at it, then scrawled a note on his own pad. It read 'Aspice ad septentriones versus.' I looked to the north as requested – and saw that once again Toth's flying instinct had served us well. East of Mestre there swayed and bobbed an immense barrier of kite-balloons: three successive layers, no less, arranged at heights from about a thousand metres up to four thousand. The Corps Air Intelligence Officer had made no mention of them when we were planning the raid. If we had followed our planned route we would have flown out of the cloud and straight in among them, slicing our wings off against the steel cables and plunging to our deaths almost before we knew what had happened. It now looked as if, thanks to Toth, we had found our way into the last gap in Venice's aerial defenceworks. It was at this point I think that I finally made the decision to abandon all attempts at back-seat driving and leave the business of flying to my pilot, realising that if I was not exactly in safe hands – Toth was still a hair-raising man to fly with – I was at least with someone who was competently dangerous.

It looked as if he had decided not to try attacking the bridge from the landward side. In fact as the domes and towers of the city appeared before us across the flat expanse of lagoon it became obvious that we were going to try an entirely different line of approach – and at extremely low level. We skimmed across the water at a height of barely ten metres. I kept watch astern as clouds of waterfowl rose into the air, screaming in alarm as we roared over them. There were few defences here apart from the odd anti-aircraft pontoon moored among the reedbeds, so poorly camouflaged that it was an easy matter to fly around them. A few desultory streams of tracer curved up at us, to no effect whatever. But I saw signal rockets arching into the sky in our wake. Venice was being warned of our approach and would doubtless give us a warm welcome.

It is a noble perspective, that approach to Venice from the sea, one of the finest in the entire world I think: the Canale di San Marco with the island of San Giorgio Maggiore to port and the Riva delli Schiavoni to starboard and the Madonna del Salute and the Basilica ahead. Yet I think that of all the millions of tourists who must have seen it over the centuries, none ever had or ever again will see it as I saw it that October morning in the pale sunlight, rushing along at full throttle in a flimsy wood and canvas biplane a few metres above the waves while the Day of Judgement crashed about us, as the men on shore and aboard the warships riding at anchor let fly at us with everything at their disposal. It was terrifying yet wildly exhilarating, with rifle and machine-gun fire coming at us from every side and the angry orange and yellow flashes of flak shells bursting above as the gunners tried to get down low enough to hit us. I looked ahead into the howling air, peering over Toth's shoulder and down the side of the engine cowling. A sudden familiar outline loomed ahead – and a strangely terrible thought flashed through my brain: that even if we survived this mad exploit I might be known for the rest of my life as 'Prohaska – the man who demolished the Basilica of San Marco'. Toth lugged at the control column and we rose to skim over the house-tops, barely missing the pinnacled roof. We rushed on across the roof-tops and the sudden chasm of the Grand Canal as I grasped the bomb-release lever and tried to make out the glass roof of Santa Lucia Station ahead. I have a vivid recollection to this day of glancing down and catching a glimpse of an Italian officer on a roof-top firing a pistol at us with one hand while he pulled up his trousers with the other and a woman scurried in terror to hide behind a chimney. We swerved to avoid a church dome. Yes, there was the station! We would make our bombing-run along the bridge instead of approaching it side-on. I waited until the station canopies had disappeared below us – then yanked at the lever and felt the aeroplane leap as it was relieved of the weight of the two bombs. There was a flash and a mighty confusion of smoke astern as Toth banked us sharply away to avoid the flak batteries at the landward end of the bridge. Our mission had been accomplished: we could now dedicate ourselves entirely to the business of saving our own skins. I later learnt, by the way, that one of our bombs had damaged a bridge support while the other had landed in the mud and failed to explode. Traffic between Venice and the mainland had been held up for all of half an hour while Italian sappers carried out repairs.

Somehow we managed to climb away and evade the flak shells coming up at us from the batteries below. I can only assume that they failed to hit us because they were expecting attack only from the landward side and we took them by surprise. At any rate, after five minutes we were clear of it all, flying over the mainland. The fighter aircraft from Alberone flying field would be up after us by now, but we had a head-start on them and, relieved of its bombs, our Brandenburger was not much slower than a Nieuport in level flight. We would head across country to the River Brenta and then follow it northward to where it entered the Alpine foothills at Bassano. After that it would be a simple matter to fly along the mountain valleys and cross the front line to reach Pergine.

The Camposampiero lay below us now as we gained height, a monotonous expanse of drained marshland east of the Brenta. It should have taken us about half an hour to reach the river and turn north – had our engine not suddenly begun to splutter and misfire. Before long we were losing altitude as the revs fell away. I suspected trouble with the ignition magnetoes, to judge by the noise: at any rate, all the cylinders seemed to be firing, but fitfully, so that the engine was shaking and jolting like a cement mixer. No, there was nothing for it but to land and try to clear the trouble ourselves, then get airborne again before we were noticed. I looked down. At least the fields hereabouts looked level – mostly green pasture – and there were few villages. I shook Toth's shoulder and pointed down. He nodded, and a couple of minutes later we were bumping down on to as remote a stretch of meadow as I had been able to find.

It sounds hazardous I know, touching down on a field in enemy territory; but flying in those days was utterly remote from anything practised nowadays, and emergency landings were an occurrence so normal as to be scarcely worth remarking upon. With her large-wheeled, generously sprung undercarriage and a landing-run not much longer than a football pitch, our Brandenburger had little to fear from a forced landing – in fact could probably have landed across a freshly ploughed field without coming to any harm. In any case, the field on which we touched down was a smooth expanse of grass preferable in every respect to the rutted, stone-littered stretch of ex-ploughland so grandly described as k.u.k. Fliegerfeld Caprovizza. As we slowed down and the tail-skid bit the grass I pointed Toth towards a clump of poplars. The Brandenburger would be horribly conspicuous on the ground with its pale yellow wings and tailplane, so I was concerned to get us into the shadow of the trees as quickly as possible. Our pursuers would not be far behind us, but I hoped that they would be too intent on scanning the sky ahead to look downwards. I have always found that people tend to miss things they do not expect to see.

This turned out to have been a very bad decision on my part. We discovered as much when our slow, wobbling progress across the field suddenly became glutinous, then stopped altogether even though the propeller was still spinning as before. I clambered over the cockpit edge and sprang to the ground to see what was the matter – and promptly sank up to my ankles in the soft cattle-trodden mud. We had taxied into a patch of grass-covered marsh and were now embedded up to our wheel hubs. Rev the engine as he might, Toth could not dislodge us, stuck now like some immense bluebottle buzzing frantically on a fly-paper. I squelched around to the tail and shoved my shoulder under the tail-skid to lift it, hoping to lessen the drag. But the wheels only sank further into the soft, black ground. We both cut brushwood to lay beneath the wheels, and tried levering under the axle with a fallen branch, but it was no use. We were trapped, stuck fast in a field deep in enemy territory with no hope whatever of getting free unless we could find horses or a motor lorry to drag us out. Toth turned off the engine as I leant against the fuselage, wiping my brow and panting from exertion.

It was only then that I saw them. They must have been standing there for some minutes watching us as we strained and heaved. They stood silent, in a row, gazing at us with black eyes and tanned, dark-whiskery faces: straw-hatted and dressed in ragged shirts and trousers, each of them carrying a bill-hook or a fork. We were captives. No doubt these villagers had come to prevent our escape while others had gone to fetch the carabinieri. I wondered suddenly what one did to pass the time in a prisoner-of-war camp. Then a sudden mad urge took hold of me. Why not? We had nothing to lose, and these labourers were certainly poor and probably illiterate as well, living in a remote area and incapable of reading even newspaper headlines, let alone aircraft-recognition handbooks. It was certainly worth a try. Why had I sweated through four years of Italian classes at the Marine Academy if not for such moments as this? I decided to address myself to a sturdy middle-aged man who looked as if he might be some sort of foreman or village elder.

'Buon giorno,' I bade him, smiling. 'As you see, we have been forced to land here by engine trouble. I wonder, might you have a telephone near by, or failing that, might you be able to help us extract our aeroplane from the mud so that we can take off and fly on our way?'

'Who are you, strangers, and where are you from?'

'Two airmen of the Corpo Aereo flying from our base at Venice to the airfield at Bassano. But tell me,' I asked, 'do you have a carabiniere or a priest in your village?' I was worried that even if there was no policeman hereabouts there might at least be a priest who would be well enough informed about the world to recognise an Austrian aeroplane when he saw one.

'There is no priest in our village, and no carabinieri nearer than the barracks in Castelfranco.'

'Good – I mean, what a pity. Can you then perhaps help us to get free?'

The man turned to a small boy standing near by, gaping at us. 'Mauro, run to the house of Ronchelli and tell him to bring his plough-oxen; also a coil of rope.'

The barefooted child scampered away. Really, this was all too easy. I supposed that it was quite possible that these ignorant rustics had never seen an aeroplane before, at least on the ground.

I began to feel myself a rotter for having deceived them so smoothly.

'My friends,' I said, 'we will see that you are well rewarded for your trouble when we reach our airfield. What is the name of this village?'

'Busovecchio di Camposampiero, if it's any business of yours,' said the foreman. 'But tell me one thing that puzzles me: what's the meaning of those black crosses on your aeroplane?'

I swallowed hard – then a brilliant idea struck me.

'There are to signify that the aircraft was blessed by the Pope, at a ceremony in Rome earlier this year. He anointed it with holy oil and the crosses were painted on to mark the places where he applied it. As you will see, they represent the five wounds of Our Lord.'

He grunted and craned his neck to look at the markings on the upper wing. 'I see. In that case then His Holiness must have used a step-ladder to get up there.' He sounded dubious, but I supposed that this was just his way, since he seemed a surly man at the best of times.

By now the small boy had reappeared, leading two wheezing, steaming, cream-coloured oxen and with a coil of plaited straw rope slung about his shoulder. We attached this to the under-carriage axle, and after five minutes or so of straining and lugging we had the aeroplane free, standing once more upon firm ground. While this was going on we had stopped to look up into the sky as a flight of aeroplanes passed by, heading north at speed. There seemed to be four Nieuports and a two-seater of some kind, but they had evidently not seen us. So much the better, I thought; we can get airborne and proceed to Pergine at a discreet distance behind them.

The farm labourers watched as Toth and I removed the aluminium panels around the engine so that we could get at the two magnetoes on the front of the cylinder block. I was thankful now that my first submarine command, *U8*, had been powered by Austro-Daimler petrol engines and that my Chief Engineer had given me a thorough course of instruction in their workings. It would be me who would have to get the engine running again. Toth was a superb flier, but with him it was as entirely a matter of instinct as with an eagle. Otherwise he was about as completely unmechanical as it is possible to be. If he had not been, then I think he would not have been such a formidable pilot, since only a man totally indifferent to machinery could have maltreated airframes and engines with such ruthless disregard.

Like most Porsche-designed inline engines the Austro-Daimler had two spark plugs in each cylinder, each row run off its own magneto and coil. This was to guard against spark failure and should have been foolproof since it was most unlikely that both magnetoes would fail it once. But as I removed the bakelite magneto cover I saw that, if both were still working, both were in an equally decrepit state. The contact-breaker electrodes were badly eroded. They must have been made from some wretched wartime alloy and the constant sparking was wearing them away. Standing orders were to change each magneto every fifty flying hours, so that one would always be near-new; but over the past month Feldwebel Prokesch had been forced to ignore this instruction owing to the lack of spares from the Fliegerettapen-park. All that I could do now was dismantle the two contact breakers and clean them up as best I could with a file, then put the whole thing back together again and hope for the best.

It was not until after midday that we finally put the cowling panels back in place and prepared to leave. While I worked on the magnetoes I had been obliged to field a barrage of embarrassing questions from the villagers, who had now been joined by a crowd of women and children.

'Your man doesn't say much does he? Is he a deaf-mute?'

'No, he's a little quiet it is true, but he's an excellent pilot. It's just that he's a Sardinian.'

'Sardinian? Looks more like an ape to me. Get him to say something in Sardinian then.' I turned desperately to Toth and whispered:

'Toth, di aliquid, per misericordiam Dei.' He obliged with a few sentences of Magyar.

'Couldn't understand a word of it. That's the trouble with the Sards: all pig-ignorant Mauritanos. Worse even than Sicilians.'

At last we were ready, I swung the propeller and at the second attempt, to my intense relief, the engine sprang into life, firing with less than perfect smoothness but certainly well enough to get us airborne and over the mountains to Pergine. It warmed up, straining the undercarriage against the logs which we had stuck beneath the wheels as chocks, while I climbed into the cockpit behind Toth. The village elder climbed up behind me and presented me with a large rush basket covered with a cloth. It contained some loaves, a cheese, a large black-smoked country sausage and a straw-wrapped bottle of brown local wine. I turned to thank him, ashamed to have practised such a suave deception upon these simple people. A sudden horrible thought had struck me. Suppose that word got around later and they were hauled in by the authorities on a charge of aiding and comforting the enemy? From what I knew of the Italian military I doubted whether a plea of terminal ignorance would save them from an army penal battalion.

'Some provisions for your journey,' shouted the head-man above the noise of the engine. 'Remember to send us a postcard when you get back to Austria.'

I was speechless for a few moments.

'Austria . . . but . . . we are Italians.'

'Don't give me that horse-shit, Austriaco. We may be poor here but we aren't stupid.'

'But . . . why did you help us then?'

'We're anarcho-syndicalists in this village. Anyone who's against the landlords and the carabinieri is on our side. If we lived in Austria we'd help Italian fliers just the same. That's why we don't have a priest here: we burnt the bugger out ten years ago and since then no black-frock has dared show his nose in these parts. We'll do the landlords next, come the revolution. Here, here's some reading-matter for your flight.' He thrust a wad of papers into my hand: pamphlets with titles like 'The Death of Property' by Proudhon and Prince Kropotkin's 'Uselessness of Laws'. There were also some copies of the newspaper *La Rivolta*. I glanced at the back page of one of them and saw an article entitled 'Chemistry in the Home, No. 35: The Properties of Nitro-Glycerine'. 'Anyway,' he said, 'be on your way now before the carabinieri arrive and be thankful you landed among us and not elsewhere.'

I shook hands with him and thanked him as he stepped down to the ground and Toth revved up the engine. As we began to trundle across the field they all waved and gave us clenched-fist salutes. 'Arrivederci!' the foreman shouted, 'and remember, mankind will never be happy until we've hanged the last priest with the guts of the last king. When you get home tell your old Emperor from us that when we've finished with King Vittorio the Short-Arsed we're coming for him next!'

So we climbed away from that field as the cawing rooks flapped around the poplars below us and the villagers stood waving. In the years since, I have never heard anarchists mentioned except as wolves in the guise of men: bomb tossers, assassins and enemies of the human race. Yet these were the only anarchists that I ever met in person, and I must say that they treated us with every kindness.

We landed at k.u.k. Fliegerfeld Pergine at about three that afternoon after an uneventful flight, following the River Brenta as far as Bassano del Grappa then climbing over the hills and the front line until we saw the twin lakes of Caldonazzo gleaming in the distance. The Pergine flying field, home of Fliegerkompagnie 7, was as rudimentary as all other airfields on the Italian Front in those days: a hummocky grass field surrounded by a makeshift jumble of wooden huts and canvas tent-hangars. What made it different from Caprovizza was the alarming approach along the side of a vineyard-clad mountain with a rather vulgar nineteenth-century mock-Renaissance castle half-way up. Down-draughts and thermals from the mountainside made us skip and bounce like a rubber ball as Toth brought us in to land.

Nor were matters at all helped by the fact that after an hour or so of relatively smooth running, the engine was beginning to misfire once more. One thing was certain: that before we flew another kilometre on our circuitous journey back to Caprovizza we would have to get the magnetoes replaced. Flying over the Alps in October would be a risky enough enterprise without having a faltering engine to contend with. As Toth taxied up to the aircraft parking area in front of the hangars (I was walking alongside to guide him since he could not see direct ahead), I had decided that I would report to the commanding officer of Flik 7, then place the aeroplane in the hands of their workshop while I telephoned Caprovizza to tell them that our mission had been successful, but that we would be getting home late.

Toth switched off the engine and climbed stiffly down from the cockpit, red-eyed and grimy-faced after four hours in the air and three hours or so standing by in a muddy field while I filed away at the contact breakers. He stretched his arms and yawned while I strode up the steps of the Kanzlei hut. We had fired the agreed yellow and white flares as we came in to land, but no one had watched our arrival. In fact there was nobody to be seen. Had there been an outbreak of cholera, I wondered? Had the Allies chosen the place to try out a death ray, or some devastating new poison gas that made its victims evaporate into thin air? I opened the door and entered the outer office. Still no one to be seen. I peered into the inner office just as a young Oberleutnant with an unbuttoned tunic and dangling braces caught sight of me. He made no effort to rise from his desk.

'Yes, who is it?'

I saluted smartly. 'Ottokar Ritter von Prohaska, Linienshiffs-leutnant of the Imperial and Royal Navy, currently attached to k.u.k. Fliegertruppe Flik 19F at Fliegerfeld Caprovizza.' He stared at me, uncomprehending. I continued. 'I have the honour to report that my pilot Zugsführer Toth and I have just landed after successful completion of a bombing mission against the lagoon bridge at Venice.'

He went on staring at me, as completely baffled as if I had just announced my arrival from Valparaiso by way of Winnipeg.

'What are you doing here then?' I began to wonder whether I was dealing with a mental case, perhaps posted here as a convalescent after acute shell-shock. So I tried to be patient.

'We are from Flik 19F at Caprovizza and we have just carried out a bombing-raid on the city of Venice. We are here on our way home, which takes us north of the lines in the Dolomites.'

'Caprovizza? Never heard of it. Is that on the Eastern Front?'

By now I was growing more than a little irritated. 'Not when I last looked. It is just outside the town of Haidenschaft.'

'Where's that?'

I was beginning to drum my fingers on the desk. 'On the Isonzo Front, in the sector held by the 7th Corps of the 5th Army. But surely you must have been expecting us: this was all arranged last week by the High Command itself?'

'Haven't heard anything about it here; not a thing.' He rummaged beneath an untidy heap of paper on the desk, muttering to himself as he did so. 'You wouldn't believe the amount of rubbish Divisional Headquarters sends us each week. Honestly, we need another Adjutant full-time just to sort through the circulars . . . Ah, this might be it.' He pulled out a crumpled telegram and began to read it, eyeing me suspiciously from time to time. He broke off to look out of the window, then addressed himself to me. 'This says two aeroplanes. How come there's only one of you?'

'Our companion aeroplane, piloted by Oberleutnant Potocznik, developed engine trouble and turned back just before we started to cross the Gulf of Trieste. I think that they must have landed safely, but I'm not sure. If you want me to find out I can ask when I telephone my base to tell them that we've arrived. Do you mind. . . ?' I reached for the telephone on his desk, but before I could touch it he had snatched it away.

'You can't use the Kanzlei telephone for operator calls: the Kommandant's very strict about economy – orders from Army Group Headquarters.'

'But that's ludicrous. I have to telephone Caprovizza or we'll be posted missing. How am I to contact them if I can't use your telephone?'

'Herr Kommandant says we've got to use letters wherever possible.'

'But . . . we'll be home long before a letter gets there.'

'Well, you could always carry it with you. Or if you're set on telephoning there's a post office down in the town.'

'Anyway, where is your commanding officer? And everyone else on this airfield, if it comes to that?'

'The Old Man's in hospital in Trient. He got the horrors from drinking grappa. Keep well clear of it if you'll take my advice: it's foul stuff. As for the rest of them, it's been a bad month for crashes, so we're a bit low on aircraft and flying crew. We no sooner get a batch of stupid bastards from the flying schools than they all write themselves off on the mountainside. We've only got one aeroplane serviceable – an Aviatik on patrol now up Asiago way – so I thought I might as well give everyone the afternoon off, especially seeing as it's Friday anyway.'

'I see,' I said, detecting the drift of the conversation, 'so would I be right in assuming that we will get no assistance at this flying field today in replacing two worn-out magnetoes?'

'Perfectly correct: we aren't authorised to carry out major engine repairs in the workshops here, and anyway we fly Lohners and Aviatiks – Hiero engines you see. Yours is a Brandenburger isn't it?'

'How perceptive of you to have noticed, Herr Leutnant.'

'Thought so: Daimler 160. No luck I'm afraid. Flik 24 uses the other end of the field but they've got German Fokkers, Benz engine, so no use either.'

'So what do you suggest? We can't stand here on your flying field until we take root.'

He yawned and swung his boots on to the desk. I was beginning to take a most intense dislike to this young man.

'Better try the Flep down in Trient, they might be able to oblige.'

I saluted and turned to leave. 'Thank you for nothing then. Servitore.'

'Don't mention it. Oh, and by the way . . .'

271

'Yes?'

'Be a good chap and move your aeroplane; it's blocking the entrance to our hangars.'

We moved the aeroplane across the field, Toth and I, laboriously pushing it along by ourselves since there were no ground crew to be seen. I left Toth on his own, bidding him to leave me something from the provisions given us by the anarcho-syndicalist peasants of Busavecchio, and set off on foot for Pergine village.

I returned empty-handed. It was Friday afternoon, so the post office was closed, and anyway the entire town was shut up for some church festival or other, St Thuribus of Mongrevejo, or the Veneration of the Authentic Elbow of Padua or something. It was late afternoon when I trudged back, footsore and dusty. There was no help for it: we would have to get airborne once more and fly the ten or so kilometres to Fliegeretappenpark 3 on the other side of the town of Trient. So I swung the propeller once more and the engine coughed and backfired into motion, pouring out clouds of smoke as we lurched unsteadily into the evening sky.

We had some difficulty finding Flep 3 from the air and making our landing. As we did so a bespectacled major came running out to us, waving his arms, and gave me a most severe dressing-down as I sat in the cockpit, even before the propeller had stopped turning. It was strictly forbidden, he said, for aircraft to land within the perimeters of the Fliegeretappenpark without first submitting a written application and being given express permission. Otherwise all aircraft whatever must arrive on a railway flat-bed truck or by a special aeroplane transporter wagon (horse- or motor-powered) with wings and tailplane ready dismantled. I said as politely as I could that this was an emergency landing, and that we were here until repairs could be made for the simple reason that I doubted whether the engine would start again. In the end he consented to let us talk with a staff-sergeant engine fitter in one of the workshops, saying that it was no business of his and we were to get ourselves off his site as soon as we could fly.

In complete contrast to his commanding officer, the

Stabsfeldwebel could not have been more helpful to us – at any rate, so far as he was able. Which, sadly, was not very far at all. He stood looking at the naked engine after we had removed the cowling panels. He shook his head slowly.

'Sorry, Herr Leutnant, but I can't be of any help. We haven't got a single spare magneto in stores for a 26-series Brandenburger.'

'But that's ridiculous: the 160hp Austro-Daimler must be the most widely used engine in the entire Imperial and Royal Flying Service.'

'Not around here it isn't, Herr Leutnant. The Brandenburger Fliks in the 11th Army sector use Mercedes 160s, on account of the mountains. They reckon the Mercedes is slower accelerating but a bit better at altitude. The trouble is that they use Bosch magnetoes, and this batch of Austro-Daimlers use Zoelly. And anyway . . .' (he glanced at his watch) '. . . it's half-past five already – sorry, 1730 hours – so my lads couldn't help you now even if we had anything in stores.'

'Why ever not?'

'Sorry, Herr Leutnant, but it's a Friday and they all went off duty half an hour or more ago.'

'Gone home? But this is monstrous. What about duty-men? God damn it, man, there's a war on: the Front's not twenty kilometres south of here.'

He looked at me for some time: the sad, mildly reproachful gaze of one who has no time for such juvenile follies. He was a solid, calm, kindly-looking man in his early fifties, with the air about him of a watchmaker; or the sort of cobbler whom you almost feel the urge to thank when he tells you that he can't have your dress-uniform boots ready for the gala on Thursday after all on account of how you just can't get the leather these days.

'War or no war, Herr Leutnant, you won't get them working shifts here. This is an aircraft-repair park so it would rate as a rear echelon even if the Italians were just across the fence. The men work peacetime hours here and go home early Fridays.'

'What the devil do you mean, peacetime hours? We've just

273

come from an extremely dangerous mission over Venice in broad daylight. I've just been counting the bullet holes and I've got up to fifty-seven already. And while we've been getting our backsides shot at your men have been pushing off early!'

He nodded in agreement, utterly incapable of being provoked to anger. 'Fair point, Herr Leutnant, fair point: there's a lot in what you say, I don't deny that. But the fact is, all my men here are reservists – 1860 class, one or two of them – who've had nothing to do with the Army for thirty-odd years, then got called up. They're in uniform, but they'll be blowed if they're going to keep army hours. Half of them are local men anyway and have families down in the town.'

'What about military discipline?'

'Oh, Herr Leutnant, Herr Leutnant. We get little enough work out of them as it is, and if I started coming the old eiserne Diszipline mallarkey here we'd get none at all. Military discipline my arse, if you'll pardon the expression: you can't get skilled engine fitters for love nor money now, so I have to keep them on a loose rein if I want to get anything done at all. As it is they're on army pay, which is about a quarter what they'd be getting if they were in the munitions factories. Anyway . . .' (he adjusted his spectacles and turned to me), 'if you like I can take out those contact breakers myself and clean them up a bit for you. That'd at least get you up the valley to Gardolo. If I remember rightly they've got a few old Aviatiks up there with Flik 17. They've got Austro-Daimler 160s, so they might have a couple of magnetoes lying around in stores.'

In the k.u.k. Fliegertruppe one word that was in constant use in those years was the noun 'Kraxe', derived from the verb 'kraxeln', which is Austro-German for 'clamber up' but which had become fliers' slang for a pile-up on landing. It was something that happened with depressing frequency around Haidenschaft, with the mountains towering above and savage, unpredictable winds whipping down the side valleys. Yet of all the flying fields of the South-West Front I think that none could have been more perfectly designed for kraxelling than Fliegerfeld Gardolo, some

274

kilometres up the Adige valley from Trient. In the gathering darkness the landing at Fliegerfeld Gardolo was even more alarming than that at Pergine. The airfield lay in the narrow valley bottom with the walls of mountain soaring almost sheer on both sides for a thousand metres or more, so that landing was rather like touching down in a vast horse trough. On balance I was glad of the gathering dusk, in that I was at least spared the horror of seeing the precipices looming above us as we lined up to land. I thought that we had had it just as we reached the edge of the flying field. An eddying back-draught of wind off the mountainsides had created a sort of air-hollow, into which we suddenly dropped ten metres or more like a house-brick, to the sound of a great squeal of anguish from the wings. It took all Toth's skill to bring us level again before the wheels bumped the ground.

But when we had landed safely we found that we might as well not have bothered. True, Flik 17 had a number of Aviatik two-seaters on the strength with 160hp Austro-Daimler engines. But, like Flik 19F, they had not seen a new magneto in months. All that they could suggest was that we stayed overnight with them and took off again in the morning to fly further up the valley to Feldfliegerschule 2 at Neumarkt, where they suspected there might be some magnetoes in the stores, because the school had once had a couple of pensioned-off Brandenburgers from an earlier series, but had recently written them both off in the course of flying lessons. We thanked them, staked our aeroplane down for the night (a chill wind was already moaning down the valley), then ate a most welcome meal with them in their mess hut before bedding down in a stores tent. Tomorrow was Saturday.

14

SUNDAY MOUNTAINEER

It was drizzling when we got up: thin rain turning to sleet. We refuelled at Gardolo after breakfast. We could not use Flik 17's petrol without a requisition signed by no less than three officers of a rank of Major or above. These were finally found for us at a neighbouring supply depot. They signed the forms for us with every sign of irritation before driving away in a pre-war sports car with luggage and two rather nice-looking army nurses in the back: off (we were told) for a couple of days touring in the Tyrol on a tank filled, no doubt, with government petrol. I could only hope that it stayed fine for them. As for Toth and me and our bullet-riddled, faltering aeroplane, it was yet another leg of our miserable begging-tour of the airfields and supply depots of the South Tyrol.

In the course of a half-century or more spent in the armed services I have often had cause to remark upon the fact that, among the military, comradeship, honour and kindliness all decrease the further one gets from the front line. In my younger days I would often wonder why this should be; but it was only with time that it gradually dawned upon me that it is precisely those qualities of honesty, selflessness and courage that tend to land men in the firing line – and their opposites that facilitate the wangling of safe little jobs in the rear. The truth of the matter is that two world wars were, for Europe, nothing but a vast experiment in negative Darwinism, in which the best died and the worst survived to breed.

Nowhere was this more apparent to me than at Fliegerettapen-park St Jakob, a repair workshops located just outside 11th Army

Headquarters at Bozen and specially attached to the army divisions in the Tyrol. We arrived there mid-morning after finding that the Feflisch at Neumarkt could be no help whatever, having just closed down for half-term. The Kommandant was anything but pleased to have two flying mendicants turn up at his door on a Saturday morning in a consumptive aeroplane, one of them a naval lieutenant and the other an apparently cretinous Magyar NCO.

'This repair park is strictly for machines from units on the Tyrolean Front, do you hear?' he shouted, waving a cane at us as we formed up beneath the balcony of the ex-Gasthof that housed the unit offices. 'We're attached directly to 11th Army Command and we aren't here to offer repairs to any vagrants who happen by. Go on, be off with you, I say! No, I don't care a copper farthing what General-Oberst Boroević will say: General-Oberst Boroević is on the Isonzo Front, not here, and as far as I'm concerned he might as well be in Patagonia. I don't care if you do either, you insolent bugger. Just clear off back where you came from – you and your pet monkey.'

Utterly dejected, we ambled back around the workshops – deserted and locked for the weekend – to where our aeroplane stood. There was no hope whatever of going on now, even if we had anywhere left to go. No, we would just have to abandon the aeroplane and make our way back to Caprovizza by train – perhaps even riding on the roofs of goods wagons, since I had barely ten kronen left in my trouser pockets. For God's sake, were we in the same army as these people or weren't we? If the Italians had captured us at Busavecchio they could scarcely have treated us worse. All that we had to eat now was the leftovers from the food that the villagers had given us. Toth sat miserably beneath a wing on the wet grass as I removed the engine cowling panels yet again to see if anything could be done with the magnetoes.

As I had suspected, they were past praying for, except perhaps via St Jude the Patron of Hopeless Cases. The contact-breaker electrodes had now worn away and honeycombed to the point of disintegration. As I tinkered I suddenly heard a voice over my shoulder, speaking in heavily accented German.

'Excuse, Excellence, but wad kin' of engine is dat?'

I turned around to find myself looking at a Russian prisoner of war, one of the many employed about the supply bases here in the Tyrol as porters and labourers. He was leaning on his broom and looking with intense interest at what I was doing: in his early twenties I would have thought, with a wide, honest, slightly Asiatic face and wearing a peaked cap and khaki blouse. I answered in Russian, which I was able to speak fairly well from Polish.

'An Austro-Daimler 160hp, soldier. But why the interest?'

'Oh, it's nothing, High-Born One. It's just that before the war I was an apprentice at the Putilov Works in St Petersburg, and I used to work on Daimler engines. We were building them under licence: the 80hp kind for motor cars. They're the same as this one only a bit smaller. But those contact breakers of yours are done for.'

'Thank you, but I had gathered that.'

'Can I have a look at one?' I handed him the corroded electrodes and he examined them carefully. 'Of course,' he said, 'I could make you some like these if I had the tools. It's not much of a job. I used to do things like that for my apprenticeship tests.'

'What's your name?'

'Trofimov, Excellency: Arkady Feodorovich, Junior Corporal, 3rd Battery, 258th Regiment of Field Artillery. I got captured at Lutsk in the summer. There's about twenty of us here, mostly Siberians.'

'Do they treat you well?'

'Well enough, Excellency. The food here's no worse than in Russia and the local people are all right. They don't give me anything interesting to do though, only sweeping up and collecting salvage.'

'What do you mean, interesting?'

'Work as a motor mechanic. I've offered to be the Herr Kommandant's driver but he only laughs and slaps me round the head and calls me an ignorant peasant from the steppes. But honestly, I could do the job much better than most of the people here.' His eyes suddenly pleaded with me. 'Let me have a go at those contacts at least. I could do you a replacement set in an afternoon if I could get some files and a vice and a grinding wheel.'

So I took Lance-Corporal Trofimov up on his kind offer. True, the workshops were locked up for the weekend. But Toth had acquired a number of strange skills in his seminary, apart from that of seducing nuns in marrow-beds, and one of these was the picking of locks. Before long Trofimov was at work in a shed, singing to himself as he filed away and the grinding wheel screeched and sparked. By the end of the afternoon he had fashioned us two perfects sets of contact-breaker electrodes; and not only that but replaced them, reset the magneto timing and removed and cleaned the sparking plugs. They were test-running the engine when I returned from Bozen carrying a large ham sausage which I had bought for Trofimov as a present with my remaining ten kronen. He was pleased, but was more anxious that I should recommend him for a vehicle fitter's course. I said that I thought this might cause problems under the Hague Convention, but I promised to see what could be done.

'You see, Excellency,' he said earnestly, 'this war's not going to go on for ever, and when I get home I'm going to help build a new Russia: a Russia of the twentieth century, with motor cars and aeroplanes and electricity. I've taught myself to read since I've been here, you know.'

I often wonder whether he got home after the war, and what happened to him later.

We spent the night at St Jakob, lying on the field under the aeroplane's wing, sheltered against the unseasonable chill only by our blankets and an old tarpaulin procured for us by the Russians. The Kommandant had returned from Bozen unexpectedly that evening and had caught us in the workshop. We told him that the door had been open, but we could see that he did not believe us.

He kicked us out, then locked up the hut and posted a sentry with instructions to fire if he saw anyone trying to break in again. For good measure he ordered us to be on our way at first light next morning, saying that he was running a base repair unit and not a hostel for tramps.

We woke and breakfasted on bread and tea supplied us by the Russians, who seemed delightfully free of petty prejudices on the matter of nationality. They even made us packed lunches to take with us, and provided us with an old winebottle full of 'samgonka', a probably lethal home-made vodka distilled from mashed potatoes. All they asked in return were some old newspapers. Puzzled, I asked why. After all, most of them looked illiterate even in Russian, and all that I had was an old copy of the *Triester Anzeiger* which someone had left in the cockpit. No matter, they said: they only wanted it for rolling cigarettes from the foul-smelling tobacco which they grew for themselves on the airfield. I asked whether they would prefer proper cigarette papers? I was a smoker myself and had a few boxes in my jacket pockets. No, they said; newspapers had more flavour, on account of the ink.

After breakfast we washed, shaved and smartened ourselves up, more for reasons of morale than of appearance. It was a good thing that we did, however, for just as we had climbed into the cockpit and were about to signal to Arkady Feodorovich to swing the propeller (a privilege which he had wheedled out of me), we heard the distant honking of a car horn. We turned to see the Herr Kommandant running across the field towards us, followed some way behind by a large, open motor car.

'Stop, stop!' he shouted. 'Wait a moment if you please!' He was panting fit to choke by the time he reached us, to a degree where a heart attack looked imminent. 'Herleutnanteinmomentbitte!' he gasped, '. . . if you please . . . just wait a moment . . .'

I must say that after our reception the day before I was in no mood to be polite.

'Herr Major,' I replied coldly, 'a letter thanking you for the particular warmth of your hospitality will be sent to you when we get back to our base. In the mean time, if you think that we are trying to leave without paying the bill I can show you the receipt.'

'No . . . No . . . There is something most important. Please to wait a moment . . . I shall explain.' The motor car was close enough now for me to see that it was no ordinary army staff car but the very plushest, most sumptuous vehicle that one could hope to find in that category, short of the Emperor's limousine itself. It was a beautiful sleek Mercedes of the very finest pre-war make, though now painted over in khaki drab. In the back were two very high-ranking officers indeed. Toth and I scrambled out to stand by our aeroplane at the salute. Could it be an archduke? No, there was no black-and-yellow eagle-pennant on the mudguard. An orderly opened the door and the two officers got down. One was a general, the other a full field marshal: a smallish, slim man in his early sixties with grey hair and a moustache in which traces of blond still showed, and with a nervous, rather irritable air about him. This, I realised, was none other than Field Marshal Franz Conrad, Freiherr von Hötzendorf, Commander-in-Chief of the entire Austro-Hungarian armed forces. As he walked up to me I saw that he had a constant faint twitch running from the corner of his mouth to his left eye. He surveyed me for a moment, then smiled.

'Stand easy,' he said. 'What's your name?'

'Prohaska, Excellency. Ottokar, Ritter von Prohaska, k.u.k. Linienschiffsleutnant.'

'Aha, a sailor. Of course, you're the Maria-Theresien Ritter aren't you? The one who commanded a U-Boat and then got bored with it and took up flying. How are you enjoying it?'

'I obediently report that I enjoy it well enough, Excellency,' I said, lying in my teeth as prescribed by regulations.

'Splendid, splendid. Well Prohaska, I've got a little errand here that's right up the street of a man of your calibre. Can I rely upon you?'

'You may rely absolutely upon Zugsführer Toth and myself, Excellency.' I saw that he looked rather doubtful about that when he saw Toth, but he said nothing.

'Well Prohaska, I have here a despatch-case of documents for you to deliver for me: papers of such importance that they must be flown direct to their destination in conditions of the utmost secrecy by a courier of the greatest courage and integrity. That is why we have chosen you.'

'I obediently report that I am flattered by your confidence in me, Excellency, and I shall guard these documents with my very life. But might I enquire where you wish them delivered?'

'You were flying to Villach, were you not? That is what the Herr Kommandant told us when we asked if there was an aeroplane ready to take off.'

'I obediently report, to Villach.'

'Well, I want you to fly a little further than that: in fact all the way to Imperial and Royal Supreme Headquarters in Teschen.' This was indeed quite a journey: Teschen was on the very north-eastern edge of the Monarchy, quite near to my own home town on the borders of Prussian Silesia. 'It should take you about four hours, my staff officer assures me, but if you could make it shorter I would be grateful. You are to make your way up to Brixen and then follow the valley to Lienz, where you can cross over into the Mur valley and fly down to Vienna before heading across Moravia. You will refuel at Judenburg, and during that stop you are on no account to leave the aeroplane, do you understand? When you arrive at Teschen flying field, for reasons of secrecy a lady will be waiting with a staff officer in a green Graef und Stift motor car to collect the documents. In the event of your being forced down by engine failure or other mishap on the way you will keep the documents with you at all times to prevent them from falling into unauthorised hands. This whole mission, I need hardly stress, is so secret that not even our own people must know about it, except for those who need to know. Is that all clear?'

'Perfectly clear, Excellency.'

'Good then, fill up your tanks with petrol and be on your way at once. Austria flies with you.' He turned to leave.

As he did so the base Kommandant bowed and bobbed his way up to him. 'Excellency, if you please, your signature will be required upon these petrol requisition forms. Aviation fuel provided for this unit cannot be supplied without authorisation . . .'

'Damn you and your bureaucratic pettifogging – fill the aeroplane up or you'll find yourself in the front line before you can draw breath.' As if to underline what he had just said, Conrad took the proferred sheaf of forms and flung them contemptuously over his shoulder to scatter in the mud. 'Furthermore, imbecile, I wish you to be aware that this flight is of such secrecy that there must be no record of it whatever in the airfield logbook, is that clear? Try to pay more attention to what your superiors say to you in future.' And with that he turned and got into the car without saying a further word to any of us and without giving a single wave or even a backward glance. I supposed that the cares of the supreme direction of the Monarchy's military effort for two long years must excuse such behaviour, which in anyone else would be considered plain rudeness.

We took off just before 0800. It was not going to be an easy flight by any means, with the weather coming down over the Alps, but it should still not be too arduous. We would by flying along mountain valleys most of the way, and beyond Vienna the country would open out into the plains of Moravia. I thought that it might take about five hours, weather permitting and inclusive of the stop for refuelling at Judenburg. My spirits rose as we climbed away from Bozen. We had been specially selected to undertake a vital mission to deliver despatches – perhaps even plans of attack for a grand war-winning offensive – which might decide the fate of the Monarchy. The gravity of our task and our pride at being chosen for it gave a keen sense of urgency to the proceedings, especially after two miserable days of creeping from depot to depot like vagrants begging cigarette ends.

But quite apart from that it was a marvellous jaunt in itself, a sudden and totally unexpected break from the routine business of wartime flying. The engine was purring like a well-fed cat, the tank was full of petrol and the sun had at last broken through the clouds to reveal the full autumn glory of the Dolomites before us. Even the aeroplane seemed to sense the mood, climbing with us like Pegasus. And of course, not the least of the reasons for a certain high spirits was that when we arrived back at Caprovizza sometime on Monday, a whole two days late, I would be able to confront the odious Kraliczek with a smug smile and say, 'Sorry, Herr Kommandant, can't tell you where we've been: secret orders from the High Command and all that. You had better ring up the Commander-in-Chief if you want further details.' Let me see now, if we arrived at Teschen about 1300 hours and waited half an hour to refuel they could not reasonably expect us to get back to Caprovizza that evening, not in mid-October. Elisabeth was staying with my aunt in Vienna now. I smiled to myself as I imagined her delighted surprise a few hours hence when the housemaid Franzi would usher me in, still wearing my flying kit, stopping off for an unexpected overnight visit.

Toth and I had conferred briefly about the route just before we took off from St Jakob. I had indicated the line on the map and he had nodded and grunted his assent. But now I saw that we were deviating from our course, heading more to the south to fly over the northern edge of the Brenta Dolomites and cut off the corner where the Rienz flows into the Eisack, just north of Brixen. No matter, I thought: these mountains were low – about 2,500 metres or so. The aeroplane was maintaining her altitude with no trouble and we would save a good few kilometres, picking up the railway line as planned at Bruneck or Toblach. I looked southward to see the great massif of the Marmolada, Queen of the Dolomites, looming on the horizon with her permanent lace cap of snow: so vast that I could make out no sign whatever of the trench lines and belts of barbed wire that now scarred the summit.

It was only after we had been flying for twenty minutes or so that I began to have misgivings about Toth's choice of route. Away to northward an indigo cliff of stormclouds was bearing down on us, its sunlit upper edges that curious orange-brown colour that betokens snow. It was moving fast, blotting out mountain peak after mountain peak of the High Alps to the north of the Rienz valley. I leant out into the rushing wind to look ahead – and saw to my dismay that, while the storm had not yet reached us, it was only because it was advancing in a deep crescent shape, with its two horns cutting off our escape both to west and to east. We could not fly under it because of the mountains, we could certainly not fly over it, and we could no longer avoid it by flying around it. Our only line of retreat now was to turn around and fly due south – straight towards the Italian lines with a pouch of ultra-secret documents on board. No. I swallowed hard; duty left only one course open: we would have to try to fly through it, hoping that it was only a line storm and that we would emerge on the other side before we ran into a mountain-top.

The edge of the storm hit us like a moving brick wall, flicking us up and dashing us down again in the violent turbulence at its edge. Toth struggled with the control column to bring us level again as we buried ourselves in the swirling eerie murk inside the cloud. I was right: it was snow, the first of that early and bitter winter. It was wet stuff, but thick and mixed with freezing rain. We had taken a compass bearing before we entered the clouds, but it was hopeless: before long any sense of up and down and sideways had been lost and jumbled, however desperately we checked the spirit-levels to try and judge our angle. Sometimes the curtains of snow were falling down: sometimes they seemed to be falling upwards. Or was it us moving relative to them? I could no longer tell, wiping the snowflakes off my goggles as demon air currents inside the cloud attempted to pull our fragile aeroplane to pieces.

I wiped the snow off my goggles once more and peered over Toth's shoulder at the altimeter in the dim yellow light. Holy Mother of God! We had lost nearly a thousand metres already. I looked up at the wings – and at once saw why. A thick crust of ice was forming on the doped canvas. Toth stood up in the cockpit with the control column gripped between his knees and tried to bang it loose with his fists. I scrambled out over the cockpit edge in the howling slipstream, too frightened to be afraid any longer, and kicked desperately at the ice on the lower wing with the heel of my boot. It cracked, and sheets flew away astern. But it was hopeless: fresh ice formed almost as soon as the old had gone, stuck to the wings by the freezing rain. We were coming down, but where? I peered out into the swirling sheets of snow, billowing like theatre curtains in a wind. At last the air cleared a little. I saw a dark smother beyond. Perhaps it was mountain forest in the distance, glimpsed through a chink in the cloud. I looked again – and realised aghast that it was indeed a mountain side: sheer naked rock-face hurtling past about four metres from our port wingtip! Toth saw it as well and lugged at the column to bank us away. At that moment the clouds chose to part to let the sunlight pour through.

These might well be the last moments of our lives, but I still caught my breath at the vision of unearthly splendour as the sun streamed through the eddying snow to reveal where we were; flying along a high mountain valley surrounded on every side by vast precipices and snow-covered pinnacles so fantastically shaped that any stage-set designer who had reproduced them would have been denounced as a madman. But we had to land. I leant out and looked below. We were only ten or fifteen metres above a level, smooth-white surface: perhaps a high mountain pasture covered in the first of the winter snow, I thought. Well, there was no choice: a sheer wall of rock towered a few kilometres ahead of us, so high that it would have taken us half an hour to climb over it even in calm weather. The snowstorm would soon close in again. It was now or never. I signalled to Toth to come down. He nodded. But amid the crazed vortices in the heart of the storm it was impossible even for such a pilot as Toth to maintain our height: in the end we managed a landing of the kind described by my old flying instructors as 'ground three metres too low': in other words dropping out of the air on the last part of the landing to belly-flop on the ground.

It was no mountain meadow under snow: we discovered that the moment our undercarriage touched and was ripped off. It was a glacier, its jagged, rasping surface of ice-lumps temporarily smoothed out by feathery, drifting snow into an illusory flat sheet. We skidded along it for perhaps fifty metres before coming to a halt: us two and what was left of the aeroplane after each ice-claw had torn off its portion. It seemed to last several minutes, even though I suppose that it must have been no more than a few seconds. I came around smothered in snow and scalded by water hissing from the fractured radiator tubes. All was deathly quiet now apart from the moaning of the wind. It was snowing again. I picked myself up from on top of Toth's still form on the cockpit floor. The forward bulkhead had collapsed and the engine had been smashed back into the crew space to join us. I checked myself limb by limb. I was shaken and badly bruised and suspected a couple of cracked ribs, but otherwise everything seemed to work. I dragged Toth out. He was alive but unconscious, bleeding profusely from a gash on his forehead. I found the first-aid kit and bandaged the wound after making a compress of snow to reduce the bleeding. Then I found the bottle of samogonka given us by the Russians and uncorked it to trickle a few drops on to his tongue. This brought him back to consciousness as brutally as if I had stuck a red-hot poker into his mouth. He moaned something, badly concussed. I tried to move him and he howled with pain. Both his ankles were broken. I found the blankets and wrapped him up as best I could, then took the saw from the tool kit and hacked off the upper wings at the roots to make a rough shelter over him. Then I huddled up with him to keep him warm and myself out of the snow.

It must have been about three hours before it let up. The sky cleared and the sun shone once more to reveal that we were in one of the very highest valleys of the Dolomites, way above the snowline and far from human help. I had to go and get assistance. Luckily I had done quite a lot of mountaineering in my youth when my brother Anton and I were junior officers, back in the days when ample leave made up in some degree for our miserable salaries. I knew in particular that I must not attempt to follow the glacier down to wherever it went, winding out of sight among the peaks: my brother and I had both nearly perished on the Oetztal glacier in 1908 when we had attempted something similar. No, I must leave Toth and head for the edge of the glacier, then climb the rock-face of the valley side and get over the ridge into the next valley, which might be deeper and extend below the snowline.

I was loath to leave him, still dazed and confused. But in the end I brought our remaining supplies up to him, gave him a half-syringe of morphine from the first-aid kit and put together a flare made from the hacked-open fuel tank filled with sump oil and petrol and with a wick of rag for him to light if he heard an aeroplane above. Surely we would have been missed at Judenburg by now. I also moved up the machine gun near him, cocked it and told him to fire it if he heard searchers. For myself I took the aeroplane compass and the rocket pistol. Before I left I assured Toth as best I could in my execrable school-Latin that he would soon be rescued: that the Dolomites were really not much more than a mountain park criss-crossed with paths, where even maiden aunts could come 'rock-climbing' in their long loden skirts and little hats with the cord around the brim. As I set off I wished that I felt as confident as I sounded about the suburban tameness of this particular Alpine range.

I took the greatest care crossing the glacier, probing gingerly in front of me with a broken wooden strut. Even so I slipped into a small crevasse at one point and spent five or so terror-filled minutes dragging myself back over the edge, lying exhausted on the ice with wildly beating heart before I was able to get up and go on. But at last I reached the edge of the glacier, a chaotic jumble of ice-blocks and fallen boulders where the mountainside and the billions of tonnes of ice had spent millennia grinding against one another. The climb up the rock-face must have taken me a good hour and a half. My flying-boots had smooth soles and the first of the winter's snow was making the crags slippery, while the wind-eddies tried their best to pluck me from the cliff as I panted in the thin air. Then at last, after an infinity of scrambling and clawing, I found myself on the saw edge of the ridge, perhaps a thousand metres above the glacier, where I could just make out the wreck of the aeroplane lying in the snow. I peered over the edge, fearful that I would find nothing but another glacier. But no; I was looking down into a deep valley: so much deeper than the one that I had just climbed out of that dark blue-green forests of pine grew in it below the snowline. I could see no sign of human habitation, but in the Dolomites forests meant trackways, and trackways led to villages. All that I had to do now was descend and follow the mountain streams down to safety. I took one last look at the wreck below, to fix its position in my mind so that I could guide the rescue party. Then I began the descent.

I had often noticed when mountaineering that coming downhill is usually far more arduous than going up. In this case the going was particularly tough because the rock-faces were mostly north-facing and were still festooned with loose and highly dangerous patches of rotten ice from last winter, treacherously masked by a light veil of fresh snow. It took me upwards of three hours to get down to the treeline. As I neared it, sliding down a rock scree and across snow patches, I paused. It was human voices. Quickly I fumbled a red flare into the rocket pistol and fired it into the air. Then I saw them, among the small trees at the edge of the forest. I ran down towards them, slithering in the snow and shouting to attract their attention. They turned and stopped. It was only as I got to within perhaps twenty metres of them that I stopped too. They were soldiers, in peaked caps with snow-goggles and with pairs of skis slung on their backs with their rifles. But there was something not quite right about the cut of the grey uniforms; also a rather un-Austrian swarthiness about their features. I stopped and we stared at one another as the awful truth dawned upon me: that these were not Landschützen as I had innocently supposed, but Italian Alpini.

Various thoughts raced through my brain in those few seconds. We were effectively prisoners of war now, but at least Toth would be rescued swiftly when the Italians sent up a search party. Anyway, I had to get food and rest for a while. My leather flying overalls were wet through from snow, heavy and clammy to feel. Nor had I eaten since that morning. I was in such a state that quite frankly I would have surrendered myself to a tribe of cannibals if they had been prepared to give me a place by the fire and some food before eating me. But then, quite suddenly, a chilling realisation struck me: the secret papers! The entire fate of the Monarchy might depend upon them. If the Italians found Toth they would also find the aeroplane, and would certainly find the pouch of documents which I had entrusted to his care when I left him. No, I must try to confuse them: play for time, then escape if I could and get back to our lines – which surely could not be far away – and get a search party sent up from our side. What could the life of my pilot weigh against the whole Austro-Hungarian war effort? A higher duty beckoned.

The patrol leader was a sergeant: a dark, sharp-featured young man who spoke with the characteristic accent of the South Tyrolean valleys, where many of the local people in those days still used a strange patois of Latin called Ladinisch. He pushed up his goggles and regarded me suspiciously.

'Aviatore austriaco? Österreichischer Flieger?'

'No, no,' I replied, 'sono aviatore italiano.'

'Why did you shout to us in German then?'

'I thought that you must be an Austrian patrol. I'm lost and I thought that I must have come down behind their lines. But thank God I'm still on our side.'

'Who are you and from which airfield?'

'Tenente-Pilota Giuseppe Falzari, Squadriglia 27ª at Feltre flying field. I was flying a Savioia-Pomilio but got lost in a snowstorm and had the engine cut out. I managed to land somewhere up there on a pasture in the snow, but I've no idea where I am now. I've been wandering all day and had to cross a glacier.'

He looked puzzled. 'Funny. We got a telephone call to go up and look for a crashed aeroplane, but that was an SP2 from San Vittorio with two men on board. There must have been some mistake. But anyway, we've found you now wherever it was that you flew from, so let's get you down the mountain. Can you walk?'

'Yes, yes, no trouble. I came out of the landing unhurt. But I'm very tired so I would be glad if you walked slowly.'

The patrol was based at a rifugio: a small wooden climber's hut perched precariously on the edge of a snow-covered precipice on the chilly north face of the mountain, about two thousand metres up. It was barely big enough to hold the ten men and their equipment, but it had a stone hearth and log fire blazing most invitingly as I entered. Before long my wet leather overalls were steaming gently as I sat by the fire devouring a bowl of spaghetti with some cheese crumbled over it. A delicious and almost forgotten smell of real coffee pervaded the hut from the enamel pot brewing in the embers. It would have been a little heaven on earth after the cold and wet and exhaustion – had it not been for the consciousness of Toth lying up there on the glacier with two broken ankles and night drawing on, with a leather pouch of top-secret documents resting beneath his head.

There was also the more pressing problem of my host, Sergente Agorda. He was a talkative man, and not only talkative but unpleasantly inquisitive, with sharp eyes and (I found to my dismay) a detective's instinct for the small inconsistencies in people's stories. My Italian was convincing enough to pass muster, I knew; the problem was rather that of making up a plausible life history for myself as I went along. The Sergeant's men were not too much trouble: to my surprise, most of them were not Tyroleans but came from the Abruzzi or even further south. But Agorda himself was a tougher proposition. He was a local man – his peacetime job had been as a mountain guide in Cortina d'Ampezzo – but he had travelled widely enough in northern Italy to be able to pick me up on more than one detail of my story.

'We've been using this rifugio as a base all summer,' he said, pouring me a steaming tin mug of coffee, 'but we're going to have to move down the mountain in a few weeks I reckon. The snow's early this year and they all say it's going to be a hard winter.'

'Has there been much fighting up here?'

'Not a great deal so far. There's been a lot going on down in the Tofane and the Marmolada these past few months, quite heavy some of it. But for the time being it looks like neither our generals nor the Austrians want these mountains badly enough to do any serious fighting over them.'

'Where are the lines? Are they far from here?'

He laughed. 'Lines? There's no lines up here, any more than there are for you fellows up in the air. The Austrians are over the other side of the massif and we're over here and so far it's been skirmishes most of the time. Sometimes their artillery chucks a few shells over and we chuck a few back, but mostly it's patrols taking a few shots at one another up among the cols. We lost two men back in March when the bastards brought a machine gun up on a sledge, but we ambushed them the next month and killed three of them, so it's about quits at the moment. Funny thing really, but we know most of them, the Landschützen I mean. In fact some of our local men and some of theirs are cousins and brothers-in-law. Crazy really: fighting over mountains when the mountains could wipe out the lot of us if they chose.' He topped up my mug of coffee. 'That happened last spring over on Monte Cristallo, you know? There were two companies shooting it out on the mountainside with their rifles. Then some stupid sod tossed a hand-grenade and that started an avalanche and neither our lot nor the Austrians have been heard of since. No, Tenente, if you've earned your living up here as a guide then believe me you treat the mountains with a bit of respect.' He paused and stoked the fire. 'But that's enough about us, Tenente, what about yourself? Have you been long in the Corpo Aereo?'

'Eighteen months, almost.'

'What were you in before, if I might ask?'

'The cavalry.' I adjusted the collar of my still tightly buttoned leather flying jacket to conceal the naval officer's jacket underneath.

'Which regiment?'

'Er . . . the Aosta Dragoons.' This seemed a good choice: in 1916 a very high proportion of flying officers in all the air forces of Europe had come from the cavalry, tired of sitting behind the lines and waiting for the breakthrough that would never happen.

'Aosta Dragoons? But you come from the Veneto don't you?'

I could hardly deny this: the Habsburg Navy had been entirely Italian-speaking until the 1850s and the version of the language taught in the Marine Academy had been the soft, lilting Venetian dialect which one used to hear in those days all the way down the Adriatic coast as far as Corfu. This man's questions were becoming impertinent, but I sensed that it would be unwise to – how do you say? – pull rank and tell him to mind his own business.

'Yes, from Pordenone if you must know. My father was a wine merchant there.' I saw at once that I would regret this lie. His face brightened.

'Ah, from Pordenone? I know it well. I have cousins there. But on which street, if I might ask?'

'The Strada della Libertà.'

'Which number?'

I swallowed hard. I was not enjoying this game at all. 'Number twenty-seven.'

'Then you'll remember old Ernesto the drunkard and his wife. Were you there when it happened?'

Mother of God, help me, I thought.

'No, should I have been?'

'That's odd then: it was all over the papers when they found her buried in the cellar.'

'I was away at military college at the time: I only heard about it later.'

'At military academy? They must have sent you there young then. It was about 1892 or 1893. She was a cousin on my mother's side. But if your father was a wine merchant he must have been a member of the Guild.'

'The Guild?'

'The Guild. Surely you know about that affair? The Guild of San Salvatore: all the wine-trade people were in it. They were making wine out of horse-beans with logwood and sulphuric acid. A lot of them went to jail when people started dying from it. The whole of Italy must have heard of it.' He got up. 'Here, let's put another log on the fire, shall we? It's perishing cold in here.'

In fact, far from being perishing cold, the interior of the hut was

293

like a Turkish bath. I divined now what the game was: to force me to open my flying jacket and reveal the uniform underneath, without the risk of being put on a charge of insubordination if he simply ordered me to open it and I turned out to be an Italian officer after all. It was a cunning ruse: inside my flying overalls I was already beginning to feel little rivulets of sweat trickling down my body. Agorda stuck another couple of logs on the blazing fire, sending a blast of sparks up the chimney. He turned to me.

'Tenente, wouldn't you like to remove that flying suit? You'll catch a chill sitting there in damp leather.'

In the end I tried to gain some relief from the stifling heat by removing my overall trousers and belt. I was wearing field-grey breeches and puttees which I hoped would look indeterminate-coloured enough in their sweat-soaked state to pass for Italian uniform. As I placed them on the table the Sergeant took the belt and the holster attached to it and removed the pistol inside. 'Where did you get this Steyr pistol, Tenente?'

'I picked it up on the Isonzo last year and decided to keep it. It's better than our issue.' This was nonsense and he must have known it: the 9mm Steyr pistol must have been one of the most substandard military firearms ever devised. I only carried mine because regulations required it – and to put a bullet through my head if need be to escape death by fire. He examined it.

'Nice piece of work. But these overalls – did you capture them from the Austrians as well? Ours are black, not brown, and they have a fur lining. I know because we had to go up last month to bring down the body of one of our fliers. But don't you want to take the jacket off?'

'No, no thank you. These jackets have to dry on the body, otherwise they get stiff.' I realised that if I did not make my escape now it would soon be too late. 'Sergente, I must go outside – you understand.'

'Ah yes, the latrine's out along the path there. I've kept it swept of snow.'

I made my way out into the air. Its chill was like a slap in the face after the smothering warmth inside the rifugio. It was snowing again and beginning to get dark. I looked about me in the swirling flakes, knowing full well that several keen pairs of eyes were watching my every move from inside the hut. Damn it! The skis had been locked away in a shed. I would have to find some other means of escape. I made my way to the rickety privy and shut the door. It was a sheet-metal box like an enlarged biscuit tin perched precariously on a creaking wooden frame above a slope of snow falling away to invisibility in the murk below. What was I to do? Only the back of the privy was invisible from the hut. I tried the back wall, above the board with a hole in it which served as the seat. A sheet of tinplate was loose. Slowly and carefully I worked it free and pulled it out. Snowflakes came pouring in through the gap. It was about a metre and a half long by perhaps three-quarters of a metre across. It might be worth a try. I placed it on the seat, stood on it and bent the front edge upwards to make a crude toboggan. I had my leather gauntlets in my pockets, so I put them on to save my hands from being cut to pieces by the edge of the metal. It seemed like suicide: for all I knew the slope below might run down into the darkness, then turn into a five-hundred-metre sheer drop. I stood on the seat holding the makeshift sledge in front of me, trying to nerve myself to jump. Suddenly the door rattled.

'Tenente, are you in there? Open this door and come out with your hands above your head or I shoot at the count of ten. Uno, due, tre . . .' I quickly said the Act of Contrition – then launched myself into space.

The belly-landing on the filthy snow beneath knocked the breath out of me, and I almost rolled over with the tin sheet on top of me. There were shouts from above, and lights, then pistol shots as I hurtled away into the dusk down a near-vertical ice-slope. But luck was with me. An unknown distance later I came to an abrupt halt in a snowdrift among trees. I quickly abandoned the toboggan and floundered away among the trees on foot. Voices could be heard further up the mountainside, but that was the last I saw of them.

I have no idea where or how long I wandered that night. I had left the compass behind and it was snowing again while the cloud had come down, so I could only wade through drifts and scramble along up rock-faces and down ice-slopes in the hope that instinct was leading me towards the Austrian lines. This went on until near dawn the next morning, when the first light revealed me traversing my way down a high north slope across a steep snowfield above a forest. I was worn out and utterly, hopelessly lost, all sense of direction gone. I paused to regain my breath, knee-deep in the rotten grainy snow of last winter. I realised suddenly that something was wrong, even if at first I put it down to the light-headedness of exhaustion: I had stopped walking, but I was still moving perceptibly downhill. I tried desperately to scramble sideways on to firm snow. Too late. I went over, then was buried by the sliding white mass, then surfaced for a moment, then went under again like a swimmer being swept over a weir. Stifled, tumbled, rolled over and over, I lost all sense of where I was in the grinding, roaring smother.

At last all was still, and I knew that I was dead: buried metres deep by the avalanche. It seemed strange that sensation should still persist after death. I wondered when they would come for me, whoever they were who acted as doorkeepers for this world beyond. I suppose that I could have lain like that for minutes or for hours: I have no idea. I remember that my first thought as I peered through snow-clogged eyes was that, whether they were angels or devils, neither type of attendant in the next world had ever been described to me as wearing puttees. I looked up. A dim shape stood over me. For some reason I spoke in Italian.

'Who are you? Take me with you.'

The mysterious being spoke at last. The accent was broad Tyrolean.

'Warum sprechen Sie Italienisch? Wir sind Österreichern.'

They sent patrols up all that day and the next, even called aircraft up from Bruneck to join the search. But the snow had been heavy that night up in the high Dolomites, and in any case after my wanderings I had very little idea where Toth and the wreck of the aeroplane might be. It was a particularly savage winter in the Alps that year. A record ten metres of snow fell on the Marmolada in December. By January 1917 the wretched troops in the line had declared an unofficial armistice in order to fight for sheer survival against the weather. Tens of thousands perished in avalanches, swept away and never seen again. Sentries froze to blocks of ice in their rock-bound eyries while entire companies were buried without trace in a few minutes by the terrible blizzards that raged along the mountain ridges. By the time the spring came Zugsführer-Feldpilot Zoltan Toth and the wreck of the aeroplane Hansa-Brandenburg CI number 26.74, *Zośka*, must have been buried metres deep in that unknown glacier.

And I suppose that they must still be there, the last flier and the last aeroplane of the Imperial and Royal Austro-Hungarian Flying Service. The glacier will make its grinding way down the mountain trough, a metre or so a year, until one summer it will melt and crumble open at the bottom of the valley to reveal Toth's frozen body and the remains of the aeroplane, perhaps thousands of years hence, when we are all dust and the Habsburg Monarchy (if anyone remembers anything about it at all) will be known only to scholars: one with the kingdom of the Seleucids, the Egyptian Second Dynasty and all the other gaudy, tinsel-and-paste empires that were to have lasted for eternity.

They gave me the job of breaking the news to Magdalena, there in the front room of her father's house in Caprovizza. I had expected tears, but the girl just became dreadfully quiet, the colour draining from her normally rosy face as if someone had opened a tap. I tried to comfort her by saying that her fiancé was not killed, just missing, and that a patrol might yet find him alive in the mountains. But I knew that it was hopeless: that he had probably died of cold and shock on the first night. And I think that she knew as well. I left her parents to comfort her and walked back to the flying field. On the Carso the guns were thundering away in the preparatory barrage for the Ninth Battle of the Isonzo, the Italians having pushed forward some three kilometres since mid-September, at a cost of about 150,000 lives. What did one more life mean, in the face of such monstrous carnage, one bereaved Slovene country girl when widows and orphans were being created every day by the thousand? The world had gone mad.

I returned to find a visitor waiting for me in the Kanzlei hut. It was a major from the Air Liaison Section at 5th Army Headquarters. He questioned me closely about the mission which had led Toth and me to our fateful flight over the Alps. In the end he shut his folder and prepared to leave.

'Well Prohaska, I can't say that this business leaves a very pleasant taste in the mouth.'

'Why not, Herr Major?'

He smiled a bitter, mirthless smile. 'I suppose that I'd better tell you, even though I ought not to according to the strict letter of regulations. Those documents of yours.'

'Yes?'

'They weren't secret papers at all: they were love-letters from Conrad von Hötzendorf to his wife.'

'They were . . . what? How do you know?'

'The field police stopped the car at Teschen flying field and questioned them. Everyone in Vienna's nervy at the moment of course – oh, you wouldn't have heard, would you? Someone shot the Prime Minister yesterday morning in the Café Meissl und Schaden. The place is buzzing with rumours of a German putsch to get rid of Karl when the old Emperor dies. Anyway, they questioned them both and it appears that Conrad's been writing to her every day of the war without fail.'

'I suppose that's very wise of him,' I said. 'He stole her from another man I hear, so perhaps he's worried she'll do the same to him if he doesn't keep an eye on her.'

'Quite possibly. Anyway, he had been away from Teschen for a week touring the Tyrolean Front, so the letters had built up and he roped you fellows in to fly them to Teschen for him: special express delivery at the expense of the War Ministry. Conrad loves little flourishes like that, I understand. Pity that your pilot had to lose his life for it.' He rose to leave. 'Anyway, sorry and all that. You were quite outrageously misled, but there's nothing we can do about it. And even if we could put our own Chief of Staff in front of a court martial for misuse of army personnel and property, it still wouldn't bring back your Hungarian chap. Sorry.'

He left, and Hauptmann Kraliczek came in. As he sat down a sudden surge of bile welled up in my throat: a violent loathing for all the field marshals and generals and desk-strategists who poured away men's lives like water to feed their own preening vanity. I gazed at Kraliczek's pasty, self-satisfied features before me and something snapped.

'Herr Kommandant, I have a request to make.'

'What is that, Herr Schiffsleutnant?'

'I wish to transfer from this unit and resign from the k.u.k. Fliegertruppe. It's all one to me where I go: the U-Boats, the trenches in the worst part of the front line – I don't care any longer.'

He smirked behind his spectacles. 'I see: the Maria-Theresien Ritter's courage has deserted him. I understand – the Flying Service is too dangerous for him. And what are your reasons for requesting this transfer, pray? I cannot simply enter "Cowardice" on the form, you understand.'

I tried to remain calm. 'My reason for requesting the move, Herr Kommandant, is simply to be as far away as possible from a creeping thing like you: a commanding officer of a flying unit who, so far as I am aware, has never once flown in an aeroplane and whose sole talent is for designing forms and sending brave men to their deaths in order to draw lines on pieces of graph paper afterwards.'

'Watch your tongue, Prohaska: what you have just said is court-martial talk and might . . . might lead me to demand satisfaction from you.' I noticed that his voice trembled as he spoke these words.

'Herr Kommandant, you will surely be aware as I am that the *K.u.K. Dienstreglement* absolutely forbids an officer to challenge his superior to a duel in wartime. If it did not then you would have been cold meat long ago.'

'But this is outrageous! You are quite obviously unhinged.'

'I obediently report that if I am unhinged, Herr Kommandant, that is because I have seen so many good men's lives squandered these past three months to no effect. In fact I have just been informed that my pilot was sent to die of cold and injuries on a glacier high up in the Alps so that a field marshal's wife could get a packet of letters a day earlier than she would have done if he had put them in the post. This does not please me and I want no further part in it.'

'Nonsense. Your duty is to carry out whatever tasks your superiors give you. An order is an order. Anyway . . .' He sniffed. 'I can't see what you're making such a fuss about. Your pilot fellow was only a ranker . . .'

They told me afterwards that when the orderlies rushed into the office they found me kneeling on Kraliczek's chest with my hands about his throat, choking the life out of him as I endeavoured to drive his head through the floorboards. Another five seconds or so, the Medical Officer said, and I would probably have been up for court martial on a charge of murder. For my part I remember nothing of it, only a blind, murderous animal rage such as I have never known before or since. I had killed men in battle before that and would do so again; but never would I be filled with such a pure, intense, single-minded, near-ecstatic lust to take someone's life. It was not Kraliczek's odious features that I saw there as I gripped his throat, it was Magdalena's pale, shocked young face; and Toth dazed and moaning glassy-eyed on that cursed icefield; Conrad von Hötzendorf's self-satisfied little nervous twitch; and Rieger's charred, grinning skull smouldering among the embers that first day on the field at Caprovizza – all the poor faceless, helpless victims caught up in this collective lunacy that called itself a war.

There was an awful row of course: Maria-Theresien Ritter or no Maria-Theresien Ritter, war or no war, most armies in the world regarded it then and (I believe) still regard it to this day as a fairly serious breach of discipline to have attempted to throttle one's commanding officer. What saved me in the end from court martial and a possible firing squad was a quite fortuitous piece of luck. For the next day, on 19 October, Flik 19F ceased to exist and was officially merged once more with its parent unit Flik 19. My new commanding officer was not therefore Hauptmann Rudolf Kraliczek, who was currently lying in hospital at Marburg, but Hauptmann Adolf Heyrowsky of Flik 19.

'Well Prohaska,' he said, 'I must say that you've gone and got yourself into a pretty little spot here and no mistake. If Oberleutnant Meyerhofer hadn't got you into the ambulance straight away and off to the loony bin in Trieste the Provost's people would have come for you and you'd have found yourself in a cell in the Caserne Grande. I gather from this report here that you attempted to inflict grievous bodily harm on Hauptmann Kraliczek?'

'With respect Herr Kommandant, that is incorrect: I tried to kill him.' Heyrowsky stuck his fingers into his ears.

'Tut tut, Prohaska; you really mustn't say things like that or there'll have to be a court martial after all. No, I didn't hear what you said. My eardrums have been troubling me lately: altitude and all that. You're a flier yourself so I'm sure you understand. No, I think that if we play this one intelligently we can still get you off the hook.'

'Might I enquire how, Herr Kommandant? I am undeniably guilty of a death-penalty offence. Court martial is mandatory in such cases.'

'Well, it is and it isn't. Evidence has to be gathered, and there were no witnesses I understand: at any rate, none who'd testify against you. And anyway, Flik 19F has just been merged with Flik 19, so while the papers are being transferred from their Kanzlei to ours I would imagine it to be quite possible that some might get mislaid. I think that if we can discreetly lose you along the way as well . . .'

'Lose me? How?'

'I gather that you were only seconded to the k.u.k. Fliegertruppe from the Navy, so you're not technically on the strength. I also understand from contacts of mine in Pola that they're short of pilots in the Imperial and Royal Naval Flying Service. Now, I may be a fighting soldier but I haven't served twenty years in the k.u.k. Armee without learning something about paperwork. If we're quick we can get you up to Divacca and on to the next train to Pola before the Military Procurator's people come here looking for you. They've still got a file open on you after that affair with the Italian pilot chap.' He looked at his watch. 'Eleven-thirty-five precisely. Get your kit together and report back here in fifteen minutes while I talk with the lorry driver. Mustn't make your departure too public I think. There'll be a rail warrant waiting for you at Divacca.'

'But Herr Kommandant . . .'

'Prohaska, you are in no position to argue, believe me. Just go, and take damned good care not to leave a forwarding address.'

So that was how I bade farewell to the k.u.k. Fliegertruppe: lying under a tarpaulin in the back of a motor lorry full of empty lubricating-oil cans, as we lumbered out through the gate of k.u.k. Fliegerfeld Haidenschaft and on to the Divacca road. It had been eighty-nine days in total. It only seemed much longer.

I met Franz Meyerhofer in Vienna in 1930 or thereabouts. I had just returned from South America and he was in the city for a family funeral, so we met for a couple of drinks for old times' sake. Meyerhofer told me that they had fought on after I left, first in Flik 19 then in other units. Meyerhofer himself had at last won his pilot's wings and had eventually led a fighter squadron over the Montello sector in the battles of the summer of 1918. The k.u.k. Fliegertruppe had fought on to the end, he said, outnumbered, and handicapped by every imaginable deficiency of equipment, organisation and training. Even in 1917, he said, the Germans would still not sell us Fokker interrupter gear to allow machine guns to fire through the propeller arc, so we had used a homemade version called the Zaparka system. This had worked, but only with the engine between 1,200 and two thousand revs per minute – which meant that a pilot had to keep one eye on his target and the other on the tachometer as he pressed the firing button, otherwise he might only shoot off his own propeller blades. Likewise they still had to soldier on with the wretched Schwarzlose machine gun and its canvas ammunition belts. At the end of 1917, Meyerhofer told me, they had shot down a British Sopwith Camel fighter and had found that its machine guns were fed by self-destructing ammunition belts, made up of a chain of aluminium clips which held each cartridge to its neighbour and which fell off when the bullet had been fired. Samples were rushed to the k.u.k. Fliegerarsenal with an urgent request for an Austrian supplier to make a copy. Weeks later a letter was received thanking Meyerhofer for the sample and saying that the matter 'was receiving the most active consideration'. It was still receiving the most active consideration a year later when the war ended – though, to be fair to the Fliegerarsenal, it had reached committee stage by then.

Of those who had flown with me in Flik 19F only he, I and Svetozar von Potocznik were still alive. Most of the rest – Szuborits, Barinkai and Zwierzkowski and the others – had survived the war, but by 1926 all were dead, killed in peacetime flying accidents. Meyerhofer was now a pilot with the Belgian airline Sabena, and a few weeks after our meeting he too would 'find the flier's death', colliding with a factory chimney as he tried to land in fog at Le Bourget.

As for Svetozar von Potocznik, paladin of the Germanic Race, I had met him already in Paraguay in 1926 when I was briefly commanding the Paraguayan river fleet during the murderous Chaco War with Brazil. Rather odd when I had known him at Caprovizza, he was by now completely crazed, but in a disturbingly calm, rational sort of way. He had flown in the shadowy little war in Carinthia in 1919 when the infant Austrian Republic had fought to prevent the Slovenes – now part of Yugoslavia – from taking the area south of Klagenfurt. And that was the reason why he was now in South America under the name of Siegfried Neumann: he was wanted throughout Europe as a war criminal after he had dive-bombed his father's old school at Pravnitz and killed some forty or so children in a ground-floor classroom. He was now flying in the Paraguayan Air Force and practising on Indian villages the theories of terror bombing he had developed during the last years of the world war.

About 1931 he returned to Germany and became a test-pilot for Junkers, then entered the Luftwaffe and became one of the leaders of the infamous Condor Legion during the Spanish Civil War – the ones who used the town of Guernica as a test-laboratory. He had risen to the rank of Major-General by the end of the war. But the Balkans which had given him his original name seemed to draw him back with some fateful magnetism. After being injured in a crash in 1941 he had been assigned to ground duties, commanding a region in occupied Yugoslavia. Partisan activity was intense, but the activities of 'Sonderkommando Neumann' – a force made up of Luftwaffe ground troops, SS and Croat Ustashis – had been even intenser, and much more systematic. He was handed over to the Yugoslavs in 1946 and hanged as a war criminal responsible for the deaths of at least twenty-five thousand people.

Meyerhofer had no idea what had become of the miserable Hauptmann Kraliczek after I had tried to choke him that day at Caprovizza: he had just disappeared from the scene. It was not until the 1960s that I remembered him, when I saw an article about him in one of the Sunday papers. It appeared that after the war Kraliczek had become a desk official with the Vienna police, collating crime statistics or something. For twenty years he had led the obscure life of a civilian police official. But recognition sometimes comes even late in life. In 1938 the Nazis arrived in Austria, and in 1940 Kraliczek's section had been incorporated into Himmler's SS empire and moved to Berlin. There he was put to work on his old job, organising rail movements. And now he came into his own. In the old days his diligence and attention to detail had been able to work only through the rickety Habsburg administrative machine. But now, as Section Head, he had at his disposal a superbly efficient and unquestioningly obedient administration, absolutely dedicated to its allotted task.

He had undoubtedly done a superb job, organising dozens of rail transports a day across occupied Europe despite the chaos brought about by bombing and the collapse of the fighting fronts. In fact the worse things got, the more effective Kraliczek's team became. When the British had arrested him near Flensburg in 1945 he had boasted to his captors that in the summer of 1944 he had been routing thirty or forty trains a day across Slovakia even as the Russian armies were pushing into Hungary. Had he ever given any thought to what was being done with the contents of the trucks when they reached their destination?, he had been asked. No, he said indignantly: that was totally outside his area of responsibility and no concern of his whatever. They gave him twenty years at Nuremberg. He came out early, about 1962, and was immediately approached for interviews by a young American-Jewish woman journalist – hence the newspaper articles later. He had taken a great liking to her for her qualities of precision and hard work, and had told her everything that she wanted to know in great detail. It was not until near the end of the interviews that she revealed that both her parents had died in the gas chambers. Kraliczek had been genuinely shocked and horrified by this revelation, quite unable to comprehend that it was one of his trains that had taken them there.

So much for the players: what about the stage? As for the Carso Plateau, if I had never seen the place again that would have been far too soon for me. Not steam winches and No. 6 hawsers would ever have dragged me back to that poisonous wilderness. But not everyone felt the same way, I understand. In fact I believe that in the years after the war there were many survivors – Italian and Austrian and ex-Austrian – who kept on going back to those barren hills, spending days at a time wandering alone among the rusty wire-belts and crumbling dug-outs in search of they knew not what, whether the comrades they had left behind there, or their own stolen youth, or perhaps expiation for having come out of it all alive when so many had not. One of these sad living ghosts was Meyerhofer's youngest brother, who had served on the Carso in the thick of the 1916–17 fighting as a twenty-year-old Leutnant in a

Feldjäger battalion, straight out of school into the Army. He had gone back every year, Meyerhofer told me, until the previous summer, when he had been killed one evening near Castagnevizza, blown up (the carabinieri said) after he had lit his campfire on top of an old artillery shell buried in a dolina.

Like myself, he had been a keen amateur photographer and Meyerhofer, while he was in Vienna, was going to bequeath his brother's album to the Military History Museum at the Arsenal. He showed it to me back in his hotel room. Many of the photographs were from the years after the war, when the Mussolini regime was dotting the Carso with bombastic war memorials designed not so much to honour the dead as to assert the grandeur of armed struggle. But one photograph showed an unofficial war memorial, erected by the troops themselves in the field. It was taken, I should think, some time after the rout at Caporetto, when the Italian Army on the Carso had abandoned in an afternoon all that it had just taken them two years and half a million lives to gain. Marked simply FAJTJI HRIB, AUTUMN 1917, it showed a pyramid of twenty or thirty skulls, piled together without any regard to their owners' nationality and surmounted by a crucifix made from two thigh bones and a screw-picket stake lashed together with barbed wire. I have no idea what became of that photograph. Perhaps it was lost, because I have never seen it reproduced anywhere. Which is a pity, since I think that if all war memorials had the stark honesty of that simple monument then we might perhaps have fewer wars to commemorate.

15

NAVAL AIRMAN

Imperial and Royal Naval Air Station Lussin Piccolo in November 1916 was really not much of a place. But then Lussin Piccolo itself was not much of a place either; though it seemed that it had once known more spacious days, perhaps a century before.

Like many another title in the Habsburg realms, even here on their furthest Dalmatian fringes, the name was confusing. There were two towns on the long, narrow, straggling island of Lussin: Lussin Grande and Lussin Piccolo. Yet Lussin Piccolo was the only one of the two that could be described as a town. Despite its name the other settlement on the opposite side of the island, though it had once been the capital, was by now no more than a dilapidated fishing village with a very large old church. It puzzled me why anyone should ever have bothered to build a town on that side of the island at all. It faced the Velebit Mountains on the Balkan mainland and was exposed to the full fury of the bora, which blew here in winter with a ferocity that, over the ages, had left the entire east-facing coast looking rather as if it had been sand-blasted at maximum pressure: every stick of vegetation shrivelled and worn away by the salt spray and the grit whipped up from the shore.

Lussin Piccolo was a typical small island port-town barely distinguishable from several dozen other such towns along the Dalmatian coast. Centuries of Venetian rule had given them all a characteristic pattern-book appearance. There was the usual great baroque-byzantine church with its fluted campanile; and the same rows of shabby yellow-stuccoed palazzi along the riva, once the homes of the ship-owning dynasties who had made this a considerable port in the days of sail, but which had long since been reduced to mausoleums peopled by a few aged survivors of the old patrician families. One saw them sometimes early in the morning on their way to mass: the shrivelled Donna Carlottas and Donna Lugarezzias hobbling along in their black-lace mantillas with equally ancient maids trailing behind them to carry their breviaries, on their way to one or other of the five or so barn-like churches where the walls were covered in memorial tablets to generations of Cosuliches and Tarabocchias lost at sea.

Lussin Piccolo had once had a marine academy of its own, and a powerful guild of ship owners. But iron steamships and the Suez Canal had finally done for the place, and it had long since sunk into shabby poverty, alleviated a little only in the early years of this century when the Archduke Karl Stefan had built a villa here and the place had become, like the rest of the Dalmatian coast under Austrian rule, a riviera for second-rank nobility and imperial bureaucrats in summer and a sanatorium for invalids in winter. This always struck me as an odd belief, I must say: that the warm, sunlit Adriatic coast was an ideal place for consumptives. I had served fifteen years in the Austrian fleet and knew perfectly well from officiating at recruiting depots that the entire coast was in fact rotten with tuberculosis.

But then, this was scarcely a matter for wonder: the diet of the common people had always been miserable here in Dalmatia. The limestone islands – no more than karst mountain-tops protruding from the water – were stony and arid to a degree where even goats could scarcely browse a living from most of them. The islanders had imported their food in peacetime and had paid for it with tourist income and remittances from abroad. But now that the war was into its third year, tourism and remittances were both things of the past. The 1916 harvest had been disastrously bad throughout Central Europe. The Hungarian government had just forbidden the export of grain to the rest of the Monarchy, so Dalmatia was indeed in a precarious state. If the people of Vienna were now subsisting on turnips and barley-meal, what would be left over for the folk of the poor, distant, forgotten Adriatic coastlands? By

November supplies to the islands were down to the bare minimum needed to prevent people from dying of starvation in the streets. Even fish was no longer available to feed the people, now that the local fishing fleet was under military control and its catch requisitioned at the dockside to be taken away and canned for army rations.

But the scarcity of food on Lussin Island in the autumn of 1916 had one good side to it: if there was nothing much for the people to eat, that at least meant that they no longer had to bother about finding fuel to cook it. Coal had been short throughout the Monarchy for a year or more past, as the blast-furnaces consumed everything that Austria's increasingly decrepit rail system was able to transport. The cities got only what was left over from the war industries. By mid-November electricity and gas were off for most of the day in Vienna, so it was not very likely that places like Lussin were going to see much coal, dangling as they did at the end of a precarious steamer line down from Fiume. About the middle of the month a violent bora tore an old three-masted barque from her moorings on the mainland and drove her ashore on the eastern coast of the island just across from the air station. Word spread to the town and within minutes the entire population were on the move, armed with axes and crowbars. I was telephoned by the local coastguards to provide a naval picket to guard the wreck; but by the time I had collected the men and got to the ridge of the island above the shore it was already too late. We stood open-mouthed, staring in disbelief as the old wooden ship simply evaporated in front of our eyes, disappearing like a piece of camphor in the sunshine, only much faster.

There were about forty of us at Naval Air Station Lussin Piccolo, lodged in a small wooden-hutted encampment on the shores of Kovčanja Bay, at the opposite end of the long, narrow fjord-harbour from the town about five kilometres distant. The flying-boat base had recently been moved here out of the way because a minesweeper flotilla was using the town harbour, and things had become too crowded for safe take-off and landing. Lussin's fjord was a splendid natural anchorage, sheltered by low hills to eastward from the bora and with only one narrow entrance, about half-way down the seaward side. The French Navy had occupied the place in the war of 1859 with the intention of using it as a base for stirring up revolt in Hungary – if the war had not ended after only a few weeks with Austria's defeat. The War Ministry had learnt its lesson though and had built a number of forts on the island in the 1860s, as well as providing a chain barrier to block the harbour entrance.

By the looks of it the War Ministry might very well have installed the personnel of the Naval Air Station at the same time as the defences, because the average age of the lower deck was (I should think) nearer to sixty than to fifty: a collection of ancient naval reservists and pensioners called up for the duration and commanded – for want of a better word – by a delightful old gentleman called Fregattenkapitän Maximillian von Lötsch. Fregattenkapitän von Lötsch had not so much been called from retirement to command the station as returned from the embalmers. Nobody knew for sure how old he was, but it was reasonably certain on the evidence of old daguerrotype photographs that he had been a Seefähnrich aboard the brig *Huszar* at the siege of Venice in 1849. Certainly he must have been eighty-five if he was a day when I knew him: a charming old boy straight out of Biedermeyer Austria, but pretty well gaga and unshakeably convinced that we were at war with the Prussians. He had not the remotest idea about aviation, or about running a naval air station. But it scarcely mattered, since he spent most of the day dozing peacefully in an armchair in his office, waking only from time to time to enquire whether the 'Pfiff-Chinesers' had managed to capture Prague yet. We just gave him things to sign every now and then and got on with running the station as best we could.

Not that our crew gave us much trouble. Apart from a few young engine fitters and other such craftsmen from our parent unit, the naval air base at Pola, the station personnel were simply too old to present us with the disciplinary problems that usually arise from having a ship full of feckless and hot-blooded young men. There was none of the drunkenness, none of the whoring, none of the fights and none of the requests to visit pox clinics that normally make life so tiresome for divisional officers; only a good deal of grumbling among a collection of aged men who had suddenly found themselves in naval uniform again when they were already grandfathers, and who had now been exiled to spend the war on a remote island in the Adriatic. They would while away their off-duty hours huddled around the stove at the Café Garibaldi in town, playing backgammon and wheezing complaints against the war and the 'verfluchtete Kriegsmarine' as they snapped their arthritic knuckles.

My servant was an ancient Pola-Italian naval pensioner called Tomassini who claimed (with what truth I cannot say) to have served as a powder-monkey aboard the wooden battleship *Kaiser* at Lissa in 1866. It was a pity, I once told him, that the Monarchy's desperate shortage of manpower should have compelled it to call up men in their sixties. Tomassini sucked his remaining teeth and thought for a while about this.

'Can't say that it bothers me too much, Herr Leutnant, if you really want to know what I think. It gets me away from the old woman for a bit, and all things considered this isn't too bad a place to sit out the war, specially now as they're copping it back in Pola. There's an air-raid every other day now, the missus says. They had a bomb come down the chimney of the house next door last week and bring our ceiling down. Frightened the life out of her it did. No danger of that out here anyway.'

He was quite right about that: Lussin Island was way outside the range of the smaller Italian aircraft, and had nothing whatever to attract the big Caproni bombers that were now raiding Austrian towns as far behind the Front as Graz and Laibach. Fighter aircraft could not get this far, and we ourselves were too far from the Italian ports to be employed for bombing-raids. So air operations from Naval Air Station Lussin Piccolo consisted entirely of the humdrum business of convoy escort, varied only occasionally by the odd anti-submarine patrol.

It was difficult to say which of these two was the more tedious. Escorting convoys meant flying over them in circles for four or five hours at a stretch all the way down from the port of Fiume through the Quarnerolo Gulf to the limit of our sector at the northern tip of Lunga Island – sometimes further, if the aeroplane from Zara had not turned up to relieve us. But, tiresome or not, it was certainly a necessary task. The Balkans in those days were a wild and primitive land, almost devoid of roads and railways. This meant that most of the supplies for our fleet at Cattaro and for the Austrian armies in Albania had to travel by sea, down a long coast which lay everywhere within easy striking distance of the Italian shore. If the convoys had not been properly protected, Allied submarines and motor boats would have been free to slaughter at will like foxes in a hen-coop. But they never managed it: in fact, thanks to our Navy's competent use of escorts, only a handful of merchantmen were ever sunk on the Fiume–Durazzo run, even though the number of sailings must have run into thousands. But it was arduous work for all those involved: both for the overworked destroyer and torpedo-boat crews who did the surface escorting and for the flying-boat pilots above.

The trouble from our point of view was that even at half-throttle, down nearly to stalling speed, a Lohner flying-boat was about eight times as fast as a convoy of elderly merchant steamers with engines worn out by lack of grease and burning lignite in their boilers. We had to circle above them all the time, turning in great slow loops as the merchantmen doddered along below at five or six knots with a couple of harassed torpedo-boats fussing about on their flanks. Sometimes we would go clockwise, sometimes anti-clockwise, for no other reason than to break the monotony and stop ourselves getting dizzy, and also because our riggers warned us that this circling in the same direction all the time gave a permanent warp to the airframe. Yet it was a job that demanded unrelenting vigilance: constantly on the look-out not only for the tell-tale white plume of a periscope but for the tiny black dot of a drifting mine or the miniscule grey outlines of a flotilla of Italian MAS boats lurking among the myriad islands and waiting to skim in and launch their torpedoes. We were looking all the time for something which was probably not there, but which would wreak disaster if it were there and we failed to see it. If there was any doubt on that point it was dispelled early in November when the Ungaro-Croatia steamer *Gabor Bethlen* was torpedoed and sunk off Lunga Island after the other Lussin aeroplane had fumbled the hand-over to the relief from Zara and a submarine had taken advantage of the gap. As an ex-submarine captain myself I liked to think that he would never have had the chance if I had been there, but secretly I was far from sure of that. Observer and pilot used to work one-hour shifts in those flying-boats; but in the winter cold it was dreadfully easy to drift into trains of thought and miss a periscope wake, especially when the sea was flecked with white-caps from the wind or if there had been a lot of dolphins about.

My feelings about all this were curiously mixed, I must say. On the one hand, after the excitements and terrors of my time as a front flier with the k.u.k. Fliegertruppe I might have been expected to have relished the boring safety of this sort of flying; and all the more so when I had a wife six months pregnant back in Vienna. But I also knew that hundreds of thousands of my comrades were risking their lives every minute of the day and dying in hetacombs for their Emperor and Fatherland. Somehow it seemed a slightly seedy thing for a Maria-Theresien Ritter to be living this semi-retired life of modest comfort and minimal risk on a pleasant Adriatic island while my fellows were undergoing the most terrible hardships and dangers in the trenches and the U-Boats.

Compared with flying over – or more usually among – the Alps, there was not even any great intrinsic risk in the flying itself. The Lohner boat in which I flew, number L149, was a comfortable and safe old bus: like all flying-boats, of very modest performance even when compared with the Hansa-Brandenburg, but soundly built and extremely reliable when fitted like ours with a 160hp German-built Mercedes engine. Built by the Jakob Lohner carriageworks in Vienna, one-time specialists in the horse-drawn hearses that still occasionally feature in horror films, it had a long, elegant boat-hull of varnished mahogany and the propeller mounted pusher-fashion behind the two long, curving, slightly swept-back wings. My pilot and I sat side by side in the open cockpit as if in a sort of airborne sports car. We could carry a machine gun for defence, mounted on a folding spigot on the observer's side of the cockpit, but since we were so far from enemy fighters we usually left this ashore in the interests of weight-saving and took a wireless set instead. For armament we carried four 20kg bombs on racks beneath the wing-roots to deal with a submarine if we spotted one.

The other half of the 'we' in this instance was my pilot Fregattenleutnant Franz (or František) Nechledil. Like myself, Nechledil was a Czech by birth, the son of a chemist from the town of Příbram in southern Bohemia. I liked Nechledil, who was seven years my junior, but we never spoke Czech together, only German. The Habsburg Army permitted – even encouraged – its officers to speak with their men in their own language, even if this meant having to learn it specially. But among officers and senior NCOs the speaking of national languages, though not actually forbidden, was regarded as bad form outside a few Hungarian and Polish regiments. The official doctrine was that anyone who put on the Emperor's Coloured Coat as an officer put aside nationality. Thus the only permissible language among officers in the Austrian half of the Monarchy was that curious, now almost forgotten tongue called 'official German': a language distinguished by the fact that, of those who spoke it, wrote it, thought in it, told jokes – even made love – in it, a good two-thirds were using it as a foreign language; like Elisabeth and myself for example, since I knew no Magyar while she could only stumble along in Czech.

But where Franz Nechledil was concerned there were other, darker reasons for his avoiding the Czech language even when we were alone together in private. His father had been founder of the local branch of the society 'Sokol' in Příbram: a Czech patriotic and sporting organisation which was officially dedicated to 'elevating the moral and spiritual tone of Czech youth', but which had for some years before the war been viewed with increasing alarm in Vienna as a secret society dedicated to Czech

314

independence, the possible kernel of a Czech underground army of resistance. When the war came, and the k.u.k. Armee had been well and truly thrashed by the Russians and Serbs, the authorities had panicked and arrested Czech nationalists by the hundred, hanging some after trumped-up trials in front of military courts and sending the rest to hastily set-up concentration camps in Austria. Nechledil's father had been found guilty of espionage and sentenced to death, but had cheated the hangman by dying of typhus in jail. His mother and younger brother had ended up in a camp at Steinfeld outside Vienna.

But worse was to follow, for it came to light early in 1915 that Nechledil's elder brother, a Captain in Infantry Regiment No. 28, had not been killed at Przemyśl after all but had gone over to the Russians and was now helping organise the Czechoslovak Legion in Siberia. Nechledil had been summoned to the Military Procurator's department and had undergone a series of very unpleasant interviews concerning his own activities in the Sokol. He had been returned to duty in the end, but had been left under no illusions but that he was a marked man and was being closely watched. The result was that he regarded anything Czech – even a Dvořák gramophone record – with the sort of mildly hysterical aversion that some people have towards wasps or spiders. Between us two there was an unspoken pact never to mention or allude to any national political question, even to the extent of never talking about our respective home towns. This sounds like duplicity, and I suppose that in a way it was. But please understand that we Central Europeans have become masters of the art of partial amnesia, of excising from our minds anything that is not convenient to those set in authority over us. How does the joke go?

'Granny, where were you born?'

'Hush, child, and don't talk about politics.'

Still, it was good to be back in my own chosen service at last, among people whom I understood and who talked a common language. The massacre of the old k.u.k. Armee officer corps in 1914 had meant that the Army's ranks had been filled up with pre-

315

war Einjahrigers; but so far its naval counterpart had escaped serious casualties and in consequence had retained much of the old pre-war mentality. I felt far more comfortable in the tiny, spartan mess hut at Lussin than I ever did among my brother-officers at Caprovizza.

Nechledil was officially the pilot of L149 and I was the observer. But in practice our duties were not so neatly divided. I had qualified as a pilot in 1912 and had flown some of the Navy's earliest flying-boats, emerging with a badly injured leg to prove it when I crashed one of them off Abbazia in 1913. I had not flown a great deal in the years since, but my residual skill did at least mean that Nechledil and I could break the monotony of patrolling over the steel-grey winter sea by changing places every hour. As flying-boats go I found the Lohner to be a pleasant and easy machine to handle: well-balanced and light on the controls, so that one did not have to spend the entire four- or five-hour flight lugging desperately at the column to keep the thing flying level.

Even so it was a depressingly humdrum business, escorting convoys: more like the life of a Viennese tram driver than that of an airman in a world war. There would be the usual checks in the hangar before dawn, then the bleary-eyed ground crew trundling the machine out on its trolley and down the concrete slipway to leave it sitting like a sea-gull on the water. This was always the trickiest part of the operation, the launching. The hull was matchbox-fragile and, although it had a shallow V-section up at the bows, the rest of the bottom was flat, which meant that it would drift sideways in the wind like a paper bag. If the sailors holding the mooring-lines let their attention wander, a sudden bora gust could snatch the aeroplane from them and send it gliding across the cove to pile up on the rocks at the other side. Once the boat was safely in the water Nechledil and I would paddle up in our dinghy and clamber aboard. As observer, it would fall to me to start the engine. I always approached this task with some trepidation, standing on the cockpit edge and straining at a hand-

316

crank above me to turn over the six-cylinder engine. It was liable to backfire on starting and if one was grasping the starting-handle too tightly, then dislocated wrists could be the result. Once the engine was thundering away and the aeroplane straining at the mooring-lines I would sit down and test the wireless, tapping out a few words on the Morse key and checking the reply from the naval wireless station up at Fort Lussin. Then if all was well Nechledil would ease the throttle forward and signal to the ground crew to release the mooring-lines, and we would begin our take-off run.

I often think that the French verb for take-off, 'décoller', must have been coined by a flying-boat pilot, because in calm weather the boat would seem to stick to the water as if to a sheet of glue, requiring the most strenuous efforts to get the thing into the air. In winter however this was not such a problem: there would usually be a breeze blowing and we would huddle behind the windscreen in the driving spray as the boat thumped its way across the waves, hurtling down the fjord on its take-off run through the short, spume-laden chop ruffled up by the wind. We would get airborne, then bank away over the entrance to this almost land-locked harbour before turning northwards to make our way to our rendezvous with the convoy.

Our pick-up point would be either the Cape Porer lighthouse, if the convoy was coming down from Pola, or (more usually) the northernmost tip of Cherso Island if it was a convoy proceeding southward from Fiume, through the Mezzo Channel and down the Quarnerolo between the outer and inner belts of islands. They would be there waiting for us, beneath their usual brownish haze of lignite smoke: six or seven merchant steamers with a couple of small warships as escorts. I would launch the agreed signal rockets as we approached and then fire up the wireless to contact the operators aboard the escorts. We would circle above the convoy while they sorted themselves out, dismiss the aeroplane which had accompanied them out of Fiume, then settle down for the next four hours of acute boredom. The steamers would shamble along below at their customary five or six knots – provided it was a good day and there was no head-wind – meandering along like a string of old-age pensioners on their way to the post office as their helmsmen struggled with worn-out steering gear to keep them on course. Meanwhile I would sweep the sea with my Zeiss binoculars, checking off the islands as we passed by: Cherso, Plavnik, Arbe, Dolin, Lussin, Asinello, Pago, Skarda, Selbe, Ulbo, Premuda, Meleda . . . Sometimes I would think to myself that the profusion of islands along the Dalmatian coast spoke of some mental disorder on the part of the Creator. Surely no one in their right mind could possibly need so many of them . . .

In the end Lunga Island would come into sight, and with it (all being well) the aeroplane from Naval Air Station Zara waiting to take over from us, with perhaps a north-bound convoy waiting to be escorted back. Recognition signals would be exchanged, I would sign off to the wireless operators below and we would gratefully turn the aeroplane north once more. The islands would pass below us again: Meleda and Premuda and Ulbo and Selbe and Skarda and Pago and Asinello, until at long weary last we would be touching down on the fjord at Lussin and skimming across the water into Kovčanja Cove. The mooring-lines would be tossed to us and we would be hauled in towards the slipway.

'Anything happen this time, Herr Schiffsleutnant?'

'No, nothing to report – as usual. Here, help me out will you? I'm so stiff I can hardly move.'

Amid such a general lack of action and excitement, trifling details of life at the air station tended to inflate themselves into major issues. Like food for instance. The rations had been mediocre for a good year past. First the daily wine ration had gone, then coffee had been replaced by the nauseous black 'kaffeesurrogat'. Then meat had come off the menu for three days each week, and the warm evening meal had been replaced by a fluid described as 'tea' with bread and cheese – or, more usually now, just bread. A thin washy soup of dehydrated turnips and barley-groats was the main meal on most days of the week. And when meat was available, it was often barely fit for human consumption.

When I was not flying, one of my duties as watch officer at the air station was that of inspecting the meat when the fortnightly supply ship arrived from Pola. And amid one consignment of beef carcasses early in November I discovered a creature so stunted and deformed that I took alarm at once. The occasional horse carcass had to be tolerated nowadays among shipments of beef, but I was damned if I was going to put up with my men being fed on dead dogs. I called over the Supplies Warrant Officer from the steamer gangway and told him that I was not going to sign for the delivery. He demurred, insisting that the creature was in fact beef. I began to suspect fraud: it was well known that many officials of the Marine Commissariat at Pola were taking advantage of the growing wartime misery and lining their own pockets by selling off government supplies to the civil population, then making up the short weight with whatever rubbish they could find. I was adamant that I would not accept the delivery, and he was equally adamant that I would. In the end I decided that I would refer the matter to higher authority and sent a rating off on a bicycle to find the station's Medical Officer.

Naval Air Station Lussin Piccolo had no resident surgeon. Instead it had been allocated the services – such as they were – of a retired naval doctor living in the town. I devoutly hoped that I would be able to avoid injury, because the physician in question was scarcely younger than Fregattenkapitän von Lötsch and not in much better mental shape. He was not in a good mood when he arrived at the jetty half an hour later, riding on the crossbar of the rating's bicycle.

'Well Herr Schiffsleutnant, what is it?'

'Herr Schiffsarzt, we have had a very dubious carcass of beef delivered here and I am refusing to accept it. I would like you to inspect it so that I can lodge a complaint with the Marine Commissariat.'

'What? Have you called me out all this way just for that? Is the beef maggoty or what?'

'With respect, Herr Schiffsarzt, I suspect that it is not beef at all but dog: possibly an Alsatian or some such large breed.'

He walked with me to the supply shed and adjusted his

319

pince-nez. But as he saw the horrible misshapen thing hanging among the mauve and yellow carcasses his annoyance rapidly gave way to wonder.

'My goodness, yes,' he said, examining the dead creature, 'I see what you mean. Thank you for having called me.'

'It is a dog then, Herr Schiffsarzt?'

'No, no. It's definitely of the bovine species, but so badly deformed that you'd almost think it was a dog, or perhaps a baboon.'

'Is it a calf, perhaps?'

'No, it's an adult animal all right, but worthy of a freak show. Look at the way the spine's bent and the vertebrae are fused with the pelvis. I wonder that the poor animal managed to exist at all. It must be a veterinary version of Pott's disease or something similar. I say – you don't think do you that when your men have consumed the meat you might let me have the skeleton to mount? The local veterinary inspector and I have built up quite a collection of lusus naturae over the years . . .'

'Consume? . . . Excuse me, Herr Schiffsarzt, but I don't understand: this meat is diseased.'

'Good Lord man, no one will ever know. Just get the cooks to wipe it down with a cloth dipped in vinegar. If there are any microbes in the meat the cooking will probably kill them. I doubt whether it's communicable to humans anyway.'

'But this is monstrous, to serve up . . .'

'Oh do be sensible my dear fellow; there's a war on, don't you know? It's not much worse than the rest of your consignment anyway. By the looks of it the other carcasses must have died of old age or disease.'

Life on Lussin was quiet, to be sure. But at least the remoteness of the station seemed to have spared me for the time being from further investigations into my assault on Hauptmann Kraliczek and my involvement in the escape of Major di Carraciolo. Each day I returned to base expecting to be given a message telling me to report to the Marine Auditor's office in Pola. But nothing came. By the second half of November things seemed to have quietened down sufficiently for me to risk a trip back to the mainland, to spend a week's leave in Vienna with my wife, who had by now left the hospital and was staying with my Aunt Aleksia on the Josefsgasse. I had urgent matters to discuss with her anyway: chiefly that of moving her out of the capital now that she was into the sixth month of her pregnancy and things were becoming so difficult. Her last letter had painted a dismal picture of life in the city: the electricity off at least half of each day; the trams not running; queues everywhere and even potatoes hard to come by. Soap was practically unobtainable, she wrote, or if it could be found, consisted of nothing more than a block of scouring sand held together by the thinnest smear of grease. By now the only food item that could be obtained regularly was the dismal vegetable which would brand that bitterly cold winter into the memory of all who lived through it in Central Europe as 'the Turnip Winter'. Already substitute substitutes had begun to appear: a new type of ersatz coffee made from roasted turnips, and a wondrous material called 'imitation leather substitute'. Buildings were being shaken to pieces now that motor lorries had finally lost their rubber tyres and been fitted with surrogates, which had originally consisted of two concentric steel hoops held apart by springs, but in which the springs had now been replaced by wooden blocks since spring- steel was in short supply. My aunt was helping run a charity clinic for children in Favoriten and said that the incidence of rickets and scabies was increasing most alarmingly among the poor.

In a word, it all sounded utterly dismal. I had already written to my cousins in Poland to seek their help. They had a sizeable estate in the country near Myślenice and had written back to say that Elisabeth would be more than welcome to stay with them for as long as she pleased, both before the birth and afterwards.

She was not pleased when I told her that evening outside the Südbahnhof, trying to find a fiacre to take us to the Josefsgasse since the trams were not running.

'But dearest, be reasonable. Surely you can't want to stay in

321

Vienna for the birth. The place already looks as if it's been under siege for a year, and this is only November.'

'Otto, I've stuck the war out so far in Vienna and I don't intend quitting now. Anyway, there's bags of room at your aunt's and we get on well together.'

'But she's old, and you've only got Franzi to look after you both now that Frau Niedermayer's gone into the munitions factory.'

'Just fancy – two grown women forced by the brutal circumstances of war to fend for themselves with only one servant to help them. Merciful heavens, how will they bear such privation? Oh wake up Otto: the day of servants and ladies of leisure has gone now and it'll never come back. If I can't do the cooking and look after a baby on my own then I must really be a prize ninny. What sort of woman did you think you were marrying?'

'But why stick in Vienna, for heaven's sake? It's hungry and cold already, so what will it be like when the snow comes? Why stay here? It's not your home.'

'I know. But I've no other home now, and as for scuttling away to hide in the countryside, be damned to it. The ordinary people of this country have had to suffer a lot because of the emperors and the generals and their precious war. People like us landed them in it, so we ought at least to stick by them now that the going's getting tough.'

'By Vienna? You always used to say that it wasn't so much a city as a form of mental disorder.'

'So it is. But its people are real enough.'

I laughed. 'Really Liserl, you're getting to sound like a socialist these days.'

'Perhaps I am, or becoming one. This war's making me into a revolutionary: or at least someone who thinks that we ought to end it by putting the Kaiser and Ludendorff and Conrad and the rest into opposite holes in the ground and making them toss bombs at each other for a bit to see how they like it.'

We woke next morning about 8.00, huddled together under the eiderdown in the chilly flat where the stove was now fired with balls of dampened newspaper. A wan, grey late-November light filtered through the window panes, grimy with lignite dust now that the building's caretaker was dead in Siberia and his successor was too old to clean them. Command of a U-Boat had given me an acute instinct for things not being quite right, and I sensed as soon as I woke that the noise from the street outside was not quite the same as on other mornings: more like a Sunday in fact.

Then Franzi came in with our breakfast on a tray: ersatz coffee, but real white-bread rolls, which my aunt had somehow managed to procure in honour of my visit. My aunt's maidservant was a girl in her mid-twenties from the suburb of Purkersdorf (or 'Puahkersdoarf' as she called it) with fluffy blond hair and great china-blue eyes. Franzi was mildly half-witted, so she had not gone to work in the munitions factories. This morning though she was not her usual equable self. Her doll's eyes were red-rimmed and she wiped them on her apron, sniffing loudly as she did so.

'What's the matter, Franzi?'

'It's him, Herr Leutnant, he's gone.'

'Who's gone?'

'The Old Gentleman, God rest his soul.' She crossed herself. 'They say he's gone and died in the night at Schönbrunn.'

It was in this manner that we learnt of the death of our sovereign lord and ruler Franz Joseph the First, by the Grace of God Emperor of Austria and Apostolic King of Hungary for the past sixty-eight years – all but eleven days. Neither Elisabeth nor I were anything but the most tepid of monarchists, but even so we were hushed as we heard the news. It was not that the man had been inordinately loved by his subjects: most in fact knew that he had been an obstinate and short-sighted ruler in peace and a blundering commander in war. Even that morning as the muffled church bells tolled through the city and the flags flew at half-mast there must have been many ancestral memories of the working men summarily shot in the city moat in 1849; of the crows flapping over the mangled white-coated bodies tumbled in the vineyards of the Casa di Solferino; of the half-mad Empress wandering Europe to get away from her dreary husband and his insufferable court; of the sleazy incompetent cover-up after their wretched son had shot

323

his girlfriend in the lodge at Mayerling and then blown his own limited supply of brains through the top of his head. No, it was just that the Emperor – 'Old Prohaska', as the Viennese used to call him – had been around for so long that he had become as fixed a feature in people's lives as the green summit of the Kahlenberg in the distance. People had excised from their minds the fact that the dear old boy spent much of his regular sixteen-hour working day signing death warrants; or that his ministers were strictly forbidden to deviate from their scheduled subject when they had an audience with him; or that he spoke nineteen languages but would never utter anything else in them but the most leaden platitudes. Instead they remembered the legendary courtesy, and the odd round-shouldered walk, the famous side-whiskers and the hundreds of little anecdotes which had accumulated around the old man over the years like ferns and wildflowers in the cracks of a mausoleum.

And now he was no more. The presence that had shaped the entire lives of all but a few of his subjects and held together his ethnic dustbin of an empire by sheer personal prestige; all that was gone. Something changed for ever that November morning. Until now, behind the battlefronts, a curious unreality had hung over Austria-Hungary's war. The casualties had been immense, but the fighting was far away in other people's countries for the most part, and café society had tended to swallow the cheerfully jaunty headlines in the newspapers without demur: 'Przemyśl Captured'; 'Przemyśl Recaptured'; 'Przemyśl Recaptured Again'; or (a couple of days before the rout of Pfanzer-Balltin's 4th Army) 'Our Defences in Volhynia in a State of Moderate Readiness'. Now there could no longer be any ignoring the Monarchy's disastrous plight. People suddenly woke up to the fact that they were cold and hungry, and that still no end to the war was in sight.

The dead Emperor's withered old body even lay between us in bed that evening. We would normally have fallen into one another's arms with joy. I had been away for two months now and I had been scrupulously faithful to my wedding vows. But when we held one another it was not the embrace of lovers reunited

324

so much as the clinging together of two children lost in a dark wood.

'Oh Otto,' she said at last, 'is it my lump? There, let me move over if it gets in the way.'

'No dearest, it's not that.'

'Why, don't you like pregnant ladies then?'

'It's not that either: you know you're more beautiful to me now than ever. No, I don't know why . . .'

She gazed into my eyes. 'Oh surely not. You don't mean you're upset over the Old Man? Really, I don't believe it: not in the twentieth century, surely.'

'It's not that, Liserl, not really. But try to understand: I've been a servant of the House of Austria for sixteen years now, and I've hardly ever met anyone who could remember when the old boy wasn't Emperor. I don't know why, but it just makes me feel odd inside. Perhaps it's the war and all I've seen these past four months. But I'm still bound by oath to the House of Habsburg.'

'And you're bound by oath to me, and to the child you've planted inside me.' She took my hand and placed it on her satin-smooth belly. 'There, feel. It's life in there: a living child who'll be breathing in a few months and walking not long after that. Why grieve for the dead? There's simply too many of them: the whole of Europe turned into one vast boneyard by Franz Joseph and his like. Let all the kings and generals rot, like the millions of young men they've sent to moulder into the earth. Come my Maria-Theresien Ritter, forget about Maria Theresa and Franz Joseph and all the dead emperors and dying empires. Long live life! Let's make love and create a dozen children: it's the only way people like us can get back at the rotten sods.'

'Liserl, are you quite mad? Have you no respect for the departed, to talk like that?'

She laughed. 'Yes, I think perhaps I am a little crazy now. After what I've had to look at these past two years I'm not surprised: all the maimed bodies and damaged minds. Respect for the departed? If we could I'd take you now to Schönbrunn and make love on top of his coffin.'

*

In the years since, I must have read or listened to several dozen eye-witness accounts of the funeral of the Emperor Franz Joseph. I am sure that you too will be familiar with the solemn pageantry of that grey November day; the muffled hoofs of the horses; the nodding black plumes on the catafalque; the thirty-four reigning monarchs following bare-headed behind the hearse as the cortège wound its way along streets lined with stunned, grieving people; and of course the traditional exchange at the door of the Capuchin Crypt:

'Who seeks to enter?', the Court Chamberlain reeling off the Emperor's name and his fifty or sixty titles. Then the reply:

'We know of none such here. I ask again, who seeks to enter?'

'Franz Joseph, a poor servant of God seeking burial.'

'Enter then,' and the doors slowly swinging open to admit the coffin.

No, I shall not bother you yet again by giving a detailed account of what happened. I have found that the aforementioned eye-witness accounts usually come either from people who were not there at all, or who were tiny children at the time, or who could not possibly have seen more than a small part of the ceremony if they were indeed present. The reports generally disagree on certain major details, while in other particulars they often show unmistakable signs of having been cribbed one from another. In any case, they almost always compress the two funeral processions into one: the cortège along the Mariahilferstrasse from Schönbrunn on 27 November, and the shorter journey three days later through the Kärntnerstrasse to the Capuchin Crypt after the lying in state in St Stephen's Cathedral.

As to the famous traditional exchange outside the crypt, by the way, while I hate to cast doubt upon a cherished legend, I once discussed this in detail with a Polish general, the very soul of veracity, while we were sitting in a shelter near Victoria Station during a prolonged and noisy air-raid one night in 1941. He had actually been within earshot of the crypt door that day, as a young

Rittmeister in an Uhlan regiment, and he assured me upon his honour that no such ritual ever took place. He thought that it might once have done, perhaps back in the eighteenth century; but certainly by 1916 it had long since fallen into disuse. As to the thirty-four crowned heads, neither of us had the slightest idea how that total had been calculated. True, the usual mob of small-time German royalty had turned up – probably more for a free meal than anything else – but Kaiser Wilhelm had pleaded other engagements and there was a war on, so in the end only Ferdinand of Bulgaria had appeared for the non-German monarchies.

The other reason for my not wishing to bore you with yet another account of the funeral of the Emperor Franz Joseph is the simple fact that I was not actually present at either part of the ceremony. I had been due to walk in the cortège from Schönbrunn on the 27th, representing the Knights of the Military Order of Maria Theresa; but at the very last moment I had received a telephone call instructing me to report immediately to Aspern flying field. It appeared that the Italian poet-aviator and daredevil Gabriele d'Annunzio had given a newspaper interview in which he had announced his intention of flying to Vienna on the day and bombing the catafalque as it passed through the streets, hoping thus to distribute the Emperor's embalmed remains among his grieving subjects. As an airman I found the whole idea quite preposterous: if d'Annunzio was prepared to fly a six-hour round trip across the Alps and back in winter then in my opinion he was even more intrepid than the Italian press made him out to be. But the local military command had taken alarm and a scratch air-defence squadron had been assembled at Aspern from aircraft out of the workshops and a collection of test-pilots and convalescents. So that is how I spent the afternoon of 27 November, sitting on the field at Aspern in the cockpit of a Brandenburger waiting for the telephone to ring. We were not finally stood down until dusk, so I missed it all.

As to the interment itself, it was the last day of my leave and my presence had not been requested either in the procession or as a pilot. The weather was fine for Vienna in late November, so

Elisabeth and I decided to take advantage of the fact that the trams were running and spend the day walking in the Wienerwald: not far, because her waist was beginning to get cumbersome, but enough to get some fresh air and just be together alone before I returned to duty. We kicked up the autumn leaves as we walked arm in arm along the woodland paths, talking of this and that and just luxuriating in one another's nearness. We drank tea in a little café near Grinzing, then climbed up on to the wooded Kahlenberg to look out over the distant city. Despite the anaemic sunshine a light November mist filled the bowl in which Vienna lies, so that only the needle spire of the cathedral and a couple of the higher buildings protruded from the golden haze. Then it began, drifting up to us where we sat: the tolling of all the city's remaining church bells. And above them all rang the sonorous booming of the Pummerin, the great bell of the cathedral cast from Turkish cannon captured in 1683. We both tried hard not to be affected by it all, but it would have taken a heart of granite not to be moved by the sound of a venerable and once-great empire pulling its own passing-bell. We did not speak to one another: there was no need. We merely sat holding hands, acutely aware that the world in which we had been born and grown up was now slipping away for ever.

When it was all over, after a quarter of an hour or so when the last tolling had died away, we got up to make our way home while the trams were still running. As we descended the slope of the hill through the beech woods we saw that others had also given the funeral of their late master a miss. Ragged and thin-faced, dressed in sacking and fragments of army uniform, women and children from the Vienna slums were out gathering wood to keep themselves warm – and berries and mushrooms to eat.

I returned to Pola that evening to catch the boat for Lussin. On my way to the Südbahnhof I had made a detour to a military outfitters on the Graben, then to the Marine Section of the War Ministry on the Zollamtstrasse to collect a small parcel. Before I kissed Elisabeth goodbye on the station platform I had gone into a cloakroom and removed the FJI rosette from my cap, replacing it with one purchased that afternoon. It was embroidered in a dubious-looking wartime gold thread and read simply KI, cipher of our new Emperor Karl the First – or Karl the Last, as people were already calling him. The parcel contained similar rosettes for my brother-officers at Lussin, and also forty or so of the other-ranks version: a disc of black-japanned metal with the letters embossed in gilt.

We held the oath-taking ceremony the morning after I got back: put on our best uniforms and paraded in the December drizzle, caps under left arms and right hands raised with first and second fingers together, standing before our commanding officer dozing in a chair, a military chaplain and a petty officer bearing the red-white-red naval ensign on a staff. There we swore undying loyalty to our prince and lord Karl, by the Grace of God Emperor of Austria, Apostolic King of Hungary, King of Bohemia, Croatia . . . and so on through a list of thirty-something fairy-book titles like Illyria and Lodomeria, finishing for good measure with '. . . and King of Jerusalem'. Mass was celebrated by the chaplain. Then the Petty Officer roared 'Abtreten sofort!', Fregatten-kapitän von Lötsch woke with a start to enquire what was the matter, we dispersed to our duties, and that was that: the Emperor was dead, long live the Emperor.

I was called from the Adjutant's office half an hour later. There was trouble in the ratings' mess hut and would I please come over, since they wished to see an officer? I put my cap and sword on and hurried across the rain-lashed square of cinders. I entered the hut to be greeted by silence. The men did not rise to attention but sat at the trestle tables, plates before them. I was met by that month's president of the messing commission, a Slovak telegraphist rating called Kučár. He stood stony-faced, holding out a plate bearing two oblong slabs of gritty-looking yellowish-grey substance.

'Well Kučár, what's the trouble? Why aren't the men eating their dinner?'

'Obediently report that we aren't going to eat this stuff, Herr Schiffsleutnant. It's polenta.'

I looked closely at the unappetising slabs on the plate. It was indeed polenta, that sad pudding of boiled corn-meal that weighs down so many a table in northern Italy. As an accompaniment to something else – for example fried and served with jugged hare in Friuli – polenta is at least tolerable, if an acquired taste, by which I mean that it is rather horrid but that one can get hardened to it in time. But served on its own it is undeniably a most depressing dish, rather like cold slices of congealed porridge only with less flavour. I prodded it with my finger.

'Nonsense Kučár, that's perfectly good polenta.'

'With respect Herr Schiffsleutnant, we couldn't care less whether it's perfectly good or perfectly bad: it's polenta and we're not going to eat it. Only the shit-poor eat polenta.'

And he was more or less right there of course: along the Dalmatian coast poverty and polenta went together like twin brothers. For the people of the port towns and the islands the consumption of polenta marked the final slide into indigence, rather as eating horsemeat would for the English or setting down black-eye peas and chitterlings in front of poor white people in Mississippi. In the end we had to get the Proviantmeister to open his stores and serve out bread and bacon to the men. But there would come a time not very far into the future when they would eat even polenta and be glad of it.

16

LAST FLIGHT

Fregattenleutnant Franz Nechledil and I made our first flight on behalf of the Emperor Karl on the morning of 4 December. For once it was not the usual business of convoy escort. We had been preparing to take off on the customary Lunga-and-back run, but at the last moment an orderly came running from the air-station Kanzlei hut. A telephone call had just been received from the Naval Air Station at Pola, our parent unit. One of their flying-boats had reported sighting a submarine about thirty miles west of Sansego Island. The aeroplane had been returning to Pola and was running low on petrol, and had anyway lost contact with the mystery vessel in a rain squall. Now we were to fly out and see whether we could catch the thing unawares before it gave us the slip. Our convoy escort would be taken over by an aeroplane from Fiume.

Well, we were bombed-up and ready for submarine hunting, so what were we waiting for? I doubted very much whether we would catch the prowler, who would certainly have sighted the Pola aeroplane and turned around if he had any sense at all. But this promised to be a welcome break from the monotony of circling endlessly above a flock of worn-out merchant steamers. Submarines, I knew from experience, had a way of turning out to be floating logs or dolphins or upturned lifeboats; but there was always just a slim chance that one day it might be the real thing. As Nechledil warmed up the engine I turned quickly to check the four anti-submarine bombs slung beneath the wings just behind the cockpit. They were 20kg contact-fuse bombs, but with an additional calcium fuse which would detonate them at about four metres' depth if the submarine had dived by the time they hit the water. One of them exploding alongside would be quite enough to do for any submarine afloat.

We arrived in the search area about 8.30. The cloud had lifted somewhat, but occasional curtains of drizzle still drifted slowly across the winter sea. For over an hour we quartered and requartered the twenty-kilometre square where I thought the submarine might be lurking, having first circled it several times to make sure that the thing was not trying to escape on the surface, where its speed would be much higher. I tried to work out what I would do as a U-Boat commander if I thought that an aeroplane was prowling above me: probably idle around at a couple of knots about ten metres below the surface, conserving batteries as much as possible and hoping that the aeroplane would run low on fuel and patience after about an hour and go home. As for us, our only chance of getting at him would be if he came up to periscope depth and lay there, dimly visible from above like a pike lurking just below the surface of a pond. In that case we had him: prismatic persicopes to search the sky for aircraft were still well into the future in 1916, and if our luck was in, the first that he would know of our presence would be the crash of a bomb alongside and the sudden rush of water as the hull plating blew in.

We were flying about fifty metres up as I scanned the sea through my binoculars. We reached the end of one of our sweeps and turned to make the next one, like a man ploughing a field. Suddenly Nechledil caught my arm and pointed excitedly below. I leant over him at the controls to look. It was an oil slick, spreading across the surface of the sea and reflecting the pallid light with the iridescent gleam of a peacock's feather. Well, that settled it: our submarine was somewhere below us with one of his tanks seeping oil. All that we had to do now was to track him until he came up to the surface. I checked our petrol gauge: three-quarters full. That gave us a good four hours. We were both filled now with the lust of the chase. As for myself, I was determined if need be to follow him like a bloodhound until our tanks ran dry, even if it meant landing on the sea and being towed back in. I was not going to let a chance like this pass us by because of any old-womanish concern about getting back home afterwards. Nechledil checked the compass bearing as I tapped out a message: 'L149 – 8.56 a.m. – Field 167 – Just sighted oil slick from submarine. In pursuit. Send assistance.' A few minutes later back came the reply, 'Good luck and good hunting. Torpedo-boat on way from Lussin.'

By now we were intent on following the oil slick. It could only be coming from a submarine, spreading across the sea like a snail track, mile after mile, marking on the surface the boat's silent progress down in the depths. We held our breath, expecting any moment to see the dim outline as the vessel came up to take a look around. But after some forty minutes of this, doubts began to creep in. Surely we had flown over that patch of seaweed before? I checked the compass bearing. The same thought had just occurred to Nechledil, and I saw him peer as well at his notepad, then at the compass on the dashboard. The realisation hit us both at the same moment: that for the past three-quarters of an hour we had in fact been flying round and round in the same huge circle about four miles across, by now on about our eighth or ninth lap. I glanced astern – and saw to my horror what was the real cause of the circular oil slick! A thin black dribble was trickling from beneath the engine and being blown astern by the slipstream to be beaten to spray by the propeller. We had been following our own track, like a dog chasing a tin can tied to its tail.

I stared at the oil-pressure gauge – and saw that the pointer had dropped almost to zero. The Mercedes 160hp engine contained eight litres of oil in its sump and had a fresh oil tank in the upper wing containing a further sixteen litres. A pump sucked oil out of this tank at each turn of the crankshaft and returned an equal amount of used oil back into the tank. The drain-tap beneath the sump had clearly shaken itself open in flight, so that instead of circulating the oil, the pump was squirting out a little of the engine's heart's blood at each stroke. It was too late to do anything now: after an hour or more of this both sump and tank must be nearly dry. I checked the cooling-water thermometer and saw that it was nearly boiling as the engine overheated. Already I heard it beginning to seize up. The best that we could do now was to thank the kind fates that we were in a flying-boat and that there was only a light swell running: also that there was a torpedo-boat already on its way.

I sent out a hurried SOS message giving our position and saying that we were being forced to ditch by engine failure. Then I remembered the bombs. I had leant overboard at the start of our fool's chase to remove the nosecaps and set the fuses. The calcium fuses could not be made safe again once they had been armed. The smallest splash of salt water would detonate them, so they had to be dropped before we landed. I placed my hand on the bomb-release levers. Then I saw it, about a mile ahead: a low, shadowy shape obscured by drizzle with a smoking funnel amidships, heading west. My heart jumped for joy: it must be the torpedo-boat. Nechledil turned towards it as I fired a signal rocket to attract their attention, then pulled the bomb releases and felt the aeroplane lift momentarily as the bombs fell away to throw up great mounds of spray astern. We certainly needed the lift: the engine was coughing and faltering now as boiling water spumed out of the radiator safety valve above us. We would try to come down in the water beyond them so that the slight wind would blow us towards and not away from them as they lowered their dinghy.

It was not until we were almost above our would-be rescuer that I realised something was badly wrong: that it was not a torpedo-boat at all, let alone an Austrian one, and that what I had taken to be signal flares were in fact tracer rounds from a machine gun being fired up at us – fortunately with very little accuracy. A few bullets flicked through the wings as we skimmed over the mystery vessel to land on the sea about eight hundred metres beyond. As I turned to see who on earth they were I saw that it was in fact a steam-powered submarine which had now lowered its funnel and was in the act of submerging. Within ten seconds the thing had vanished like a ghost, leaving only a patch of foam to prove that it had ever existed. So that was it: the submarine we had set out to hunt had been a submarine after all, one of the large French steam-driven boats of the *Ventose* class which had been operating in the Adriatic now for two years with somewhat patchy results. Nechledil and I sat down and awaited developments. Would they leave the scene as quickly as they could, not bothering about us? Or would they realise that we had ditched and come back up to take us prisoner?

In the event they did neither. The submarine had been submerged for only a minute or so when suddenly it reappeared in almost the same place, bows breaking surface in a tumult of spray, submerging and then bobbing back up again. We watched fascinated. Within a few seconds the entire forward section of the submarine was sticking out of the water at forty-five degrees. Soon it was almost vertical, like a sporting whale. It hung there for a good two minutes, pirouetting slowly, until the forward hatch burst open to cascade human figures scrambling into the water. They did so among an evil-looking yellowish cloud which I knew must be chlorine coming from the batteries as the seawater poured in. A minute later and it was all over: the bows had disappeared beneath the surface in a boiling heap of air bubbles, leaving only flotsam and the heads of swimmers to mark its final exit. Had we been the agents of its destruction? Surely not: our bombs had fallen into the sea a good thousand metres short. No, all that I could imagine was that they had panicked as they saw us coming towards them and had dived with a hatch left open. It was an easy enough thing to do in any submarine, and doubly so in these steam-powered boats with their telescopic funnel and numerous ventilator trunks. I had good cause to know about these things, since I myself had narrowly escaped drowning aboard just such a vessel, the *Réamur*, during a visit to Toulon before the war, when a piece of driftwood had jammed beneath the funnel hatch during a demonstration dive. Apart from that, what I particularly remembered about these French boats was the nonchalant, hair-raising disregard for any sort of consistency in their design. Some valves, I recalled, opened anti-clockwise, others clockwise; some electrical switches worked down, others up; certain cocks closed with the handle parallel to the pipe, others across it, others still at an angle to it. Sailing these contraptions must have been hazardous enough in peacetime: what they were like to operate in a war zone hardly bore thinking about. But what would become of her crew, swimming now in the sea thirty-odd miles from land? We had inadvertently sunk them, but now we were their only hope of staying afloat long enough to be picked up. The breeze was drifting us gradually towards them. As we drew near I hoped that they would understand the situation and not simply slake their desire for vengeance upon us. Just in case, Nechledil and I drew our pistols.

As it turned out we need not have worried about being lynched. In fact when we finally drifted among them we found that they barely noticed our arrival, being too busy trying to lynch one of their own number, the unfortunate diving coxswain whom they clearly blamed for having dived the boat with a window left open, so to speak. Fortunately for him it is far from easy to beat up a man swimming in the sea – especially when his assailants are also treading water. So Nechledil and I laid about with our paddles at the wet heads around us, then took hold of the wretched man and dragged him aboard. It was not until we had placed him safely on the bows of the boat in front of the cockpit that we set about rescuing the others: twenty-three of them in all, the boat's entire complement of two officers and twenty-two men.

Our most immediate concern was to prevent them from swamping us by clambering aboard all at once. Nechledil, whose French was excellent, explained the position to them and be-seeched them to behave sensibly in the interests of us all. They did, and we took them aboard one by one, distributing them carefully around the flying-boat to spread the strain upon its flimsy hull and wings. Lohner flying-boats were sturdily built as aero-planes went in those days; but getting on for a tonne of wet humanity was a load that they had never been designed to carry. In the end the best that we could do was to sit six on each of the lower wings inboard of the floats, huddled together for warmth like swallows on a telegraph wire. Six more perched around the cockpit where the hull was broadest, and four were seated on the hull aft of the wings. The space beneath the engine was used to lay out two engine-room ratings who had taken in too much chlorine and were not feeling very well at all. When the loading was finished the boat sat evenly in the water, though very low. It would do for the time being; but if even a moderate sea got up before help arrived the aeroplane would break up and we would all drown for sure.

I sent out a distress message in clear. The wireless was normally driven by a wind-powered dynamo. We had a small battery to allow us to transmit while standing still, but it was too small for more than three repetitions of the message 'L149 ditched 44.27N by 13.55E with crew of French submarine aboard. Send help urgently.' It would be heard I knew. But by whom? And who would reach us first?

While we sat waiting to be picked up there was not much for us to do but exchange introductions with our dripping guests. The submarine, I learnt, had been the *Laplace*, based at Brindisi. The crew were as surly as one might have expected in the distressing circumstances, but at least the Captain did as courtesy demanded and shook hands with me to introduce himself. I would have expected no less: he was plainly a very aristrocratic sort of Frenchman indeed and was not at all averse to letting me know it. His name was Lieutenant de Vaisseau the Chevalier Dagobert St Jurienne Gréoux-Chasseloup d'Issigny: about the same age as myself or a bit younger and very aloof indeed. I sensed that he was not much liked by his crew, and that he had no great liking for them either. He sat with his legs dangling over the cockpit side and talked with me while wringing out his trousers with as much refinement as one can manage in such circumstances.

'Enfin, mon cher lieutenant,' he said, 'while I must congratulate you on your rare chivalry and Christian spirit in landing to rescue me and my crew, I regret very much to tell you that you are now our prisoners. However, do not despair: I shall personally contact Admiral Boué de Lapeyrère at Brindisi to make sure that you are courteously treated, and I shall make every effort to see that you and your gallant companion are given parole. You will find I think that even in this frightful war, towns like Limoges are far from disagreeable places in which to be held captive. But tell me, are you also a nobleman? I understand that most Austrian officers are.'

'Only by recent creation. I am a Knight of the Military Order of Maria Theresa, but my father is only a Czech postal official I'm afraid.' He sniffed a little and looked down his nose at me. I continued though. 'However, my dear Lieutenant d'Issigny, I am afraid that I have to inform you that you are in fact our prisoners rather than the other way around. An Austrian torpedo-boat was on its way even before we sighted you, so I imagine that we shall all be picked up shortly. I am grateful though for your concern for Fregattenleutnant Nechledil and myself, and I shall do my utmost to see that you and your men are treated with all the hospitality at our disposal. By the way though – I am afraid that I must set you right on one small point: we did not sink your vessel. We mistook you for one of our torpedo boats and were trying to land. The bomb-splashes you saw were when I jettisoned our bombs before landing. I imagine that you sank because you dived with a hatch left open. I was once a submarine captain myself and I com-miserate with you: these things happen. In fact I myself was very nearly drowned aboard one of your steam-driven boats in Toulon harbour back in 1910 in very similar circumstances. If you ask me it's an idiotic system for driving a submarine and I feel sorry for you fellows having to sail aboard such vessels.'

He looked more than a little concerned at this news and, after mumbling that it had not been like that at all, he set to work with a will on wringing out his clothes.

We soon gathered that the *Laplace* had not been a happy ship, too long at Brindisi and far too long without a refit. We learnt as much by talking with her Second Officer, a fellow called Handelsman. Handelsman had been the *Laplace*'s Second Officer since before the war and clearly felt that, being a Jew and a staunch republican, he had been unfairly passed over for com-mand in favour of the aristocratic, Catholic and probably crypto-

338

royalist d'Issigny, even though the latter was a poor leader of men in small ships and had paid very little attention to training. I gathered that such things were far from uncommon in the French Navy, which was manned largely by Catholic Bretons and which had consequently been viewed with very little favour by the anti-clericals of the Third Republic.

'Our matelots, you understand, they are very dévot,' Handelsman had confided in me. I replied that so far as I could see, with boats like the *Laplace* and captains like d'Issigny that was probably just as well. As for the matelots themselves, they seemed a thoroughly dispirited lot even after making allowance for their recent narrow escape from drowning and their present plight sitting dripping wet in the middle of the Adriatic with nothing to support them but the flimsy structure of an enemy flying-boat. They sat and glowered at us with their glum, heavy-moustached faces, and nothing seemed capable of cheering them up: not even Nechledil's well-meaning attempts to generate a little animal warmth by getting them singing the 'Marseillaise' and 'Sambre et Meuse'. All that we could offer them by way of hospitality was a single boiled sweet each from the aeroplane's emergency ration pack, and a capful of schnapps from my hipflask.

This merely seemed to increase their dejection – until Nechledil started to sing a song which he had learnt some years before at a Sokol summer youth camp among emigrant Czech miners in the Nord coalfield. It was called 'Revenant de Nantes' and seemed to be a ditty peculiar to the French Army, which was perhaps why our devout Catholic matelots appeared never to have heard it before. It certainly did the trick of raising spirits, as he sang each verse and then taught it to them. There were about seventy-five of them I think, each of them more luminously bawdy than the last as the song wound its picaresque way among blond-haired farmer's daughters, cuckolded station masters, rapacious widows and lascivious curés. It was all tremendous fun, and soon our sailors were steaming away nicely as they roared out each chorus with the utmost zest. When it was over Nechledil bowed modestly to a round of applause and sat down in the pilot's seat. I wondered as he did so whether this was quite the sort of thing that the Sokol movement's founders had in mind when they set out to improve the moral and spiritual tone of Czech youth.

It was about 3.00 p.m. that we saw the smoke on the horizon – to westward. That, we realised with sinking hearts, meant a French warship, and for Nechledil and me a spell of indefinite duration in a prison camp. True, it was better than being drowned, but I still felt a certain chagrin that rescuing these Frenchmen had landed us in that predicament. If we had come down on an empty expanse of sea we would have sent a distress signal in code instead of giving our position in clear and would have been picked up in due course by our own people. But there: the fortunes of war I supposed. With heavy heart I loaded a red flare into the rocket pistol and fired it into the air, almost hearing as I did so the sound of a key turning in a lock. I would probably survive the war now, but how long would it be before I saw my child?

Our rescuer hove into sight to a loud cheer from our guests. As I expected it was a French two-funnelled destroyer: *Branlebas-*class. As it approached I saw that d'Issigny and his maltreated diving coxswain were deep in a whispered consultation. Twenty minutes later a whaler from the destroyer had come alongside and the *Laplace*'s crew were being loaded on to it, one by one so as not to overbalance our aeroplane. Nechledil and I were the last to leave as the French prepared to take the machine in tow. I had my cigarette lighter ready to set her on fire and swim for it, but the French had thought of that possibility. Three men with rifles kept us covered, and when we boarded the whaler we had to do so with our hands on our heads.

I saluted the destroyer's captain at the head of the gangway, and shook hands with him in as curt a fashion as I thought the occasion demanded. Then Nechledil and I were politely relieved of our pistols and escorted below to the wardroom. So this was it at last: prisoners of war. But I supposed that it could have been worse. At least we were prisoners of the French and not the Italians. I suspected that life as a prisoner in France might not be quite the gentlemanly eighteenth-century affair that Lieutenant the

Chevalier d'Issigny had made it out to be; but at worst a prison camp could hardly be more lacking in amenities than Lussin Piccolo, while as to the food, I was sure that it would be a good deal better. But would we be prisoners of the French? That thought preoccupied me as I sat there in the wardroom under armed guard, gratefully drinking the coffee laced with brandy which a steward had brought me. Imprisonment on parole in Bizerta or Toulouse might be quite agreeable, I thought. But suppose that they handed us over to the Italians after all? My old U-Boat comrade Hugo Falkhausen had been taken prisoner with his entire crew earlier in 1916 when his boat had been caught in nets by British armed trawlers in the Otranto Straits. The British had handed him over to the Italians and since then his accommodation and diet had been so poor that he had been bombarding the Red Cross and the Swiss government – even the Vatican – with letters of complaint. I wondered also whether and how soon I would be able to get a telegram off to tell Elisabeth that I was safe. The alarm would have been raised by now at Lussin and if we were not found by nightfall tomorrow we would be posted missing. In her present condition I was anxious to spare her any upset.

These thoughts were interrupted as an orderly entered: I was cordially requested to attend an interview with the commanding officer. The Captain of the destroyer *Bombardier* was a portly little man in his fifties called Kermadec-Ploufragan: a Breton like most French seamen. He invited me to sit down and offered me a cigar, which I gladly accepted. For some reason he insisted on speaking with me in English, though my French was reasonably good. It was only as the conversation progressed that I realised that this might have something to do with the presence of a fusilier marin standing sentry on the other side of the door.

'My most dear Lieutenant,' he began, 'Lieutenant d'Issigny has just related to me of your quite incredible chivalry: that you sink his submarine after long and bitter struggles, then you land on the water to rescue him and his equipage even though you yourselves will become prisoners.' I was about to point out that we had not sunk the *Laplace* after long and bitter struggles, that on the

341

contrary, so far as I could make out the *Laplace* had sunk herself through incompetence. But he went on before I could speak. 'Yes, my dearest Lieutenant, it is indeed a most sad and pitiable thing that yourself and your pilot should have become captive solely because of your honourable and gentle behaviour.'

'Captain, think nothing of it. These are the fortunes of war I am afraid. If our torpedo-boat had found us before you did then Lieutenant d'Issigny and his crew would now be our prisoners. Lieutenant Nechledil and I can at least console ourselves that we managed to rescue twenty-four of our enemies from drowning once they could no longer wage war on us. We are both seafarers like yourself and regard ourselves as waging war on the French government, not on the human race.'

Kermadec almost wiped away a tear at these words. 'Ah, my dear Lieutenant, your noble words, they move me so deeply. Such distinguished sentiments. We French have always considered you Austrians to be a civilised people like ourselves, not beast-brutes and savages like les sales Boches. Your actions today confirm me only in this. But . . .' his face brightened, 'but courage; it must not that we despair ourselves of the situation. There may yet be a solution.'

'A solution, Captain? I'm afraid that I don't understand. Lieutenant Nechledil and I are your prisoners and that's all there is to be said on the matter.'

'Please, please to wait a little moment. I have spoken with Lieutenant d'Issigny and we are agreed that perhaps it may be possible to de-capture you, if you understand my meaning.'

'I'm sorry, but I don't follow you . . .'

'It is almost dark. Your aeroplane, it is towed astern. You may still get into it and we will cut you loose. Voilà – you have escaped. No one will say anything or know anything. But you must first promise me two things.'

'And what are they, if I might ask?'

'The first, that you will not start your motor and take off until we are out of hearing; the second, that you will give me your paroles as officers never again in this war to fly against France. Against the

Italians – pah! they are crapule: it signifies nothing. But not against France.'

It certainly looked an attractive offer. I sensed now that both d'Issigny and the Captain of the destroyer were intensely anxious to have us both out of the way. Of course – d'Issigny himself must have been in the conning-tower hatch firing the machine gun at us as we roared overhead. A submarine has no portholes, so only he and his unfortunate diving coxswain knew that their boat had been sunk purely through accident and not from our bombs. If Nechledil and I conveniently disappeared from the scene then he and his crew might get medals from this action instead of facing a court of enquiry. He and Kermadec would explain away the rescue by saying that we had flown away before we could be captured, leaving the *Laplace*'s crew swimming in the water for the destroyer to pick up. The professional honour of La Royale would be preserved and everyone would be happy.

The only question now was, what was in it for us? Our engine was defunct, so we would be set adrift and left to our fate. It would be a long, cold night and perhaps by morning a bora would be blowing. In the end we might merely have exchanged a prison camp for a watery grave.

'Captain,' I asked, 'if we were to be landed by you, whose prisoners would we be?'

'Ah, that is simple. We would have to hand you over to the Italians. The Marine Nationale are guests at Brindisi and we have no faculties for holding prisoners. There is an agreement for this.'

That settled it: five minutes later Nechledil and I were seated once more in the cockpit of the flying-boat L149 as it drifted away astern into the Adriatic night. A few minutes more, and the noise of the *Bombardier*'s engines had been swallowed up by the darkness. We were on our own once more.

Many years later, about 1955, I happened to see a recently published book entitled *A Sailor Remembers*, by none other than Rear-Admiral Dagobert St Jurienne, Chevalier Gréoux-

Chasseloup d'Issigny, French Navy (Rtd). Written in a most entertainingly florid style, it told of his adventures from the time when he had chosen the seafaring life up to his retirement in 1953. I must say however that I found it to be more interesting for what a sailor had managed to forget than for what he had remembered, particularly as regards his own murky activities during the Second World War when he had served as Deputy Minister of the Marine in the Vichy government, then attached himself to Admiral Darlan in North Africa, then deftly changed sides in 1943 and emerged among the ranks of the victors. My main interest though was in finding out what (if anything) he had to say about certain events one day in December 1916. I was not to be disappointed:

After a ferocious battle lasting over an hour with the many Austrian aeroplanes, the immortal submarine *Laplace* slid at last beneath the waters of the Adriatic, overwhelmed by the superior might of the enemy. As the waves closed over them our brave matelots raised three cheers of 'Vive la France!' and sang the 'Marseillaise' while the perfidious enemies circled above them like odious vultures.

Yet even in the darkest moments of war some sparks of humanity may be found in the adversary, and as we swam among the wreckage an Austro-Hungarian hydroplane alighted on the waves beside us and supported me and my brave fellows in the water until succour arrived. These very chivalrous and gentle Austrians, by name the Chevalier von Parchatzky and the Vicomte de Nec-Ledil, would have supported us longer even at the cost of themselves becoming prisoners, but I bade them leave with a cry of 'Save yourselves while there is still time, my braves!' So they started their motor and climbed into the air, waving to us as they did so in farewell. Alas, we later heard that these noble fellows were both lost soon afterwards, and that the sea had swallowed them up for ever.

I was unable to resist sending a postcard to the Admiral's

publisher saying that while sadly the Vicomte de Nec-Ledil was no more, the noble Austrian Chevalier von Parchatzky was very much alive and would in fact be glad to meet him if he were ever in London. I read a few weeks later in *The Times* that he had died suddenly of a stroke. I hope that there was no connection.

For the time being though, Lieutenant d'Issigny's surmise about our being engloutis par la mer came uncomfortably close to being fulfilled. A north-west wind got up during the night and soon raised a sea that would have been uncomfortable in any small boat, let alone one like ours with a great venetian-blind structure of wings and tailplane on top of it. By dawn we were wet through, frozen and exhausted by lack of sleep and continuous bailing. Nor had we the slightest idea where we were. The hazy sun came up to reveal a heaving grey disc of water with our flying-boat tossing and lurching in the middle of it as its flat bottom slithered down into each wave-trough. We were being drifted along at about six or seven knots by the wind, I thought. But at least drifting was better than staying still. In an almost land-locked sea like the Adriatic drifting with the wind would bring us eventually to one shore or another. I decided to aid this process. I took out my clasp-knife and clambered out on to the lower wings. I slit open the fabric on the under-surface of the wings above and pulled this down in flaps, which I fastened to the lower wings to make crude sails. Steering with our paddles and the rudder, this would help us to make better speed before the wind and might get us to land before we were dead from exposure and fatigue.

Even so it was a miserable business to huddle there in the cockpit, soaked through with spray, each trying to snatch a half-hour's sleep as the other bailed. Yet despite the chill and wet, we were soon tormented by thirst as the salt spray caked on our lips. We had no water apart from a couple of litres milked from the engine radiator, barely drinkable from rust and engine oil. As for food, there was none apart from a packet of ship's biscuits which we had been too ashamed to offer to the survivors from the *Laplace*. Crunching these and trying to swallow them with our parched throats was like trying to masticate broken bottles. About

345

midday I decided to try and get the wireless working, charging the battery by attaching a makeshift crank to the wind-driven dynamo. It was a bitter disappointment: an hour or more of strenuous cranking produced barely enough current for four repetitions of the message 'L149 – SOS.'

This purgatory lasted until early afternoon, when the breeze dropped and the sea lessened to leave us drifting aimlessly once more. Then we both saw it together: the smoke on the horizon to northward. I fired three flares as the upperworks came into sight. Through my binoculars it looked like an Austrian *Tb1*-class torpedo-boat, in fact a small two-funnelled coastal destroyer. But had they seen us? They seemed to be steaming at about seven knots and were within three thousand metres of us. A drifting flying-boat is hardly something that a look-out can miss, but still they steamed on past us and disappeared in a bank of haze, ignoring us as I desperately fired our last flares.

'Nechledil,' I said through cracked lips, 'how could they have missed us? Surely they must have seen us at this range.' Nechledil said nothing, merely sat staring glumly as the vessel faded into the murk. I could see that the apathy of exhaustion was already creeping over him. I too gazed at the spot where the torpedo-boat had vanished, lost for words. So imagine my surprise about five minutes later when the boat reappeared, heading in the opposite direction and turning towards us. I waved and shouted as if they would hear us at that range. Why had they ignored us the first time? They were coming to pick us up, no question of that.

The dinghy bumped alongside us a few minutes later. To my surprise the two ratings in it refused to answer us when we spoke, only told us curtly to sit down and shut up. I was even more surprised when one of them proceeded to take a crowbar and smash holes in the floor and sides of the flying-boat – and told me to be quiet when I asked him what he thought he was doing. My suspicion that something was badly amiss was confirmed shortly afterwards as we came alongside the torpedo-boat *Tb14*. We were greeted by two ratings with levelled rifles and a petty officer with a pistol. I asked what the devil was going on – and was told to come

346

aboard with my hands up. As I was bundled across the rail the incredible truth finally dawned upon me. The vessel was in the hands of mutineers.

17

FIAT JUSTITIA

As Nechledil and I were being searched before being hustled below decks I overheard an argument going on between the petty officer who had greeted us at the gangway and a senior rating. Both were Czechs, and the rating was plainly not all pleased with the Petty Officer.

'For God Almighty's sake why did we have to pick them up? I told the helmsman to keep his course when I saw them. They'll be out after us by now and we've still got three hours left until it gets dark.'

'Shut up Eichler. Who's giving the orders here, me or you?'

'I thought there weren't going to be any orders any more. You and your finer feelings, Vačkář. We ought to have left the bastards to drown. They're only officers.'

'They're human and we're socialists. They were men like us once: only Austria turned them into officers.'

'Oh be quiet and get them below with the others then. I've got a ship to run.' He turned to us. 'What's your names?'

'No business of yours, sailor,' I answered. 'And stand to attention when you speak to an officer. Who's in charge here?'

He laughed. 'Don't come that tone of voice here Herr Leutnant or you'll both end up back in the sea. We're all in charge here.' A sailor stuck a pistol into my stomach as he reached down the neck of my flying tunic to pull out my identity tag. He collected Nechledil's by the same means and handed them to Eichler, who examined the names stamped on the back. 'I don't believe it – both Czechs as well. And one of them the celebrated Ritter von Prohaska of the U-Boat Service. Well meine Herren, remember any of our Czech do we? Or did they wash that out of you at cadet school as well? Filth – you'd forget your own names if the Austrians told you to do it. Your sort make me sick.'

With that we were pushed down the narrow companionway and shoved into the Captain's cabin. The door was locked behind us. We found ourselves packed into the tiny steel cubicle with five other men: the ship's captain, a Seefähnrich and three NCOs who had remained loyal when the ship had been taken over. The Captain was a fellow called Klemmer whom I knew vaguely from the Marine Academy. He was in a bad way, shot through the left lung and coughing blood. They had bandaged him with a torn bedsheet and laid him out on a bunk. We gathered that *Tb14* had been operating with the 5th Torpedo Boat Division at Sebenico, engaged day-in, day-out for the past ten months on convoy escort along the Dalmatian coast. Working-hours had been long, leave minimal and the food increasingly poor. Likewise the First Officer, one Strnadl, had been very unpopular, combining tyranny with incompetence in about equal measure. Yet no one had suspected anything until just before eight bells that morning off Premuda, when the Captain had suddenly found himself barricaded into his cabin just as he was about to relieve Strnadl on the forenoon watch. He had finally managed to lever the cabin door open with a chair-leg, but had emerged on deck pistol in hand only to be knocked over by a rifle-shot from Eichler on a conning tower. Our fellow prisoners said that, so far as they knew, Eichler and Vačkář had taken an equal part in organising the mutiny. Both had been heard talking some days before about a Czech Legion which was being formed among Austrian prisoners in Italy. Quite clearly the boat was bound for Ancona to surrender.

As for the rest of the eighteen-man crew, they thought that most were undecided about the mutiny: a few of the South Slavs disposed to join it, others probably against and the engine-room crew wavering. No one knew what had happened to Fregatten-leutnant Strnadl. He might have been locked up in the fo'c'sle, but shots had been heard and it seemed more likely that he had gone overboard with a bullet through his head.

It looked then as if, having been generously released from French captivity, I was now on my way to become a prisoner of the Italians after all. That was a matter for regret to be sure, and for acute shame on behalf of my service in view of the circumstances in which it had happened, but at least it cast no slur upon either my loyalty or my professional competence. As for poor Nechledil though, I sensed that he would gladly accept life imprisonment in a cesspit with scorpions for company and bread and water to eat in exchange for his present predicament. His father had been condemned for treason, his brother was a deserter and his relatives were sitting in Austrian internment camps on suspicion of Czech nationalist subversion. And now he found himself through no fault of his own aboard a warship about to desert to the enemy after having fallen victim to a Czech-led mutiny. He was in a pretty mess and no mistake. What would happen if *Tb14* were captured before nightfall by Austrian ships? What would happen to his mother and brother when he arrived in Italy and the news got back via the Red Cross? Suppose that Italy finally lost the war and Austrian deserters were handed over? I could vouch for his loyalty, but who would listen to me? I was a Czech myself after all, and already under investigation for various breaches of military discipline. Something had to be done.

I knew the *Tb1*-class torpedo-boats quite well from having served aboard one as second-in-command back in 1909; not only served aboard her, but worked on her in the shipyard where she was being built. In order to get the Hungarian parliamentary depututation to vote money for them, half of the *Tb1*-class orders had been placed with the Kingdom of Hungary's only salt-water shipyard, the Ganz-Danubius AG in Fiume. Although only set up a couple of years before, Ganz-Danubius had already established a formidable reputation for poor design and shoddy workmanship. The Danubius *Tb1* boats were no exceptions to this unhappy rule. Long, narrow steel canoes driven by a single propeller, they were unstable and top-heavy at the best of times. But Danubius had managed to make the basic design even worse by taking no account whatever of the enormous torque-effect from the propeller. The result on speed-trials had been a list to starboard which grew more alarming with every knot, until I had been obliged to have men hanging on to the port rails to trim ship and the crew below moving every available piece of gear over to the port side. The boats had been refused acceptance by the Navy and had returned to the yard for months of modifications.

I had been at the Danubius yard throughout those alterations. And now, seven years later, I was sitting in the captain's cabin of one of these boats with a pencil and sheet of paper, trying to remember what had been done. At last I had it: below the cabin a certain lubricating-oil tank had been taken out and moved to the other side of the ship. So far as I could remember the holes in the frames had never been plated in because there was no need for it. It was worth a try. I pulled open the door of the captain's locker on the starboard side, up against the forward bulkhead, and dragged out a couple of suitcases, then ripped up a sheet of linoleum from the steel deck beneath. Yes, there was an inspection plate as I had expected: a removable section of deck to allow workmen to look inside the ship's bottom during a major refit and find any sprung rivets before recoating the bilges with rust-proofing compound. It might just be possible . . . I rummaged in the drawer of the captain's desk and found a clasp-knife with a screwdriver of sorts then returned to the wardrobe floor and got to work on the counter-sunk screws holding the plate in position. They were well rusted in, but after half an hour or so of exertion we had wormed them out and levered up the plate. I lowered my head inside the hole and stuck a match. Yes, there was a hole through the bulkhead, about the size of a largish dinner plate. A thin man with very narrow shoulders might just be able to wriggle through into the next compartment of the boat's bilges, which happened to be below the vestibule at the bottom of the companion ladder where a sentry was now standing to keep guard on us. The vestibule contained several lockers in addition to the officers' lavatory. If he could then force open the floor of one of the lockers . . . But who would undertake the task? He would need to be a circus contortionist or a human eel. I looked around. Franz Nechledil

351

was the obvious choice: tall, but so thin that he was difficult to see when he stood sideways.

As for Nechledil, in his present predicament he would cheerfully have volunteered to jump into a vat of boiling acid to prove his loyalty to the Austro-Hungarian Monarchy. But it was still going to be extremely tricky. He would have to go down into the bilges head-first, we decided, then worm his way through the hole and bend in the middle to come up on the other side. In the end he had to strip himself naked while we smeared him with the contents of a large pot of cold-cream which Klemmer had been taking home to Pola as a present for his wife. Then we lashed a bedsheet about his ankles in order to haul him up if he fainted. He took a pocket torch, and down into the musty blackness he went.

Just as Nechledil's feet disappeared the key sounded in the lock and the door swung open. Two armed ratings entered and laid hold of me to drag me out to Vačkář, who was waiting on deck. Fortunately they were in such a hurry that they failed to notice that they were one prisoner short. Was this it, I thought to myself as they hustled me up the ladder? Was I due to be shot and dumped overboard in order to impress the others? When we were on deck I shook off my captors and stood as straight as I could, rearranging my disordered clothes as I did so.

'Herr Schiffsleutnant Prohaska?' said Vačkář.

'Yes, in what may I perhaps be of service to you now that your ruffians have dragged me up on deck?'

'Come with me if you will. I wish to talk with you in private.'

I was tempted to stand on my dignity and refuse. But a rifle muzzle stuck into the small of one's back is the most pressing of invitations, and in any case the longer I kept the ringleaders of this mutiny preoccupied the longer Nechledil and the rest would have to break out of their prison.

Vačkář led me to the fo'c'sle crew-space and shut the door after bidding the two ratings stand guard outside. He sat down at the mess table and indicated that I should do the same. I considered standing, but felt that I could talk better with him sitting down. He seemed very anxious to speak with me.

'Care for a cigarette, Herr Schiffsleutnant? They belonged to Herr Leutnant Strnadl, but he won't be needing them now.'

'In that case, no thank you. I don't touch stolen property.'

'Please yourself. You don't mind if I light up, do you?'

'Feel free.' He lit his cigarette, and turned to face me across the table.

'Look here, Prohaska . . .'

' "Herr Schiffsleutnant", if you please . . .'

'Prohaska: you're not in a position to get on your high horse. Look, I'll come straight with you: I'm inviting you to join us.'

'Join mutineers and murderers? You must be out of your mind. But why on earth do you think that I'd want to join you anyway?'

'You're a Czech like Eichler and me, and I think it's high time you began to consider where your real interests lie.'

'Perhaps you ought to have done some thinking about where your best interests lie – or, rather, lay, since as far as I can see it's far too late for it now. Mutiny, murder, desertion to the enemy and offering violence to your superiors are all death-penalty offences.'

'So they shoot me four times if they catch me? Come off it: we're within thirty miles of Italian waters now and it'll be starting to get dark in an hour. No, we'll make sure they don't catch us – one way or another. I think I ought to warn you though that Eichler's talking of shooting you one by one as hostages if they come after us. He's a much harder nut than I am, as I think you may already have noticed.'

'But if you're so sure of reaching the Italian side before nightfall why should it matter to you whether I join you or not?'

'Partly concern for your own long-term interests . . .'

'Thank you. I'm most touched.'

'. . . And partly concern for ours.'

'What do you mean?'

'There was a flying-boat overhead half an hour ago, and it certainly wasn't Italian. The Wireless Operator managed to get a message off before we took control of the ship. Also the boilers are in bad shape.'

'Why are you telling me all this? You're beginning to sound as if you aren't quite so sure of getting to Italy after all.'

He was silent for a few moments. 'It's the stokers down in the engine room. They can't make up their minds whether to join us or not and they're just dawdling, waiting to see what happens. If we could get an officer to tell them to do it they'd certainly come over to us and put their backs into it. They're mostly Croat peasants and used to doing what they're told.'

'I see. But why should I come over to you? If I don't your friend Eichler might shoot me and tip me overboard like Fregatten-leutnant Strnadl; but if that doesn't happen the worst I can expect is a spell in an Italian prison camp.'

'Because you're a Czech like us, that's why, you and your pilot.'

'I'm sorry; I may have been born a Czech but I became an officer of the House of Austria a long time ago now and gave up my nationality.'

'Well, perhaps it's high time you considered applying to rejoin. Austria's dead, Prohaska: had been dead for years, even before the war. Now the Old Man's gone the corpse has finally fallen to pieces.'

'I beg to differ: Austria-Hungary is probably going to win this war.'

'Austria won't win this war, whatever happens. Austria can't win. But Germany might, and what's going to happen to us all then?' He leant across the table and stared into my face. 'For God's sake, Prohaska, wake up will you? They say that you're an intelligent man. This whole precious Austria-Hungary of yours is nothing more now than a way of forcing us Slavs to fight for Germany. What sort of future do you think there'll be for any of us if they win? Come over and join us, you and your pilot. When we get to Italy we'll all volunteer to join this Czech Legion of theirs.'

'You seem to know a lot about these things for a petty officer telegraphist, Vačkář.'

'I've made it my business to know. We wireless operators talk to one another a lot, despite the war. I've been in touch with Masaryk and the National Council through Switerland for a year or more now. There's a lot of us organising in the fleet and the garrisons, just waiting for the day. It hasn't come yet, but when it does then believe me there'll be a lot of us Czechs ready to do what needs to be done.'

'All very impressive. So why all the trouble aboard this ship?'

'The Croats and the Slovenes. We could still get them on our side, but for the moment they're more frightened of the Italians than of Germany. And anyway, they're half of them long-service men: heads of solid wood. If an officer told them to jump over a cliff for their Emperor they'd do it.'

I must admit that what Vačkář had to say to me in the fo'c'sle there that morning did disturb me a good deal; brought a number of uncomfortable half-formed ideas to the surface about the direction the war was taking. But please understand that if the pull of my old nationality and language was strong, the bonds of loyalty to Dynasty and Fatherland were still much stronger. Things looked different in those days from how they look now, seventy years on. All of us officers – even first-generation officers like myself from the old peasant peoples – had been subjected to years of very subtle and effective mind-shaping as we went through the schools and military colleges of the Old Monarchy. Loyalty to our Emperor; loyalty to our ruling house; loyalty to our multinational Fatherland and to our ship and service; loyalty to the officer's code of honour and to our oath, loyalty to the Catholic Church and to our country's allies: all these were extremely powerful ties. And just because we had been indoctrinated to accept these things does not necessarily mean that they were themselves worthless: in fact, looking back on it now, I think that even if the Habsburg multinational empire was a pretty disastrous affair in practice, not all of its ideals were ignoble ones.

But any inner struggle that I might perhaps have undergone was rapidly forestalled by a shout from the other side of the door. Vačkář sprang to his feet and rushed out on deck, leaving a very young Croat sailor with a pistol to guard me. Before long shouting and confused sounds of struggle came to me from amidships as the boat began to lose way. Something was happening in the engine room. I set to work upon my guard, who was clearly very perplexed by it all.

'Sailor,' I said in Croat, 'do you hear that?'

'Obediently report that yes, Herr Schiffsleutnant.'

'What will you do now?'

His voice trembled as he replied. 'Obediently report . . . Obediently report that I'll . . . shoot you dead if you move – by your leave, Herr Schiffsleutnant.'

'Shoot me, sailor? Oh dear, you shouldn't have said that you know: offering threats to an officer is a death-penalty offence in wartime.' 'Tod durch erschiessen . . .' Is that how you want your parents to remember you?' The poor lad was almost in tears by now. I held out my hand. 'There, there. You're a young lad and no doubt they threatened you into joining them. Give me that pistol and we'll say no more about it.' He handed me the pistol almost thankfully and I rushed up the ladder on to the deck abaft the conning tower.

A strange scene greeted me in the gathering dust. A naked man, covered from head to foot in grime and rust, stood at the conning-tower rails with a pistol in his hand and a naval cap on his head. He was haranguing a crowd of open-mouthed, staring ratings below, like some crazed prophet just arrived in Jerusalem from the wilderness to tell everyone to repent and escape the wrath to come. It was only with difficulty that I recognised this bizarre, staring-eyed figure as Franz Nechledil.

'Sailors,' he yelled, 'sailors, don't listen to these fools and deceivers who would lead you to the enemy, who would entice you to destruction and sell your country to the perfidious King of Italy. Czechs, Slovenes, Germans, Croats – we all fight for one another, for our Emperor and King and for our common Fatherland; for God and for our honour as sailors of Austria. Will you let these reptiles make you into traitors and mutineers? No future awaits you in Italy but a prison camp, a prison camp which will take in the whole of the Adriatic coastlands and all your families as well if the Italians win. Be true to your oath; true to your comrades; true to the Noble House of Habsburg!' Out of the corner of my eye I saw a movement behind the after funnel. It was Eichler, levelling a rifle at Nechledil on the bridge and about to fire. But I fired first. Hitting someone with a pistol at twenty metres is by no means certain, but my luck was in. He dropped the rifle and fell to his knees, clutching his arm. That was the hair that tipped the scales: within a few minutes the waverers had joined us and the mutineers were firmly under lock and key in the fo'c'sle with sentries posted at every door and skylight. S.M. *Tb14* had rejoined the Imperial and Royal Fleet.

The full story only came out later: how Nechledil had almost fainted in the foul air of the bilges, but had still managed to turn that tight corner and worm his way up into the base of the oilskin locker at the foot of the companionway ladder. The plate that made up the locker floor had given him some trouble, but luck and the slipshod workmanship of Messrs Ganz and Danubius had been on our side: instead of a steel plate the floor of the locker was nothing but plywood. He had managed to prise it open, climb up into the locker – then burst out upon an astonished sentry at the foot of the ladder. The man had given no trouble when Nechledil appeared, naked and black as the devil with rust and bilge-grime: in fact had run for his life yelling that the murdered officer had come back aboard to haunt everyone. This unexpected turn had so thrown the engine-room crew off balance that they had barricaded themselves in and drawn the boiler fires. Nechledil had unlocked the door of the Captain's cabin and the prisoners had then rushed out armed with legs from the cabin table. Things had hung in the balance for a few minutes, but in the end it was undoubtedly the awesome spectacle of Nechledil's naked speech of Kaisertreu devotion from the bridge that had finally swung the crew against the mutineers. Just before dusk we fell in with the destroyer S.M.S. *Sneznik* and were escorted back to Zara, all of us under arrest pending investigations.

In the end Vačkář and Eichler paid with their lives for their humanity in stopping to pick us up. That much is indisputable, for without the half-hour's loss of time, and without my special knowledge of the detailed construction of *Tb1*-class torpedo-boats, and without Nechledil's determination, I am pretty sure that they would have got away with it, boilers or no boilers. I pleaded extenuating circumstances as vigorously as I could at their court martial aboard the flagship *Viribus Unitis* in Pola Harbour the following week, but it was a hopeless task from the outset, Mutiny, murder and desertion are all death-penalty offences in wartime, whatever the country, and in 1916 they would have suffered death for them in any other country in Europe as well. The best that I could do was to get more lenient sentences for the lesser mutineers, particularly for the young Croat sailor who had handed me his pistol and who got off with eighteen months. As for the rest, two men got twelve-year sentences – of which they served only two, thanks to Austria's collapse – while the remainder were landed and dispersed to shore establishments.

Vačkář and Eichler were shot at dawn on the morning of 12 December, against the wall of Pola's Naval Cemetery, where two graves had been dug ready for them. Like all the rest of the fleet in harbour I had to stand to attention on deck and listen as the volleys crashed among the black cypress trees on the hill and the crows rose cawing from their roosts into the early morning air. Old Austria was good at pageantry, and no effort had been spared here to drive home the lesson that mutiny did not pay. The lesson sank in, to judge from the pale, tense faces of the ratings paraded on the decks of the warships at anchor as the Articles of War were read out to them by their captains.

First one volley rang out, then another – then a third, more ragged than the first two, and finally a disorderead spatter of shots. I felt sick: clearly something had gone badly wrong. It has always amazed me that human life can be snuffed out so easily by falling backwards off a chair or inhaling a cherry pip or – as a Polish great-aunt of mine is supposed once to have done – through dislocating one's neck with a violent sneeze, yet when the state's professional operatives set out to achieve the same end they so often botch the job. I heard afterwards that Eichler had died at the first volley, but that poor Vačkář had only been wounded, and shouted, 'You can kill us, but not our ideas!' as the blindfold fell off. The second volley also failed to kill him, and the third, by which time the firing squad's nerve had gone. The officer stepped up and tried to administer the coup de grace with his pistol, but it missed fire and jammed. In the end the municipal gravedigger had to put Vačkář out of his misery with a couple of well-aimed blows from his spade. He had been a horse slaughterer before he went to work for the town council and knew about these things.

For me at least that was not the end of the affair. The very next day I was summoned, not to my own court martial as I had half expected, but to the Imperial Residence at the Villa Wartholz, near Bad Reichenau. When I arrived I was ushered straight into the Emperor's audience room. He had heard about my part in suppressing the mutiny aboard *Tb14* and was anxious to meet me. I must say that my immediate reaction after the events of the previous day was one of nausea. No doubt I would be fulsomely congratulated on my dog-like fidelity to my imperial master and would receive some disc of metal on a bit of ribbon to reward me for having procured the deaths of two of my fellow-countrymen. But it was not like that at all. The Emperor shook my hand and said all the usual things: asked about my family and how long had I been an officer and so forth. Then he sent out his aides and bade me sit down in the armchair opposite him in his private study.

'Prohaska,' he said, 'this was a bad business and must have been very distressing for you.'

'I obediently report that not in the least, Your Imperial Majesty. I merely did my duty as an officer of the House of Austria.'

'Yes, yes, I know that: I can read as much in the *Armee Zeitung* any day of the week. But mutinies don't just happen. Tell me what you think were the reasons – and mind you, tell me what you really think, not what you think you are expected to say. If people can't tell the truth even to their Emperor then we are indeed lost.'

So I told him what I thought: about this mutiny, and others, and the near-mutinies that had never got into the papers. I told him

359

that it was not socialist agitators or secret nationalists or agents of the Entente as the hurrah-press said, but boredom, too little leave and bad food piled on top of a system of discipline which might have been appropriate for the armies of Maria Theresa, ruled by the pace-stick and the lash, but which was grotesquely ill-adapted to running units made up from intelligent young technicians. As I spoke he made notes and kept interrupting me to ask a great many very intelligent questions. Then he said something that made me stare in goggle-eyed disbelief.

'Prohaska, you have told me what you think. And I will now tell you as one of my bravest officers what I think about it all. I think that the Monarchy cannot survive another year of this war; nor can it survive in its present form even if peace should come tomorrow. My first priority as Emperor will be to bring about a negotiated end to this dreadful butchery – without Germany if necessary – and then set about a programme of root-and-branch reform at home. What you have told me here today only confirms me in the correctness of these views. But,' he picked up a bulky folder from his desk, 'I have something else to discuss with you before you leave. When we met at Haidenschaft back in August we spoke briefly, did we not, about the circumstances of your transfer from the U-Boat service to the k.u.k. Fliegertruppe?'

'I obediently report that we did, Your Imperial Highness.' Well I'll be damned, I thought to myself, he remembered after all . . .

'Well, I was as good as my word, and I got Baron Lerchenfeld to look into the details of the case. As a result of what he discovered – and also, I might add, as a result of petitions from your brother-officers and your former crew – I have reached the conclusion that a grave injustice took place. I also have the satisfaction of telling you that new evidence has come to light which throws doubt on whether the submarine which you torpedoed off Chioggia that night was in fact the German minelayer. I gather that in August an Italian submarine ran aground off Cape Galliola and when its crew were taken prisoner several of them asked whether they would be going to the same camp as the men from the *Anguilla*, which they said had left Venice on the night of 3 July and had not been heard of since. In short, Prohaska, I think that the German Navy's case against you – which was never too strong in the first place – now collapses entirely. Tell me, would you wish to be reinstated in the U-Boat Service or would you like to go on flying?'

I said that while I was prepared to serve my Emperor and Fatherland on land, sea or air, I felt that my particular talents might be better employed back in my old trade rather than in flying round in circles above convoys.

'Good then. The Marineoberkommando tells me that your old crew from *U13* are for the moment ashore following a navigational error on the part of their Captain. Now Prohaska, what would you say to rejoining them aboard one of our newest submarines currently completing at Pola Naval Dockyard?'

The interview ended and we shook hands as I left, taking with me a feeling – which I still hold to this day – that if the old Emperor had done the decent thing and died about (say) 1906, and if Franz Ferdinand had already died from tuberculosis – as he nearly did in 1893 – then perhaps with the earnest young Karl as Emperor and King, succeeded about 1950 by the Emperor Otto, the Austro-Hungarian state might still be with us today, transformed from a rickety, bilious, shambling quasi-autocracy into a rickety, bilious, shambling constitutional monarchy. Perhaps.

So I returned officially to the Imperial and Royal U-Boat Service on Christmas Eve 1916. I had been exactly five months in the Flying Service, yet it had seemed so much longer. I handed in my flying kit, removed my airman's wings from my jacket and, from that day to this, have never flown in an aeroplane except as a passenger. The events of my brief but hectic career as an aviator for the House of Habsburg were soon put behind me, then gradually buried and lost beneath the detritus of all the years and all the lives that followed.

And Franz Nechledil, my pilot in the Naval Air Service? The trial and shooting of the mutineers caused something to snap inside him I think. He became a great Czech patriot and rose to the rank of general in the Czechoslovak Air Force in the 1930s. He stayed in Prague after 1939 and was deeply involved from the beginning with the Czech Resistance, taking part in an early attempt in 1941 to kill the infamous Reichsprotektor Heydrich. The Gestapo caught him in October of that year. He knew a great deal about the organisation of the Resistance, and his captors knew that he knew. Yet still he appears to have kept his mouth shut for ten awful days, resisting the worst that they could do to him until he finally died of heart failure. I have no way of knowing, but I imagine that what sustained him through his atrocious ordeal was the memory of how he had turned in two of his fellow-countrymen a quarter-century before. But he gave away nothing, and when the Gestapo arrested his fellow-conspirators two days later it was because someone had betrayed them for money. They put his name on a monument to the Martyrs of the Nation in Prague in 1946 – in the next row to Vačkář and Eichler as it happened. The Communists demolished it two years later I understand.

Memories, memories. You must think me an awful old bore. Yet for sixty-five years I scarcely breathed a word about my time as a U-Boat commander, until the photograph album turned up again this spring. And I would also like to be able to say that I never told anyone about my brief flying career. But this is not strictly true: just once, not many years ago, I was persuaded to talk about my days with the k.u.k. Fliegertruppe.

It was in 1978 I think, in the Home at Iddesleigh Road in Ealing, where I had already lived for several years after Edith died and I could no longer look after myself. It was one wet summer afternoon as I was sitting in an armchair in the lounge trying to read. Gradually I became aware that I was being irritated by a loud, honking voice with an American accent. It came from over in Mr Kempowski's corner. I turned around to look, and saw the old fool sitting in an armchair with a blanket over his legs being interrogated by a large – not to say gross – individual in his early thirties with a great curly mane of hair, heavy horn-rimmed spectacles and a drooping moustache in the style of the late

Pancho Villa. The young man was holding the microphone of a tape recorder towards Kempowski and trying to induce him to talk into it by bawling into the old man's ear. He was evidently not having much joy: Kempowski was near-senile by then and his English had always been minimal, while the young man's German was ludicrously poor. This puzzled me: why German in a Polish old people's home? Then I remembered: some weeks before, Mother Superior had received a letter from an American air-historian – or 'aviation buff' as he styled himself – asking whether he might have an interview with the noted World War One flying ace Gustav Kempowski. I thought 'flying ace' was a bit thick: Kempowski had flown briefly as a junior officer in Jasta 2 – Richthofen's old squadron – in the autumn of 1918 and had then transferred to the Polish Air Force.

It appeared that the interview was not going well: Kempowski was pretty well gaga by then – he died a few weeks later – and in any case, he regarded the Polish–Soviet war of 1920 as vastly more interesting and important than the earlier conflict in which he had flown for the German Kaiser. At length the old man cackled maliciously and pointed across to me.

'Prohaska zere – he also flieger in First Weltkrieg – fly in Austriacki Fliegertruppe gegen Italia – you speak him also, yes-no?' The old rogue had remembered, as people sometimes will when their minds are failing, an interview which I had given to a Berlin paper in 1916 after I had brought down the Italian airship. I got up to leave, but my lines of escape were blocked: the young American had also got up and was advancing to pin me into the corner with his bison-like bulk. I saw Mother Superior simpering in the background. I would have to be polite or there would be trouble for me later on.

He proferred me a huge, flabby paw to shake. It was like having a giant toad placed in my hand.

'Wow! I mean, this is incredible – another First World War aviator in the same afternoon – I can hardly believe this.' Without so much as a by your leave he sat down opposite me and loaded another cassette into his little machine. I was already irritated by his evident belief that we old people have no minds of our own, no independent value except as historical relics and memoir-quarries. But with Mother Superior eyeing me in that sinister way of hers I had to sit still and try to be civil.

Without looking at me he introduced himself.

'Hi there. I'm Frank T. Mahan of the Lansing Michigan World War One Air Enthusiasts' Society. I'm over here in Europe collecting reminiscences from those who flew in that great conflict and you, sir, are the first person I've met so far who flew in the Austro-Hungarian Air Force on the Italian Front.'

'Then I congratulate you on your success. But what is it that you want to know? I am no historian myself and I can only tell you what I happened to see, which was not a great deal really. It was all rather confused and quite frankly I have not given it a great deal of thought in the years since. I was a naval officer you see, and only seconded for a while to the k.u.k. Fliegertruppe. And anyway, I flew as an observer in two-seaters, which was usually rather boring.'

'But sir, do you realise that you are one of the privileged few who had the honour to fly in that first great war in the air?'

'It was a privilege that I would gladly have foregone. And what do you mean by "privileged few" anyway? That I was privileged to be able to do it, or that I was privileged to be among the few who came out of it alive? I think that I might disagree with you on the first count at least.'

He appeared not to have heard this remark; only stuck the microphone impertinently under my nose. 'Tell me, how many missions did you fly in all? And how many aerial combats were you involved in? What was your personal score?'

'Really, I have no idea. I was with the Fliegertruppe on the Isonzo Front for about three months, then for a month of so with the Naval Air Service on convoy patrol. I don't think that we ever thought of them as "missions". We went up in the air when we got an order from Army Headquarters or from the division, and most of the time it was reconnaissance or artillery-spotting or a little bombing behind the lines. But usually we just sat on the ground because of bad weather or lack of aircraft. As for combats, I don't really remember. Certainly the Italians shot at us a good deal, and we shot back at them where we could; sometimes with less success, sometimes with more. But "combats" is a grand-sounding name for what took place. Usually it was so quick that it was over before we realised it had happened. You pressed the trigger and shut your eyes, and when you opened them again they had either gone away or you were lying in hospital.'

This person's manner was already beginning to irritate me intensely. I usually get on well with Americans – far better than the English in fact – but when I meet one whom I dislike, the aversion usually borders on the homicidal. What right had this fat buffoon to come digging around among the bones of the dead to feed his hobby, collecting our pain like stamps? Already the memories were coming back: the smells of acetone and petrol and cordite; the sound of Mizzi Günther and Hubert Marischka as the Carso wind rattled the tent sides; the pock-pock-pock of machine-gun fire and the dreadful crunching as we slithered across the glacier. What could he know of it all? He had not even been in Vietnam, he said, having wangled a draft exemption (though he did not put it quite as bluntly as that). At last he fixed me with a bovine gaze through his thick spectacles. I sensed that the Big Question was coming. When it came it was of such stark imbecility that it fairly knocked the breath out of me.

'Tell me sir, what was it really like to be a flier in that war?'

Well, I thought, a question as asinine as that deserves some sort of answer. So I thought for a moment or two.

'If you really want to know what it was like, to fight in the air in the Great War, then go up to someone you have never met before and who has never done you the slightest harm and pour a two-gallon tin of petrol over them. Then apply a match, and when they are nicely ablaze, push them from a fifteenth-floor window, after first perhaps shooting them a few times in the back with a revolver. And be aware as you are doing these things that ten seconds later someone else will quite probably do them to you. This will exactly reproduce for you and your fellow enthusiasts the substance of

365

First World War aerial combat and will cost your country nothing. It will also avoid the necessity for ten million other people to die in order for you to enjoy it.'

I saw that the interview was now at an end: Mother Superior moved in to usher the man away, saying, 'Please – you must not mind him – he old man, head not so good any more.' After he had left it was only my advanced age which saved me from ten days' solitary on bread and water.

A couple of months after this I happened to pick up a library book: *The Traveller's Guide to Northern Yugoslavia*, published the previous year. Curious, I looked up the chapter on the Carso region. One paragraph caught my eye.

The lives of the people of mountain-Slovenia often take on the quality of Greek tragedy, of something as stony and unyielding as the landscape itself. In one village where the entire male population was massacred in 1943 by the SS the women swore an oath that thereafter, as long as they lived, no man would ever enter the village again. Likewise in a village just outside Ajdovščina there lived until about 1975 an old woman who had once been the sweetheart of an Austrian airman, during the First World War when there was an airfield near by. He was posted missing over the Alps in 1917 and we were told that every day from then until her death she had walked into Ajdovščina to ask at the post office whether there was any news of him. We saw her in 1973, dressed in black from head to foot like a crow, quite mad as she hobbled along the dusty road in the midday heat.

'What was it like?' The question stuck in my mind, and now, eight years after I met that odious young man, I have tried to answer it for you, confident that you my listeners will have a maturer understanding of what it all meant – if indeed it meant anything at all, which I sometimes doubt. That war which we fought there above the Alps in those fragile, desperate aircraft with their unreliable engines and flimsy petrol tanks and no parachutes was not a light-hearted, boy's-story-book adventure as some would have you believe. But neither was it remotely comparable to the monstrous butchery that was going on below us. The death rate was enormous – a good half of those who flew I should think – and of those deaths, the majority were by burning. But in all that war and all the years since I have never heard of anyone who ever applied to transfer back to the trenches. Likewise nearly all of those who flew in that war went on doing it afterwards, test-flying aeroplanes and mapping out the world's air routes – like young Leutnant Szuborits of Flik 19F, who went to work for the French Bréguet company after the war and disappeared without trace in 1925 while trying to fly across the Sahara.

And soon the memory of it will have vanished, now that the gorse and willow bushes have grown back over the rubble-filled trenches of the Isonzo and the last of the old men who saw it all are being carried one by one to their graves. May they rest in peace, those warriors of three-quarters of a century ago, gone now to join those who never came back. What was it all for, that so much blood should have been spilt for so little? I cannot say, only tell you what I saw and hope that you will know about it when I am no more: know about it, and perhaps understand better than we did.